What Might Have Been Me

Yvonne Cassidy

HACHETTE
BOOKS
IRELAND

First published in Ireland in 2012 by Hachette Books Ireland

A Hachette UK company

Copyright © Yvonne Cassidy 2012

A CIP catalogue record for this title is available from the British Library.

ISBN 978 1 444 70480 8

Typeset in Sabon MT by Hachette Books Ireland

Printed and bound by Clays Ltd, St Ives plc

Hachette Books Ireland policy is to use papers that are natural, renewable and recyclable products and made from wood grown in sustainable forests. The logging and manufacturing processes are expected to conform to the environmental regulations of the country of origin.

Hachette Books Ireland
8 Castlecourt Centre
Castleknock
Dublin 15

www.hachette.ie

A division of

Hachette UK
338 Euston Road
London
NW1 3BH

For Granddad, my first writing teacher and for Nana, who gave me the inspiration for this story.

PART ONE

ONE

It was a Sunday night near the end of the summer when I first saw Eddie on stage in O'Dowd's in Montauk. When I came in, late from work, they were playing Red Hot Chili Peppers' 'Under The Bridge'. It was a song they always played towards the end of their set but I didn't know that then, just like I didn't know how corny it was to fall for someone on a stage. I was twenty, that Sunday night in August, and young enough to think that the first time something happened to me it was the first time it had happened to anyone.

You could still smoke in bars in New York back then and at first I couldn't find the others in the smoky dark. It wasn't until after I'd got my beer I spotted them, made out the shape of Ange's curls next to the counter by the wall. As I pushed my way towards her the band moved on to the Rolling Stones. 'Hey,' I whispered, 'they're playing your song.'

The joke was getting old. Nearly every band that played that summer had 'Angie' in their set. Usually they made a balls of it, weighing it down with more emotion than the music could carry so it dredged along or did the opposite, tripped through the verses like Angie was some chick they'd just met. But the guy on stage was doing a decent job, balancing everything just right.

'How come you're so late?' Ange said.

'Just as we were about to close, a table of eight showed up. Do you think Steve would turn them away?'

Ange rolled her eyes. The band had finished 'Angie' and the singer said something I couldn't hear over the clapping.

3

'I called Pete,' she said. 'He says he's never going to fail an exam again. He sounded miserable to be home.' She smiled.

'You don't look too upset?'

'Well, I'm missing him like mad, wouldn't want him to be too happy!'

We laughed and chinked bottles. On stage, the band was starting another song and I recognised it straight away: 'You're a Big Girl Now'. Dylan, *Blood on the Tracks*. As the singer played the opening guitar chords he closed his eyes, as if the music was taking him out of the bar to somewhere far away inside his own head. It was years since the days when I'd listened to that album over and over, lying on my bedroom floor, watching the vinyl spin so close I could practically see the music between the grooves. It was Dad's before it was mine, but now it was nobody's, put away on the top shelf of my wardrobe, along with the rest. I couldn't listen to Dylan, not any more.

'Pete said Damien was giving him the third degree about you. He kept asking if you'd been with anyone over the summer, why you never wrote back to him.'

I could feel Ange's eyes on me but I concentrated on the stage. There was something mesmerising about this guy, the way he was rocking backwards and forwards on the balls of his feet in the disc of light. Only a minute ago he'd been channelling Jagger, and now if I closed my eyes, it could have been Bob Dylan up there. He was getting to my favourite part, the part about the corkscrew.

'Did you hear what I said about Damien?'

A guy in front of us turned and glared.

I shot Ange a glance in the dark. 'I'm just trying to listen to the music, OK?'

She was quiet then, but a pissed-off quiet that I could still hear, and when the song ended she turned to talk to Pat on her other side. I didn't care. I was sick of talking about Damien, analysing whether I'd done the right thing. It seemed like I'd spent the whole summer doing that. The singer pulled over a stool from the edge of the stage and said he was going to play one of the band's own songs, a song called 'Falling'.

You could feel the restlessness in the crowd when he said that. They wanted him to sing more Dylan, one of the big ones, and so did I at first, until I heard him sing. His voice was pretty high for a guy, and it was funny how different he sounded, Dylan and Jagger gone completely. The bass and the drum were barely traces of noise so it was just his guitar, simple and clear as drops of rain. As he sat on the stool, the yellow stage light lit one half of his face, catching the edge of his sideburn, making his eyebrow-piercing glint.

I can still remember that feeling, that sudden wash of sadness that came from nowhere. It might have been because of the melancholy melody or because Dylan had made me think about Dad or knowing that I'd probably never hear the song again, but whatever it was, standing there with the hot empty beer bottle in my hand, I was afraid I might cry. Not that I ever cried then.

When it was over, I clapped as loudly as I could, my ring clinking on the glass. They barely waited for the applause to stop before pushing into the last song, a lively rendition of 'Like a Rolling Stone'. By the end of it everyone who wasn't already on their feet was on their feet and I could hardly see them any more over arms waving and hands clapping.

'They were good, weren't they?' Ange said.

'The best band of the summer. Typical that I missed most of it.'

As the crowd dispersed we found ourselves in a circle with Catherine, Rachel and Pat, who said the band had played before, back in June. The debate started, whether to stay where we were or to move on to the Starfish, if it was too early for shots of Jägermeister. I offered to get a round in and that settled it.

Pushing through the crowd, I noticed it was mostly Americans, stressed-out New Yorkers on a mission to relax. At the start of the summer, us Irish had outnumbered everyone, but our numbers were dwindling as people went off travelling or home to repeat exams. Every night, every round, every drink was another part of the summer edging away and I wasn't ready for it to end, to go home. Not yet.

It was three deep at the bar, the worst time to be there, right after the band ended. As I waited, something made me look down the corridor towards the loo. A guy was on the phone, one finger in his ear. It was the diagonal line of sweat on his back that I noticed first, the barcode tattoo on his neck. It was only when he hung up that I realised it was him, the singer with the sad voice.

I wriggled my way into the narrow space in front of me. I felt a tap on my back and turned to see Pat leaning through the crowd. 'Nialler just got here − can you get him a bottle of Miller?'

'Sure − help me carry them, will you?'

The barman took my order fast, like I knew he would: I'd been tipping him well all summer. Pulling a twenty from the roll of notes in my pocket, I thought again how it was easy to be generous here, where the roll of notes never seemed to run out. When I turned to pass the drinks back to Pat he was bending down to talk to someone.

'Pat! Here, take these.'

Someone shifted in the crowd and I saw it was the singer Pat was talking to, his hand heavy on his shoulder, like he was pinning him there. He let go to reach for the bottles, shoving one in the top pocket of his shirt. 'I was just telling this fella here how great they were tonight, even better than back in June.'

The guy was smiling but looked embarrassed.

'Thanks, man,' he said. 'Unless we really sucked in June.'

Pat laughed. 'I wanted to ask you about your name, Long Night's Journey. Where'd you get it from?'

'It's a line from a Bob Dylan song,' I said.

The singer was rubbing the back of his head and he stopped to look at me, raised his pierced eyebrow. 'That's right,' he said. '"Tough Mama". You know your Dylan.'

'You should meet Nialler,' Pat said. 'Now, he's a real Dylan fanatic. I'm Pat, by the way. Patrick. Patrick Kennedy.' He held out his hand.

'Eddie Salerno.'

'Eddie − a good Irish name! And this is Carla.'

Eddie: it suited him. He turned to me and I moved the bottles to my left hand so I could take his.

'Carla Matthews,' I said, 'since we're being formal with the last names.'

'Nice to meet you, Carla Matthews.'

He had a good handshake, a nice smile. His T-shirt had a picture of a tree on the front with a guitar as the trunk. It said 'Natural Rhythm' underneath.

'Sure, come over and have a pint with us,' Pat said. 'Meet the gang.'

'Pat, Eddie probably has loads of friends here.'

'No,' he said. 'I don't know anyone other than Nick and Rob, who seem to have ditched me. How about I find them and then we'll find you guys?'

I'd seen them earlier by the door, chatting to two American girls, but I didn't say that. I thought once he found them we wouldn't see him again, that he was only being polite, but I barely had time to tell Ange what had happened before he was back again with the two others in tow, Pat dragging over some more high stools and introducing them to everyone as if he'd known them all his life.

Nick, the drummer, was the best-looking one, tall with intense eyes. I wished he'd sat next to me instead of Eddie. Eddie was nice but he wasn't my type, too small and skinny, like the bass player sitting on the other side of Ange, the one she practically had her back to. But Eddie was better-looking than him – he had nice hair, dark and shiny and soft. It was a pity he ruined it by letting it splay into the sideburns that took up half his face.

'I think Pat might be what you'd call a fan,' I said.

He blew his fringe from his eyes. 'I should talk to him, try to perfect my formula.'

'Your formula?'

'I've noticed the appreciation of our performance increases in direct proportion to the volume of beer consumed. I need to do more research to find out exactly at what point that is.'

I laughed. 'Well, I just arrived from work and I really enjoyed it. Especially that song, the second last one.'

'That's one of my all-time favourite Dylan tracks.'

For a second I was confused. 'No, not "You're a Big Girl Now". *Your* song – "Falling", was it?'

'Oh, "Fallen"? You liked that? Thanks. It's the first time we played it at a set like this.' He smiled and looked down at his beer bottle, peeled off the label.

'You should play more of your own stuff. It was really good.'

He shook his head. 'Nah, you've got to be careful. People come to hear the songs they know, not our stuff. One of the first things you learn: give the audience what they want.'

'Sounds like you've been doing this for a while?'

'We've been on the circuit for a couple of years. Rob and I got together first, in Philly. Then Nick came along when we moved back to New York. But I've been singing and playing since I was this high.' He waved his hand around the level of his knee. 'So, like, since last year!' He laughed at his own joke and I did too, he had stolen it before I could make it.

'My mom gave me my first guitar when I was five. A plastic thing with a handle that you wound up. It played "Old MacDonald Had A Farm". I was so excited when I got it that I bit it. I sank my teeth right into the plastic.'

I kicked towards the guitar case on the floor next to him. 'Should I check that one for bite marks?'

He smiled his nice smile. 'I think I'm over that now. But my mom says that's how she knew I had a taste for music.'

It was a terrible joke but I laughed anyway, a proper laugh, not faking it. He was talking a bit too much but maybe he was nervous. 'So you'd your career mapped out from the age of five?' I said.

'Not totally. That took till I was seven, when Mom brought me and my sister to see Springsteen in the Garden. Ever hear of the No Nukes concert – I swear I remember the moment he came on stage. And that was when I knew that that was what I wanted to do.'

I nearly made a joke about O'Dowd's not quite being Madison Square Garden but there was an earnestness in his brown eyes that stopped me. I tried to imagine my mum bringing me to a Bruce Springsteen concert at seven – at any age. 'When I was seven I wanted to be the back half of a cow in the school nativity play.'

He'd just taken a swig of beer and he burst out laughing, nearly spitting it all over himself.

'You know, that's the first thing you've told me about yourself,' he said.

'You never know, it might be important.' I drank some beer. 'Anyway that's not true, I told you my name.'

'Carla Matthews,' he said. 'Matthews doesn't sound Irish, is it?'

'No,' I paused. 'English.'

'Your dad is English?'

'Yep.' I didn't correct his tense, swung my legs. 'Nat Matthews. From Brighton, it's a seaside town, in the south.'

'Nat Matthews,' he repeated. 'Cool name. He should be in a band.'

I don't know what had made me bring up Dad, except maybe that they'd played Dylan earlier on. I glanced around to see if Ange had heard but she was deep in conversation with Nick, their heads close. Eddie chatted on, talking about the sets they usually played in New York, a weekly slot in a bar in the Village. They were hoping to do a tour of the east coast in the fall, he said, to play in Philly and DC and some college towns in North and South Carolina. When he spoke about the band his face lit up, his excitement infectious and, listening to him, I envied his passion, his certainty.

After a while Pat interrupted to say he and Nialler were going to the Starfish. Catherine jumped down off her stool to go too, Rachel finished her beer. Ange turned and caught my eye and I could see she wanted to stay, just like I did, so I suggested one more, before we decided what to do next.

We got one more and when we were finished Rob called it a night and went back to the band's motel. We got another and then one for the road after that. Now that there were only four of us we talked in a group, telling funny stories that became funnier as the night wore on. I told them about the time Ange went for an interview in McDonald's and got locked in the loo, and she told them about the time I got my leg stuck in the railings outside McCormack's. Eddie liked that one, laughed a lot, until Nick told his story about Eddie falling off the stage at a college gig they'd played in Buffalo. Nick was quieter than the rest of us so we all listened properly when he started talking, even Eddie, who sat there with his arms folded, shaking his head. I liked Nick, how he told the story, the way he made us wait, and I wished he was looking at me the way he was looking at Ange.

It was when I came back from the bar that the group seemed to have broken up, Eddie sitting facing the door while Ange leaned in closer to talk to Nick. Now that it was two twos instead of a foursome it was a bit awkward between us, until we went back to talking about music, an intense discussion about Bob Dylan, Guns N' Roses and Neil Young that took us the rest of the way through the night, until the lights came on.

Nick had gone to the loo and Ange leaned over towards us. 'What are you two talking about?' 'Two' and 'talking' kind of slid into each other.

'Music,' I said. 'It's nice to have a conversation with someone who has decent taste for once.'

Ange made a face. 'Oh, God, do you like all that miserable stuff too? Morrissey and The Smiths?' She steadied herself on the counter with one hand and spoke to Eddie in a pretend whisper: 'She's my best friend and all, but between you and me she can be a bit depressing.' She slipped off her stool and Eddie had to half catch her. I remember thinking then that I was glad I didn't fancy him because I'd have gone mad about that comment in case it put him off.

'I'll leave you to cheer Eddie up, Ange,' I said. 'I'm off to the loo.'

Walking to the toilet I could feel the beers getting a foothold. I wasn't as drunk as Ange, but I was getting there. The bar was

10

closing. What now? Ange might be flirting with Nick but she was on her way home – she'd never be unfaithful to Pete. Waiting for the cubicle to open, I made a face at myself in the mirror, a smile, a frown. Eddie was interesting and funny, a great musician, but he wasn't my type. Damien was six two, rugby build. But Damien wasn't there. An image of him flashed into my head: his head grazing the ceiling of his mum's car parked outside my house the night before I left. He'd been talking on and on, how we didn't need to break up, what I was feeling was only natural after everything that had happened, I just needed time to think. I'd been thinking all summer and I was sick of it. Why shouldn't I have some fun like everyone else?

When I came back, Eddie was on his own. 'Where are the others?' I said.

'Gone to get some fries. Apparently there's some late-night diner around.'

'That's right – Joel's.'

'You hungry?' he said.

The feeling in my stomach wasn't hunger. 'Not really.'

'You want to go down to the beach instead?'

'At four in the morning?'

'I vowed after last time that I wouldn't come back to Montauk without seeing the beach and we leave first thing tomorrow.'

'What about Ange?'

'Nick'll make sure she gets home. He's a good guy. C'mon, it'll be fun.'

He downed his beer in a final gulp and jumped down from his stool, bending down to pick up his guitar case. His T-shirt pulled up and I saw part of another tattoo across the base of his back. His skin was tanned.

'What?' he said, when he stood back up and saw the indecision in my face. 'I'm sorry, is this a bad idea? You said you were working. You're probably beat – you probably want to go home.'

Home. In a few weeks I'd be at home for good.

'No,' I said, 'I'm not even tired. I'm coming with you.'

11

Two

His guitar bumped between us like a third person on the walk to the beach but he didn't move it to his other shoulder. All night I'd been refusing his cigarettes but he held out a box of Marlboro anyway. I was about to refuse again but something made me take one. There was a crack as he lit it for me, I remember that, and the forgotten rush of the first inhale, the way he tossed the match on to the road so the tip glowed in the darkness before it burned out. He was a few inches shorter than me – it was more noticeable now that I was walking alongside him. But it was only a few inches, and it's not like I ever wore heels.

We took the back road to the closest part of the beach. It was nicer at night because you couldn't see the rocks and the seaweed that rose up with the tide, like dead girls' hair. Crunching my ass into the sand, I listened to the waves sucking out over the stones. It was like one of those movie-clear moments right then, like everything existed just for us. I couldn't think of a single thing to say.

Eddie had his head tipped back, looking at the sky.

'The stars are gorgeous here,' I said, 'so much brighter than at home.'

'The stars of heaven. You know them?'

'Some. I think that's the Plough over there …'

'No!' he laughed. 'The band. The Stars of Heaven – Dublin band in the eighties?'

'Never heard of them.'

'They were good. I don't know what happened to them. They had two really cool albums and then they just, like, disappeared.'

There was nothing to say to that and we were quiet. He grabbed a fistful of sand and let it escape into a pile next to his leg. I was looking at it, thinking about what to say next, when he spoke first. 'Shit. I'm so bad at this stuff. I have no idea how to talk to a girl like you.'

'A girl like me?'

'You know – a beautiful girl.'

'Ah, Jesus! Would you ever fuck off!'

'What?'

'Those cheesy lines might work on American girls you pick up after your gigs but if I was you I wouldn't try them on the Irish ones.' I laughed to make the words sound lighter, conscious of the way he was looking at me.

'What do you Irish girls like, then? Some guy who swills Guinness until he throws up over your shoes?'

'That sounds like the perfect date.'

'It's not a line. I am really bad at this stuff. Usually I end up talking to some music nerd in the corner after gigs. Usually that nerd is a guy and he doesn't look like you.'

I scrunched deeper into the sand.

'I don't go around telling girls they're beautiful. But I think you are.'

I stared out into the darkness where I knew the waves were. 'Sorry if I don't know what to say to that,' I said. 'My sister Suzanne, now she'd have the right response.'

'How come?'

'She's had a lot of practice. She's the good-looking one in the family.'

'Is that right?'

I could hear the sarcasm in his voice but I still didn't look at him. 'That's right. She's just like my mum, sallow skin, dark hair. I got Dad's looks, which basically means I have to rely on my glittering personality.' I thought that would make him laugh or at least smile but when I turned, his face was more serious than it had been all night. He picked up another handful of sand. I wished I hadn't made that comment about Suzanne but it was the closest I could get to the truth: that no one had ever told me I was beautiful before.

'Don't let your dad hear you say that,' he said.

I watched the sand flowing through his fingers, slow at first, then faster. 'He used to say it himself,' I said.

I knew what he was going to say right before he said it.

'Used to?' he asked. 'Your parents split up too?'

I shook my head, a tiny movement in the dark that he didn't see.

'My dad split when I was seven, moved to Philly,' he went on. 'Me and my sister had to move there, too, when I was ten.'

'My dad died,' I said, pushing my feet deeper into the sand. 'He split permanently.' It was a stupid thing to say, childish, but I didn't care then. All of a sudden I felt cold and stupid sitting with this guy on this beach, a guy who knew nothing about me.

'Shit,' he said. 'I'm sorry. Earlier – you never said. I just assumed?'

'It's OK.'

It seemed like it was time to go, a good place to end whatever it was that hadn't even started, and I stood up, my feet slipping in the sand. He reached out to grab my arm and missed. 'Hey,' he said, pushing himself into a stand too. 'Sit down. I'm sorry. I didn't mean to bring something like that up. Please don't go.'

Behind him the dunes were dark against the lighter sky. It couldn't be getting bright already, but it seemed like it was. I dusted the sand off the seat of my jeans.

'What did I tell you, Carla? I'm no good in situations like this. If you stay you can be the one asking the questions. I'll tell you anything you want.'

'Who were you calling after the gig?' The question came out before I knew it was going to, and as soon as I'd asked I wished I hadn't. It had been a girlfriend. Who else would he have been calling?

'My mom,' he said, folding his arms.

'Your mom?'

'Yep.'

'You always rush off stage to call your mother?'

'Actually, yeah, I do.'

His face was half in shadow so I couldn't see if he was messing, but something in his voice made me believe him.

I giggled.

'I know it's lame. Not the macho image girls want to see.'

I shrugged. 'What did you tell her? About tonight?'

'She wasn't there. I knew she wouldn't be. She's in a folk band and they were playing tonight too. But I left a message on her machine so she'd hear it when she got home.'

I only realised my muscles had been tensed when I felt myself soften, just a little. He sat down again, cross-legged, waiting for me to join him. I had to ask him. 'So, it wasn't your girlfriend?'

'I don't have a girlfriend.'

I sat back down, a little further away this time. I was surprised by the relief I felt to know he didn't have some girlfriend back in New York. 'By the way, you guys get it all wrong. Most girls don't want some macho type. They love to see a sensitive side. Next time you're chatting someone up you should tell her that thing about your mom straight away.'

'I'll remember that.'

'Do.'

'So, what about you, Carla?'

'What about me?'

'Is there a Mr Carla at home in Ireland?'

I laughed. Mr Carla – it almost suited Damien. 'There was – but now there's not.'

'What was he like? A macho guy? Or a sensitive soul?'

I thought for a minute. 'He's nice. I've known him all my life. We were in school together. Played rounders together. Now we're at university together. He stayed at home this summer to work in the bank. His father's a bank manager.'

Eddie waited for me to say more.

15

'When he told me that, I realised he was growing into his father. Literally turning into him. That in twenty years from now we'd be living in a house just like our parents' houses, him driving a Ford Mondeo, me driving a Fiesta. And we'd have two kids, a boy and a girl, who'd look like us and go to the same schools we did. They'd grow up to be like us and the whole damn cycle would start all over again. It just seemed so pointless. And boring. So fucking boring.'

The words flowed out on to the sand. It must have been the beer or the freedom of talking to someone who didn't know anything about Damien, or even about me, that let me be so honest, and after all the months of agony over my decision, everything suddenly seemed as clear as the moon over our heads. I waited for Eddie to ask me more, but he didn't.

When I turned to look at him, he made an imaginary steering wheel with his hands. 'That's a car? The Fiesta? You could have driven around in a party for the rest of your life and you turned it down?'

'You've obviously never seen one.'

'So this guy, the Mondeo guy, he's a maybe or a no?'

'A no.'

Eddie nodded and stretched back on the sand, resting his hands behind his head. 'You only have one life,' he said. 'You got to spend it doing what you're passionate about. It's an obligation to yourself.'

'Yeah,' I said, 'that's it. That's totally it.'

He sat up again, quick and cross-legged, facing me. 'So tell me, Carla Matthews, if that's all so boring, what is it you want? What is it you're passionate about?'

His eyes were on mine, shiny in the moonlight. I wasn't expecting such a direct question. I pushed my heel into the sand. Any indecision from earlier was gone and I wanted to tell him something that would make me sound intense and interesting, someone he would have to get to know. I ran through a list in my mind of things I'd tried and given up: painting and piano, even a pottery class once. The gap between the question and my answer was getting too long. And then I remembered.

'I don't know,' I said, 'I suppose the only thing I'd put into that category is writing.'

'Writing?' He raised the eyebrow with the piercing. 'That's awesome. What do you write?'

I was the one to look away now. It had been over a year since I'd written a word, I'd probably forgotten how. 'Oh, just stuff, you know. Bits and pieces.'

That was when I remembered the play I'd written once. I'd forgotten about it but then on the beach the memory opened inside my head and I could see it all so clearly. Using an old copybook I'd written it out in marker pen, with scenes and acts and everything. There were even little drawings down the side. I'd hidden it where I knew Dad would find it, next to the ashtrays on the window ledge in the kitchen. He read it aloud while I did the drying up and Suzanne did the putting away; Mum was away on an overnight. I remembered that he read both parts, making us laugh, and that I hadn't known it was funny until I heard it in his voice instead of mine.

I must have spent a while thinking about that because when I looked at Eddie I saw he had moved much closer. His hand wasn't draining sand any more and he put it on my side, in the gap of skin between my T-shirt and my jeans. 'Don't go all shy on me,' he said. 'Tell me about these bits and pieces. You love lyrics – I bet you write awesome poetry. I can tell you're the poetry type.'

His face was nearly touching mine, his breath nearly in my mouth so I could smell the cigarettes I was about to taste. His skin looked soft, and even though it was dark I could see the tan that made it even and smooth, not pink and bumpy, like Irish guys'. Right then, at that moment, more than anything, I wanted to be his type.

'You guessed it,' I said. 'I love writing poetry.'

It was the first lie of our relationship, out there before we'd even kissed.

THREE

It was weird how fast we became Carla and Eddie, Eddie and Carla, how suddenly you couldn't say one of our names without the other. Anyone I'd known before, I'd known my whole life and I never knew you could do that; find someone on the other side of the world and slot your lives together, like two pieces of Lego.

He came out to Montauk whenever he could over the next few weeks, and when he couldn't he called me at the restaurant, all the time, until my boss, Steve, had to tell me to cut it out. He sent me things in the post, letters in his slanty black writing with articles cut out of music magazines that he knew I'd like. He sent me a postcard of the Brooklyn Bridge with two stick figures drawn on the front, and a beer mat from a bar he'd played at in the Village where he said he'd take me when I came up.

I'd already planned to spend time in New York at the end of the summer, with Ange and the rest of the girls. We'd had our places booked in the Y for ages, saved up our summer money, but now that Eddie was there I decided to go earlier, so we could be together as much as we could before I had to go back.

'Have you decided yet what you're going to do? Are you going to try and keep things going long distance?'

Ange asked me that, the night before I left, the two of us leaning against the wooden railing on the deck outside Salinger's watching the sun blending with the line of the horizon across the bay. It was getting cooler by then: you needed a sweatshirt at that time of the evening and I'd goosebumps on my legs. We both had bottles of Miller in our hands, and I had a cigarette in mine. I

18

remember I'd inhaled right before she asked it and I blew the smoke out slowly, not rushing the answer.

'I don't know,' I said.

'But you've talked about it? You must have. It seems pretty serious.'

'You make it sound like a disease.'

She laughed but didn't say anything. Instead she turned to hear my answer. I kept facing the sea, looking at the sky, lines of purple, lavender, tangerine. From the corner of my eye I saw her push her sunglasses further back on her head, moving her curls off her face.

'We could come back next summer,' she said. 'I'd be on for that and I know Pete would. Eddie could come over and see you in the meantime, maybe for Christmas.'

She said it so lightly, next summer, like it would be here before we knew it. My stomach flipped and I finished my cigarette, grinding it under my runner.

'Uh-oh,' she said, when I turned to her.

'What?'

'You have that expression on, the one that means you've something to tell me. Spit it out.'

I smiled. I recognised her expression too – her top teeth were biting her bottom lip, the way they always did when she was worried about something.

'I was thinking of pushing my flight out a bit.' I said the words quickly.

'How long's a bit?'

'I don't know, Ange, a week or so. Maybe two.'

'But we fly out on the tenth and college goes back on the fourteenth.'

I made a face. 'Sure nothing happens in the first couple of weeks.'

'It'd probably cost a fortune to change it now.'

'It's not bad, fifty dollars or something.'

'You checked it out already?'

'Yeah. I called them this morning.'

19

There was silence for a minute and I leaned on my arms again, looking at the boats tied together, bobbing against their moorings. I thought about lighting another cigarette but the one I'd just put out had been my last.

'Have you said that to your mum?' Ange said. 'She'll probably go spare.'

I drank some more beer. 'Not yet. She'll be grand. She'll hardly even notice.'

'What's that supposed to mean?'

'Nothing, just she's so wrapped up in this psychology course she's going to be doing.'

'In fairness, Carla, she's had a lot on her plate, with your dad and everything. And Suzanne—'

'I know Ange, I know she has.'

I really wanted another cigarette. I should never have started again. Across the bay the sun was blazing now. I swung my foot, bounced it off the railing. 'Look, it's only a couple of weeks. It's no big deal.' I turned to her, but she'd put her sunglasses back on so I couldn't see her eyes. 'I'm just not ready to go back, Ange. Not yet.'

Her teeth were pushing into her lip again, turning it pinky white. She nodded slowly. 'You *are* coming home, Carla?'

My answer came without hesitation. 'Don't be silly, Ange. Of course I am. Of course I'm coming home.'

★

The first time I'd gone to America it was to Florida. I was eleven and even then I knew it wasn't the real America, not like New York, but Mum said New York wasn't a place for kids, that we'd go when we were older. On the flight everyone made a fuss of Mum, and I remember Suzanne and I being mortified as we were brought up to see the cockpit. Afterwards Dad teased me, saying maybe I'd be a pilot when I grew up, but that was silly because we both knew I was going to be an English lecturer in Trinity, just like him.

Florida was fun but it wasn't like the America on TV, it wasn't New York and we never did make it there like Mum had promised we would. And that October walking along the narrow Manhattan streets with my hand in Eddie's, I was glad I hadn't been there before. He showed off the city like it was his alone, unfolding it for me, a movie set; the TV shows of my childhood coming alive. As we wandered through Central Park, I told him how, as a kid, I'd always include the little girls in America in my prayers, little girls who were in school when I was going to bed, in bed when I got up. I remember him laughing at that, the idea of me saying prayers for these little girls on the other side of the world, girls just like me but doing everything in reverse.

The day before Ange and the others came up, we went to Coney Island and I knew we were going to talk that day, about us and what we were doing. And I don't know if I'd made up my mind already, or if I made it up that day, sitting on the beach. All I know is there was still heat in the October sand and that sitting cross-legged, opposite Eddie, his knees touching mine, I could feel his touch in my whole body. And that there was only ever one decision I was going to make.

'I used to think that Van Morrison song was about here,' he said, 'until I listened to the words properly.'

'I think it's about Coney Island in Sligo, where my mum's from. It's gorgeous there.'

'Maybe we'll go some time,' he said. He was looking at the sand, doing what he'd done that first night, picking up fistfuls of beach, letting it ooze from his hands.

'We'll go,' I said. 'I'll take you.'

'Jeez. I can't believe you're going next week. The time has gone so damn fast.'

'Like a jet plane,' I said.

He looked up and smiled. 'We haven't really talked about it, like what we're going to do.'

'No,' I said, 'we haven't.' I put my hands on the sand, steadying myself for whatever was coming next. Over Eddie's shoulder I

21

watched two little girls in matching pink togs run towards the sea, a little boy trailing behind. Every time one of them got close to the water, they'd let out a scream and run back up the beach again.

'This might sound crazy, Carls, but I feel like you know me better than anyone else, anyone in the world.' His eyes were still glued to the beach. In my chest, my heart picked up speed. 'I know it hasn't been that long, but I know – I know I want to be with you.' He reached out his fingers towards me, so they were on my knees. 'Having you here – it's, like, everything's better. I'm writing better, playing better. I love you, Carls. I don't know if I can handle it if you leave.'

I remember the way he sounded, the words hesitant and afraid and slightly raised over the noise of the fairground, the call of the gulls, the collective screams from the people on the Cyclone, speeding along its rattling rail. Behind him a woman was shouting at the little boy to stay near the edge as the white foam lapped over his ankles, his shins. All around us life was going on, crazy, colourful, New York life, and it seemed like Eddie and I were at the centre of it, right at the heart of it, a pearl of stillness and silence.

I put my hands on his, felt the soft skin of his fingers, the smoothness of his nails. 'Eddie,' I said, 'I don't want to go home.' I'd had the thought in my head but saying it out loud made it worse somehow, more real. For the first time I pictured what it would mean, being back in Dublin, walking to lectures in the rain, the cobblestones wet and slippery under my feet, trying to remember what Eddie looked like. In a week, all this could be over. I stared into his face, imagining not being able to see it. He'd shaved his sideburns a bit and his hair was longer, brushing his eyebrows, hiding the piercing. I loved his eyebrows. It was the thought of never seeing them again that made the tears come.

'Sorry,' I said, wiping the side of my eye, feeling the scrunch of sun cream and sand on my skin. 'Must be the heat.'

I tried to laugh and I nearly did, but I was half crying too. Eddie shuffled closer on the sand and took my hand, held it properly. 'So, why don't you stay?'

YVONNE CASSIDY

'I can't.'

'Why not?'

'You know why not! My visa runs out next month. And I've to go back to college.'

He pushed my hair off my face. With his thumb he wiped away another tear that had followed the first. 'I love you. We love each other, don't we?'

I nodded.

'So don't you think that's more important than all this visa bullshit? It's only red tape – we can sort it out.'

'But what about college?' As I asked the question, I knew he'd have an answer. I hoped he would.

He blew his fringe out of his eyes and he smiled, for the first time since the conversation had started. 'Are you kidding me? The best colleges in the world are here. Columbia. The New School. NYU.'

'NYU.' The name had power over me. I pictured myself in a dimly lit bar having a heated discussion about Hemingway and Frost over pitchers of beer, the clack of billiard balls in the background. Like Trinity, but not like Trinity. Not like Trinity at all.

'I'd never be able to afford NYU, Eddie. Mum wouldn't have the money for that.'

'But that's the best part!' He grabbed both my hands, pulling them up and down on the sand. 'They have all these scholarships especially for overseas students. I was talking to Nick about it and his sister's friend is from England and she got one.'

'Yeah, but I'd never get a scholarship—'

'Why not? You're smart, and there's hundreds of different ones. Pages and pages, in this book I was looking at.'

'You bought a book about it?'

'I was looking at one in Barnes & Noble. We can get one. You'll be as excited as I am. Imagine it Carls, you at NYU, writing, me getting the band off the ground once and for all. It'll be amazing! There's nothing stopping us!'

23

It was impossible not to smile, and he knew by my smile that I'd made up my mind. He leaned over to kiss me, a soft kiss that seemed to seal something between us. I broke away first and he hugged me tight to his chest. Over his shoulder I saw that the two little girls were crouched together on the sand now, filling a bucket, tired of their earlier game. The boy stood watching them before running back down to the water. 'Look at me,' he called, splashing in the sluggish spray. 'Look at me!'

We talked for hours then, making plans about the kind of apartment we'd rent and what schools to apply for and all the places we wanted to go together. We talked until the kids had gone and the whole beach was empty. When Eddie pulled me to my feet, my legs were stiff, and it was only when we turned back to the boardwalk and I saw the Cyclone all lit up that I realised we'd talked our way through the whole afternoon and into the October night.

'Come on,' Eddie said. 'You can't come to Coney Island and not ride the Cyclone.'

'OK,' I said. 'I'll try anything once.'

The closer we got the more rickety it looked. It seemed to defy gravity, this giant hurtling, hissing hunk of metal balancing on wooden scaffolds. I felt a wash of fear and almost changed my mind, but we were at the top of the line by then. Sliding after Eddie into the bucket seat, I imagined all the other legs that had worn away the leather, all the other people who'd been scared, just like me.

Eddie turned to me and squeezed my hand. He'd been smiling all day, it seemed. I loved him and he loved me, really loved me. It seemed that the version of me he saw was the version of me I wanted to be, the version that only one other person had ever been able to see. And as the ride clanked off to a start I told myself that that was the most important thing, that nothing else really mattered at all.

FOUR

Telling Ange hadn't gone well and I dreaded telling Mum even more. At least Ange had met Eddie, could understand a little, even though she pretended not to. Every day she asked if I'd called Mum and I'd say I would, that I'd call later, and when later came it was too late in Ireland to phone and I'd say I'd call tomorrow. Until tomorrow was the day of her flight home. The flight that was supposed to be my flight.

I remember sitting on Eddie's bed, dialling the number on the phone shaped like a hamburger. As I listened to the ring-ring at the other end, I hoped Mum wouldn't answer, but of course she did.

'Ah, Carla,' she said, 'it seems like ages since I heard your voice. You must be all packed up and ready now. What time do you land tomorrow?'

I could hear her sitting down, making herself comfortable. I hadn't expected such warmth in her voice, for her to ask me about the flight straight away. I was going to tell her, but I wasn't ready, not yet.

'Carla?' Mum said. 'Carla, are you there?'

'I'm here.'

'I think there's something wrong with the line.'

It was tempting, when she said that, to hang up. To throw the phone away and never answer it again. I tried to remember the sentence I'd decided on, the thing I was going to say first. 'I think the line's OK,' I said instead.

Mum made her voice louder. 'I was asking about your flight. Am I picking you up, or is Ange's mum?'

I took a deep breath, pushed the words out. 'There's something I need to tell you, Mum. I won't be on that flight tomorrow.'

At first she misunderstood and thought that the flight had been cancelled, that none of us were on it, but I talked over her, not wanting to stop in case I couldn't start again. As I talked about Eddie I was conscious that I'd never mentioned him before, not in a phone call, not in a letter. I stumbled through sentences that seemed to go on and on, getting stuck in them, like quicksand. I couldn't seem to get to the point, until there was nowhere to go, except the point.

'So the thing is, Mum, I've decided to stay,' I said, 'to stay here.'

I waited for her to say something, but the dead air stretched between us, thousands and thousands of miles of dead air. I could picture the hall, the green curtains matching the cushion of the stool that she'd be sitting on. I could picture it more clearly than where I was now. I focused on a pair of Eddie's runners on the floor.

'What do you mean you're staying? For how long?'

I swallowed. 'For now. For a while.'

'What's a while?'

'A while, Mum, I don't know. A few months, a year maybe.'

'What about college?'

I was ready for that one, more prepared. 'I've been looking into colleges over here—'

'What? Sure you're in college here!'

'Mum, the best colleges in the world are in New York! They've all these fantastic courses—'

'And fantastic prices to match.' She laughed, but it wasn't a real laugh.

I switched the phone from one hand to the other. 'They've scholarships, Mum, loads of them. Some of them are even just for Irish people—'

'Have you any idea what college fees are like over there? Thousands! Tens of thousands! I can't afford that, Carla, not when you get Trinity for free.'

We were talking over each other and I raised my voice. 'Mum, you're not listening! I'm not talking about fees, I'm talking about getting a scholarship.'

'A scholarship? Carla, do you have any idea how hard that is?'

'Dad got a scholarship to Trinity.'

'That was years ago. It's much harder now, especially in America. Impossible.'

'Dad would never have said it was impossible!'

'Your dad would have said that Trinity is one of the best colleges in the world and that you're lucky to go there.'

We were both shouting, and I hoped Eddie couldn't hear the argument, how Dad had suddenly become part of it. My eyes flicked to my copy of *Animal Farm* on the dresser, the green elastic band that held it together. There was a photo of Dad in there, between those yellowing pages, a photo I hadn't looked at since I left.

Something Ange had said came into my mind, something that might help. 'Look, if it makes you feel better, I can defer the year,' I said. 'So that way I have a back-up, in case it doesn't work out.'

In some way I didn't understand, it seemed disloyal to Eddie to have a back-up plan, but at least it got Mum to listen. When she spoke next she wasn't shouting. 'That'd be better, of course,' she said. 'But I don't like you deferring at all.'

'You didn't mind when Suzanne deferred her finals.'

'That was different, Carla, you know it was.'

A bit of silence passed between us. I reached my foot out for Eddie's runner and pushed it inside as far as it would go. I imagined I could feel some of Eddie still in it, some warmth left over from hundreds and hundreds of wears, and the thought was somehow comforting. I heard her sniff. I hoped she wasn't crying. 'You haven't asked me about Eddie,' I said. 'Don't you want to know anything about him?'

'Go on then.' She sighed. 'Tell me about him.'

'He's a singer,' I said, 'in a band.' I waited for her to say something, and when she didn't, I went on. 'They're really good.

They get great write-ups in all the papers here. His mum's in a band too. And she's a photographer.'

'So, you've met his parents?'

'His mum, Bonnie. She lives in Brooklyn. His dad lives in Philadelphia.'

'They're separated?'

'Divorced.'

The word hung between us, a death knell of a word. I wanted to get away from Eddie's parents, to say something that would make her understand. 'We get on so well, Mum. It's like I've known him all my life. I've never felt like this about anyone else.'

'What about Damien?'

'No.' I shook my head. 'I never felt like this about Damien. We were kids. It's different with Eddie. I love him – we really love each other.'

Mum laughed. 'Carla, you're twenty years old, you've known him two months. You think you know what love is but, believe me, you don't.'

I hated her then, her certainty, how she wanted us to fail. I thought of something important. 'You and Dad got together when you were my age.'

'We were both very young, too young.' Mum started going on then, about faraway hills being greener, how she'd counted down the days till she could leave Sligo and come up to Dublin. I stood up and walked over to the window, pushing the slats of the blinds apart to look at the cars and the people five storeys below. My eyes followed the delivery boy from the takeaway downstairs, pedalling the wrong way through the lines of stopped cars, disappearing out of sight at the end of the block.

I cut across her. 'You loved Dad. If he was still here, you'd still be together.'

It was a statement, not a question.

'If he was still here, would you be doing this?'

The words were designed to hurt me and they did, but I knew how to hurt too. 'If he was still here, he'd understand! He'd have

28

asked all about Eddie! He'd say it was important to follow my heart, that he wanted me to be happy.' My voice cracked on 'happy'. As I'd imagined what Dad would say, I could almost hear him inside my head, and suddenly more than anything I wished it was him I was having the conversation with, instead of Mum.

When she spoke again, her voice was quieter. 'Is that really what you think? That I don't want you to be happy? I just don't want you to throw your life away over some summer romance, that's all.'

I sank back on to the bed, twisting the phone cord tight around my index finger so the tip turned white. Something about the conversation had changed, and when Mum spoke next she sounded defeated, exhausted. I agreed to phone an old friend of hers in Boston, whose husband was a lawyer, and find out more about visas. I gave her the phone number of the apartment and Bonnie's number too, in case she needed to get in touch and I wasn't at home.

It was getting dark by then and my hand ached from holding the hamburger phone.

'How's Suzanne?' I said, to fill the silence.

'She's doing well. Out tonight with some new guy, a few job interviews lined up. I think it's only just hitting her that she's finished college, while I'm getting into the swing of it.'

'How's your course going? Do you like it?'

'It's very interesting, nice people.'

We both heard it, how we sounded like two people who'd only just met.

'I thought I might miss the lecture in the morning, because of the airport, but I suppose I've no excuse not to make it now.' She gave a little laugh after she'd said that, and there was something about it that jolted a sudden twist of love for her, the kind of love that made me want to jump down the phone line, to be there with her on the little wooden stool, and have her put her arms around me the way she must have when I was a little girl, when I fitted into the curves of her body as well as I fitted into my own.

'I love you, Carla,' she said. 'You do know that, don't you?'

She'd never said that before, and hearing it then was sad somehow, a burden, when it should've made me happy. I wanted to say it back but the words were stuck somewhere else. 'I know,' I said. 'I know you do.'

'You'll always have a home here, whatever happens.'

I bit my lip, nodded a nod she couldn't see. 'I know.'

'I hope you find whatever it is you're looking for over there.'

There was nothing more to say to that, at least nothing I could see then and we said goodbye. I remember that she hung up first, so the dial tone came on, before I folded the phone closed.

It was strange the feeling I had, freedom and fear, mixed up together. I sat on Eddie's bed, the phone still warm in my hands. I pictured her putting the phone back on the table before turning to pull the curtains across the front door to stop the night coming in through the glass. She might make herself a cup of tea to take up to bed, and when she passed the mirror in the hall, she'd check her hair, just like she always did.

And as I pictured all of that, what she might be doing on the other side of the world, the one thing I was certain of was that there'd be tears on her face, just like the tears on mine.

'I love you too, Mum,' I whispered, into the empty room. 'I love you too.'

FIVE

It was hot that fall and the tiny apartment was a sweatbox, hotter than it ever seemed in Montauk. I don't know if the air-conditioner did much good but at least it drowned the noise of the TV that Eddie's flatmate Greg kept on all night.

Eddie was doing some sound work then, when he could get it, and with rehearsals he was pretty busy. I called into loads of bars and cafés looking for a job but in the end it was Eddie who got me one in a bar along the strip in Coney Island that was open year round. His friend Danny owned it and it was so quiet he could've run it on his own but he hired me anyway. Eddie came down every night to pick me up after work and I introduced him to my customers, big-bellied guys in baseball caps who drank Seven and Sevens, and taught me to play euchre.

On the days we were both off he showed me more of the city, not the tourist spots this time, the real city, so real it seemed like it was nearly alive, the steam from manholes its breath, the black seams of tar its battle scars. East Village, West Village, Chelsea, Hell's Kitchen, block by block I got to know New York, as much as you can ever know New York, because once you know it, it changes again.

In Brooklyn we searched for apartments in neighbourhoods that were up and coming but still affordable. We saw one near where Bonnie lived in Williamsburg, and walking along the broken sidewalk, I remember hoping Eddie wouldn't like it and being relieved when it was gone already. Apartments went quickly in New York, even the bad ones, and in the end we found ours on Thanksgiving, when everyone else was eating turkey and watching football.

The price was right because it was on the wrong side of Nostrand but if you came at it from Dekalb it was safe enough. It was the top floor of a brownstone and I knew I was going to love that apartment before I even got inside it. I could feel my excitement building as we climbed the stairs up and up and up, the banister wobbly in places under my fingers. When Eddie turned to smile at me over his shoulder I knew he'd love it too.

We moved in the next day, borrowed Bonnie's boyfriend's Honda to do the journey and filled it with boxes of Eddie's records and clothes, his guitars and amps. My stuff still fit in my backpack, and I joked that I needed to go shopping straight away, just to make things even.

The only furniture in the apartment was a bed and a bottle-green corduroy couch. We filled the rest of the space with stuff we found on the sidewalk in areas nicer than ours, amazed at what people threw away. We painted everything, every inch of that apartment, even the light switches. We thought we'd be done in a few days but it took forever, all that painting. Not that we minded. We were in no rush. We'd Eddie's little CD player for company, the pizza and soda special from the place on the corner when we needed a break. And we talked all the time, all day painting and later at night when the candles flickered on the walls so you couldn't see the mistakes we'd made.

There was always so much to say then, it seemed we'd never run out of words.

★

One night, after we'd made love, Eddie told me about the day his dad had left. Even though he was right next to me in bed, he felt far away, his arm tucked behind his head, his gaze somewhere in the corner of the room. His dad had slammed the door so hard one of his mum's photographs had jumped off the wall. That was what Eddie remembered most, the glass cracking down the middle when it landed on the floor.

'It was my favourite of all her pictures,' he said, 'one she'd taken in Alaska, these two polar bears looking like bumps in the snow.'

He turned his head to look at me over his raised elbow and I waited for him to say more.

'She was crying in her room, I could hear her, and I didn't want her to be even sadder, so I tried to fix it. But I sliced my thumb when I picked up the glass. See there, right across the top.'

He held it out to me, the thumb with the shimmer of a scar, still there after all those years. I held it between my fingers and kissed it. 'You poor thing,' I said. 'That must've really hurt.'

'You know what's funny? I don't remember it hurting. I only remember watching the blood trickle down my hand first, then my whole arm. It was crazy, like blood from a movie, that real deep red. I guess I passed out because the next thing I remember I was in the ER.'

'That must've been scary.'

'Yeah, but it was kind of cool too. The doctor who stitched me up was Chinese, and he said if I was brave he'd get me any kind of candy I wanted. I asked him if he could get my dad to come home.'

I cuddled closer to him, resting my head on his chest. His arm wrapped around my shoulders, holding me tighter.

'Jeez, that sounds lame now that I think about it,' he said.

'No, it doesn't,' I said. 'It sounds horrible and scary. And sad. You were only a little boy.'

'I've never told anyone that before,' he said. 'I didn't even know I still remembered it. There's something about being with you, Carls. It's like I've a seam down my middle and you unzip it and everything comes out.'

We lay there in the dark, breathing in his memory.

'I know what you mean,' I said.

'You do? Sometimes I feel like I'm always the one telling you stuff. Tell me something. Tell me something about your dad.'

Before he'd finished the question an image came alive in my head, too close and too fast to stop it. Grass. Crumpled flowers – daffodils. A leg bent at the knee. Three tea-towels on a washing line. I pushed it away, wouldn't let myself see it, reaching straight away for something else.

'He was great fun at my birthday parties,' I said. 'He let me and my friends chase him all over the garden, cover him with that stickleback grass.'

'Stickleback grass?'

'You know, the weed? It's got some kind of gooey stuff on it, sticks to your clothes.'

'Must be an Irish weed, we never got none of that in Brooklyn.' He'd put on a fake New York accent, like he did sometimes, and I laughed.

The fan over our heads swished around, a shadow on the ceiling. Now that I'd remembered that memory, another came, Dad's office, reading The Famous Five. I remembered the sunlight catching in his glasses, the reflection of the notes he was reading, looking up to find him smiling at me. It might have been a memory of one Sunday in Trinity or a thousand Sundays. I thought about trying to explain it to Eddie but I was afraid to, as if out loud the memory might disintegrate into nothing.

'What about your mom? Did you chase her around with this sticky weed too?'

I imagined the scene, Mum being chased around by a bunch of five-year-olds, letting herself be pinned down on the grass. I giggled. 'No way,' I said. 'She'd never have let us do that. My mum never has a hair out of place.'

'Just like her daughter then,' Eddie said. 'So where was Mama Matthews, then, when all this garden fun was going on?'

I hesitated, tried to picture her, but all I could see was her smiling and pretty in her green Aer Lingus uniform, her hair shiny and dark like a conker. The image was static, like a photograph, I might have been picturing a photograph. 'I'm not sure how often she was there for my birthdays. She was away a lot.'

'You missed her?'

I thought about it, trying to be honest, with me, with him. 'Not really,' I said. 'Olivia, her sister, picked us up from school and Dad collected us from her on his way home from work. It was way more fun anyway, being with my cousins.'

'I'd say so,' Eddie said. 'I missed my cousins in Philly.'

'And when she was there she was always stressed, busy, that's what I remember. She'd always be cooking food and freezing it and labelling it with the name of the dish, even the day we were supposed to eat it.'

Eddie laughed.

'We got this cleaner then, Mrs Fox. To give Mum more time, I suppose. But even then I remember Mum running around, cleaning before Mrs Fox came.'

'Cleaning for the cleaner?' Eddie said. 'That's awesome. Hey, I bet you got those little cans of soda, though. A kid in my class in Philly always brought them in.'

'Yeah,' I said. 'Suzanne and I got those with our lunches, little cans of Coke.'

'His were Pepsi. I was so jealous.'

The conversation circled back to Eddie again, to his school in Philadelphia and what it was like having to move in with his dad and step-mom when Bonnie's drinking got really bad. I listened as he described the journey, his new room. As he talked about his class in school, my mind wandered back to Mum, the blank where it seemed my memories should have been. I remembered her schedule on the fridge, the smell of her perfume in the hall where'd she spray herself in front of the mirror before she left. But she was home a lot too, she must have been. Why didn't I remember those times?

Eddie played with my hair absently. Anytime she'd been there, she was getting ready to leave again. Maybe that was why I didn't remember. As I snuggled in closer to his warmth, I realised I'd told him the truth but a lie as well. I had missed Mum. Not when she was gone, but I missed her those other times, the times when she was actually there.

★

By Christmas my visa had run out, and even though Mum offered to pay for my flight home, I couldn't risk not being allowed back in. She didn't try to convince me, only said they'd miss me, and I felt a pang of guilt, picturing her and Suzanne at the dining-room table, two of them where there used to be four.

Christmas in New York was bigger and better than Christmas anywhere else. Midtown was wrapped up like a giant present and Eddie said the lights were so bright you could see them from outer space. There was snow on the sidewalk when we came out of the subway the day he brought me out to get my surprise.

'Where are we?' I said. 'Is this Alphabet City?'

Eddie smiled. His orange woolly hat was pulled down low over his sideburns, making him look younger somehow. 'Come on,' he said. 'This way.'

I followed him down a street I knew we'd been on before. A street where he'd told me his friend Vinny had a tattoo parlour. I felt my stomach drop. 'You're not thinking of getting me a tattoo?'

When he didn't answer, I pulled my hand away from him. 'Eddie! What kind of present is that? I thought you were taking me into the city to go shopping.'

We stopped outside a black door with a neon sign in the window. He folded his arms, bounced on the balls of his feet. 'I had this idea that we could both get the same one. Tatts are cool, Carls, memories on the outside. I thought you liked mine.'

'On *you*, Eddie. I never said I wanted to get one.'

'I'm not going to force you, Carls. If you want, I can get you earrings or a sweater or whatever. I just thought you might want something different. Something permanent. Something that'll always make sure we remember our first Christmas together.'

The ice in the wind stung my cheeks and I pulled my scarf higher, breathing in my own warm air. 'I'm only going to look,' I said, 'because we're here. I'm not saying I'm getting one.'

Eddie kissed me and pushed a buzzer on the door. A second

later Vinny was there, twice as tall as Eddie with a belly that hung below his black polo shirt. He made us coffee while we sat around on low stools leafing through pages of symbols, crosses, animals, spirals, stars. I didn't know if it was all the smoke in the air or looking at so many pictures that was making me nauseous. When Vinny went to get us more coffee I leaned towards Eddie. 'I don't think I want to do this,' I whispered. 'I think we should go.'

His hand found my thigh, kneaded it. 'We just haven't found the right one yet,' he said. 'When we do, we'll just know it's meant for us.'

Before I could answer him, Vinny was back, with a drawing that he placed on the table in front of us. It was a black swirl on white paper, simple and complicated and perfect. 'The infinity symbol,' he said, 'with a tribal twist. Kind of cool, huh?'

Eddie looked at me and raised the eyebrow with the piercing so it disappeared under his fringe. 'I think it's perfect. Carls?'

We decided to get it done on the outside of our ankles, my left and Eddie's right, so they'd line up when we stood next to each other. As Vinny held my ankle tightly, the relentless buzzing pain seemed to go on for ever. I crushed Eddie's fingers hard with my own when he told me I was really brave because getting it done on bone was sorest of all.

It was days before the scab came off and I'd nearly forgotten about it until one morning when I was in the shower and looked down to see this new addition to my body, the clear loopy black line that had caused so much fuss. I soaped over it and rinsed it so the skin was white and shiny. It was still there.

I ran back into the bedroom in my towel. 'Eddie, Eddie, look! I've got a tattoo!'

'What?' He rolled over, still half in the duvet. I put my foot on the bed and he held it, inspecting my ankle, rubbing his thumb over it before he kissed it. 'Wow! My girl, tatted up!'

'What about yours? Check and see if it's ready too.'

He stretched his leg out from under the duvet and there it was: a swirl of black on the triangle of his bone, just like the one on mine. He shuffled over in bed, so I could lie next to him. We lined up our feet. Our ankles touched so the swerve of black ran into itself. You couldn't tell where my tattoo ended and his began.

'That,' he said, 'is awesome! Perfect! You happy we got them?'

'Yes,' I said. 'Very.'

In one move he scrambled out from under the duvet and on top of me. He propped himself above me, pushing my wet hair off my face. 'Infinity,' he said. 'This is for ever, you know.'

There seemed to be ages after he said that, a big gap between the words ending and the kiss beginning, seconds that were full of his face, his eyes brown and deep, telling me he wasn't just talking about the tattoo.

It was a moment that became one of those touchstone moments, a memory I polished up, that over the years I came back to, again and again. Because no matter what else was going on, how lost I ever felt, remembering that morning, our love, our certainty, always seemed to help.

Six

Mum's first visit was in March, over the Easter holidays, almost a full year since I'd last seen her. It was strange to be back in JFK, the whole airport totally unfamiliar, as if I'd never been there before. Watching people come through the double doors, I made up a game to take my mind off my nerves – I had to guess if they were on vacation or coming home. A woman and a little boy, a trolley load of cases: coming home, definitely. An old couple, wheelie bags: probably vacation.

My bladder twinged but I wasn't going to leave my spot and risk missing her. What if I had already? She'd reminded me last night about her hair, said it made her look very different, but I'd recognise her, of course I would.

The doors opened again. A couple with backpacks, his navy, hers red: vacation. Watching them disappear into the crowd, I wondered when Eddie and I would be able to make a trip like that, not with the band, just the two of us. I checked my watch: forty minutes since her plane had landed. When I looked up a cluster of young girls were standing there, blocking the door, and when they moved she was there, really there.

For a second I let myself just watch her like that, tall and graceful, pushing her trolley in a way that said she knew where she was going, not at all like the other crumpled passengers who stood around like prizes, waiting to be claimed. When she'd said she wasn't dyeing her hair any more I'd expected it to be grey, but it wasn't grey at all, it was silver and chic, cut along the line of her jaw.

'Mum!' I called. 'Over here!'

Her hair swung as she turned, her whole face becoming a smile, just for me. 'Carla!'

I stepped around the people in my way and she hurried over with her trolley, letting go of it to hug me with a fierceness I hadn't expected. Dad had always been the hugger, Mum preferred kisses that landed in awkward places – the side of your forehead, an ear sometimes – but that day we hugged for ages, swaying a little back and forth. She must just have reapplied her perfume, it was the same one I remembered from the hall.

'How was your journey?'

'Have you been waiting long?'

We talked over each other and stopped, then did it all over again. I took hold of the trolley, swinging it towards where I knew the buses went from. It felt good to be in charge.

The bus was half full and we took a seat near the back, Mum next to the window. She took a mirror from her purse and checked her makeup, reached into her bag to reapply her lipstick.

'I look like the wreck of the Hesperus,' she said. 'I'd forgotten how exhausting flying is. I don't know how I used to do it all the time.'

'You look great. I really like your hair.'

'And yours is lovely too. You never told me.'

'I wanted to surprise you.'

'Well, you did. I didn't know we'd a redhead in the family.' She clipped her compact back together.

She did look great. I wasn't just saying it, there was something different about her but I wasn't sure what it was.

'You sure you don't mind about me staying in a hotel?'

'No,' I said, 'of course not.' I heard the edge of the lie in my voice and something told me she'd heard it too.

'I just didn't want to land in on top of you and Eddie,' she said. 'Not for five days.'

'I know,' I said. 'It makes sense to be in Manhattan, the centre of things. It's not like our apartment is the Ritz or anything.'

Eddie had laughed at me getting upset that Mum wouldn't stay, reminding me how much I'd been dreading the three of us cooped up together in the apartment. It was silly, I knew, but it wasn't just the hotel, it was the fact that she was heading to Boston straight after. She was entitled to see her friends, of course she was. It just made me wonder if I was the reason she'd come over at all.

'Well, Ritz or not, I'm looking forward to seeing your apartment. And getting to know a bit of Brooklyn – Eddie too, of course.'

Her smile was genuine. It seemed like a long time since she'd insisted on referring to him as 'that Eddie'. Last week they'd even spoken on the phone. The bus driver said something I didn't catch into the intercom and the engine rumbled to life. I raised my voice so she could hear me over it. 'He can't wait to meet you too.'

★

They got on great, Eddie and Mum, from the moment they met in the hotel lobby and she came straight over and hugged him, without waiting to be introduced. Over dinner she asked him about the band and what his musical influences were, and he teased her about loving Neil Diamond, said if she came to see them play, he'd sing 'Sweet Caroline', just for her. He asked her all about her travelling, places she'd been, things I'd never thought to ask her. Sitting between them in the semi-circular booth, I laughed at the stories she told us, stories I'd never heard before, stories that sounded like they were about someone else and not my mum at all.

The next morning in the lobby, waiting for her to finish chatting to the concierge, I was nervous all over again and wished Eddie could have come, so we could laugh again the way we had the night before.

'That's Mauricio,' she said, smiling as she walked over. 'He remembered me from the Aer Lingus days.'

'You obviously made an impression,' I said.

We pushed our way through the revolving doors and out on to Fifth Avenue, turning right towards Central Park. 'Your first glimpse of New York City by day,' I said, sidestepping a Japanese couple reading a map. 'Has it changed?'

She shook her head. 'Still the same energy as ever,' she said. 'But I was out already this morning. I went for breakfast in Grand Central.'

At the corner the lights were red and we stopped next to a pretzel vendor.

'You did?' I hadn't pictured Mum venturing out for breakfast. I'd assumed she'd eat in the hotel restaurant, that she'd wait for me to show her around.

'It's one of my old haunts. I used to love getting breakfast there, watching everyone dashing about. I've always had this idea that I'd love to jump on a train, any train, just as it was pulling out to see where I'd end up.'

'Me too!' I said. 'I've always wanted to do that too!'

'We'll have to do it some day,' she said.

She smiled and I did too, and I remember being grateful for that moment, even as it was happening, her wide smile, the lift of her chin, the rectangle of blue sky behind. And I remember thinking that out of our five days together, if all we had was that moment, that it might just be enough.

*

She'd booked a table at the Boathouse and it was even nicer inside than I'd imagined, filled with light, the tinkle of cutlery and conversation. The waiter showed us to a table by the window. The lake was clear of greeny sludge that day so the water was multicoloured, a reflection of trees and sky and clouds.

'It's really expensive, Mum. Are you sure this is OK?' I said, scanning the menu.

'Relax. It's not every day I get to have lunch with my daughter in Central Park.'

When the drinks arrived we toasted, my Diet Coke against her glass of red wine. I shook a cigarette into my hand from the box of Marlboro in my pocket. Even though I'd smoked the night before, I felt suddenly self-conscious, alone with her in the daylight, and it took me three strikes to light it.

'It's chillier here than at home,' Mum said.

She'd already said that, in the park, and I hoped we weren't running out of conversation already, with four and a half days to go.

'Yeah,' I said, inhaling deeply, letting the smoke hit the back of my throat.

'Although, once the weather turns fine, I'll know that my exams are only around the corner.'

'You've probably done loads of study.'

She tilted her head to one side. 'A bit. It's just, it's so long since I've done anything like this. And I'd hate to fail.'

'You won't,' I said.

'The assessment during the year helps,' she said. 'I'm not someone who rises to the pressure of exams. Some people do. You were always good at exams.' She took another sip of wine, left some lipstick on the glass.

I didn't like where this conversation was going.

'Crab cakes?' The waiter had reappeared, standing over us with huge white plates. I put out my cigarette. In one seamless motion he replaced the dirty ashtray with a clean one from his pocket.

'He's deadly efficient, isn't he?' Mum said, when he was far enough away not to hear. 'If a bit severe. Are they all as efficient as him in your restaurant?'

She hadn't seen the diner in downtown Brooklyn where I worked, with its sticky ketchup bottles and sticky tables and sticky tiled floor.

'The only people who pocket the ashtrays there are the customers,' I said, taking a bite of crab. 'Along with the salt, pepper and cutlery.'

It wasn't as bad as I was making out, not really. Like the apartment, I wanted it to sound worse than it was so that when she got to see it she'd be pleasantly surprised.

'How long are you going to stay there? What's happening with the college applications?' She put a forkful of salad into her mouth after she'd asked, chewed slowly.

The question had been coming since she'd walked through the doors at JFK, since before then, but somehow I still didn't have an answer. I drank some of my Diet Coke. 'I meant to tell you. The ones I applied for didn't come through.'

'Oh,' she said. 'Sorry to hear that. How many did you go for?'

'Three.'

'Three?'

She didn't say 'only' but she might as well have.

'A lot of them were already past their closing date and I hadn't realised how much effort each one was. It takes days to put them together.' I heard defensiveness in my voice.

'Well, they're not going to make it easy, I suppose. I'm sure you know it's a numbers game, that you'll have to apply for a lot more than three.'

'Yes, Mum, I know that.' I ate some more crab, mixed it with the salad. I realised that some part of me had thought three applications would be enough. I didn't remember Dad talking about any other scholarship applications.

She paused, a forkful of salad in mid-air, and I waited for what I knew was coming next: that I had to do something one way or the other, that I couldn't leave things as they were. 'They're much harder to get, these days, scholarships, very competitive. Don't go beating yourself up that you didn't get one of those three, sure you won't?'

I wasn't expecting her to have guessed that the harder it was to get a scholarship the more I'd want one, that the feeling of not being good enough, of failing, would gnaw away at me, no matter how long the odds were. 'I won't.' I swallowed the last bite and pushed my plate away.

'Did you ever hear of community colleges?' Mum said. 'Andrea Clarke from the badminton club was telling me her niece is in one over here and it's much cheaper than the universities. If you got into one of those maybe I could help you out with the fees a bit.'

44

I twisted my glass on the coaster, thought about the ads on the subway, smiling middle-aged men and women who went back to school to get associates' business degrees. 'Thanks, Mum,' I said. 'But they're not proper universities. They're like a tech or something.'

She finished her food, lined up her knife and fork. 'Well,' she said, 'wouldn't that be better than nothing?'

Better than working as a waitress, was what she meant.

'Not really,' I said. 'They're all business courses. I don't want to do business. I want to study English, to write.'

She wiped her mouth with her napkin, taking her time over it as if she was thinking about what to say next. When she moved it away from her lips, her smile was tight. 'They can't all be business courses. Maybe you could look into it.'

I reached to take another cigarette. She watched me but didn't say anything.

'You're right,' I said, 'I will.'

Over the rim of her wine glass, her eyes held mine for a second too long and I felt that she could see right through me, that she knew I'd no intention of going to some night school in the back end of Brooklyn or Queens to take courses with people twice my age. That was what she was thinking and maybe she would have said it, but then the waiter was clearing our plates away and it was time for the conversation to move on to something else.

★

Outside, the clouds had rolled in, threatening rain. A guy sat on a bench playing the saxophone to the pigeons at his feet. I recognised his stripy fingerless gloves and realised I'd seen him before.

'I think we should head back the quickest way,' I said, 'skip the Rambles.'

'Probably a good idea,' she said.

'Let's go this way,' I said. 'I'll show you my favourite bit of the park – it's called the Mall.'

When we got to the tree-lined walkway, Mum stopped, looked around. 'I remember this part,' she said. 'They filmed that scene in *Kramer vs. Kramer* here, when he's learning to ride his bike.' She walked on slowly, her arms wrapped around herself, tipping her head back to see the branches over our heads. 'I remember going to see it with your father. I cried my eyes out and he hated it. Said it was sentimental American rubbish.'

Unbidden, a memory surfaced. A white-blonde kid, a wobbling bike, watching it in my pyjamas on the couch, leaning up against Dad, Suzanne lying next to us, on her stomach in front of the fire.

'Dad liked it,' I said. 'I watched it with him too.'

She shook her head. 'You must be thinking of some other film.'

I felt myself tense. I didn't want to talk about this, remember this, but now she was making me. 'No, I'm not. He liked it – he even let us stay up until the end. Ask Suzanne if you don't believe me.'

'I don't remember that.'

'You weren't there,' I said. 'You were away.'

The breeze had picked up and the leaves rustled in the branches over our heads. I waited for her to argue with me, to tell me I'd got it wrong – part of me even wanted her to – but instead she turned to me and smiled. 'Sounds like he grew to like it,' she said.

We walked on in silence then and I was thinking of a safe topic to bring up when she spoke first. 'I ran into Ange's mum the other day,' she said. 'She was saying they're all heading back to Montauk. You must be dying to see them.'

A man in a neon pink jacket jogged directly towards us, swerving around us at the very last minute.

'Yeah,' I said, burying my hands in my pockets. 'I am.'

'Would you think about getting a job out there for the summer?'

'I'd love to,' I said, 'but the timing doesn't suit. It looks like Eddie'll have a tour in June and July, all the way down the coast as far as Florida and I said I'd go with him.'

'What about the apartment?'

'We'll have to give it up. We've no choice.'

She didn't say anything, and I wondered if Ange's mum had mentioned the argument we'd had about it, how Ange couldn't understand why I had to go, was still guilt-tripping me.

'You must miss your friends, though?'

I kicked a pebble along the path. Was it her psychology course that made her able to mine a nerve or had she always been like that? 'Yeah, but we talk on the phone. Write. And I'll see her at the end of the summer.'

'It's probably easier not to miss people here,' she said, 'somewhere new, where you've no real memories of them.'

I glanced at her, wondering what she was getting at, but she was looking the other way, towards a woman practising t'ai chi, a silhouette in the light, legs bent, arms raised into a curve, turning so slowly to one side she was barely moving at all.

'Did you ever try that?' she asked.

'T'ai chi? No.'

'If I was your age now, in this city, I'd love to try all these things. I want to do a yoga class, while I'm here, if I can fit it in.'

'On your holidays? Would you not give yourself a break?'

She laughed. 'Yoga *is* a break for me. I love it.'

I asked her what she loved about it and she talked about it all the way out of the park, and for most of the twelve blocks home. She lit up as she spoke, explaining the philosophy behind it, how it opened up your body and your mind. That she was thinking about going to India in the summer, with her new friend from college, Lily-Anne. By the time we reached the hotel even I was curious.

'It does sound interesting,' I admitted. 'Maybe I'll try it some time.'

'Would you?' She looked genuinely pleased. 'If I found a class here, would you come with me?'

'I meant some time in my life, not in the next few days.'

'Sure what is life if it's not the day we have today?' She opened her hands to the sidewalk around us, the people streaming past.

47

'I've no mat, and I'm not buying one just for one class.'

'They'll have some at the studio.'

I hesitated. 'But we wouldn't be in the same class, would we? I'd need a beginners' one.'

'We could find an open class,' she said. 'Although I have to warn you, you might not like it. Suzanne didn't take to it at all.'

'Really?' I said.

'I think it was too slow for her. You know Suzanne, likes to be all go.'

Suzanne always liked the same things Mum did and the fact that she didn't like yoga made it suddenly more appealing, that we could have something that we did together, on our own. 'OK,' I said. 'If you find a class, I'll think about it.'

★

They went quickly, those five days, in a blur of shopping and sightseeing, and a yoga class in Greenwich Village. Mum came to see the apartment and said she really liked it, that it had character. We went to see the band in the Sidewalk Café on her last night and Bonnie showed up unexpectedly with her new boyfriend John, and Eddie sang 'Sweet Caroline', just like he'd promised.

She'd checked out already by the time I met her in the lobby, was taking a ticket for her bag. I wished that she wasn't going to Boston, that I could have two more days with her, and I wondered if she thought the same thing.

'So,' she said, fixing a red and grey scarf around her neck. 'What do you want to do today? We have till about four.'

Suddenly the whole of New York seemed tiny and uninspiring, as if we'd done every single thing there was to do already.

'Bonnie says there's an amazing exhibition on at the Whitney. I've never been there.'

Mum made a face. 'Do you feel like an art exhibition? Is there any place in the city you haven't shown me yet? One of your favourite spots?'

If Dad had been there I'd have taken him to the library. That was the thought that came and she read it as it crossed my face.

'There is somewhere,' she said. 'Where?'

That was how we ended up there on her last day, taking photos of each other at the lions outside before we walked past them and up the steps. I told her they were called 'Patience' and 'Fortitude' and she was interested in that, how they'd got their names, was impressed by the marble columns and staircase inside. I took her to the reading room, where the arched windows let in just enough of the city above the shelves of books and journals. She asked me to show her where I liked to sit and we walked past the rows of long tables towards the one second from the back. We sat down side by side, tilting our heads so we could see the pinks and golds of the clouds on the ceiling.

'It's beautiful,' she whispered.

We spent ages in the gift shop and we thought we were out of time, but when we got to Penn there was half an hour before her train. Standing around drinking coffee, I wanted it to be over, for her already to be gone.

'Geraldine was saying that you and Eddie have an open invite to go to Boston,' she said.

'That's nice of her. I'll tell him. I'd like to go to Cape Cod too – the beaches look amazing.'

'You and Suzanne always loved the sea. I can still picture you in Rosses Point, running in and out of the waves, squealing. Thick as thieves, the two of you.'

'Really?'

'Oh, yes, you always got on great on holidays.' She nodded, remembering. 'The rows only started on the way home.'

I laughed. That bit I could remember, drawing pictures on my fogged-up window so I wouldn't have to talk to her.

'I wish you were closer,' Mum said suddenly. 'I wish you'd stay in touch a bit more.'

I'd known she thought that but she'd never said it before and I wished she hadn't. I swished my coffee in a circle. 'I try, Mum.

I'm always asking you how she is. And I sent her a birthday card.'

Mum sighed. 'Don't get defensive, love. I'm not saying it's your fault — it's not anyone's fault. It's just that she's your sister. I'd have been lost without Olivia, after your dad died. Sure she was the one who encouraged me to go back to college and everything.'

I drained my coffee cup and threw it into the garbage. 'Not all sisters are as close as you and Olivia,' I said. 'Suzanne and I don't have anything in common.'

An announcement came over the Tannoy, and as we listened to it I hoped it would be her train, that it would end this conversation. When it stopped she turned to me again.

'Yourself and Suzanne are different in lots of ways,' she said. 'She's not as strong as you are. But you've a lot in common too. All I'm saying is maybe both of you could make more of an effort. Send her the odd postcard — she'd be delighted. I worry sometimes. If anything happened to me, it'd be important for you to have each other.'

For a second I felt the grip of panic that she was going to tell me she was sick, dying. Until I realised she wouldn't tell me that, not here, that it was only one of those theoretical conversations, the kind that it was easiest to agree with and move on from.

'OK, Mum,' I said. 'I'll make more of an effort. I promise.'

*

She went to the newsagent, and by the time she came out the platform number was on the board and the crowd had lined up.

'Gosh,' she said, bending down to take her ticket from her bag. 'They're on the ball.'

When she looked up her eyes were a shinier brown than usual.

'You have everything?' I said. 'Your passport?'

She patted her jacket pocket. 'Yep.'

'And you'll call me when you get to Boston?'

I was in control again, like when I'd collected her at the airport.

'Yes, Carla, I'll call you when I get there.'

When she hugged me, I hugged her back and it was hard to let go.

'I'd a great time, love,' she said, 'and I'll come back soon, or maybe you'll come to see us soon.'

I forced a smile.

'And I'm so glad I met Eddie finally, tell him I said 'bye.'

'I will. And say hi to Olivia. Tell her if she gets over her fear of flying I'll take her out to the Waldorf for dinner.'

'I think it'll take more than that to get her over here.' She had her bag in one hand, the newspaper she'd just bought in the other. The crowd in front of her gate began to move.

'You'd better get going – you don't want to miss it.'

She looked like she wanted to hug me again, but we'd already hugged. 'OK then, I love you. Bye.'

I wanted to say it to her, was about to, but before I could, she was striding, tall and straight, into the crowd. The queue moved quickly through the door to the platform and I watched her progress. Just before she went through, she turned back and waved with the paper still in her hand. I waved too, standing on my tiptoes to make sure she'd see me, even though I knew she had. For a moment I thought about getting another coffee, waiting till the train actually left, but that was silly, she was already gone.

I dug my hands deep into my pockets, took one last glance over my shoulder, then made my way downstairs to the subway that would take me home to Brooklyn, to Eddie.

SEVEN

New York did rain like no other city did rain and even after three years I couldn't get used to it, the relentlessness of it that made rivers on the roads, shin deep at the corner of each block. Manhattan was always worse than Brooklyn in the rain – all the concrete I supposed – and that was where we were going that rainy night, to meet Suzanne. The subway had been on a go slow for the whole journey and at Canal Street it stopped entirely. A garbled voice announced the track ahead was flooded.

'Great,' Eddie said. 'That's just fucking great! We're never going to get a cab. You want to just go home?' He raised his eyebrow like it was a joke, but something told me it wasn't, at least not entirely.

'Eddie, we can't go home! She's only here for one night!'

'Who comes to New York for one night?'

The carriage doors opened and he was on the platform before I could answer. I hurried after him as he weaved through the crowd. 'She probably doesn't want to meet us either,' I said. 'If it wasn't for Mum she probably wouldn't even have told me about her stopover here.'

Eddie didn't respond, just kept pushing ahead. When we got to the steps he took them two at a time, hunching into the rain when he got to the top. I hitched my jacket over my head and followed him. Within seconds I was sopping, trickles of rain finding their way down my sleeve, and I wished I hadn't binned my umbrella, broken or not.

Eddie turned around, his denim jacket almost black, his fringe dripping on his face. A cab drove by and splashed him.

'Fuck!' he said, shaking his leg out. 'Come on, let's try and find a bus.'

I followed him up the block and across the street, my head down. Water poured along the sidewalk, my Converse squelching through it, not white any more but dirty grey. The bus shelter was full so we huddled together under the awning of a sex shop, next to a garbage bin full of broken umbrellas. Eddie looked the other way, hands in wet pockets, sighing every so often to remind me that he didn't want to be here. Something about his stance turned my guilt to irritation and I felt bad, suddenly, for slagging Suzanne off in front of him. It didn't seem that long ago since he'd wanted to know everything about my family, and now she was actually here, he didn't seem to care.

On the street the cars weren't moving now, most of them cabs with steamed-up windows, all with their lights off. A man stood at the edge of the sidewalk holding out one drenched arm. I looked up the block and a bus was there, caught way behind. Slowly, it lurched towards us and we moved from the awning out towards the kerb, but when it came close we could see the bodies packed tight inside and it drove past without stopping.

'Jesus H. Christ!' Eddie said.

A girl joined our group, standing in the place just where the rain was bouncing down on to the sidewalk and we shunted close together to make room. Eddie folded his arms, drummed his fingers on his sleeve. His shitty mood had nothing to do with Suzanne, not really, I knew that, and as we stood there, I tried to put myself in his shoes: stuck in the middle of all this fighting between Rob and Nick and then losing their Saturday night in Solomon's. It was enough to put anyone in a shitty mood.

'You going to get the chicken wings tonight?' I said.

He shrugged. 'I can never decide between those and the meatballs. They're both great there.'

'Why not get them both?' I said. 'My treat.'

He smiled. A little smile, but still a smile. I smiled back. Couples went through phases, people got in shitty moods. Soon things would be back to normal. Even as I thought it, another thought formed right behind it. But what if this became normal? A new version of normal. A version I didn't like quite as much as the one before.

*

I didn't wait for the hostess. I'd spied them in the corner of the room, by the window.

'I'm sorry, I'm sorry – I'm so sorry! The subway was flooded and we couldn't get a cab and it's just horrible out there.'

My excuses started when I was three tables away, Eddie right behind me. Suzanne was standing up, elegant in a black dress, her hair longer, down past her shoulders.

'Oh, my God,' she said, 'look at you – you're soaking.'

She reached out to hug me, pulling away when she realised just how wet I was.

'Don't!' I said. 'You'll get drenched!'

'You sure you didn't swim here?'

She looked more like Mum than ever, her laugh, her wide smile just the same, except for a little too much pink gum. 'You look great,' I said. 'It's good to see you.' As I said it, I realised it was.

'You too,' she said. 'Here, meet Ian.'

Eddie and Ian had already introduced themselves and were shaking hands. Ian was exactly Suzanne's type – handsome, designer shirt tucked into dark jeans, sleeves rolled halfway up. Eddie peeled off his jacket and his T-shirt was slicked to his skin, making him look scrawnier than ever. I felt a twinge of tenderness.

'Ian, Carla; Carla, Ian.'

I went to shake Ian's hand but he acted faster: he put one hand on my shoulder and planted a firm kiss on my cheek. His aftershave smelt nice, not too strong. Eddie never wore aftershave.

'Great to meet you, finally,' he said. 'I've heard so much about you.'

'It's all true, I'm afraid. The Tabasco sauce on her recorder mouthpiece, the time I drew moustaches on her Five Star posters.' I laughed, looking at Suzanne.

'You never told me you were a Five Star fan.'

'Was I?' she said. 'I don't remember having any Five Star posters.'

She frowned, trying to remember, and I felt foolish for bringing it up until I felt Eddie's hand on my shoulder as he reached over to kiss Suzanne.

'You've probably repressed it,' he said. 'Post-traumatic musical stress or something.'

They laughed, and I loved him for rescuing me, for leaving his shitty mood outside on the sidewalk. Ian pulled out a chair and I sat down facing Suzanne. 'Let's order,' he said. 'You guys must be starving.'

'I know what I'm having,' Suzanne said.

I looked up from the menu. 'Lasagne?'

Suzanne smiled and drank some water. 'Surprise, surprise!'

Ian looked amused, reached over and held her hand on the table. 'Wow, from this huge menu, that's a good guess. How did you know?'

'What can I say? My sister's a creature of habit.'

'By creature of habit, Carla means boring,' Suzanne said.

'Creature of habit is what I said. Boring's your word, not mine.'

I went back to the menu, half reading, half listening to Eddie telling the story about the time Bonnie was here when some woman recognised her and asked her to sing 'Happy Birthday' to her husband. The waitress came and took our order, and Eddie moved on to another story, about a gig in South Carolina. Across the table, hand in hand with Ian, Suzanne looked like a lady, an adult. In the pictures in my head she was in her school uniform, hockey clothes. I'd no clear memory of the last time we'd seen each other. The closest I could pinpoint was that day when I'd opened the front door and she'd fallen into the hall, makeup and tears and snot on her face. That was the day she'd broken down in the exam hall, but it was ages ago, more than a year before I left.

Eddie turned to me to take up the story at the same point he always did, both of us sharing the punch line that made everyone laugh. Ian took his hand off Suzanne's long enough to slap the table before starting a story of his own.

The waitress came back with more wine for them and beers for us. Suzanne's nails on her glass were pink and shiny, long but not too long, the way nails should be. I held my bottle so she wouldn't see mine. Under the table my jeans felt wetter against my skin and I wanted to be at home. But I wasn't home, I was in an Italian restaurant with the lights of Times Square blurry in the rain behind us. Ian's story finished and I jumped into the gap of conversation. 'Are you excited about going to Mexico?'

'I can't wait,' Suzanne said. 'Work's been manic and I'm just dying for the break.'

'It's our first holiday together,' Ian said, rubbing his thumb on her fingers.

'Our first holiday outside Ireland,' she corrected. She looked from me to Eddie. 'We've been to Kerry and west Cork.'

'Where in Mexico are you going?' Eddie asked.

'Cancun,' Suzanne said. 'Well, a resort, just outside.'

'Cool. Sounds awesome.' Eddie drank more beer.

We'd talked about going to Mexico, Eddie and I, planned a trip around the country but we'd never made it happen.

'So, how did you guys meet?' I said, directing the question at Suzanne.

'Guess,' she said, smiling.

'Not hockey?'

She nodded.

'I didn't think guys and girls played on the same team.'

'We're in a mixed club,' she said. 'It was a charity game so we were playing together.'

'She was the captain,' Ian said, 'and she was amazing – she scored three goals.'

Suzanne looked down at her wine. 'It was only a bit of fun.'

'Don't be so modest,' he said. 'You played a blinder that day.'

He leaned over then to kiss her, right on the lips in front of us, and I became conscious that Eddie and I hadn't touched each other since we'd sat down. In fact, when I thought about it, I wasn't sure if we'd even kissed that day. I reached over and touched his thigh, his jeans still wet. He put his hand on mine for a few seconds, before he let it go.

★

My lips in the mirror were red at the edges from too much wine. I pulled them back to check there was nothing in my teeth. As I did, I saw Suzanne coming in through the door behind me.

'Hi,' I said.

'Those two were having some debate about David Bowie. I don't think they even noticed that I left.'

I smiled at myself in the mirror, at her. 'Once Eddie's in full flow about music the whole restaurant could leave and he wouldn't notice.'

'It's good that they're getting on well, though,' she said.

I nodded. They were. It seemed like they'd dominated the whole conversation tonight, that Suzanne and I had hardly said anything at all. She leaned into the mirror to check her hair, folded it behind an ear.

'Are you OK?' she asked.

'Me? I'm fine. Why?' I reached for the soap, washed my hands slowly, feeling the water warm on my skin.

'I don't know,' she said. 'It just feels like you've been away with the fairies for half the night.'

Mum used to say that all the time, but I hadn't heard the expression in years.

'I'm fine, a bit tired. It was busy today at work.'

'At the restaurant?'

There was something in the way she said it that made it more than a question. 'Yes,' I said. 'At the restaurant.' I dried my hands with a paper towel and we stood in silence.

'I'm knackered too,' she said. 'The jet-lag. We should call it a night soon. Wait here, will you, while I go to the loo?'

She disappeared into the cubicle and, looking at the white plastic door, I realised that in an hour, less, she'd be gone. We hadn't seen each other in nearly three years, there had to be other things that we should be talking about but now I had her on my own I couldn't think of what they were.

'I ran into Ange's mum last week. I hear her and Pete are engaged,' Suzanne called, her voice disappearing into the flush. The door opened. 'Do you think you'll come home for the wedding?'

She had her back to me now, at the washbasin. She kept her voice light.

'I don't know yet,' I said. 'I'd love to.'

'I'm sure it'd mean a lot to her if you could make it. And to Mammy.'

She glanced up into the mirror and caught my eye. I looked away. Mammy. It sounded ridiculous, like she was six years old.

She threw her paper towel into the silver bin, turned back to the mirror and took a lipstick from her bag.

'So, things seem good with you,' I said. 'You seem much better.'

'Yeah,' she said. 'I am.'

'Good,' I said. 'That's great.'

She opened her mouth, sliding the colour over her lips, licking them. 'Everything just got on top of me, after Dad and everything.'

I nodded, fiddling with my necklace. 'Mum seems like she's in good form, loving college. She'll miss it next year.'

'It's given her a new lease of life, I suppose, but it hasn't all been easy.' She clicked the top on her lipstick and her dark hair fell across her face as she put it back in her bag. 'She worries about you, Carla, a lot. She'd love it if you came home every now and then, maybe for her graduation.'

Two mentions of coming home in as many beats of conversation. I slid the beads up and down my necklace. 'Suzanne, I'd love to be there and for Ange's wedding. You know it's not that easy.'

She turned back to the mirror again, fixing her hair with a brush she took from her bag. I dropped the necklace and folded my arms.

'You'll have to sort it out, though, Carla. I mean, whatever about working illegally for a few months, but it's coming up to three years.'

She was still facing the mirror, and over her shoulder I could see me as she saw me, my cheeks red, getting redder. My hair flat from the rain. In this light it looked yellow, not blonde, and I decided, then and there, to go dark again, as soon as I could.

'I mean, what if something happened, Carla? Something where you needed to come home?'

I held my arms tighter, felt my body hardening. 'If I needed to come home, I'd get home. It's complicated, not something I can sort out overnight, but I will. OK?'

It hung in the air, that 'OK', floating between us and the white bathroom tiles. She picked up her bag and slung it over her shoulder. She smiled a little at herself in the mirror and wiped some lipstick off the corner of a tooth.

'Fine,' she said. 'OK.'

When she looked at me, her eyebrows creased, just a little.

'I know it's none of my business, and this is the last thing I'll say, but what I don't get is why you two don't get married. Wouldn't that solve everything?'

Responses formed in my head. That no one ran up to you on the steps of the City Courthouse and gave you a Green Card as soon as you got married, that there was time involved, legal fees. That me and Eddie getting married was none of her damn business.

I opened the restroom door, let in the dining-room noise, the hum of conversation, music, laughter. 'It's not as simple as that,' I said. 'And you're right, it's not really any of your business.'

★

By the time we left the restaurant the rain had stopped and Eddie was up for going to another bar, but Ian glanced at Suzanne and said maybe next time, when they weren't so jet-lagged. We said goodbye on the corner of 42nd and 8th at the top of the steps to the subway, a kiss on the cheek again from Ian, a light quick hug with Suzanne as if we'd only met that night.

The subway carriage was almost empty and we sat near the door, Eddie the one, this time, chatting through the night, his arm around me on the back of the seat. It turned out Ian had a friend who worked in a record company in London and they'd exchanged contact details. Tomorrow he was going to put together a CD to send him, some of their newer tracks. 'Your sister's nice,' he said. 'I'm glad I got to meet her. She's quiet, though.'

'It was hard for anyone to get a word in edgeways,' I said, 'with the two of you.'

Eddie pulled back his arm and gave me a wounded look. 'Jesus, Carls! I can't win with you! Earlier you were all about making an effort, then I make an effort and I'm talking too much.'

'I'm sorry,' I said, suddenly contrite. 'You're right, I'm being a moody bitch. Suzanne brings that out in me.'

I reached for his hand and he let me hold it, wrapping his fingers slowly around mine. 'Good thing they were only here for one night,' he said.

'I'm still surprised they stopped over. I guess there're no direct flights from Ireland.'

'You're kidding, right?' Eddie said, his eyebrows knotted. 'When you guys were in the restroom Ian told me they were supposed to fly direct but Suzanne insisted on coming this way. They had to pay more, apparently.'

I looked down the carriage at a homeless guy asleep and back to Eddie. 'Really? Ian said that?'

'Sure. They were trying to get longer but they could only do the one night because of the connection or something.'

'She never said anything.'

'He made a point of saying it. Said they'd talked about maybe coming back for longer next time.'

I looked out the window at the tunnel. Next time. After our conversation in the loos it didn't feel like there'd be a next time. Maybe I should've apologised but I'd been right – us getting married was none of her business. Outside in the blackness a white light sped by, then another. Marriage. Even when Eddie brought it up I shied away from talking about it, not that he'd mentioned it for a while. Just because Ange and Pete were doing it didn't mean we had to and there was no law that said I had to be at their wedding. Or Mum's graduation. We wouldn't be able to afford the flights anyway. What was it Suzanne'd said? Getting married would solve everything, as if there was some big problem.

But there was no problem. No problem at all.

EIGHT

The Christmas after Olivia died was the only one Mum ever spent in New York, my fifth Christmas there. She wanted Suzanne to come too, so we'd all be together, but she was still with Ian then and they'd agreed to spend it with his family. It was the first time Mum stayed with us in our apartment. Hotels were double the price at that time of year, she'd said, and it was nice to be with family at Christmas.

Bonnie said she didn't mind having one more for dinner, and when she opened the door to us she was more festive than usual with tiny flashing Christmas trees that hung from her ears, her hair slicked back in a bun to show them off.

I bent down to hug her, and her hands were cold on my face as she kissed one cheek, then the other. 'Carla, honey, happy holidays,' she said. 'And, Collette, you look fabulous!'

'You too,' Mum said. 'I love your earrings.'

'Canal Street, five bucks,' Bonnie said, turning her head so the earrings swirled in a flash of colour. 'I should've picked them up for you guys too.'

She kissed Mum on both cheeks and then Eddie, standing on the steps behind us. 'Merry Christmas, honey,' she said.

'Merry Christmas, Mom.'

Inside the apartment a Christmas tree blocked most of the window and filled the air with the scent of pine. A table I'd never noticed before was in the centre of the room, covered with a holly-patterned cloth. Nightlights glowed on every surface, the table, the shelves, the window ledges, reflecting in the glass of the photo

62

frames that covered the walls. As we streamed in I was thinking how crowded it was with the four of us, until I saw there were five.

'This is Aaron,' Bonnie said, leaning on the arm of a man twice her height, wearing a red apron. 'Aaron, this is everyone.'

Aaron smiled through a full beard, edging around the table to shake our hands in his giant ones. I hadn't known anyone else was joining us, that she was even seeing someone, and from the look on Eddie's face, he hadn't either.

'Nice to meet you, Ed,' Aaron said, pumping his hand up and down. 'I've heard a lot about you.'

'Something smells wonderful,' Mum said, putting her bag of presents on a chair. 'Here's a little something to go with it.' She handed a bottle wrapped in gold paper to Bonnie. At first I thought it might be a bottle of something else, some kind of soda. 'It's a Merlot,' she said. 'I know that technically white would be better with turkey but red's so much nicer in winter, don't you think?'

I caught eyes with Eddie. He raised his pierced eyebrow but neither of us said anything.

Bonnie passed the bottle to Aaron without removing the paper. 'I'll leave that in your capable hands, honey,' she said. 'Aaron's doing the cooking today. We're having a vegetarian king.'

Aaron laughed a deep laugh that came from somewhere in his chest. 'It's called a vegetable crown, hon.'

'Well, it smells great, whatever it is,' she said, standing on tiptoe to kiss his cheek.

Eddie took our coats and we squashed around the table, Bonnie and Aaron opposite me and Mum, so Eddie took the stool at the end when he came back in. Aaron started to speak but Bonnie cut across him, her face excited. 'Well, Carla honey, did you love your present?'

'Yes, I did. It looks like a fantastic camera.' I smiled hard. I'd felt self-conscious this morning, having Mum there as Eddie and I exchanged presents, and I'd struggled to find the right reaction to the old-fashioned camera that felt so heavy around my neck. That Bonnie had helped him pick it out meant another audience, finding the right reaction all over again.

'I used to have one – did Eddie tell you? That's the camera Garry Winogrand used. Remember I told you about him?'

'He's the one who took all the photos of the zoo?' I said.

'That's right, and Coney Island. All over New York.'

'What is it? A Leica?' Aaron said. 'Let me see it.'

'It's an M4,' Bonnie said, 'chrome and black. Show him, Carla.'

I'd left it at home, the camera, in its box, with two types of wrapping paper, on the bed in our room and realised, suddenly, just how bad that looked. On the other side of the table, Eddie uncorked the wine and plopped a can of Dr Pepper in front of Bonnie. 'I don't have it with me,' I said.

'What?' Bonnie sat back in her chair.

'I left it in the apartment.'

'In the apartment?' Her voice rose to a pitch I thought might shatter the wine glasses. She was looking from me to Eddie, standing with the bottle of wine in his hand.

'You didn't bring it?' he said.

'I told you I wasn't going to, that it was a bit heavy.'

'I never heard you say that. I thought it was in your bag.'

'The bag was full of presents. There wasn't any room for the camera.'

I was aware of the tone of our voices, that it could sound like we were arguing and Eddie and I never argued, hardly ever. Especially not in front of other people. Especially not on Christmas Day.

Mum was the one to break the silence.

'Sure not to worry,' she said, rummaging in her bag. 'I've got one somewhere. We can use that and I'll make copies for everyone.' She found her camera and took it out, put it on the table between us. It was a disposable one, made from yellow and black cardboard, with stamp-sized pictures along the side of the Empire State Building, the Statue of Liberty, Times Square.

Eddie put the bottle on the table and went back into the kitchen.

*

The vegetable crown took two hours to cook. We exchanged presents and drank wine and then more wine, listening to Aaron's stories about growing up in Montana, how he hadn't been back in eight years, that it was hard to find the time since he'd discovered Europe. Bonnie hopped up from the table at intervals: to replace a nightlight that had gone out, to take a call from some girl she was sponsoring, to find another packet of cigarettes. The longer we waited, the harder it was not to take one, and I was glad they were her funny herbal kind.

The crown, when it came, had a thick crust of pastry that puffed up like a turkey.

'You serve it up, Ed,' Aaron said, handing it to him. 'You're the man of the house.'

Eddie looked hesitant, holding the carving knife and fork in mid-air, unsure where to make his first incision. He opted for the middle. Under the knife the pastry crumbled, then split, half of it crumbling into the brownish liquid below. 'Shit,' he said, trying to fish out the remains of the pastry lid with the knife.

'Eddie, honey, you're ruining it!' Bonnie said, her eyes big and round in her small face. 'Aaron, you do it. He's messed it up.'

'Sorry,' Eddie said, stepping back to make way for Aaron.

'Don't worry, man,' Aaron said, as he salvaged what was left of the crust and put it on Mum's plate. 'As my ma used to say, it all goes down the same way.'

'That's right,' Mum said. 'It's the taste that counts.'

As it turned out the crown wasn't big on that either but that didn't stop us making short work of it. There was silence for a while as we ate and Mum was first to break it, folding her napkin over the remains of the food on her plate, pushing back her chair. 'I can't take my eyes off your photographs,' she said. 'There's so many of them, like being in an exhibition.'

I followed her gaze around the room, the frames so close there was barely any wall between them. Snow-covered mountains, birds in flight, a drummer with his hair thrown around his head, blocking his eyes, his arms a skim of movement.

'Is that Mick Jagger in that one?' Mum asked. 'It looks like him.'

Bonnie smiled and lit a herbal cigarette, then told Mum about the time she'd met Jagger. I'd heard the story before, here, in this apartment, the first time Eddie had gone on tour without me. Bonnie had taken me under her wing, brought me out for dinner and then back here so we could smoke a joint together. Afterwards I'd told Ange and I remember us laughing, trying to imagine our mums doing anything remotely like that.

'I love the way you use all the space,' Mum was saying. 'I like walls covered with pictures like that.'

'I never remember much stuff on the walls at home,' I said.

'Before you were born we used to have maps all over the walls,' she said. 'We used every inch of wall space in our little bedsit in Ranelagh.'

'Maps?' Bonnie said. 'Why maps?'

'We'd all these plans to travel, me and Nat, my husband. We put the maps up with pins in them, to mark out our route.' Mum smiled, tilting her head to one side.

Aaron sat back and folded his arms. Some pastry clung to his beard. 'Where did you guys go?'

'Nowhere, as it turned out. He got a permanent position at the university where he worked. It was just too good to turn down, so we stayed.'

'I never knew that,' I said. 'I never heard that story.'

'We always went away, though, to Brighton to see his parents or Sligo to see my mother. And of course I travelled all over with work. But it's not the same, is it?'

Mum reached out to fill her glass again.

'You could travel now. Are you guys still together?' Aaron said.

'Collette's a widow, honey.' Bonnie put a hand on his arm.

'I'm sorry,' Aaron said. He looked down at his wrist, playing with a little band of leather he wore around it, sliding it over the skin. I thought that was it, that he'd finished with his questions, until he looked up and asked another. 'You never thought of marrying again?'

The words rolled out on to the table, sitting among the dirty plates and scrunched-up napkins. Where did this guy get off, asking Mum these questions, questions I'd never ask? I looked to Eddie for support but he seemed in another world, his arms folded, tipping back on his stool and leaning against the wall.

Mum twisted her wine glass around on the coaster. 'No,' she said, shaking her head. 'I suppose once was enough for me. I immersed myself in my course afterwards, and now I have my therapy practice, my clients. And my friends – I've great friends. I go to India with one of my friends every year.'

I reached across to take the wine bottle, refilling first Mum's glass, then Eddie's, then mine. I hoped the movement might change the conversation's direction but it seemed unstoppable. The smell of clove from Bonnie's cigarettes seemed to penetrate the whole room and I longed to open a window.

'Big change,' Aaron said, 'airline stewardess to therapist.'

'Yes and no. I always seemed to be someone other people turned to with their problems. It was Olivia who suggested I might try it, that I needed something different.'

As Mum mentioned Olivia her voice changed. I could hear the tears in it and hoped Bonnie had told Aaron about her, that he wasn't going to ask about that too.

'It's got to be different doing it 24/7, though,' Bonnie said, lighting another cigarette. 'I couldn't handle it. Listening to people's shit all the time.'

'Me neither,' I said, grateful for her interjection. 'Neither could you, Eddie. You'd go crazy. You can't handle listening to Rob going on and on about his girl problems.'

'That's because Rob always has the same problem,' Eddie said, dropping his stool back on to the floor. 'He goes after girls with zero interest in him who are usually total bitches.'

Aaron and I laughed, but Bonnie shook her head. 'Maybe if Rob put as much time into showing up to rehearsals as he does worrying about girls then you guys could land some decent sets again.'

'Don't start, Mom.'

'I'm just saying—'

'Well, don't, not today.'

Aaron dabbed his mouth with a napkin, dislodging the pastry. I glanced at Mum, but she didn't seem to have heard anything. Her cheeks were a little pink and she was staring at the Christmas tree as if it was the first time she'd ever seen one.

'I spent some time in therapy,' Aaron said. 'Let me ask you something. Even though I hardly knew a thing about my shrink I felt like we had all this stuff in common, like we would've been best buddies if we'd met somewhere else. Does everyone feel like that?'

Mum looked from the tree to Aaron. 'They say you get the clients you need, for you and them. I think that's true.' She pushed out her bottom lip and I noticed it was stained a little with red wine. 'One of my first clients had all this unresolved stuff around her father who had walked out on the family when she was eleven. She was a real daddy's girl, you see. Reminded me of Carla.'

I wasn't expecting her to say that, or the kick of my heart when she did.

'You were a daddy's girl?' Aaron said, reaching over to scuff my elbow with his hand.

'Oh, yes,' Mum said. 'When Carla was seven or eight, she'd tell everyone how her daddy was an English teacher in the big school and she was going to be a teacher just like him.'

'Mum!' I said, forcing a laugh. 'No one wants to hear this.'

'That's what mothers are for,' said Aaron. 'I'm nearly fifty and my ma still does it.'

Mum turned to me as if she'd suddenly remembered I was there. 'Remember those stories he used to make up? About the dragon family who lived in Brighton in the terraced house? You used to gobble up those stories. I only had the ones in the book, not the same at all.'

I'd forgotten all about the dragon family that lived in a terraced house in Brighton. Daddy Scorcher who lit fires in factories for a living. What was she doing, raking up all this old stuff? Before I could find an answer, Bonnie did.

'Fathers and daughters,' she said. She pulled one of her earrings down hard, so it nearly touched her jaw and I noticed it had stopped flashing. 'Just like Janie. She's a real daddy's girl, isn't she, Eddie?'

'You always say that, Mom. I don't know.'

'That's because it's true! Where is she today? With him and Monica.' Bonnie stubbed out her cigarette too hard and sparks jumped on to the tablecloth. There was a bit of silence then and Joni Mitchell filled it. I recognised the jumpy rhythm of *For the Roses*, an uneasy album and the only one of hers I didn't like. I realised I was holding my breath.

Mum reached over and took a cigarette from Bonnie's open pack without asking. Aaron lit it for her. I'd never seen her smoke before, and if she could, so could I. I reached for one too but, seeing Eddie's face, I slid it back into the box. We'd quit together so it wouldn't be just me I was letting down.

'When Nat died, I thought Carla'd be the one to go to pieces, but she held it together better than any of us.' She blew out a thin grey line of smoke. 'She did so well in her exams, she seemed fine. I thought she was fine.'

My heart was bang-banging by then, hard in my chest like it wanted to escape. I wanted to escape from this table, from this conversation, from this whole day. Mum turned to me. 'It was only later I realised how silly I'd been, that of course you weren't fine at all.'

Mum started to cough, put the cigarette in the ashtray. When I looked at her I saw there were tears in her eyes, on her face. They weren't just tears from coughing, she was crying in front of everyone, in Bonnie's apartment, on Christmas Day.

What Might Have Been Me

*

The next day we walked the Brooklyn Bridge while Eddie was at rehearsals. Beneath our feet the boardwalk was slippery, icing up again already, the air in our faces cold as a pane of glass.

'It's funny being away at Christmas,' Mum said. 'I keep forgetting what day it is. How long before I go back.'

'Me too. Bonnie asked us to come over again but I don't think we'll have time.'

The boardwalk widened into a viewing area and we stopped, looking out towards the Statue of Liberty, clear and constant in the winter sun.

'That was nice of her,' Mum said. 'She probably wants to give you a tutorial on your camera.'

The wind was whipping up a little, making white peaks on the water below. I glanced at Mum and there was a twitch in her smile.

'Probably,' I said. I pushed my hands deeper into my pockets. 'She's so damn good it's a bit daunting. You saw all those photos on the wall – they're amazing.'

A gust of wind caught Mum's hair, blowing it upwards, a funnel of silver. 'Yes, they are,' she said. 'I was wondering where she keeps the ones of Eddie and Janie. There were none on the walls.'

She said it in a normal way, like it was just a question, but I heard something else in it: her therapist's voice. Of all the times I'd been in Bonnie's apartment, I'd never noticed what Mum had spotted. 'I've only ever seen a couple of photos of Eddie as a kid. He said most of them are in Philadelphia.'

We started to walk again, past a couple holding a camera at arm's length, taking a photo of themselves.

'Maybe if you phone Bonnie later, I could speak to her,' Mum said. 'To say sorry.'

Above our heads the wind rattled the cables.

'It's fine,' I said, 'don't worry about it.'

'It's not fine,' she said. 'I upset everyone. I didn't mean to. I don't know what came over me, bringing all that stuff up. I'm just finding everything hard, much harder, since Olivia—'

I ground my hands harder into my pockets, leaning into the wind. It had started to make my eyes water. Since Olivia had died. That was the end of her sentence but she couldn't finish it and I couldn't either. Turning, I saw that she'd stopped a couple of paces back from me, that she'd pulled her hood up around her face.

'I know, Mum,' I said. 'It's OK. Really. It's the first Christmas and it's only natural you'd be upset.'

The words came easily, making a sentence I'd heard before, more than once. The first Christmas. The first anniversary. The first year. Mum reached into her pocket for a tissue. 'You're right, of course,' she said. 'And I know feeling it is better than not. It's taken me the longest time to accept that she's dead. I'm sure it must be the same for you, worse even, because you weren't at the funeral.'

I'd been waiting all week for her to bring that up.

'I said I was sorry, Mum. You know I wanted to be there. The tour was last-minute and I never thought to tell you. The timing was terrible.'

I started to walk again, faster, towards the looming vastness of the skyline. It always shocked me how close up it felt, how vivid. Did she not think I'd wished I was there? That I wouldn't rather have been with people who knew Olivia, who loved her, instead of hearing the news on a payphone in a diner on the interstate, only a slice of Perspex between me and the guy waiting, jingling quarters?

'I know, love,' she said, catching up with me. 'And I'm not trying to get at you. But even if you had been here, if I had been able to let you know in time, what would you have done?'

I'd been prepared for this, rehearsed it. 'I'd have come home, Mum.'

'But would you really? What about getting back in?'

The wind sneaked into the gaps between my scarf and my jumper, finding slivers of bare skin.

'Eddie and I have been talking about getting married,' I said. 'He's under a lot of pressure right now with the band – things have come to a bit of a head with Rob. With all that going on, it's just not top priority right now—'

'For who? For Eddie?'

I took a deep breath. 'For me, for both of us. We'll get it sorted, Mum, I promise.' I glanced across at her but she wasn't looking at me. 'What?' I said. 'That's what you want, isn't it?'

'Carla, this isn't about what I want or what Eddie wants. What do *you* want?'

'Jesus,' I said, tipping my head back.

Above us the sky was thick white, edges of pink. More snow. Every time she'd come over lately it had made things so much bloody harder – she'd made things so much harder. That's what I wanted to say, only I couldn't say that.

'Just be my mum, will you, not my therapist?'

She took so long to answer that I thought maybe she wasn't going to. 'I'm sorry if it feels that way. I'm trying to do my best. I'm worried about you. I just want you to be happy. That's all.'

We walked on in silence, the bridge narrowing, the wood giving way to concrete. A bike whizzed by close to her and I felt her shoulder touch mine, her arm.

'Mum,' I said, 'I know you want the best for me, and I'm happy. Very happy. Eddie and I, we're both happy.'

The more I said 'happy' the less convincing it sounded. Mum smiled a little smile, and I linked my arm in hers. We walked the rest of the bridge like that, arms linked, steps in time with each other, just us and the cold and the shape Manhattan made, stark and uneven against the clouds.

PART TWO

ONE

The morning the phone call came, I was still in bed. I should've been up by then, but Eddie had had a gig in the Bronx the night before. The ringing was part of my dream, or I thought it was, until I felt Eddie roll into me, his elbow in my side.

'The phone,' he said. 'Get the phone.'

Eleven years of being together and I knew the pitch of his voice as well as my own, could hear the trace of something in it and I remembered that we'd argued last night. Again.

The only people who ever called the landline were telemarketing companies and Mum. As I reached over to answer it, I misjudged the distance, knocking the receiver on to the floor. It landed next to my handbag. 'Hello?' I said, picking it up.

The ringing had stopped but then it started again, obscuring the voice at the other end. For a second I looked at the handset, not understanding until I realised it was another phone, the sound of Eddie's cell. As I watched him unfold from the bedclothes and rummage in his jeans a memory surfaced from the night before; the two of us outside the bar, his voice raised, mine. I was the one who started it this time, twenty minutes of pent-up frustration of waiting for him, finally exploding when he bounded down the stairs and out onto the sidewalk. We were supposed to be getting something to eat, just the two of us, and he'd said he'd be right out. I'd probably overreacted, not caring then about the music blogger he was talking to and how influential he was, only that I was starving and that Eddie had promised we'd leave as soon as it was over.

The person at the other end was speaking.

'Carla? Hello, can you hear me?'

'Mum? Hi!'

Eddie's phone stopped ringing. 'Dawn,' he said. 'What's up?'

I sat up properly in bed, pushed my hair out of my eyes. Why was Dawn calling Eddie so early? It was only hours since we'd seen her. Over his voice, I could still hear Mum's.

'Did I wake you up?'

'No, you didn't.' I pushed the covers back and swung my legs out of bed, a movement that jarred the shadow of a headache into proper pain. 'I was just getting ready for work.' In the mirror I caught sight of myself, black tyres of makeup under my eyes, my T-shirt on inside out.

'Really?' Eddie was saying, behind me. 'When? That's awesome!'

I tuned back in to Mum, conscious suddenly that it wasn't like her to call unarranged on a weekday. 'Is everything OK, Mum?' I said.

'Oh, yes, fine. Grand.'

Grand. The Irish word for everything and nothing. I waited for more.

'Is it a bad time?' she said. 'If you're on your way to work?'

I pushed my hair back from my face. 'Mum, it's fine. What's up?'

There was a pause before she spoke, a beat of silence. 'Nothing really. Except, well, I have a bit of news.'

The sun was strong already, penetrating the thin curtains. Eddie walked out of the bedroom and down the hall, still on the phone. In the space he left behind I could hear Mum's breathing. News usually meant bad news. The last news had been Suzanne and Ian breaking up.

'Did Suzanne and Ian get back together?'

It was a stupid thing to say, not even a joke, really, but she laughed anyway. 'Two chances of that I'd say. Fat and slim.'

'I suppose,' I said.

'No,' she said. 'It's not Suzanne's news, it's about me.'

My breath clenched. This was it, the call I'd been dreading for so long it felt like for ever. This was the phone call where Mum told me she was dying. That she had months to live, weeks. 'I don't like telling you this on the phone, love, but I told Suzanne this morning and I want you to know as well.'

I stood up, moved towards the window, as far as the phone cord would go. Breathed in, breathed out. From the living room I could hear Eddie's voice, high, excited, just like it had been the day he told me she'd joined the band.

'There's no easy way to say this, so I'll just say it. I've been diagnosed with Alzheimer's.'

The air-conditioner was off – no wonder the room was stifling. I turned it on full, holding my T-shirt out so a blast of freezing air hit my clammy skin. 'Alzheimer's?'

'Alzheimer's disease. I'm sure you've heard of it.'

A giggle bubbled but I stopped it just in time. Of course I'd heard of it. Alzheimer's. It was something people said when they misplaced their keys. It sounded like the name of a German bakery, not a disease at all.

'Of course, yeah. But doesn't it . . .' I paused, tried to line up the right words in the right order. 'I mean, isn't it something old people get?'

Mum laughed again. 'It's nice to know that sixty-one isn't old. Sometimes I think you and Suzanne think I'm ancient.'

'Sixty is the new forty – at least that's what Jan says in yoga.'

'I think I feel about twenty years older after her yoga classes, not younger.'

'Me too,' I said. 'I could hardly walk the other day.'

We should've been talking about the disease, what it was and what it meant, but instead we were making jokes, laughing, talking about yoga. I pushed my feet into flip-flops and paced to the end of the bed, then back again. The apartment was almost silent, with only the hum of the air-conditioner, Eddie's footsteps in the hallway, the click of the bathroom door.

'Before I told you I meant to check if Eddie was there,' Mum said. 'Is he?'

As if on cue, the shower burst into life.

'Yep,' I said. 'He's here. He says to say hi.'

'Good,' she said. 'I'm glad. I didn't want to tell you when you were on your own.' She started to tell me more about it then, the disease and the different types, how she had 'early onset'. Her voice was clear, normal, factual, and I couldn't marry the things she was saying with the way she was saying them. I kicked the flip-flops off and lay back in bed, pulling the sheet up to my chest. Mum was in full swing, telling me there was no need to worry. Yes, Alzheimer's was degenerative but it took a long time, ten years, fifteen sometimes. The disease had lots of different stages that took years to develop. She was in stage one. And a cure was very close.

When Eddie came back in he was humming, a towel around his waist. He never dried himself properly and I counted the tattoos I could see on his wet skin. Two, three, four, not including the one on his other shoulder that I couldn't see. He rummaged in the drawers and took out boxers, a clean T-shirt, shorts. I watched him dress, listening to Mum talk about the different types of drugs there were, the ones she was on and how she was feeling so much better. As he tied the laces of his runner I saw the loop of infinity on his ankle, black against his tanned skin.

'You haven't said much,' Mum said. 'I wish I could be with you, face to face. It's so much harder, telling you like this. But I didn't want to wait until I came over next. It didn't seem fair.'

I switched the phone to my other ear and sat up straighter in bed.

'I'm OK, Mum,' I said. 'I'm fine. I suppose I'm just, I don't know, taking it in.'

Eddie raised his pierced eyebrow. He picked his wallet out of the jeans on the floor, put on his watch. He was about to go but I could stop him, tell him what was happening, ask him to stay.

'Can you hold on one second, Mum?' I said, placing my hand over the receiver.

'Sorry to interrupt, but I've got to go. Dawn got us an

78

interview! Can you believe it? It's on Shine FM! We're on between twelve–thirty and one.'

He leaned down and kissed me, whatever bad feeling there had been from last night chased away by his excitement.

'That's great,' I said, smiling.

'Don't forget to tune in, will you?'

'I won't,' I said. 'Good luck.'

At the door he turned back, nodded towards the phone. 'Everything OK with your mom?'

I kept my hand clenched over the receiver, held it slightly further away. 'Sure,' I said. 'Everything's fine.'

★

There was one bagel left in the back of the freezer and I shoved it into the toaster. On the table Eddie's laptop was open on the band's Myspace page, their new name, Homespun Heroes, in brown and beige across the top. Renaming the band had been Dawn's idea and it was a good one. They needed something to show they were going in a new direction, she said, to show that things had changed now Rob was gone and they'd a female bass player. We sat around for hours one night in the Bridge, throwing out names over half-price pitchers. It had been Bonnie who'd come up with the name in the end, the only one that everyone could agree on.

Eddie had posted something on the wall, a reply to a fan, some girl from Canada who said she loved their music and couldn't wait to see them live when she was in New York. I shut the page down and opened Google. Typed in what I wanted.

'Did you mean Alzheimer's disease?' Google asked.

Behind me the bagel was burning. I unplugged the toaster so I could shove in the knife. I tried to remember what Mum had said but none of the words from the forty-five-minute phone call seemed to have stuck. I'd seen Alzheimer's in films. Old people had it, people in their seventies and eighties who sat in chairs and looked out of windows. People who couldn't speak or recognise anyone, remember who anyone was. Mum was young; she'd explained it to me, everything about it. She was herself. She'd sounded herself. It didn't make sense.

Eddie had finished the cream cheese and put the empty box back into the fridge. I put it back too, used the butter instead. I'd seen Mum in May, been on the phone to her on Sunday. I tried to remember the conversation, what we'd talked about: the weather, a cousin's new babies. Everything was normal. She'd seemed fine.

The bagel was finished and I couldn't remember eating it. I opened the fridge, hung on to the big door as I perused the shelves. Maple syrup, peanut butter, an opened pack of flatbread. My shift didn't start for another three hours and the time between then and now seemed to hang there, empty and inevitable. I wanted to talk to someone, someone who would help fill it with me. Rhonda was the obvious choice, my American Ange, but she was at work – she hardly ever seemed to get a lunch break any more – Eddie was going to be on the radio. Mum was in Ireland, going out somewhere for the afternoon with her friend Lily-Anne as if nothing had changed. Maybe nothing *had* changed.

I closed the fridge. Maybe I'd call Rhonda on the off-chance she could make a quick lunch, even a coffee. I picked up the phone but before I could dial, it rang in my hand. I recognised the number.

'Hi, Mum,' I said.

'Carla?'

'Hello?'

'It's me, Suzanne.'

My heart sank. Thirty seconds later and I'd have been on the phone to Rhonda, she would've gone to voicemail.

'I wanted to talk to you about Mammy. I heard she told you the news.'

I walked back into the kitchen, pulled myself up on the counter. 'She did, yeah. We spoke this morning.'

'I know. Are you on your way to work? I waited to call you till she was out.'

I glanced at the kitchen clock. 'I've to leave soon enough.'

'Well, can I call you later, then? Tomorrow? What time would be good? We need to talk about this.'

I sighed, jumped off the counter. 'I have a few minutes now, sure.'

Once she heard that, she started to talk, about how she'd suspected for ages something was wrong – ever since Mum had given up the practice she hadn't been herself. I remembered an email she'd sent me earlier in the year about Mum not showing up to meet her for lunch; when Suzanne had called around to the house, the fridge was full of milk going off. Halfway through, a question rose to the surface, something that had been bugging me since the start of the call.

'Suzanne, are you ringing me from Mum's?'

'Yes, I told you, she's gone out.'

'How come you're not at your own place? Or at work?' Even as I asked some part of me didn't want to know.

'I've been here since last night. I couldn't face going in today, not after being up half the night.' When I didn't reply, she spoke again.

'She did tell you, Carla, what happened last night?'

I could've said yes, pretended I already knew, or that there was a problem on the line or that I had to leave, right then, to go to work. In the heat of the apartment I felt suddenly cold.

I took a deep breath. 'No, she didn't.'

'She didn't tell you?'

'No.'

'She really didn't tell you? She said she was going to—'

'Jesus, Suzanne! Tell me what?'

'There's no point in biting my head off – I'm only the messenger.'

She sounded irritated and, despite everything, I smiled. The more I said, the longer she'd hold out, so I sat silent, waiting for her to start.

'It was half one last night when I got the call,' she said. 'It was lucky because usually I have my mobile turned off at night but I must have forgotten before I went to bed.'

'Mum called at half one in the morning?'

'No,' she said, 'her neighbour, Ray. You don't know him and his wife, Margaret. They moved in a while ago, on the side the Phelans used to be.' I nodded a nod she couldn't see. 'He'd just got home – he'd been to a work do or something. When he drove into his driveway, he saw someone in our garden, kneeling by the hedge. When he looked in it was Mammy, in her nightie. She was weeding, Carla, at one o'clock in the morning.'

I didn't know him, this Ray guy, but I knew the angle his car would take, could see the lights sweeping the hedge, the cherry tree, grey in the dark. I could picture all of that, and in the circle of colour his headlights made, my mother, in her nightdress, weeding.

I'd walked back into the bedroom by then. It was cool, cold, from the air-conditioner. Eddie's jeans were a pool by his side of the bed, his socks half inside his runners. I kicked one hard enough to hurt my toes. 'Maybe she couldn't sleep,' I said. 'Mum loves that garden. It wouldn't surprise me that she'd get some notion into her head and—'

'Carla, she'd pulled up the peace lilies.'

Suzanne's voice snagged. We both knew the story, how Mum had planted one each for her and Dad the year they'd moved in, two white ones with purple centres. Later she'd planted two more, a pink one for each of us. At the end of the summer they died back into the ground, the leaves and everything wilting into the soil. But the next year they grew back, they always grew back.

'Listen,' I said. 'She told me she's on medication. Maybe it's messing up her sleep, maybe she was just having a bad reaction to it.'

'Carla, it's not the medication. She did tell you she has Alzheimer's? Alzheimer's disease?'

Her voice edged higher every time she said it. The headache that had been fading in and out all morning seemed to twist a little tighter, a single point of pain somewhere behind my eyes. 'Calm down,' I said. 'She told me all about it.'

'She's playing it down, but it's serious, really serious, Carla.'

'I know it's serious but we can't start to panic about it. It's not like she has cancer. She was telling me how many different stages there are, and it can take ten or fifteen years. There's no immediate need to worry.' Mum had said that, or something like it. Down the phone line I heard a long sigh. Suddenly, more than anything, I wanted to end the conversation, hang up the phone and get out of the apartment on to the sidewalk, where I could walk, move, run.

'Carla, do you have any idea what this disease can do? Look it up on the Internet and you'll see pretty quick. I'm going to have to move home with her. I can't handle this on my own, Carla. I can't. Not on top of everything else.'

This was the Suzanne I knew, Suzanne the martyr. I had no idea what 'everything else' was, and I wasn't going to ask. 'No one said you'll have to handle it on your own,' I said.

There was silence on the line then, Suzanne's breath, mine.

'Look, I have to go,' I said. 'I'm going to be dead late for work.'

The clock said one-fifteen, it was nearly true.

'Can we talk later?' she said. 'Or tomorrow? I want to talk about this properly. We need to make a plan.'

'Sure,' I said. 'I'll call you tomorrow evening.'

We said goodbye without even pretending to do small-talk. I threw the phone on to the bed, continuing the argument in my head as I pulled my work clothes from the wardrobe, found clean underwear. It was only as I was stepping into the shower that I realised I'd missed Eddie's radio interview, forgotten all about it. And, as the hot water hit my skin, I cursed Suzanne. Now I had something else to blame her for.

TWO

Walking down 43rd, I had the sensation that the whole block was on a conveyor-belt, the buildings, the lights, the people, so many people, sliding past, as if I wasn't moving at all. On the side of a bus an ad urged me to open my heart to Taiwan. A man in a cap stood on the corner, waving flyers, his mouth moving, but all I heard was my own soundtrack, replacing the city's.

I tried to remember the name of the band but it wouldn't come. The album was one that Eddie had downloaded on to my iPod and all I remembered was him telling me they were from Iceland. It was strange, this music – more like a collection of sounds – and listening to it added to the feeling that I wasn't really there, that any of the crowd streaming along the sidewalk could pass right through me. The songs had no words, or at least none that I could understand, and I was glad. It was nice to have a break from words after all I'd heard that morning.

At the corner of Sixth, I stopped. There it was, Bryant Park, the green treetops dwarfed by buildings but still somehow holding their own. In front of me a couple stopped to take a picture of the Empire State Building towering above the rest, sunlight on steel. I remembered Eddie telling me it was the second highest building in New York. As I watched it coming closer I realised I wasn't sure, anymore, if that was still true.

At 42nd I waited for the lights to change. The Icelandic band slipped into another song. Across the street the park offered shade, a type of New York silence, but I was cutting it fine now after having so much time earlier. By the time the traffic stopped I'd decided I was going in anyway and I walked up the corner steps, past the people at the green metal tables reading books, eating sandwiches, talking into cell phones. A man stood up, shrugged on his jacket and I sat down in his place.

Above me, the trees let in just enough sun, the shape of the buildings, cut-outs in the August sky of glass and stone. Two women at the table next to me were talking intensely, one of them laughing hard. I could see the laugh but I couldn't hear it – the shape her mouth made could just as easily have been a scream.

If I sat there much longer I'd be late for work. I was probably late already. If I'd called Toni earlier she might have covered my shift but it was too late now. Suzanne had called in sick today, Suzanne who never called in sick. Somehow, out of all the things she and Mum had told me, that had shocked me most of all.

I turned my music off, took out my phone to call the restaurant. Holding it in my palm I didn't seem to have the energy to make my fingers work or to speak, and even if I did, I didn't know what to say. Across from me, a homeless guy slumped forward on to the table, asleep on his arms. He was dressed in gold, like someone had spray-painted him from head to foot – baseball cap, jacket, ragged sweatpants, all dirty gold. I looked at him and wanted to make up a story about him, about his life, how he'd got there. Why did I want to make up stories about other people's lives? Did it take me away from what was going on in mine?

Behind my eyes, the headache was getting worse, the pain pulling tighter, the way it always did before the hangover got better.

Mum was sick.

The thought was clear, precise. A thought carved with a scalpel.

I stood up.

She wasn't going to get better.

I had to move.

On the lawn they were rolling out mats for yoga. We'd done

yoga together, me and Mum, the last time I'd seen her, that Mother's Day weekend. I'd been organised for once, booked us into that motel in Montauk ages in advance, booked our tickets on the bus. When we got there, the motel had messed up our reservation so we'd ended up sharing a bed that sagged in the middle, rolling into each other in the night. How had I not noticed then, a whole weekend together? Or maybe I had. Maybe it was possible to know and not know something at the very same time.

I walked past the ping-pong tables, the people waiting to play. The ball missed the table, made two hollow hops on concrete before someone picked it up. She'd been writing in her journal a lot, that I noticed, but she always journalled. She'd lost things – mislaid them – the room key, her sunglasses. I'd bought her another pair and she'd forgotten to take them off when she ran into the waves, lost them in the spray. Later, she laughed at her own silliness as she squeezed the water from her hair on to the sand.

'The art of losing things,' she'd said. 'Like the poem.'

A couple were walking towards me, hand in hand. They let go of each other long enough for me to walk between them, but when I looked back they were holding hands again. I should call Eddie, find out how the radio interview had gone. It was the band's first and he'd be excited, probably on a high when I got home. He wouldn't bring up the fight last night, not that he ever would anyway.

On the railing a tiny bird sat absolutely still, its blink the only flicker of movement. For a second I watched it before it flew away into the clamour of the city, my city: despite everything it was still my city. At every turn I could still see how I'd been seduced by it, how I would be again.

Suzanne expected me to come home. She hadn't said it, but it was there in the things she hadn't said. *I can't handle this on my own.* She'd said that, something like that, as if I expected her to, as if anyone did. But my life was here in New York. Did she expect me to give it up?

Out of the park and on to Fifth, I could imagine her response if I'd actually said that: *Working illegally waiting tables isn't a life, Carla.* I could hear her voice in my head and I continued the conversation, arguing back at her. Eleven years, a third of my life, more, eleven years with Eddie, eleven years of working, eleven years of friends, of watching movies, making love, doing laundry, going to yoga. These things made up a life, didn't they? And if they didn't, what did?

In front of the library, a team of workmen were watering flowers, shaping shrubs. Mum had pulled up the peace lilies. The peace lilies! Why hadn't she told me that? Next to them the lions were waiting in the sun, their stone white in the heat. They'd been waiting a long time for me. In front of one of them a woman posed for a photo, just like I'd posed that day for Mum.

She hadn't read much in Montauk. She'd never opened the Anne Tyler book I'd bought her for her birthday, or any of the meditation ones she'd carted with her to the beach every day. She'd held one of them on her lap as she slept and she'd slept a lot that weekend, her head nodding in the sun. I remembered adjusting her hat, so she wouldn't get burned, even though I was always the one who got burned.

At the bottom of the steps, I paused, looked up. I hadn't made a decision to come here, didn't think I had, and yet maybe this was where I'd been heading all along. There were no tourists queuing at the bag check, only me. I took the right-hand staircase up, like I always did. I'd come down on the left. The air was cool on my face, my neck, as I tipped my head back to see the arch of marble above. My fingers trailed on the wood banister, shiny and worn away by the touch of millions of hands. Mum's fingers had touched it, helping to wear it away too. I couldn't remember the last time she'd been here. Would she come again?

I held the question in my head and looked at it before I pushed it away. In here it was OK to do that, OK for there not to be an answer yet. The steps were steeper than I remembered and my calf muscles were starting to ache a little as I pulled myself up to the next, the one after that.

It was only when I got to the top that I realised I'd been holding my breath. I pushed both hands into the cold stone of the balustrade and exhaled.

THREE

The hill up to the visitors' centre was the hardest part of the circuit and I felt my legs slow down, so I was barely running at all. I pressed on, around the curve of the incline and up to the fountain.

The arc of water was cold against my teeth. My chest heaved. This was the problem with running, miss a few months and it was like starting all over again – you were right back at square one. Through the trees I could see the city, the shapes of the buildings against the darkening sky. Despite the pain I knew I'd feel tomorrow, I was glad I'd come, to get out of the apartment, away from the phone and the pack of cigarettes hidden in the bag on the floor of my wardrobe. I hadn't smoked one yet, hadn't even known I was going to buy them until I did. If Eddie found them he'd go nuts. And he'd know something was going on.

I started to run again, my footsteps following the path around the monument. For the last three weeks I'd been dreading the ring of that phone, wished it was a telemarketing call rather than Suzanne to panic me more, Mum to calm me down. Every call was a jolt, another prod to do something, to act, but somehow I hadn't done anything yet. And I hadn't told anyone, not even Eddie.

I ran to the top of the steps, looked down at a woman in yellow and black, bounding up two at a time. There was a time when I couldn't have gone three hours without telling Eddie something like that, never mind three weeks. I didn't know if that was important or just my brain's way of distracting me from the real fear by throwing up another one. Before I could think about

89

an answer I started down the steps, running a diagonal line down one flight, then two. At the bottom of the third it was shady and cool, the swing sets and slides empty for the evening. The run back up was going to be a killer; a quick lap of the playground would make it easier.

I didn't see the first poster on the tree, I ran past it. It was the second that caught my eye, the third that made me stop. I always stopped at 'missing' posters, always read the details of the cat or dog or person, memorised the photo in case I found them, but I never did.

In this one a man was smiling in a black-and-white photo alongside someone else's shoulder, all that was left of the woman or man who'd probably been smiling too. His name was Federico Gameroz and he was seventy-three. Underneath the photo the typing was smaller. He'd been last seen on Wednesday, eight days ago, on Willoughby and Myrtle. He'd been wearing a short-sleeved shirt, brown pants, sandals. A phone number. Below the square of text there was another line, handwritten in red marker: 'Federico is suffering from dementia. Please help him to come home.' The writing was loopy, childlike. I wondered who'd written it, if Federico was home, if anyone had called.

Abruptly, I started to run towards the first flight of steps. It wasn't the same. My feet pounded on the concrete, in time with the words in my head. It wasn't the same. The second flight was harder but I pushed on, tipping my body at an angle, leaning into it. He was older than Mum, much older and much sicker. And, anyway, there were loads of types of dementia.

By the time I dragged my exhausted body up the last steps I'd made up another story about Federico. He hadn't got lost at all. He'd left his family, disappeared, taken a lover; they were living it up now in Mexico or Cuba. I stopped for more water, the idea making me smile, but not for long. And as I jogged back down the darkening streets, stepping over the bumps in the sidewalk where the tree roots pushed up the paving stones, I couldn't get his image out of my mind, his half-smile, the way he wasn't looking at the camera but at something outside the photograph, something only he could see.

★

I stopped at the basketball court, and through the wire fence I watched Eddie dribble the ball, double back on himself around an imaginary player, then shoot. The ball ricocheted off the backboard with a crash. He ran to retrieve it, allowing it only one bounce before he scooped it up and turned to throw again, this time his aim so precise it flew through the hoop without grazing the edge.

I almost clapped but something stopped me, it would change things if he knew I was there. There was something calming about watching him in the fading light, the movement of his body, flowing and jerky at the same time, the sound of the ball on the tarmac, the rhythm of the game. He was too small to play properly, felt self-conscious around other guys. He'd never told me that but soon after we moved in together I'd figured out why he always waited till the court was empty so he could play on his own.

The ball hit the edge of the hoop and bounced on the ground behind him, bouncing again and once more before the bounce turned into a roll. He turned to chase it and saw me standing by the fence.

'Hey!' His fringe was wet and he pushed it away from his face. The ball rolled over and hit the edge of the court. 'How long have you been there?'

'A few minutes, long enough to admire your moves.'

He smiled and reached down to pick up the ball. He held it in front of him, spinning it, so it skimmed between his hands. 'You were out running again?'

'Yeah, second time this week. I'll feel it tomorrow.' I lifted my leg behind me, holding on to my ankle as I squeezed my calf against my thigh.

'Your sister called,' he said, bouncing the ball off the tarmac and catching it again. 'I didn't know where you were. I told her to try your cell but I guess you didn't have it with you.'

'Suzanne? When?'

He bounced the ball again. 'I don't know, just before I left, I guess. Maybe half an hour ago.'

Half an hour ago was after midnight in Ireland, too late for Suzanne to call. My heart pounded. 'Did she say anything?'

'Not really, just asked when you'd be back, said for you to call her. I figured it was pretty late over there. Is everything OK, Carls?' Eddie asked, his eyebrows knotting.

'Yeah,' I said. 'I'm sure it is. Suzanne's been going through some stuff lately.'

'Oh,' he said. 'And she's calling *you*?'

'I know, right?' I laughed. 'She'll be fine.'

Eddie spread his feet apart and bounced the ball between them, first with one hand, then the other. I watched the V the ball made in the air, the predictability of each bounce, the tap of his hand.

'Anyway,' I said, 'I guess I should go back, call her.'

I lifted up my other leg, pulling my foot into my buttock. 'Have you got rehearsals later?'

'No. Dawn has to work late and Nick's on a date with that chick from the Jersey City gig.'

'The twenty-year-old?'

'Actually, I think she's nineteen.' He shook his head, laughing, and I did too. It would be just the two of us tonight, the perfect time to tell him. I should tell him.

'You want to go to Roman's? Get something to eat?' The words came out quickly and I could feel the awkwardness in them. Since when had it become hard to ask my boyfriend to eat with me?

'Sure,' he said. 'Sounds good.'

He walked close to the fence and he looked as though he was going to say something else but instead he leaned down and kissed my fingers, wrapped through one of the diamond-shaped holes in the wire, before turning away, dribbling the ball with him.

For a second I stood there, listening to the noise echo around the empty court, watching the shape of his shoulders, his back, before I let go of the fence and started to jog towards home.

★

I willed the phone to go to voicemail. The short double rings always reminded me of being a kid, standing in the hall, Dad telling me not to be so lazy and go up the road to see Ange instead of running up the bill.

'Hello?' Suzanne's voice was sleepy. 'Carla?'

'Sorry it's so late. I only just got the message. Is everything OK?'

'No, no,' she said, 'it's fine. I'm glad you called.'

I could hear movement as she pushed herself up in bed. I imagined her reaching for the light. 'What's up? Is everything OK with Mum?'

A sigh. 'I was calling you to tell you she's decided to give up driving. I thought you should know.'

I sat down on the edge of the bed, kicked off my runners. I felt the fear loosen a little. Mum had called to tell me that yesterday, she'd said that safety was the most important thing, other people's, hers. She'd talked about Dublin's new public-transport system, the environment.

'I know,' I said to Suzanne, but she didn't hear me – she was too caught in her flow about how this was concrete proof of where Mum was at in the disease, how Mum hadn't told her herself, she'd had to find out from Lily-Anne.

'I know,' I said again, louder. 'She called to tell me.'

'What? When? Why didn't she tell *me*?'

'I don't know.' Despite everything, I felt a twitch of pleasure that I'd known first. 'She rang yesterday. She sounded happy about the decision. I think she's being very responsible.'

Mum had been logical as she explained it: people with epilepsy had to give up driving, she'd said. She'd sounded herself, and that was half the problem: the imbalance between the Mum I spoke to and the picture of her that Suzanne insisted on painting.

'I'm not saying it's not responsible, Carla,' Suzanne said, unable to hide her irritation, 'but who's going to drive her around? Take her to yoga? To work?'

So that was what this was about – more work for Suzanne, and I wasn't there to help. It wasn't about Mum at all.

'What's wrong with public transport?' I said. 'And she has Lily-Anne too. She said they work practically the same hours at the Buddhist Centre so she can go with her.'

'Public transport!' Suzanne made a noise that was somewhere between a laugh and a snort. 'It's not New York, Carla. You know what it's like here. And who's going to help her with her grocery shopping? Is she going to drag that home on the bus?'

'Only yesterday you were telling me she can't go grocery shopping any more,' I countered. 'So, what's the difference?'

Outside the door I heard footsteps, the key in the lock. 'Suzanne, it's late, you're tired. I think we should talk about this another time.'

Eddie's head came around the door. He smiled at me and placed the basketball quietly in the corner.

'There's never a good time to talk about this, though, Carla, is there? Just because you can't see it doesn't mean it's not happening. You seem to think it's all going to be fine. Well, it's not fine. Nothing about this is fine!'

Suzanne's voice was rising and I wondered if Eddie could hear it. I cupped the phone in both hands, turning away from him. He walked past me with a towel and pointed towards the bathroom.

'Listen,' I said, as he closed the door, 'I know we need to talk about this more. It's just hard, with the time difference and everything. Why don't I call you at the weekend?'

From the bathroom I heard the radio go on. At the other end of the line, Suzanne had gone silent.

'How about Sunday?' I said. 'I'm working that night, but I could call you in the afternoon – say, three my time? We'd both have ages then to chat about it.'

'OK,' she said. 'Sunday at three your time. You'll call me.'

'Yep,' I said. 'I'll call you.'

I felt the wash of relief that I'd bought another few days, that Eddie couldn't have heard us over the noise of the radio.

After we'd hung up I looked in the wardrobe and pulled out a dress I knew Eddie liked. I had until Sunday, a few more days. Time for me to figure out what I wanted from him. There was no need to bring it up tonight and spoil our evening together. I couldn't remember the last time we'd had dinner, just the two of us. That was what tonight was going to be about: Eddie and I relaxing together, having fun, not about Suzanne and Mum.

This had waited a few weeks, it could wait a few more days. At least until Sunday.

FOUR

Inside the laundromat it was barely any cooler than outside, the heat from the dryers offsetting any benefit offered by the air-conditioning. The first batch of Rhonda's clothes made a pile between us on the stainless-steel table. I grabbed a T-shirt, the cotton hot against my hands, and started to fold.

At the other end she lined up her delicates, still wet from the washer.

'What do you think would happen if I put these in the dryer?' she asked, holding up a pair of see-through cream knickers with green ribbons.

'Well, they can't get any smaller, that's for sure.'

She laughed. 'The smaller the underwear, the higher the price. I swear seeing Michael's going to have me broke soon – and he knows how much I earn.'

'You should ask him for a raise.' I made a face and she was about to respond when her phone rang from under a pile of socks. She snatched it up, her face breaking into a smile before she answered. She raised a finger at me, then strutted towards the door in heels that only Rhonda would wear to do laundry. I smiled, continued folding. I was on a run of pillowcases, cream and navy. How many pillows did one person need?

Through the window I could see Rhonda on the phone, her hand in her hair. It was Michael calling – it had to be for her to run out like that. I hadn't met him yet and I wasn't sure I wanted to. My eyes drifted towards the line of underwear she'd been putting away – lacy creams and pinks, a black bra with so much support it practically had a cleavage of its own. It all looked expensive, probably a week's tips there at least. I couldn't remember the last time I'd made an investment like that for Eddie.

The trolley was full and I pushed it away, pulling the other one towards me. I'd have done it all by the time she came back but I didn't mind helping her with her laundry. There was something nicer about it somehow than meeting at the opening of another of the trendy bars she was always inviting me to, bars that were a million miles away from the Blarney Stone on 34th where we used to spend our tips after our shifts in O'Callaghan's.

At the line of washers a skinny young woman commandeered three in a row, filling them from two black bags on the floor with the help of her daughter. When they were full she picked the little girl up, holding her on her hip so she could feed in the quarters. Each time the water started to flood into the machine the little girl clapped her hands and swung her feet in jelly sandals. 'Let's do it again, Mommy! Let's do it again!'

I looked down at my hands. I'd stopped mid-fold, watching them. Behind me, I heard the clip-clop of heels and grabbed a pair of jeans from the pile.

'I'm sorry,' Rhonda said, 'that was Michael.'

'These are still damp,' I said, holding the jeans up. 'You want to put them in the dryer?'

She made a face, creasing her makeup. 'Are you kidding me, Matthews? They're my True Religion jeans. They cost two hundred and fifty dollars!'

'Holy shit! Have you lost the plot? I remember the days when you were in your orange-tab Levi's! And you loved them.'

'I know — the Missouri hick in the big city. I didn't have a clue.' She shook her head, bundling the jeans into a bag.

'Maybe it's now you don't have a clue, spending two hundred and fifty dollars on a pair of jeans.'

A young guy came in with a sports bag, dumped it on the floor and got change from the machine, a slush of quarters.

'Michael wants me to go round to his place later. There's some problem with the power and ConEd has to come. He's stuck with his kids. You wouldn't ask someone to do that if they weren't your girlfriend, would you? I mean it's a couple kind of thing to do. Isn't it?'

I kept folding. Shorts, a tank top, another T-shirt. She was standing there, watching me, and I knew what she wanted me to say but I couldn't say it.

'What, Matthews?'

'Nothing. It's just – I don't know. How long have you been together? Six months? Longer? And you still don't know if he sees you as his girlfriend?'

She leaned down to pick up the black bra from where it had fallen on the floor, her sunglasses dislodging themselves from her dark hair and landing on her nose. When she looked back at me, they were perched there, too low. She looked like a prudish secretary. 'I hate you sometimes, Matthews, you know that? You go for the jugular every time.'

'Rhons, look—'

'No!' She held up a hand. 'You're right. It's eight months since we've been seeing each other. Eight and a half. We could nearly have a freakin' baby by now! Imagine me with a baby?'

Behind the half-pitched sunglasses her eyebrows rose and she held them there for theatrical effect.

'No, I can't. You're too much of a career woman these days.'

She opened the dryer door and the clothes inside threw themselves over each other, slower and slower, until they stopped entirely and collected at the bottom of the drum. As she took them out and put them on the table I noticed men's shirts among them, boxer shorts too.

'I've said it to two of the girls at work,' she said, 'Shelley and Michelle. And the thing is, they get it. That Michael has to be careful because he's my boss, because his divorce isn't fully through yet, but when I talk to you, I can see in your face that you think that's all bullshit.'

'No,' I said, reaching for a polo shirt. 'I never said that.'

'You didn't have to, and the shit part is you're right. You are. But we can't all be the perfect couple. We're not all you and Eddie.'

'Perfect couple? Yeah, right.' My laugh sounded weird, fake.

'What? I've known you how long? Seven years? Eight? And I've never seen you fight, not even once.'

'Sometimes I think it might be better if we did fight.'

'No, you don't. Remember Patrick and me? How much we fought? You don't want that, believe me.'

'We seem to end up fighting when we're drunk.'

'Everyone fights when they're drunk.'

I reached for a pillowcase that turned out to be a fitted sheet so big that it obscured Rhonda. I rolled it into submission, and when I did I saw she was staring at me, her glasses back in her hair.

'Are you OK? Something's up. I can tell.'

Now that I had her attention, I didn't want it. Didn't know where to start.

'Is it that Dawn chick again?' she said. 'I didn't trust her from the minute I saw her. That pixie hairstyle, those tiny hands and feet. Never trust people with feet that small.'

'Rhonda!'

'I'm sorry,' she said, pushing a bag of laundry into the trolley she was going to take home. 'I was never this much of a bitch before I worked in PR.'

'Rhons, you were a bitch when we were waiting tables in O'Callaghan's. That's why we got on so well.'

Her burst of laughter joined mine and it felt so good then to see her as she always used to be, to know that some things didn't change.

'Touché, Matthews. You should work in PR yourself. I only brought her up because that night in Zola's you were saying about how much time Eddie was spending with her. And I know I wouldn't trust Michael within five feet of that chick.'

I handed over my bag of laundry and she shoved it on top of the others. 'That was ages ago, when she first joined the band,' I said. 'Before I got to know her. She has a boyfriend anyway. And she's nice, really nice.'

'Sickly nice?'

'No,' I said. 'Just nice. Sound. Dead on.'

'Dead on,' Rhonda said. 'I love that. Dead on. I hope people say I'm dead on.'

'I'd tell people that, if you weren't such a bitch.'

Rhonda swatted at me with a tea-towel, then shoved it into the trolley. I lifted the remaining bag and we shuffled towards the door, past the mother and daughter sitting in one chair reading a story book, stepping around a little boy who rolled his basketball on the floor. We were supposed to be going for coffee afterwards, but the call from Michael meant Rhonda had to go now. We'd wasted all this time talking about Eddie and Dawn when that wasn't what I'd wanted to talk to her about at all.

Out on the sidewalk the sunlight was blinding and I put my shades on too.

'Would you care if we skipped coffee? I don't know what time these ConEd people are supposed to show up.'

'It's fine, don't worry.'

'What kind of shifts are you on this week? I've a launch Wednesday night. And Thursday. But I was thinking we could hang out next Saturday, maybe go to the beach. He's at some party in Long Island.'

Next Saturday, a week away. I was supposed to be talking to Suzanne tomorrow. I couldn't wait until next Saturday. 'I'll see,' I said. 'I'm not sure. There's some stuff going on. With Mum.'

Rhonda looked up from where she was making room in the trolley for the bag I was holding. It was the wrong time to tell her now, too hot and too loud, her laundry bag heavy in my arms. But I had to tell someone.

'She's sick,' I said. 'Mum's sick.'

'Sick? What's wrong with her?'

I glanced across the road to the deli on the corner. It was a nice one, old-fashioned looking, everything organic and fresh, not like the ones where we lived. I could pick up something for dinner on the way home, make something healthy.

'She has Alzheimer's.'

'Alzheimer's?' Rhonda lifted her sunglasses back into her hair. 'Yeah.'

I rolled my eyes, shifted the weight of the laundry bag in my arms. It was slippery with sweat where it had made contact with my skin.

'Isn't that what she had in that movie *The Notebook*?'

I'd seen it the week before, one night when Eddie was out. 'Yeah, but she's really far gone, at the late stages. Mum's only just been diagnosed – she's on medication.'

'I'm sorry, that's not what I meant,' Rhonda said. 'I'm sure it's nothing like that – your mom is years younger than the woman in that movie.'

'It's OK.'

'Plus she seemed fine when I last saw her – when was that? May?'

'Yep.'

Rhonda took the laundry bag from me and rested it on top of her trolley. 'She looked amazing – she could be in her freakin' forties! I'm sorry for bringing up that stupid movie. I'm sure what your mom has is probably nothing like that.'

She smiled and I did too. It felt good to let the words out, to hear someone else tell me that it wasn't so bad instead of how much worse it was going to get.

'I'm sorry for blurting it out now, I was going to tell you, later, but—'

'Don't be silly, it's fine. I'm just sorry I don't have more time but I have to drop this off before I go to Michael's. I can call you from there. What does Eddie say by the way?'

An old man shuffled by, wearing layers in the heat, his shoulders forward. He mumbled something about looking for change and moved on. My eyes followed him up the sidewalk.

'Matthews?'

'Nothing yet. I haven't told him.'

'You haven't told him? Why not?'

'I don't know. He's been so up and down lately. One minute he's on a high – Sony liked their demo, there might be a national tour – then a hundred and fifty people show up to their gig in Jersey City and he's suicidal again.'

'I remember when a hundred and fifty people in Jersey City would've made his head spin.'

'I know,' I said. 'It's just different now. It seems like they're on the cusp of something, tantalisingly close.'

'That type of career is always going to be like that. He's going to have to learn to stay balanced on his own. My dad had a saying – "Don't let success go to your head and don't let failure go to your heart." You've always been there for him through thick and thin with the band, now it's his turn to be there for you. And he will be.'

'I know,' I said. 'I know that.'

'So, tell him.'

'I will. There just never seems to be a good time.'

'Make time, Matthews,' Rhonda said. 'That's my advice. You're going to need to go home to see your mom. Sounds to me like it's time for you guys to get married, sort out your visa stuff once and for all.'

I folded my arms across my middle. 'I know,' I said. 'I know.'

'Look, why don't you come with me? To Michael's.'

'No, it's fine.'

'OK, then, I'll call you when I get there. I'll only be waiting for the ConEd guy, we can chat some more.'

'Maybe,' I said. 'I'm not sure what I'm going to do. I might go to yoga or something.'

She reached out then and gave me a hug. We weren't the kind of friends who hugged a lot but it felt nice then, her arms around me before she let go.

'It'll be OK, Carla,' she said, putting her sunglasses back on before she turned to go. 'You know it'll be OK.'

Carla. She never called me Carla, always Matthews, like some of Dad's friends used to call him. I stood there and waved as she made her way up the street. When she got to the end of the block, she turned and waved again before she disappeared around the corner.

★

I could've got the subway right there but I didn't. I walked instead down Atlantic towards the water. I never used to like Atlantic, but it was changing now, store by store, block by block and somehow the people on it were changing too. I turned Rhonda's words over in my mind, her certainty about me and Eddie, her assumption that we'd get married, that it was what I wanted, what he did. That night in Zola's over too many vodkas I'd spilled everything out to her, about how things weren't the same as they had been in the beginning. I'd expected sympathy, concern, but she'd laughed and told me that happened to everyone, that if it didn't then women's magazines would have nothing to write about.

I crossed the street, passing a store with rails of clothes outside, furniture, luggage. Next to it closed shutters were spray-painted yellow and pink. Dawn had lived near here before she'd moved into the city. I'd meant it when I'd told Rhonda I liked her. Eddie spent a lot of time with her but I didn't mind. Part of me wondered if maybe I should.

As the street sloped down, I saw cranes reaching into the sky. I became aware then of the noise that had been there all along, the rasp of drills, metal on concrete, a tremor beneath my feet. I turned and went back the way I'd come. I wasn't that desperate to see the water.

Something about telling Eddie scared me. It was true what I'd said about the band but I wasn't sure if it was the only truth. I tried to remember what Rhonda's dad had used to say, the thing about success and failure. Her dad was dead too, had died in an accident in the factory where he worked when she was only ten, much younger than I'd been when my dad died. She seemed to have everything he'd ever said filed away in her head. As I walked back past the shutters full of graffiti, the cheap rail of clothes, I wondered what it would have been like if Dad had died when I was ten, instead of eighteen. And even though we'd have missed out on all that time, part of me felt it would've been better to lose him then, when we knew each other best, before the wasteland of teenage years in between.

FIVE

Eddie was sitting at the table in front of the computer, checking the comedy listings. The five of us were supposed to be going, Nick and Dawn and her boyfriend Chris. I wasn't in the mood for comedy.

'Four Legs Bad. Are they those two guys we saw in the Village that time?'

I was drying the dishes. We never dried the dishes and I waited for him to ask me what I was doing.

'Suzanne called today,' I said, watching as he scrolled down a page of text. 'The third time this week.'

'"This Kentucky duo will have you saddling up for more every time . . ." Kentucky duo? I'm not sure. Sounds kind of cheesy.'

'Eddie, are you listening to me?'

He looked up. 'You were saying Suzanne called. What's going on with her anyway?'

'It's not her, it's Mum.'

He turned to face me, giving me his full attention. I could hear my heartbeat in the silence between us. I swallowed before I spoke. 'Mum's been diagnosed with Alzheimer's.' As I towelled the glass it squeaked.

'What? Like, dementia?'

'Yeah, it's called early-onset Alzheimer's, for people who get it young, younger.'

'But are they sure? I mean – can they do anything?' He swung back on the chair, his bare feet hooked around the legs.

'It's kind of fucked up, they can diagnose it, but they can't confirm one hundred per cent until – until after.'

'Until you're dead,' was what I wanted to say, but I didn't.

Eddie rubbed his shin up and down the chair leg. The apartment was quiet, no music on for once, only the air-conditioner and the fridge humming. 'Wow,' he said, running his hand from the back of his head to the front. His hair was still as thick as it always had been and it needed a cut, just like his sideburns. 'Jesus. Alzheimer's. That sucks.'

I waited for him to say more, to come over to me and take me in his arms. I put the glass down on the counter and covered my face with my hands.

'Hey,' he said, 'hey.'

I heard the chair legs hit the floor and he was there next to me, his hands in my hair, pushing it back from my face, before his arms pulled me into him. 'I'm sorry, Carls. That was a stupid thing to say. I'm such a dumbass sometimes, I'm sorry.'

I nuzzled my face into his neck, found his shoulder-blades and pulled him closer. It was going to be OK, here in his arms I could forget the whole world, this was the one place where everything was always OK. I waited for him to tell me that we'd get through this together, to whisper into my hair that we were invincible, like he always used to. I held him tighter, as if I could push the words out.

'Let me make you a cup of tea,' he said, releasing me. After the warmth of the hug I felt cold, exposed. I pulled myself up on the counter, kicked my legs, watching the tattoo on my ankle swing back and forth, back and forth.

He filled the kettle, switched on the gas. When he turned back, his arms were folded across his chest. 'So, like, how is your mom? Have you talked to her about it? Or just Suzanne?'

'She seems fine, she says she's fine, that things aren't as bad as Suzanne is making out.'

'She's on meds?'

'They have some new kind. She says it's good to start taking it early and she's in the very early stages.'

Eddie nodded, taking it all in.

'But it's weird, Eddie. Ever since I found out it's like I'm noticing all these changes. Every week there's something, but half the time I don't know if it's real or if I'm imagining it.'

He frowned. 'What do you mean "every week"? How long have you known?'

I shrugged. 'I don't know. A few weeks?'

Four was a few, it wasn't a lie.

'You've kept this to yourself for a few weeks?'

'You've been so stressed with the band – I didn't want to add to that.'

He shook his head. 'Since when do we not tell each other stuff like this? There was a time you'd have told me straight away.'

'Yeah, and there was a time when you'd have noticed something was wrong, a time when you'd have asked me.'

He shook his head. 'Hey, don't act like this is my fault for not asking. Anyway, it's not like you being in a bad mood is anything unusual these days.'

I kicked my heels hard against the cupboard door, held his gaze until he turned back to the kettle, turning the gas up so it hissed louder. 'What's that supposed to mean?'

'Look, you're upset. I can see that. I don't want to get into other stuff. We should be talking about your mom.'

'What other stuff?' I knew, of course I knew, but it was the stuff we never talked about and I wanted to hear him say it, to put a name to this weight of nothing and everything that seemed to hover over us both all the time now.

He fanned his toes on the tiles. 'I guess I mean you never seem happy any more. You're always bitching about everything – the apartment, your friends, your job—'

The kettle whistled and he turned it off. He was doing what he always did, shying away from the words before they became a fight. Right then, more than anything, I wanted to fight with him and I wanted him to fight me back.

'Eddie, would you be happy waiting tables? Asking people

how they want their fucking burgers all day long?'

'I guess it's a job, Carla.'

'It's OK for you, you've got the band. Your ideal job.'

His cheeks reddened. 'Recording advertising jingles? Ideal?'

'So it's not ideal, but you're your own boss. You can work it around the band.'

'Hey, that didn't just happen. I worked hard to make it happen!'

He was getting mad, I could see it in the line of his shoulders through his T-shirt.

'You mean your dad did!'

I knew then I'd hit the spot to make him really angry, raging, just like I was.

'That's bullshit, Carla, and you know it! I'm the one that built the business up, I'm the one who keeps it going—'

'Yeah, but the work from your dad's ad agency makes it a lot easier. You can't say it doesn't.' I kicked my heels on the door again, two sharp bangs, like a gavel. He opened his mouth to say something, then closed it.

'What?'

He shook his head.

'What, Eddie?'

'Everyone else has it so easy, Carla, don't they? All I ever hear is how you hate waiting tables, how you'll need a knee replacement by the time you're forty. If you hate it so much, then quit! Do something else!'

I jumped down from the counter, landing hard. 'Do what? I'm illegal! I can't get a job in an office—'

'Since when did you want a job in an office?'

'That's not the point! I can't get any job! A job in a bookstore or the library—'

'You want to be a librarian now?' He raised the eyebrow with the piercing.

'Don't be so fucking condescending! The point is I can't just walk into any job, Eddie, you know that. It's like – I don't know

108

– being some kind of fucking invisible person over here. I can't work, I can't vote, I can't even get home to see my mother.'

He'd started to walk away but when I said that he turned back. His eyes were dark. 'Hey! Back up there!' He jabbed the air with one finger. 'Don't throw this shit at me about not being able to go home. I'm the one who wanted to get married, to do this right. You know that.'

I went to speak but he held up a hand in my face.

'You know what I think? I think you've never wanted to go back. And it's easier to blame everyone else, to blame me.' He blew his fringe out of his eyes. 'It's not my fault your mom's sick, that you're not happy. It's not my fault your life didn't turn out the way you wanted it to.'

His words hung between us and for a second I thought I might hit him. I imagined a slap, cold and hard, like in the movies, the red stain growing on his face. 'Fuck you, Eddie!' I elbowed my way past him and out of the narrow kitchen. 'Fuck you!' I said again, as I shoved my feet into my flip-flops by the door and grabbed my bag from the hook, checking for my wallet. My keys were in the kitchen, by the window. I strode back in past where he was still standing at the counter. Anger caught in my voice, a jerk of breath between each word. 'I can't believe you! I really can't! I tell you my mother's sick – that she's got a terminal fucking illness – and this is your response? Nice, Eddie. Very supportive!'

I snatched the keys from the window ledge. I wanted him to say something, to curse back at me, maybe even to hit me. But all he did was stand there. When he glanced up I saw his anger had softened into sadness and he looked as if he might cry. Suddenly I was sad too, so very, very sad, for him and me and for Mum. For a second I wanted to tell him I was sorry for everything – for blaming him, for not being the person who he wanted me to be.

But then he looked away and I shoved the keys into my bag and walked past him into the hall, opened the door and slammed it behind me.

★

I don't know what time it was when I came back. I was trying to open the door quietly, my anger, if not forgotten, at least diluted by beer and laughter with Rhonda. Later on, Murray came out too, and we laughed even harder, but I couldn't remember anymore what was so funny. I couldn't figure out if I wanted Eddie to be in or not, but he was sitting on the couch in the light of the lamp, reading. On the stereo, Leonard Cohen was playing.

'Hi,' he said.

'Hi,' I said. I giggled. 'How was the comedy?'

'It was OK. I've seen better.' He closed his magazine. 'Where'd you go?'

'Millie's. And then Union.' I hiccuped.

'With Rhonda?'

'And Murray. And some new boyfriend of his. Tim. Or Tom. Maybe Jim. Yep, it was definitely Jim.' I put my hand over my mouth to stop the hiccups.

Eddie smiled and stood up. 'Look, I know I might need to say this again tomorrow but I want to say sorry about earlier. I talked to Nick about it. You were right. Your mom's sick, you're upset. I shouldn't have brought up all that other stuff. I'm sorry.'

He'd told Nick about Mum without even checking with me, probably Dawn as well. But there was no point in starting another argument before we were even done with this one.

'That's OK,' I said. 'I'm sorry too.'

I wasn't sure yet if I was, but it seemed like the right thing to say and it was better than earlier, seeing Eddie smiling again, to feel his hand on my waist, pulling me into a hug before we walked into the bedroom, arm in arm.

As we undressed, he asked me more about the night and I told him some of what had happened but I couldn't remember what was so funny. We took turns in the bathroom, me first, then him. We fell into the rhythm of getting ready for bed, like we'd gotten ready for bed together every night for years and years. When we lay down, he turned off the light and leaned over me, his face near my shoulder. I could feel his breath on my neck.

'Tomorrow I want you to tell me all about your mom, how she is. I love her, you know that.'

I remembered when they'd first met, all those years before, how he'd played Neil Diamond for her at the Sidewalk Café. A tear slid down the side of my face and on to the pillow. Under the covers, his hand reached for mine and he wriggled closer.

'Things will be OK, Carls.'

'I know.'

Sleep had started to come already, sudden and heavy. Through it I heard his voice, quiet in the dark, jerking me awake again.

'You know what, Carls? I was thinking it's about time we got married.'

Six

I didn't remember it right when I woke up. Other things came into my mind first: the fight, the night out, the first bar we'd gone to, the second. I lay there, piecing it all together. And then I remembered.

Eddie was on the computer when I came into the living room. 'Hey!' he said, without turning. 'How's the head?'

'Sore.' I walked past him into the kitchen. The glass on the counter looked clean and I filled it with water. Eddie was saying something I couldn't hear over the noise of the tap.

'What?' I shut it off.

'It says here that you can get a marriage licence right away, if you go down in person. Then you can get married the next day. Isn't that cool? No waiting list or anything.'

I leaned against the counter, rubbed my temples. 'What are you talking about?'

'City Hall, silly!' He glanced over at me, smiled and went back to the screen. 'We need photo ID, a money order and us both to show up. That's it. Oh, and one witness. You think Rhonda might want to do that? If she can't get off work I can see if Mom's around. She might want to come anyway.'

I drank some more water, watched him flick through the screens to find the information he needed.

'The Brooklyn office to get the licence is down by Borough Hall. They close at four. What time are you working today?'

'Today?'

'Why not?'

Too many answers to that question jammed together in my mind so I decided to answer the other one, the one he'd asked first. 'Two,' I said. 'Till closing.'

Despite the swish of nausea in my stomach I was glad suddenly of my shift, a concrete reason not to be able to do anything else today.

Eddie glanced at the clock. 'Shit, that's not going to work. How about tomorrow, early? I've a recording session at eleven but we could go before that.'

I walked over to where he was sitting and took the chair at the end of the table. He reached for my hand, squeezed it and went back to the screen. 'Did you know you can marry your first cousin in New York? No marriage for gay couples but it's OK for immediate family members. That's fucked up.'

'Eddie,' I said.

His face was lit by the glow from the screen. My brain swirled. I needed to speak, but even saying his name had been an effort. I wanted him to look at me. 'Can you just shut that down for a minute?'

I pushed the laptop gently closed. 'What?' he said. 'What's going on?' He leaned back in his chair, his hands behind his head, two leaks of sweat on his T-shirt.

I started to speak, then stopped. It was hard to get the words straight in my head. 'That's what I feel like asking you, what's going on? Last night, we're fighting, you say all these things …'

'I said I was sorry.' He landed the chair with a clunk.

'… and today we're getting married?'

'I apologised last night – don't you remember? We talked about this.'

'I do remember,' I said. 'But I didn't think that meant we'd be getting married today. Or tomorrow or whenever. Don't you think we're rushing into this?'

Outside on the street a fire truck screamed and honked. It was only after it was gone that I noticed the music playing softly in the background – Yo La Tengo. The soundtrack to our first apartment in Fort Greene.

'I wouldn't call eleven years rushing into it,' he said. 'Loads of marriages don't even last half that. And we nearly did it before the west-coast tour, what was that, eight years ago? Nine? If we'd gotten married then, we'd be married now.'

I tried to imagine what it would've been like to be married all this time, if things would've been different, better.

He took both my hands in his. 'Look, I was thinking a lot last night after you left. You're right. This whole thing is fucked, this visa thing. It's not fair. The only way to solve it is to get married. You can go home, be with your mom, come back. It's what we should've done a long time ago.'

I looked at the face I knew so well, the Sounds of the City T-shirt we'd bought together at a street market in Hell's Kitchen. I'd never been one of those girls to dream about proposals up the Eiffel Tower or weddings in a big white puffy dress.

'What?' he asked. 'You've got your thinking face on.'

I looked down, at his hands around mine, our knees almost touching, our feet, bare on the floor. When I spoke my voice was low, as if I didn't want either of us to hear the words. 'If Mum wasn't sick, would we be doing this?'

He didn't answer straight away and when I looked up his smile was gone. 'Does it matter?' he said. He dropped my hands so he could fold his arms across his chest. 'It'll sort things out, right? It's the next logical step. And we love each other.'

Behind my head the fan blew. We loved each other. I wished he'd said that first.

I swallowed. 'Eddie, this feels like a very big thing to decide when I'm hung-over and you're feeling guilty about what you said last night. Of course it's what I want, but I don't know if getting married will fix everything. It's not like you say, "I do," and they hand you a Green Card.'

'I checked it out,' he said, jerking a thumb towards the closed laptop. 'We'd have to go for an interview and there're these weird biometric tests where they scan your eyes and shit. Online it says it all takes about three months. After that you can travel.'

Three months. It was the first block of time that morning that seemed to make any sense. Three months from now was nearly Christmas. After that, I could go home, see Mum, come back again.

He took my hands in his. 'Look, if you're asking if I'd've jumped up this morning wanting to get married without this stuff about your mom, then I guess the answer is no. But so what? I mean, look at my mom and dad. They waited to get married till I was four and they split when I was seven.'

'Meaning what?'

'Meaning no one can see into the future. No decision ever feels totally right, does it? Life doesn't come with guarantees.'

He was trying to convince me, and I wanted him to. I let him talk.

'What's important is what we need to do right now. I don't want you to be unhappy, trapped here. Why would I? I love you.'

I scanned his face, his eyes, his pierced brow, his sideburns. I saw the love that was there, the memory of love. He was right. Why was I making this so complicated? The answer should be simple.

'You're sure I'll be able to travel home and get back in?' I said.

'I'm sure. We'll get a lawyer to help us with the paperwork. They do these packages online. It's not that expensive. It'll be OK, Carls.'

Carls. He'd called me that right from the beginning, and now something in the way he said it made me start to believe him, believe that this really could happen, that everything could be all right.

'Thank you, Eddie,' I said. 'I love you.'

I hugged him tight and he hugged me back and then we kissed, a soft light kiss. And it was only after that, when he'd opened the computer again, that it occurred to me that maybe I'd said those things the wrong way around.

*

Eddie kissed me before he left and reminded me to call Rhonda about being a witness. I turned the music off and called Mum first. When I told her she sounded uncertain, as if maybe she was supposed to know my news already and had forgotten it. When I explained everything, she couldn't understand why it was happening so fast, why we couldn't wait for her and Suzanne to come over.

'You got engaged today and you'll be married by the end of the week?' she said. 'What's the rush?'

I'd borrowed Eddie's line: 'Eleven years, Mum, it's hardly a rush.'

She put me on to Suzanne so I could tell her too and I remembered how she sounded when she was genuinely happy about something. After we hung up I thought of Ange: now they knew, she might find out too. I called her before I could think too much about it. I hadn't spoken to her since her mum had died – I'd been meaning to for months, but I'd never got around to it. If she was annoyed she didn't show it. She sounded excited for me, and told me to say congrats to Eddie.

Calling Rhonda was easier but her phone went to voicemail so I left a message that just said I had news. Once she'd called back, I'd call Murray. The first thing they'd both ask was what I'd wear. I knew that as sure as I'd known Suzanne would ask when it meant I could come home, that Ange would want to know how he'd proposed. People were predictable, mostly, once you'd known them long enough.

After I'd made the phone calls I poured a glass of orange juice and sat on the counter to drink it. Only last night I'd been sitting there fighting with Eddie and now we were getting married. Getting married. I held the words in my head, took another drink. It still felt unreal, even after telling people, as if it was happening to someone else.

I licked some juice off my top lip, sticky and sweet. As I did, another thought crept in, a question through the back door of my brain: if Dad was here, if I told him, what would be the thing he'd say?

SEVEN

We were the last couple of the day – in fact, we were the last couple of the week. It had been strange, that morning, going to work, knowing I was getting married later on. I'd only told Toni so she'd know why I wanted to switch shifts. I hadn't expected her to tell anyone else or for the whole gang to arrive in with a cake and champagne.

The couple ahead of us had their whole extended family with them, the clutches of women chattering in what sounded like Portuguese. It was easy to pick out the bride, a tiny woman in a floor-length dress. The groom could have been any one of the men in dark suits, laughing loudly.

'I knew we should've got more dressed up,' I said to Eddie.

Eddie folded his arms across his T-shirt. 'By "we" you mean me.'

'Well, those guys are all wearing suits.'

'You know I don't own a suit. Relax, they're not going to say we can't get married because I'm underdressed.'

That was the third time he'd told me to relax since I'd come in from work. I'd planned to take in a lunchtime yoga class but, with the cake and champagne, I'd run out of time. 'I *am* relaxed!'

'It's no big deal. Nobody here cares what you wear.'

I cared, but I didn't say that because if I did we'd be on the verge of an argument and I couldn't handle an argument. Not today.

Two little boys pushed through the crowd, chasing each other, wearing shirts so white they could only have been brand new.

One was carrying a bunch of blue flowers and the other swiped for them, trying to snatch them away.

From nowhere a tall woman swooped down on the boy, grabbed the flowers and smacked the side of his head with her palm. Instantly he started to cry. As I turned to roll my eyes to Eddie, the door opened and Nick was there, red-faced and out of breath. 'The happy couple!' He leaned in to kiss me, his hand on my shoulder. 'Sorry I'm late, guys, that damn N train. You look fantastic, Carla.'

He turned to Eddie and held his arms open. 'As for you, man, you could've made an effort.'

'What did you expect? A damn penguin suit?'

They hugged in a way I'd never seen Irish guys hug, Eddie reaching up, Nick slapping a hand on his shoulder. I remembered the first time we'd all met, in O'Dowd's, how Nick had been the one I'd liked first. If things had worked out differently, maybe we'd have been the ones getting hitched today.

The double wooden doors behind us opened and I turned to see a couple coming out. They were old, older than Mum, well into their seventies. I wanted to congratulate them but before I could think of what to say they had filed past us already. The Portuguese family swarmed around them, through the open door and for a second I saw beige carpet, wood, before it closed again.

Nick leaned against the wall, telling Eddie about a rave review in the *Village Voice* for a new band. Above his head there was a laminated sign, 'No rice throwing', with the Spanish translation under it.

Eddie was rolling on the balls of his feet, his eyebrows knotted into a frown as he mulled over what Nick was saying. Was he nervous at all? If he was, he was hiding it well. But then again, he was good at hiding things. When Bonnie had said she wouldn't make it, he'd only let me see for a second how upset he was, before wrapping it up inside him.

'Hey there, Matthews, wakey-wakey!' Rhonda squeezed my arm tight, her makeup perfect, just like it had been before she'd gone to fix it up. 'You were totally in your own world. Any last-minute jitters on the brink of becoming a married woman?' She made her voice deep on 'married woman', like it was something from a scary movie.

'No!' I said. 'Course not.'

She squeezed my arm tighter. 'You sure? Tying yourself to one person for the rest of your life doesn't freak you out?'

The smell of her perfume was too sweet. I pulled away a little. I reached for some smart comment to make her laugh, but couldn't find one. 'I thought we were the perfect couple, according to you,' I said. 'And what about Michael? Wouldn't you love to be tied to him?'

She dropped my arm and smoothed her silver dress, miles dressier than what I had on. 'I'm only kidding. I guess I was thinking of some of the creeps I've dated before. Not you and Eddie. You and Eddie are perfect.'

She smiled and I smiled back. Something was going on with Michael – I knew by her face but I wasn't going to ask.

'And you look great,' she said. 'That green really suits you. I'll make sure to get plenty of photos.' She waved a tiny sequined bag that looked barely big enough to hold a camera.

'We don't need millions,' I said, 'just a few. I'd like to send some to Mum.'

Rhonda looked like she was about to say something but I never had a chance to hear it because the double doors opened and the Portuguese family were there again, even louder this time. The tiny bride clung now to the arm of a short overweight man whose hand fixed one of the blue flowers behind her ear. She beamed.

'Come on,' Eddie said. 'We're up.'

The last of the crowd spilled out of the room. I wondered what they thought of us, our party of four, or if they'd even noticed us. As I walked in I realised that this was the part I'd been dreading most, walking up the aisle, but of course there was no aisle, not really, only some plastic chairs and a table at the other

119

end, a woman behind it in a black suit. It had the feeling of a room that had just been full of people. I thought of all the people who weren't there to fill it now: Mum, Ange, Suzanne, Dad. But Dad wouldn't be there no matter where I was, so he didn't count.

If Mum was there she'd have rivalled Rhonda. She'd probably have worn her grey dress, the wool one, with her sequined black cardigan, or maybe she'd have bought something new. Thinking about it, she'd definitely have had something new for her daughter's wedding, even if it was in City Hall.

Eddie handed the folder with everything in it to the registrar. His fingers drummed on his thigh as she went through it all, jotting some details on another sheet of paper.

'Can I have the rings?' she said.

I looked at Eddie, but the light from the window was in my eyes and I couldn't see his face properly, only the outline of his shape. 'Rings?' I said.

'We need rings?' Eddie said.

'It says it on the website. Two rings. One each.'

Usually I wore one on each hand but not today. Today we'd been running late and I couldn't find the silver one when I came out of the shower, only the one that went with the dress – a green flower with a navy centre. I pulled it off my finger. 'Will this do?' I said.

'Sure, but you need one more.'

I turned to Rhonda, who was one step ahead of me. She held out her hand. Her two rings were big and clunky, one with a glass square, bubbles of air, caught inside. The other was one I knew Michael had given her, silver with tiny diamonds dotted in the groove along the middle.

'Sorry,' she whispered.

I started to giggle as I chose the glass one and handed it to Eddie. He was laughing too.

I was still giggling when the registrar started the ceremony, as if I was ten years old and back in mass, in school. She turned to Eddie to ask the questions and I tuned in. Before I knew it, it was my turn and I realised I hadn't even put down my handbag, that it was still swinging from my shoulder.

When it was time for the rings Eddie put Rhonda's on my finger, but it was too loose so the glass part rolled around to the back. I started to giggle again. Mine was too tight for him and I couldn't get it over his knuckle. His hand was shaking and I thought he was laughing too, but then I wondered, suddenly, if it was nerves. I thought about switching the rings and giving him Rhonda's but it didn't seem like the right thing to do so I left it there, halfway down his finger. I glanced at the registrar to see if she was smiling, but she wasn't. She looked tired, as if she couldn't wait to get out of there.

The sun was in my face again and I squinted, moved out of its glare. I was conscious of the light spots in front of my eyes, of Rhonda reaching for the camera, Nick's face behind Eddie's and the weight of my bag digging into my shoulder. Eddie reached for my hand and I caught his ring just before it fell off. The registrar's voice got to the part I knew, the part we all knew, which was said for thousands of people every day. Now she was saying it for Eddie and me.

'I hereby pronounce you husband and wife.'

PART THREE

ONE

The bus jerked to a stop so my pen slipped across the page, making a blue line across what I'd written. Below me some tourists got off on O'Connell Street, which didn't look much different from how I remembered it, except the old horrible fountain had gone, replaced with a dizzingly high spike of stainless steel. I went back to my journal.

I was supposed to be writing about coming home, that was the idea. When the plane had landed and the captain had welcomed us to Dublin, I'd looked out the window at the white-grey sky, the line of green, and waited to feel something. An hour later, I was still waiting so instead I filled the pages with other things, a list of people to meet up with in the next six weeks, places to visit. I was going to find a yoga class, that was one of the things I'd decided.

The guy in front of me had been on the phone since the journey started, to someone called Ray, and now another someone called Colin. I took my phone from my pocket but didn't turn it on. Suzanne was going to freak – I was supposed to call her when I was on the bus so she could collect me from town but if she really wanted to collect me she'd have come to the airport. And anyway, something about being uncontactable was nice, creating a pocket of space that was all my own.

The bus crossed the bridge, and up the river I could see more bridges that I didn't recognise. Eddie might have tried to call but he'd still be asleep now, so he wouldn't be worried. I still felt bad about missing his gig, they'd never played Terminal 5 before and

125

it was amazing to get the chance, even if it was playing support. He didn't seem to mind though and he'd taken me for lunch to say goodbye. Afterwards we'd walked around a bit, our hands clasped despite the freezing February air that made our knuckles raw. He told me that he'd miss me, that the apartment would be empty without me. I realised then that, in all the years we'd spent together, it was the first time I'd been the one to leave.

The bus stopped again. Trinity. There it was, just like it had always been, black railings, the grass on the playing field so green it was like some kind of ad for Ireland. I didn't want to look at Trinity, and I turned to the shops on the other side of the street.

More people got on and eventually the bus pulled away. I rested my arm on my backpack, ready to move it. It was falling apart, the gaudy pinks and purples showing its age, but I liked it still. I remembered the day I'd bought it, me and Ange venturing over to Capel Street, past the shops with tents and Doc Martens hanging outside, getting ready for our big adventure. When Eddie'd seen how much I was packing he asked if I was going for six weeks or six months. I'd laughed and told him not to be silly, even though we both knew enough to know that whenever you left anywhere you never really knew when you'd come back.

The bus stopped again. Red-brick buildings with steps and paned windows, arches over the doors. Merrion Square? Or Fitzwilliam? A girl walked past and glanced at me, smiled slightly, then looked away. Shit, did I know her? I pushed the backpack higher on the seat and opened my journal again. I'd forgotten the Russian roulette of Dublin public transport, that any journey could put you next to someone from school you never wanted to see again, a friend of your mother's, an ex.

I closed my eyes, rubbed them. It seemed amazing how easy it had been, after all this time, to get here, that it had been just a journey, like any other, a taxi, a plane, a bus and here I was. In some way it seemed that the places I'd been yesterday, the Brooklyn streets with the slanting paving stones, the call of kids racing home from school, would cease to exist now that I wasn't there. Even Eddie, after only seven or ten hours or whatever it was, seemed static, like a photo. He might have been someone I'd made up.

Tiredness was making me think like that, jet-lag. When I opened my eyes I saw the bus had picked up speed as we'd left the city. We passed hotels, restaurants, a garage. Everywhere was the same, but different.

We got stuck at the lights at the hospital, the one I hated where Suzanne, Olivia and I had waited and waited in a sunny corridor, me in my pyjamas, like a patient. It looked bigger now, a plush new entrance, but I bet it smelt the same.

I took my iPod out and scrolled through the artists: John Lennon, Johnny Cash, Joni Mitchell, José Gonzalez. I didn't want any of their company, didn't need it, now that the bus was flying along, with only me and an old lady, two rows ahead, upstairs. We were on the coast road, my favourite part of the journey. Over the low rooftops I could see a sliver of sea, grey against grey sky.

In my backpack, the book on Alzheimer's remained unopened. I'd bought it weeks ago, had planned to read it before I came home and then, at least, to skim through it on the journey. There was too much information online, that was the problem, millions of results from Google, billions of words. It was even more confusing than listening to the patchwork of contradiction between Mum and Suzanne, who gave me different accounts of the same things.

The bus slowed down, stopped. The old lady was on the move and I waited for her to negotiate the stairs before pulling on my backpack. It felt heavier than before, too wide for the narrow stairwell, and for a second I thought the doors were going to close before I had a chance to get off, but the driver saw me and waited. I thanked him as I got off.

Out on the sidewalk the air was cold; it smelt different. The sweetshop that used to be there was a jeweller's, long silver necklaces glinting under lights. When I went to cross the road a car beeped and I realised I'd been looking the wrong way.

I knew this route well, had walked it so many times, up to MacDaid's on the corner, only it wasn't MacDaid's any more – it was painted white, and had a swinging brass sign with its new name: the Junction. I took the turn alongside it, past the empty beer garden with empty white metal tables and chairs. That was new too.

Now that I was nearly there, I found myself walking faster, nearly running. I remembered something Jan, my yoga teacher, always said about remembering to be in your body, to feel your feet: heel, toe, heel, toe.

I turned into the estate. How many times had I walked this walk? My backpack could've been a schoolbag – I could almost feel it, the books, the pencil case rattling up and down. I walked past the houses, remembering the names of the neighbours: the Clancys, Miss Dillon and Miss Fitzsimons, the Dorgans, the McCarthys. I wondered which of them was still there, if they knew about Mum, if they were peeking out, saying, 'There she is now, there's Carla Matthews. You know, it took her mother having Alzheimer's to get her home.'

I turned the corner and there it was, our house, at the top of the hill, windows like eyes looking down. It was a steeper walk than I remembered and I was out of breath. Two little girls were taking turns on a bike with pink stabilisers. They were laughing but stopped when they saw me. I smiled at them and they stared back. The house was getting close now and I could see it really did look the same. The hedge poking over the wall, the red-brick pillars. The cherry tree, just like I remembered but without any blossom today.

As I got closer I saw the garage door was gone – of course it was. There was a window where it had been, with wooden blinds and a door to the side. The room Mum had used for her clients.

I stopped walking. Even though it was only one o'clock there was a light on in the sitting room, and the gate was open. We used to keep it closed. When we went out in the car my job was always to close the gate, Suzanne's was to get out and open it when we got home.

Through the window, I could see someone moving. A hand shoved the blinds to one side and there was a face: Suzanne. Shorter hair, thinner cheeks, a half-wave, a smile. I waved back, crunching over the gravel between the two cars. Something made me think of all the times I'd walked up that driveway, made me picture all those other versions of me – in a communion dress, my school uniform, those twelve-hole ox-blood Docs. The long black skirt I'd worn to Dad's funeral.

The light in the hall came on. The hedge needed a trim. Underneath it the earth was wet in the flowerbed. I saw weeds, and a gap where the peace lilies should have been. The front door was opening and Suzanne was there and someone else behind her. Mum. She was talking but I couldn't hear her yet, the glass porch door still between us, overlaying them both with my reflection. I slid it back and somehow Mum was in front of Suzanne now, reaching out to me. Standing on the step, she towered over me, so I had to reach up to hug her. Her arms slid around my shoulders, solid and soft. She smelt the same. 'Welcome home, love,' she said, into my hair.

Two

There were fresh flowers in the hall, like always, white tulips in a square vase, a new carpet, beige, a wooden mirror hanging on the wall where the old one used to be.

'How was your journey? We were worried about you.'

'You should've called. Why didn't you call?'

Their sentences overlapped. I smiled from one to the other. Suzanne's hair was really short, almost shorn – it made her look older, her face fatter. 'I'm sorry, the bus was just there and it goes all the way out—'

'It doesn't matter,' Mum said. 'You're here now.'

'I'll put this up in your room,' Suzanne said, grabbing my backpack from where I'd left it on the floor. 'Out of the way.'

My room. She started up the stairs and Mum turned me towards the living room, her hand on my shoulder. A wooden floor, a swirly bright rug, the same door handles. Everything was the same but somehow different too.

'Sit down there, you must be exhausted.'

I sat on a navy couch in the same place as the old one used to be. 'You've done so much to the place,' I said. 'It looks great.'

She kept standing, looking around, her arms folded, her hands holding her elbows, and I was grateful her focus had moved away from me. From the side, her hair showed the sleek line it always had, sliding along the curve of her chin. Her makeup was perfect and I realised then how worried I'd been that she wouldn't be wearing any.

'I suppose I have,' she said. 'You don't notice, really, doing stuff bit by bit.'

130

I remembered phone calls in Brooklyn, half listening as she told me about walls painted, new floors, things she'd picked up in markets, on holidays. Why hadn't I paid more attention?

Suzanne was back, smiling. Her face was pale without makeup. I still couldn't believe she'd cut her long dark hair – what I wouldn't have done to have it. She stood next to Mum, beside her I could see she'd put on weight. 'You must be knackered,' she said. 'Are you hungry?'

'I was eating lasagne around three in the morning,' I said. 'It's hard to know where I'm at food wise.'

Mum rolled her eyes. 'It was either that or chicken, I bet. I'd say they haven't changed that menu since I worked that route.'

'The other option *was* chicken!' I said, laughing with her. She remembered working there, the whole menu.

'Why don't I make you a sandwich?' she said. 'Or some breakfast? Toast, a boiled egg?'

Suzanne reached out and touched Mum's arm. 'I'll make it, Mammy,' she said. 'You catch up with Carla.'

'She thinks I can't boil an egg,' Mum said, rolling her eyes again, only this time she wasn't laughing. 'A piece of toast, she thinks I'll burn the place down.'

I laughed even though no one else was.

'I'm not hungry,' I said. 'A cup of tea would be perfect.'

The two of them were still standing and I felt as if I should be on my feet too.

'I'll put the kettle on,' Mum said.

'Mammy, I'll do it. It's only a cup of bloody tea.'

Mum lifted her hands out to her sides. 'OK, then, I'll have a coffee while you're at it. And bring in some biscuits, the nice ones. They're in the back of the press.'

Suzanne looked like she was going to say something else, but she didn't, only nodded and walked past me towards the kitchen. Mum sat down. Her black jumper was one we'd bought together in New York. She folded her hands in her lap. Her nail polish was wearing off in strips, as if she'd been picking at it. She covered her fingers quickly with her other hand. I decided right then that I'd treat her to a manicure. 'I'm not used to being fussed over,' I said.

'Well, it won't take too long for the novelty of having you around to wear off and you'll have to fend for yourself.'

'I'd rather that.'

'So would I. Your sister's carrying on as if I'm not capable of making a cup of tea.'

She rolled her eyes for the third time since I'd come in.

'So, you two are getting on well, then?' I asked. She smiled. 'We are, of course we are. It's just different, you know, having to share the place again. I was used to my own space.'

'It's not that long since Suzanne moved out, though,' I said. 'Two years? Three?'

'Five,' Mum said.

Five years. I'd never have thought it. 'Still, at least you're used to living together.'

'I suppose so,' she said, looking down at her hands again. 'It's a bit different now, though, you know.'

It felt like we were into something already, before I even had my jacket off, before the kettle had boiled. I didn't want to talk about it yet but I had to. Ignoring the reason I was home, even for five minutes, seemed somehow worse than not coming home at all. 'How are you feeling?' I said.

'Very good,' she said. 'Very well.' When she looked back at me her smile was wide, her real smile.

'Are you still enjoying working in the Buddhist Centre with Lily-Anne?'

Her smile dropped a little. 'Oh,' she said. 'Didn't I tell you? I'm not there any more.'

'No?'

She shook her head. 'I enjoyed it and it was fine when they only wanted me the days when Lily-Anne was there – she could drive me and if I got stuck she could help. But then they wanted me on other days and, with the bus and everything, it was a bit much.'

132

It didn't seem that long since she'd been telling me how perfect the job was, that it was a great way to be around people without too much responsibility. 'When did you finish up?'

'Not long ago,' she said. 'Around Christmas.'

We'd spoken loads of times since Christmas and she'd never mentioned it. What else hadn't she told me?

'I still go,' she said, 'on Tuesday nights, with Lily-Anne. They have a meditation class. You might like to come one evening.'

She was still meditating, going to classes. That was a good sign.

'Yeah,' I said. 'Maybe.'

Suzanne was back with a tray, three mugs in different colours and a teapot with a stripy cosy I recognised. 'Oh, my God, I'd forgotten about that,' I said. 'I knitted that in fourth class.'

'As I remember it, you attempted to knit it but it was all going wrong so you convinced your auntie Olivia to knit it for you,' Mum said, smiling.

I took a mug from the tray. 'OK, it was more of a joint effort.'

Suzanne passed around a plate of chocolate biscuits. 'That's your idea of a joint effort?' she said. 'Olivia doing all the work?' She took a biscuit and chomped into it. I opened my mouth to retaliate but something told me to let it go, for now.

★

It started to rain, fat drops on the window that slid into each other. My mug was empty and I cradled it in my hand. My eyelids were heavy.

'I'll take the clothes in,' Suzanne said.

Mum looked at the window and stood up quickly. Her napkin slid on to the floor. 'I'll get them,' she said. 'You stay where you are.'

'OK,' Suzanne said. 'Use the blue basket. It's by the back door.'

'I know where it is. I've been putting clothes in it since before you were born.'

'Let me give you a hand,' I said.

'Don't worry,' she said. 'There's only a few bits.' She went into

133

the kitchen. We both heard the back door open, close again. We waited for a second of silence to pass.

'How do you think she is?' Suzanne said. She was leaning forward, sitting in the chair where Dad's used to be, her hands on her knees. Her jeans were too short. I could see her socks, pink and purple stripes. There was no point in mentioning the Buddhist Centre.

'She seems fine,' I said. 'She seems really good, actually.'

Suzanne sighed. 'She's having a good day. She's excited about you coming home, on a high.'

'That's great.'

'Plus she's better at this time of day – mornings and afternoons are her good times,' Suzanne said. 'She tends to get worse as the day goes on. You get to notice the signs when you spend a lot of time with her.'

There it was, the first dig. She hadn't even waited an hour to remind me about the things she'd done and I hadn't.

'Well, hopefully, me being here will be good for her. We can do some nice things together. I'm dying to walk the pier. And I want to go into town to see all the changes everyone talks about. Oh, and a manicure – where does she like to go?'

'A manicure?' Suzanne's voice rose with her eyebrows. 'Her nails are the least of her worries, Carla.'

'What's wrong with a manicure? She'd love that. We used to do it in New York,' I said. 'You know how into her grooming she is.' It was on the tip of my tongue to add that Suzanne used to be too, but I kept the words in.

She was shaking her head. 'I'm not saying she wouldn't enjoy it, only that we have a bit of a routine going. She's best in a routine. She spends a lot of time with Lily-Anne during the day. If you're planning on doing something different, maybe say it to one of us first.'

Those words were carefully chosen to make my blood boil. Check with her? With Lily-Anne who wasn't even family, who I'd never even met?

'What?' Suzanne said.

'I'm not a complete idiot. I'm not going to make her do something she's not able for.'

'I know that,' Suzanne said. 'I'm not saying that. Only it's tricky – what works for her one day might not work the next.'

I resolved to learn every bit as much about the disease as she knew. If I was going to be part of this, I was going to be part of this, informed and proactive, not some understudy of Suzanne's.

We both heard the back door open and stopped talking, listening instead to the footsteps in the kitchen. When Mum came back in, her hair and jumper were wet.

'Mammy, you should've put your jacket on. You'll catch a cold.'

Suzanne stood up to feel Mum's shoulders but she jerked away. 'It's only a few drops. Would you stop fussing? I'm not a child!'

Suzanne muttered something I didn't hear. Mum sighed. When had all this started? This sniping? Was it part of the disease too, or something else? All of a sudden I felt exhausted, as if I could lie down on the floor and never get up. 'I am pretty jet-lagged. I think I might go for a lie-down.'

'That's a good idea, love,' Mum said. 'You sleep well.'

'I will,' I said.

It was only when I reached out to hug her, I saw that my hands were clenched.

THREE

I knew where I was as soon as I woke up, as if I hadn't slept at all. It was a different darkness, proper night, and the house was quiet. I checked my watch. Ten past eight, but that was New York time. Just after one here. I'd done the exact worst thing, slept all day, and now I was awake with the whole night still to go.

There was a nice lamp by my bed, a new one, and I clicked it on. I checked my phone but Eddie hadn't responded to my text yet; I hoped texts would come through OK over here. Scanning the room I saw my posters were gone but my concert tickets were still pinned to the noticeboard, faded now. On my desk the ink in the pens had surely dried up. I pulled the duvet up to my neck so my feet poked out the end of the bed. I was like a giant trapped in a doll's house. I had to get up.

Mum's door was a bit open and I could hear her snoring. I'd never known she snored until that weekend in Montauk. The stairs had a new carpet but the same creaks and I took each one slowly. I knew them by heart, these creaks, had become an expert at coming in late without waking her.

In the hall, no one had pulled the curtains so the night looked in through the glass. On the door there was something I hadn't noticed before: two new locks beside the one that had always been there. I went to pull the curtain cord, but something stopped me and I turned towards the kitchen.

I clicked on the light and the brightness was dazzling. As my eyes adjusted, I took everything in – the sharp black and white tiles, the stainless-steel appliances. In the middle was the solid wooden table we'd always sat around, the same matching chairs.

The fridge had a built-in icemaker and one square magnet on the door, white with black typeface: 'If we are unwilling to be aware of the dark, we cannot see the light'. Inside, the shelves were full, and suddenly I wanted everything – salami, Cheddar, ham, tomatoes. As I made my sandwich I ate just as much as I put in, and when I was finished I took a bite where I stood at the counter, eating with a savage hunger I hadn't known I had.

Afterwards I made tea. I watched the water bubbling in the see-through kettle, heard the click as it turned itself off, loud enough, it seemed, to wake the whole house. In New York no one had electric kettles. I remembered a garage sale in Fort Greene and my excitement as I saw one on the table. Eddie and I had paid five dollars for that kettle and it had never worked, despite his best efforts. I could picture him sitting on the floor of the apartment, frowning in concentration as he opened the plug and snipped off bits of wire. The image was like a snapshot, too perfect. It made me wonder if it'd happened at all.

I thought about phoning him, but my phone was upstairs, next to my bed, and I didn't want to be trapped in my room again. The dining-room door was closed and I felt myself drawn to it, to explore. It had always been a cold room and, other than on special occasions, I never went in there except when Mum made me practise the piano. Dad had liked it – he used to work in there at night. He'd said the cold didn't bother him, that it kept him awake.

Opening the door I saw it wasn't the dining room any more. The old table and chairs were gone, and the sideboard had been replaced with symmetrical bookshelves, as high as the ceiling. I scanned the authors' names, books on their sides, crammed in on top of other books. Thich Nhat Hanh, Oliver Sacks, Nuala O' Faolain, Erich Fromm, new books I'd never seen in the house before. The Jane Austens were still there, though, leather-bound and lined up, like a family. And on the bottom shelf I recognised books from Dad's office – Oscar Wilde, Samuel Beckett – and a book with no cover that I knew before I picked it up would be *Nineteen Eighty-Four*. It was even more battered than my copy of *Animal Farm* upstairs in my backpack, the only thing of mine that had made it all the way to America and back again. The cover fell open. On the first page his name, faded but still there, 'Nat Matthews, English Department, TCD'. I closed it over and put it back.

Turning, I saw the rest of the room. The piano was still there, next to an old desk with a black leather top I'd never seen before. I trailed my fingers over everything – wood, glass, leather, finding a home for my mug of tea on a coaster next to a box of dog biscuits. Why did Mum have dog biscuits? We had never been allowed to get a dog. Next to them big leather headphones were attached to a radio and I tried them on, liking the feel of their weight along my neck. A photo had been stuck into the frame of the mirror over the fireplace, Mum, and a woman with a small pale face, a purple headscarf and a big smile. It could only be Lily-Anne.

I sat in the office chair at the desk, gazing at the books, the piano, the sliding doors that led into the new conservatory. It wasn't until I lived in New York that I remembered Mum reading books; before she'd always been too busy, preferred magazines. That was the Dublin Mum, the Mum who cleaned before the cleaner came. Of course, in New York I had known she was different, but somehow I'd imagined she'd stayed the same here in Dublin.

I walked back to the bookshelf, hugging myself. There must be something for me to read to pass the night. I picked up Oliver Sacks and put him back, then Alain de Botton. Most of the books were too demanding. Scrunching down, I saw something familiar between Dad's books, a sliver of blue. *Five on a Treasure Island*, always my favourite. Just looking at it I was back in his office, my feet tucked under me, socks sliding on the leather couch. I stood up and turned away.

The room was still cold, or maybe the whole house was. I

picked up my tea, and it was then I noticed the framed photos on top of the piano. There was Suzanne in our school colours, holding a hockey trophy, the sun reflecting on silver. Next to her, me and Eddie smiling from the Brooklyn Bridge. Beside us, Suzanne again, graduating this time, shoulder to shoulder with Mum. Her hair was still long and dark so they could've been sisters. I picked it up for a closer look and that was when I saw the other one, hidden behind the rest, waiting to ambush me. It was of my birthday party, my sixth or seventh maybe, judging by the front tooth missing from my wide smile. Suzanne's smile was a fixed one, for the camera. Between us, Dad was bent down, a hand on each of our shoulders. He still had hair. It had been taken in the garden: behind us, the roses were in full bloom and we were all squinting into the sun.

I put Suzanne's graduation photo back, its bigger frame obscuring my birthday party as it had before. It was silly to expect that there wouldn't be photos of him. Of course there would – it would have been worse if there weren't. I just hadn't expected one like that, coming on top of the Famous Five. As I looked around the room I could almost see the memories in the shadows cast by the desk, the piano, waiting to come alive. Again, tiredness was making me think like that, that and being the only one awake in the middle of the night. I'd be better off going back to bed, calling Eddie.

I turned out the light and went through the kitchen into the hall. At the bottom of the stairs I saw a wooden door I'd noticed earlier, but then forgotten. There'd never been a door there before. For a second I thought my mind was playing tricks on me until I realised, of course, that it led into Mum's therapy room.

I half expected it to be locked but it wasn't. As I went down the two steps into the room I felt like an intruder. The night was coming in through the slatted wooden blinds and I closed them, then turned on the lamp on the low table. There were two green chairs, sage, that's what that colour was called, parquet floors, cream walls. A bare room, a blank canvas.

I sat in one chair first, then the other. This was the client's chair, I decided. Mum's must be the one that faced the window. I let my hands slip down the rounded wooden arms, bounced a little back and forth. How many people had sat here over the years, telling Mum things they wanted to tell their own mothers but couldn't? Who did they talk to now that the only evidence that she'd ever been there was the creases in the green fabric?

She'd worked so hard for her degree, and had been so proud. The day she'd told me she was winding up the practice I'd known that something was wrong, that I could hear something else behind her words, a catch of the thing she wasn't telling me. Why hadn't I pushed her? Maybe I hadn't wanted to know.

On the table between the two chairs there was a book, a box of tissues and a clock. I picked up the book. *Co-dependent No More: How to Stop Controlling Others and Start Caring for Yourself.* A shelf-help book, that was what Rhonda and I called books like that. We'd a good laugh one day in that section of Barnes & Noble, laughing at all the titles, each cheesier than the last. Rhonda said she thought it was sad, people wasting their hard-earned money on books like that and I'd agreed. I remembered that comment because it hadn't been long after that I'd seen one of the same books in her bathroom. I never said anything, and I don't know if she knew I'd seen it, but the next time I was there, it had gone.

I turned the book over in my hand. On the back there was a picture of the author with a big smile. Apparently it had sold four million copies. I'd have been smiling too. It fell open at a page with a checklist to find out if you were co-dependent or not. I skimmed the list, stopped on the ones underlined in pencil. Apparently co-dependents tended to ignore problems, to pretend things weren't happening, that circumstances weren't as bad as they were.

I closed the book, held it in my hand. I sat down in Mum's chair, held the book in my lap and drank some tea, but it had gone cold. I decided I liked the room. It was a clean room, calm, a pocket of the house that didn't feel like our house at all. I tucked my feet under me on the chair and opened the book again, back at the list. Even as I was reading I was thinking how typical of me this was, to be drawn in, just like I was with magazine quizzes, recognising myself in every symptom. The statements were so broad they could have applied to anybody; sometimes they blatantly contradicted each other.

But it was easy to read and I was comfortable and even though I laughed at it in my head, as the clock on the table ticked towards morning, something made me keep reading.

Four

The restaurant was full, tables of families out for Sunday lunch, just like us. Across from me, Mum rubbed one of the pearls in her necklace between her fingers as she studied the menu.

'I can't decide between the sea bass and the lamb,' she said. 'I try not to have too much red meat, but I love the way they do the lamb here.'

'Have the sea bass, Mammy,' Suzanne said. 'Remember what Dr Glavin said about eating fish?'

Suzanne kept doing that. Bringing doctors into the conversation, reminding us that even if we looked like other families, we weren't the same.

Mum didn't answer her, just put the menu down and drank some water. 'I think I'll go for the lamb,' she said. 'What are you going to have, Carla?'

I'd been staring at the list of dishes but now that the waitress was on her way over I realised I hadn't registered what any of them were. I'd been too busy watching Mum to find out if she was disoriented by being somewhere new and if she could read the menu properly. I'd been doing that all the time since I'd got home, looking for changes I knew were there but couldn't really see.

'I'm going to take your recommendation and have the lamb too,' I said.

'Excellent,' Mum said. 'We can get a nice bottle of red to go with it.'

'A bottle, Mammy?' Suzanne said. 'I'm driving.'

'I know, love, but there's three of us. Sure three glasses would cost the same.'

I checked the prices on the menu. She was right, they would.

★

The service was slow but I didn't mind. It was nice to be out of the house, toasting each other with big glasses of red wine. All the toasts seemed to be for me: welcome home, belated congratulations to me and Eddie.

'You must miss him,' Mum said. 'How's he getting on without you?'

I drank some wine. 'Grand, I think. We've mostly just been on text, apart from a quick call the other day. It's tricky, you know, with the time difference.'

I reached for some more bread and buttered it. It was strange only speaking to Eddie once in four days yet I couldn't say for sure that I missed him. It was different, a novelty to be without him, and part of me was nearly enjoying it, this feeling of being not quite free exactly, but to be totally and completely myself.

'I don't know what they're doing with our starters,' Suzanne said. 'At this rate we'll be here till next Sunday.'

'We haven't been waiting that long,' I said.

She checked her watch. 'Half an hour.'

'Yeah but it's only fifteen minutes since we ordered.'

Just then the waitress arrived with bowls of soup that she put down in front of Mum and Suzanne, breaking up a conversation that had had the potential to go everywhere and nowhere. As she went back to get my salad I wondered if all sisters were like me and Suzanne, if all sisters had this urge to disagree with each other all the time, and if it would ever go away.

We ate in silence, the three of us, at a table for four, just one of the reasons I'd hated going out to eat after Dad had died.

'What do you think of Dublin these days?' Suzanne said, pushing her bowl away a little. 'All the changes.'

'I haven't been into town yet, so I haven't really noticed things being different.'

'Ah, you can see it everywhere!' Suzanne said. 'Dun Laoghaire – even Glasthule is smarter than before. There were no restaurants like this here when you left.'

I looked around the restaurant again: wood floors and big windows, fresh flowers on the bar. It could've been one of a hundred places in New York. 'I guess,' I said. 'The main thing I noticed were the prices. It's very expensive.'

'Everywhere's like that,' Mum said. 'Now that there's a bit of money in the country everyone thinks they can rip us off.'

'You're exaggerating, Mammy,' Suzanne said. 'I think it's great to see some choice, that Dublin is so multicultural these days.'

Following my gaze, she saw what I saw, a restaurant full of white, middle-class people like us. She frowned. 'Not here, I don't mean right here. If you go into town you'll notice it – people from all over Europe, the Philippines, China. There's even ads in Chinese on the DART.'

I was about to respond when another waitress came to collect the plates and, as if to prove Suzanne's point, when she asked if we were finished her accent was foreign. I glanced at Mum, who smiled into her napkin. I drank some more wine.

'I suppose after New York it's hard to see anywhere else as multicultural,' Mum said, when we had the table to ourselves again. 'But you're right, love, Dublin has changed.'

Suzanne seemed to soften. She turned to me again. 'I suppose New York is in another league. What would you be doing if you were there now? You and Eddie.'

I put my glass down. It seemed like a funny question, maybe a trick. 'Eddie has rehearsals on Sundays so if I'm not working, Rhonda and I usually meet up. She's moved out to Brooklyn so we might go for a walk or brunch.'

Mum smiled her wide smile. 'I love walking around Brooklyn – it's so green. I can't wait to go back.'

I smiled too. She was going to come back. I took another sip of wine, thinking about the city, the sound of it, the smell. 'We'd probably be having pancakes at Jack's Diner. I was craving some

144

this morning. I don't know how I'm going to last six weeks without them.'

I hadn't meant it to come out like that, the six weeks thing.

'Six weeks?' Suzanne said. 'I thought you were here for a couple of months. That's what you said.'

My heart kicked in my chest. Six weeks, two months, it didn't make much difference, surely – except it obviously did to Suzanne. 'I did, but that was before I found out Eddie's probably going on tour at the end of April.'

She didn't say anything and it might have been better if she had, if she'd balled her hands into fists. Instead she sat there, slightly forward in her chair, elbows propped on the table. Her eyes on mine were dark brown, shiny, Mum's eyes.

'Jack's Diner,' Mum said. 'Oh, I love the pancakes there!'

I was grateful to her for rescuing me, the conversation, maybe even the lunch, although even as I smiled at her something about that comment nagged at me as not quite right.

It was when the waitress served our main courses that I realised what it was. Mum had never been to Jack's for pancakes or anything else. Her last visit had been in May and I was sure, absolutely sure, that Jack's had only opened in the fall.

★

Suzanne was quiet for the rest of lunch, leaving Mum and me to reminisce about New York, places we'd been together, but since her slip I didn't know when she was telling me the truth. All three of us had the lamb and we all said how great it tasted, but when the waitress took away my empty plate I couldn't remember even one bite.

The rain saved us the walk we'd planned, and when we got home Mum said she was tired and wanted to lie down. Suzanne went up to her room too, so I thought I was safe to make some tea and read my book, but just as the kettle boiled she came into the kitchen in a tracksuit, her hair pulled back in a band.

'Want a cup?' I asked.

She shook her head. I could feel her eyes on me as I poured the water and took the teabag out. I waited for her to say something. When I turned, she was standing, looking out into the garden.

'Carla, what you were saying at lunch.' She paused. 'I didn't know that you were only here for six weeks.'

I sat down. 'You never asked. My flight is booked for the end of March but I could change it, push it out a bit, if you want.'

'If *I* want?'

'If *we* want – you know what I mean.' I blew on the tea, making ripples on the surface. It was my old Take That mug. The band's faces were nearly washed off from too many trips in the dishwasher – only faint circles of colour on white.

She sat down across from me, her arms folded on the table. After a minute she bowed her head, until her forehead rested on her hands.

'What?'

She didn't answer. I hated that I couldn't see her face. Overhead I heard Mum's footsteps.

'What, Suzanne?'

She lifted her head up, cupped her chin in one hand. 'I don't think you've any idea what we're dealing with here, Carla. I don't know what you think you can do in six weeks.'

I took a breath, thought of Mum upstairs, how I didn't want her to hear us fighting. 'Suzanne, I'm not stupid, I know this will get worse but for now she's OK. She's herself – playing the piano. She was fine in that restaurant.'

Suzanne shook her head and said something I couldn't hear.

'What?'

'She's fine so long as someone brings her there. So long as she can time her trips to the Ladies with someone else so she doesn't get lost on the way back to the table. So long as she doesn't have to pay because she doesn't know how to handle money any more.'

I hadn't known that, that thing about the money. Mum had gone to the bathroom once over lunch, at the same time I went.

146

'Look, I know things aren't perfect but she could be worse. I'm here now and I'll do what you want me to, and if she gets sicker, I'll come back.'

'She *will* get sicker, Carla.'

'OK. When she does I'll come back.'

There was silence then, only the echo of my words in the air. Suzanne had said hardly anything.

'What? Just spit it out. Say what you have to say instead of looking at me and thinking it. What do you think I should do? How long do you think I should stay for?'

She fiddled with her ring. It was the one from school – she'd won it for playing hockey. I couldn't believe she still wore it.

'I don't know,' she said, looking at the ring as she took it off and put it on, off and on. 'I thought maybe you might look into the possibility of moving home for a while.'

'Move back here?'

She heard the shock in my voice and held my gaze. 'Why not? The economy's great, you could both get good jobs—'

I cut across her. 'Suzanne, I can't just move back! My life is in New York, Eddie's band – I can't expect him to throw in everything and follow me over here.'

Something crossed her face then, scorn or anger, maybe a mixture of both.

'It seems like you've no problem doing exactly that, following him whenever he needs to go on tour.'

The irritation that had been flickering inside me all day ignited into anger. 'Oh, fuck off, Suzanne! You don't know anything about it. It'd take more than the promise of a job to bring me home. There's more to life than work – well, for most people anyway.'

It was a low blow but I didn't care. I hated her at that moment, hated her knack of finding the one place she knew she could hurt me. She looked out into the back garden.

The house was so quiet you could hear the rain falling – I kept noticing how quiet it was. I imagined a lifetime of listening to that

147

quiet, all alone in the house with Mum. 'Listen, Suzanne, people with Alzheimer's can be sick for ten or fifteen years. Mum said that. Do you expect me to be here indefinitely till then?'

'Do you expect *me* to?'

The words were directed at the window, not at me. I wanted to hit the table, but I forced my hand to stay where it was. 'You're here anyway. You moved back from Sandyford – it's hardly the same! When Mum needs my help, I'll be here.'

She shook her head. 'Mammy needs help now, Carla. She's great at pretending but you'll see it – even in six weeks you'll see how bad things are and they're only going to get worse.' Sitting there, picking at her nails, she looked beaten. Had she always been like that?

'Suzanne, listen—'

'No, *you* listen. If you read the books, you'll see what's going to happen, the different stages. I can't stop reading about it. It's horrific. *Horrific.*' She put her hand over her mouth, looking like she might cry.

'Maybe you shouldn't,' I said. 'It's upsetting you.'

'I have to,' she said. 'Someone has to. There's things we need to plan for, to make sure Mammy's looked after properly, that we've enough money to pay for the things we'll need to pay for. She may need care for years, Carla.'

I sat there looking at the mug of tea, nearly full. When Mum died, we'd be orphans, Suzanne and I. We both knew about death, the shape it made, that if it could show up on a Saturday morning in spring it could show up at any time at all. Death could take seconds or it could take years, I knew that, but I didn't know which was worse.

'We're both saying the same thing, Suzanne, that this disease can go on for years. You can't expect me to just stay.'

She wouldn't look at me, just stared at her nails. I gazed at the ceiling, at the new light fitting, spotlights, stainless steel, three of them pointing different directions. Mum, Suzanne and me.

I thought of something else, something I wished I'd thought

of before. 'My Green Card is still pending, Suzanne. I was told I couldn't stay out of the country for more than six months.'

'Six months is better than six weeks, Carla.'

'Suzanne, my husband is in New York,' I said. I liked the way it sounded.

She lifted her eyes so they held mine. 'And your mother,' she said, 'is here.'

FIVE

I knocked on Mum's door, more gently than she used to knock on mine. When I opened it she was a diagonal hump under the covers. I couldn't hear her snoring. What if she was dead? The thought ricocheted around my head and out again.

'Mum?'

I walked closer, the cup of tea in my hand jangling in its saucer. On her locker the pile of books was a messy tower, the one on top with a picture of a white feather and the title Stillness. Next to the books there was a photo of me and Suzanne in bright swimming togs on the stones of Brighton beach. I pushed it over to make room for the tea.

'Mum? You awake?'

'Hmm.' She rolled over so she had her back to me. Maybe I should leave her to sleep more, let her rest. I picked a stray silver hair off the pillow. Suzanne had given strict instructions, though, about what time to wake her, had told me twice about the importance of early starts, sticking to a routine. She must have reminded me four times about the locks.

I opened the curtains to let in the pale February morning. Outside the rain was coming down so the garden was almost fluorescent green. Things were going to get worse, that's what Suzanne had said, and she seemed so focused on that, installing all those locks even though Mum had never even come close to wandering.

'More rain,' I said. 'I was hoping we could walk the pier today.'

When I turned, Mum had propped herself up so she could

150

reach her tea. 'This is nice,' she said.

She looked happy, sitting there in the lamplight. I sat down next to her, moving her knees so there was room. 'How did you sleep?'

She put the teacup back in its saucer. 'I had that dream again. I hate it.'

'What dream?'

'The one I told you about,' she said. 'It's so vivid at the time, all these weird things, and then when I wake up it's gone, only the fright still there.'

She looked scared, her face childlike, remembering. She'd never told me about a dream like that. 'Is it the drugs?'

'Who knows what's the drugs and what's the disease?' She shook her head, as if she was trying to dislodge the last fragments of the dream. 'All I know is it's a long time since I woke up feeling myself.'

Her words hung in the air, but when she saw my face she laughed, as if it was a joke. 'Anyway, how about you, love? Did you sleep well?'

'Like a baby.'

The lie came out before I'd had time to think about it. I didn't know what was going on, if it was delayed jet-lag or being in a new bed but I hadn't slept again last night. I'd already finished the shelf-help book, was halfway through one on Alzheimer's that Suzanne had given me.

'That's good. At least one of us is refreshed this morning.'

I stood up and she got out of bed, her back to me in her thin nightdress. I took a deep breath and said what I didn't want to say. 'Suzanne said you might need a hand, with your clothes and that . . .'

She took her dressing-gown from the chair and wrapped it around herself before she turned to face me. 'No, love. Thank you. Your sister means well and she's a great help. But she drives me mad, laying out my clothes. I always choose something else, just to annoy her.' She laughed then, her proper laugh, the one that made no sound, that was only breath.

I started to laugh too. 'That sounds like the kind of thing I'd do.'

'Don't I know it? Sure you were like that as a little girl, always wanted to pick your own outfits. Even if I had your favourite things laid out – your Mork and Mindy T-shirt or whatever – you wouldn't put them on unless we went through this rigmarole of choosing them.'

'I don't remember that.'

'Well, I do. And as long as I remember how to open that wardrobe I'm going to decide what I'm going to wear.'

As I went downstairs, I smiled to myself. It was great to see Mum like that again, determined, sure of herself. It was great to hear the stubbornness in her voice, even if it meant she had to get annoyed, it was worth it.

★

I cracked the eggs into a bowl and turned on the radio. It was a classical music station and I didn't change it, hummed along. The tune was so familiar – from an ad or a movie maybe – but I'd no idea where I knew it from. I'd ask Mum.

Oil swirled in the pan, the kettle boiled. I heated the grill for toast, added a sprig of parsley to the smoked salmon on the plates. Making Mum's breakfast felt good. I was in control again, no Suzanne here to tell me what I was doing wrong. This was a breakfast I used to make for Eddie when we'd first moved in together. As I poured the eggs into the pan with a swoosh I remembered him coming up behind me, fresh from the shower, his hair wet, sliding his arms around my waist. It was a long time since I'd cooked him breakfast and I resolved to do it more often when I got home.

The toast was on, the tea was made, the eggs were nearly ready. I couldn't hear Mum moving around upstairs any more. I turned the music down and opened the door into the hall.

'Mum! Breakfast's ready!'

It was funny this role reversal, me calling up the stairs, rather than being called by her or Dad. The hall held echoes of their voices and I wondered how many meals had been cooked for me, how many had burned because I was late.

Back in the kitchen the toast was ready and I buttered it. Arranged the eggs over the salmon. What was keeping her? I opened the door again. 'Mum! It's going to be cold!'

This time I stayed in the hall, listening for a response, but it was quiet, no shower sounds, no hairdryer. I closed the door into the kitchen and walked to the end of the stairs.

'Mum?'

In the silence, everything sounded extra loud, my foot on each step, the ads on the radio. I could hear my heart too, bang-banging like I'd just come in from a run. There was nothing to worry about, no need to panic. I'd just seen her. She was fine, everything was fine.

On the landing, her door was ajar, a triangle of beige carpet. As my hand reached out to push it open I was conscious of my breath.

Behind me there was a crash.

'Jesus!' I whirled around. No one was there – then Mum was there in the bathroom doorway, a makeup bag in her hand. 'Jesus, Mum! You scared me!' My hand was on my chest, I could feel my heart pounding.

'Sorry. I was doing my makeup and I knocked the soap dish into the sink. The light is so much better in there.'

She smiled. Her makeup was perfect, no lipstick on her teeth.

'Did you not hear me calling you? Breakfast will be cold.'

I waited for her to put away her makeup, wondering, as I followed her downstairs, what was making me so jumpy. She looked well, in her stripy cardigan, black jeans. She hadn't needed my help at all, just like she said. When we got to the kitchen something made me look at her feet. Inside her slippers her socks were different, one blue, one black. It looked funny, Mum in mismatched socks – but it didn't matter, I wore mismatched socks all the time.

'Voilà,' I said, taking our plates from the counter and putting them on the table with a flourish. 'Eggs à la Carla!'

She clapped her hands. 'My favourite, just like you used to make me in Brooklyn.'

She'd remembered. I'd known she would.

'Come on, sit down, eat up. I'll pour the coffee.'

We sat in the same places where we'd always sat, the ones I set out automatically. The eggs were a bit rubbery and the toast was cold but it didn't matter. We ate in silence, smiling at each other now and then.

'I just remembered we were supposed to do yoga earlier,' I said, as I finished. 'I completely forgot!'

'So did I,' Mum said. 'But I've a good excuse, haven't I? Speaking of which, it's time for my tablet.'

She stood up and took a glass jar of tablets from the top shelf of the cupboard. Then she was back at the table, swallowing a small white pill that might have been a Panadol. She wiped her mouth, and as she brought her napkin down, I noticed something not quite right with her cardigan: the stripes didn't line up, the black running into the white, the grey into the black.

'What's wrong?' she said, seeing my face. Her hand went to her neck and felt the left side of the wool collar sticking up too high over the right.

'It's just your cardigan,' I said. 'You're a button out. It's no big deal.'

She undid the top button, then stopped. 'I'll do it in a minute,' she said. 'I'll have my coffee first.'

She smiled and I smiled back. I drank some more coffee and looked out the window into the rain. It was only a button, only a little thing. No big deal at all.

★

When we left the house the rain wasn't too bad, but on the pier it was coming down hard again. I was grateful for Suzanne's rain jacket, that Mum had suggested it, and I pulled my hood tighter.

With the noise of the wind and the sea and the halyards from the boats jangling it was impossible to talk and it was nice, in a way, not to have to.

The pier was different from how I'd remembered it, smaller and narrower. I had forgotten the shiny stones that made up the surface and mirrored the legs and feet of other people out walking in the rain. Halfway down we came to the bandstand and that was where memory caught me – Suzanne and I cycling round in circles, stabilisers on my bike, none on hers. Before I knew it, I was somewhere else, in the back garden, with Dad's hands on my shoulders, wobbling on my bike, just before I fell off. What age had I been then?

The wind in my face was getting stronger and I realised we were nearly at the end of the pier and that I'd missed most of it, caught so deep in the spirals of my own mind. I glanced over at Mum, her hood up, hands in her pockets and wondered what it was like to be in hers.

Suzanne had recommended a café for lunch, but Mum agreed when I'd suggested going to the new bagel place at the end of the pier instead. We were almost there when I saw someone waving, a woman, small in a navy jacket, her hood pulled low over her face.

'Carla! Carla? Collette!'

It wasn't until I heard Mum's name that I knew it was definitely us she was waving at. I raised my hand and waved back. When we were a few feet away I saw who she was.

'Carla, I knew it was you and your mum! My gosh, it's been a long time.' She gave me a loose hug.

Her voice was the same as ever, a country voice hidden under a Dublin accent, the same voice that had seemed to take up every last bit of air that Saturday in Olivia's kitchen, when all I wanted was for her to leave. For them all to leave. 'Mrs Nolan, how are you?'

'Mrs Nolan! Go on out of that. Call me Rose.'

'Rose.' I nearly laughed. Nosy Rosie was what Ange and I used to call her, although never in front of Damien.

'I'd heard you were home, not that I hear half of what goes on any more since we moved. Did you hear we'd moved?'

I remembered Mum saying she was unbearable, telling everyone how much they got for the house.

'Yes, I heard,' I said. I asked the question I had to ask. 'How's Damien?'

Inside her hood she smiled, her cheeks red from the wind. She'd been waiting for this. It was probably why she'd called me over.

'Damien's great. Flying it, so he is. A fully fledged accountant now in Goodbody's. Married to a lovely girl. Rebecca. English. They've a gorgeous little fella. Jack. Twenty-six months. Their second is on the way.'

The potted summary was well practised. I hadn't really thought about Damien since that first night on the beach in Montauk, as if he'd stopped existing right then. But he was real, living a life, making one. Eddie had christened him 'Mr Carla'. Now he was 'Mr Rebecca'.

'Tell him I was asking for him,' I said.

'I will, of course. And tell me, how's your mother doing? It's desperate, especially after everything with your poor father. And she's so young-looking.'

The pitch of her voice was carefully chosen, a tone of fake sympathy that I recognised only too well. Mum was standing back, somehow out of the conversation, her gaze directed across the bay. I linked her arm and pulled her in close. 'Sure she can tell you herself better than I can. She's a full house at the moment, don't you, Mum?'

I was grateful for Mum's smile, her nod. 'Oh, yes, I've a full house at the moment,' she said.

'And will you stay, Carla?' Mrs Nolan asked, barely acknowledging that Mum had spoken. 'I heard you finally tied the knot out there. Will your American husband come back with you?'

Finally tied the knot. Fuck her. Just because I'd dared to break up with her precious son. And how did she know all this stuff anyway?

'He's not back this time. He's in a band and they've a tour coming up so he can't really get away.'

'Oh, lovely. What're they called?'

'Homespun Heroes. They're big in the States.'

'I've never heard of them,' she said, making a face. 'Still, I suppose the young people like them. Is he away a lot?'

'A bit. I go with him sometimes.'

She raised an eyebrow, turned to Mum. 'Very glamorous altogether, isn't it, Collette? Still, not the most stable, for the long term, you know, if you ever had children, Carla. Although maybe you won't? Not everybody does, these days.'

My cheeks burned in the cold wind. Just who did this woman think she was? Before I could answer, Mum was there first. 'It's good for the soul to follow your passion,' she said. 'Too many young people are following the money now, all solicitors and accountants and into property.'

I thought I'd misheard her but when I looked at her she was smiling, as if she hadn't said anything bad at all. Nosy Rosie looked from Mum to me and back to Mum. I felt the laughter like a bubble at the back of my throat. I couldn't wait to tell Ange.

'I'd better be getting on,' she said. 'I've to mind little Jack this afternoon. I'd hate to be late.'

There were no hugs as we said goodbye. At the traffic lights, the wind seemed to have eased a little, and as I glanced over the roof of the town hall, there in the middle of the rolls of smoky cloud was a small square of blue.

★

Inside the bagel place it was bright, beaming spotlights reflected on the orange and turquoise plastic furniture. It was noisy too, with the din of children, and I realised too late that's who this place had been designed for – mums and their four-wheel-drive buggies. 'Do you want to stay here?' I said to Mum over the noise. 'Is this OK?'

'It's fine,' she said.

I watched the mothers as they laughed and chatted, feeding their children things from ziplock bags and cartons of juice, seemingly oblivious to the noise. They were my age, those girls, those women, younger than me some of them. Standing in line with Mum I felt suddenly self-conscious, dramatically out of place. I studied the board over the counter.

'What are you going to have?' I asked. 'They've a wholewheat one with hummus and roasted vegetables. Or soup?'

Mum was staring around her. She seemed not to have heard. I touched her lightly on the shoulder. 'I was just asking what you wanted? A bagel or soup? I reckon it's a soup kind of day.'

'I'll have that,' she said. 'The same as you.'

There was something in her movement, her voice, a jerkiness I hadn't seen before. She still had her hood up and a strand of silver hair poked out from under it, stuck to her cheek. I scanned for a table that would be insulated from the chaos, but the only space was at a long communal one, between three sets of children. Maybe we should leave, go somewhere else, but outside the rain had started again, streaming down the floor-length window.

I turned back to Mum. 'That was classic, what you said to Nosy Rosie. Her face!'

Mum's forehead rippled in a frown. 'I hope I didn't offend her.'

'Who cares? It was priceless. Wait till I tell Ange.'

The girl in front of us placed her order, then struggled to turn her double buggy. Mum didn't seem to notice she was standing in the way and I pulled her arm gently.

'Angela knows her too?' Mum said.

The girl pushed around us, one of the babies screeched. I rooted in my bag for my purse. 'Of course she knows her, Mum. She had to put up with her being next door – at least we were four houses away.'

I waited for her to laugh, to shake her head and ask what she'd been thinking. But she didn't do that. She didn't say anything at all. In the swirl of colours she looked pale, a little lost.

158

The guy at the counter was poised at the cash register. 'Next?' he called.

I ignored him, kept looking at Mum, waiting for recognition of her mistake.

'Next, please. Can I take your order?'

Behind him the menu offered too many choices. I couldn't remember what we were supposed to be having. Mum was reading it too, her head tipped back. Part of me didn't want to ask, but another part needed to. 'You know who that was, Mum, don't you? Nosy Rosie, Damien's mum.'

When she turned to me, she was still frowning, two little lines between her eyes. 'Sorry, Carla, but I've no idea who you're talking about.'

*

The pedicure was a good one, much more pampering than in Brooklyn, but I couldn't relax, straining instead to hear Mum's chat with the beautician doing her manicure. Neither of us had said a lot over lunch – it was too noisy to talk – but she seemed to have become more herself again since we'd left.

I'd forgotten to bring flip-flops so by the time my toes had dried it was nearly dark and raining again. When we got home, it was nice to light the fire and close the curtains. Mum had said we should watch *Pride and Prejudice*, that I'd really enjoy it, but as soon as we got the first disc out of the box set she'd fallen asleep, her hands outstretched as if to protect her new nails.

I kept it on anyway, the volume low, but I couldn't stop thinking about the day's events, trying to figure out exactly at what point the Mum I knew had gone missing and when I'd got her back.

The phone rang. Her head stirred, but she didn't wake. Eddie had said he'd call today and it was twelve in New York, about when he'd be waking up. I ran to the kitchen to answer it, suddenly certain it was him.

'Hello?'

'Hi, it's me. Just thought I'd give you a quick ring, see how you're getting on.'

Suzanne. In the background there were voices, fingers tapping on keyboards. It surprised me how pleased I was to hear her. 'Great. Grand.'

'Did you get out for a walk?'

'Just about. We got soaked, though. It's a miserable day.'

'Good. That's good.'

She wasn't listening properly and it sounded like the phone was between her chin and her shoulder. One of the voices in the background was closer now.

'Hold on a second, Carla.'

I watched the rain on the window as I listened to the muffled voices.

Suddenly she was back. 'Sorry about that. What else did you get up to?'

I wanted to tell her about Nosy Rosie, but I didn't want to, as well. 'We'd lunch. Then a manicure – well, I got a pedi. I'm watching TV and she's asleep.'

'In bed? She's not meant to be in bed, Carla.'

I'd deviated from the plan. 'She's dozing, Suzanne, by the fire, not in bed.'

'Just don't let her doze too long.'

'What time will you be home?'

'After seven or so.'

'After seven? You said half six.'

'I said half six or seven. It's a nightmare in here, two weeks of stuff backed up. Someone put a meeting in my diary for five.'

I let a beat of silence pass.

'It's only half an hour, Carla.'

'I know,' I said. 'It's fine.'

'I've got to go. This meeting is about to start. I'll see you later.'

She hung up and I replaced the receiver quietly. From the living room I could hear the voices on the DVD as it played to no one. I felt the first prickle of tears. This was silly. What was wrong with me? I took a breath, yoga breathing, in and out, in and out. I was emotional, that was all. Not enough sleep, a long day, missing New York, my friends, Eddie.

Even as I listed the reasons I knew they weren't the real ones. What I was feeling was the residue from earlier on. No matter how often I went over everything in my head, I still didn't know what had happened with Mum, what fixed it. And if I couldn't figure that out, how was I supposed to stop it from happening again?

Six

In the background one of her CDs was playing, light piano notes rising and falling and rising, the deeper ones behind. I put my book to one side. I noticed hers was on the floor, closed.

'Who's this, Mum?'

She opened her eyes, smiled. 'It's Bach. "Jesu, Joy of Man's Desiring".'

'I like it,' I said. 'Could you play it for me one morning?'

It had become a daily ritual – every morning Mum played for me while I drank my second cup of coffee, three or four pieces that she knew by heart. I loved watching her fingers, so confident of finding the right keys in a way mine had never been.

'I used to be able to play it but I'm not sure I remember it. It's been a while.'

'We could get the sheet music. It'd be fun to learn a new piece.'

Before she could answer, the doorbell rang. 'Ah, here she is,' she said, with a smile.

'Who?'

'Lily-Anne.'

'Lily-Anne's coming today?'

'I'm surprised she's managed to keep herself away so long. She's dying to meet you. I think she's been trying to give us some quality time together.'

I shoved my feet into my runners. 'I've been looking forward to meeting her too.'

That was a lie. I stopped at the mirror in the hall and ran a hand through my hair, which was extra frizzy today. She was only a friend of Mum's, some old crony. There was nothing to be nervous of.

Through the knobbly glass, I saw her, a purple shape, bending down. When I opened the door, something ran at my legs, black and brown, jumping up at me. A dog.

'Chips! Get down! Get down!'

The dog jumped around me. His hair was curly over his eyes. He pushed his nose into the crease behind my knee and I rubbed his snout, cylindrical like a tin of beans.

'Chips, come here! Relax!'

She'd said 'Relax' the way most people with dogs said 'Behave'. He kept circling my legs but slowed down a little, as if he understood.

'Chips gets a little excited around new people, a bit like his mother.' She gave a loud laugh that filled the hall. She bent down to bring Chips under control, her scarf getting tangled around his paws. When she looked up I saw her properly for the first time: a round face, no makeup, long white hair pulled back in a ponytail, a purple mac with pink spots.

'He's gorgeous,' I said. 'I like dogs.'

'Lovely, lovely, lovely to meet you, Carla.'

I put out my hand to shake hers but she was stretching out her arms. It was only then that I realised how small she was, I had to bend down to hug her. Her perfume was strong and I wanted to pull away quickly but her grip was firm. Chips jumped up again and bounced around our ankles.

'I'm so glad you're here,' she said, pushing me away so she could study my face. 'You've your father's eyes, same expression, from all the photos I've seen.'

I wasn't expecting her to say that, even though people used to all the time. I folded my arms, laughed. 'Suzanne got Mum's looks.'

'Ah, you've a look of her too, I can see it. Where is Mother, anyway? Does she think you're here to wait on her hand and foot?

That she doesn't need to answer her own front door any more?'

She laughed her big laugh again.

'She's in the dining room,' I said.

'The dining room?' She took off her mac, ignoring Chips as he put his head between her thighs, which were covered with purple leggings and, below them, knee-length woolly socks.

'She means the back room. We used to call it the dining room.'

We both turned to see Mum in the kitchen doorway, watching us. Lily-Anne smiled, like she hadn't seen her for a long, long time. Then she crossed the hall and hugged her for longer than she'd hugged me, rocking a little back and forth. So, she was the one who'd turned Mum into a hugger.

'Dining rooms and butlers,' Lily-Anne said, when she'd let go. 'Everything seems to have changed a lot in only a few days.' She winked at me and led the way through the kitchen into the 'back room'. Mum followed her and Chips followed Mum, his claws clicking on the wood. I picked up Lily-Anne's mac from where it had fallen off the cloakroom door and hung it up properly inside.

'Reading?' she was saying, holding up Mum's copy of *Jane Eyre*, as I came in.

'I know it so well I hardly need to read it. It comes alive nearly from holding it,' Mum said. 'I was just dozing, listening to music, really.'

Lily-Anne tilted her head to one side. 'Is that one of the CDs we made? The *Calm Days* one?'

She sat down where I'd been sitting, knocking my book off the arm of the chair on to the carpet. Chips sniffed it and curled up at her feet

'No.' Mum shook her head. 'I can't find that one. This is from the original.'

'Well, that's why I kept the masters, so we could make more.' She laughed, and explained to me, 'We made some CDs, she probably told you. CDs for *Calm Days*. CDs for *Angry Days*. CDs for – what was the other one?'

Mum shrugged. 'Happy Days?'

'I don't think so,' she said. 'We'd probably get sued for copyright!'

She laughed again, and Mum joined in. I wondered how she stuck that laugh. There was nowhere for me to sit so I folded my arms and bounced on the balls of my feet. 'Since I'm the butler for the day, why don't I make some coffee?' I said.

'Peppermint tea for me,' Lily-Anne said, 'and His Highness will have a couple of those doggie biscuits, maybe some water.'

'He can have that outside,' Mum said. 'You know the rules. He's lucky to be allowed in the house at all.'

Lily-Anne reached down and rubbed Chips's head so his fur went even deeper into his eyes.

'I'd love a coffee,' Mum said.

Lily-Anne frowned slightly. 'It's nearly four, Coll.'

Mum followed her gaze to the clock. 'Gosh, I hadn't realised. I'll have a peppermint tea then.'

'Mum, have what you want,' I said. 'Have coffee if you want coffee.'

Lily-Anne didn't say anything, just played with her scarf, her fingers pushing through the tassels. No wonder Suzanne got on with her, both of them so controlling. Mum looked from her to me. 'No,' she said. 'It's a little late. Peppermint tea is fine.'

★

Through the transparent kettle I could see the water bubbling. I shovelled coffee into the plunger. I was going to have coffee – she couldn't stop me. Just who did she think she was? Coming in here like she owned the place, taking over with her purple and her dog. At the bottom of the plunger there was a thick rim of coffee and I couldn't remember how much I'd put in. I reached in with the spoon to take some back out. The grains spilled on the counter.

I hadn't realised how much older Lily-Anne was than Mum. Her skin was deceptive, so pale it was almost transparent. Her hippie-dippy clothes had thrown me a bit, but all that long white hair – and her hands, she could've been seventy, easily.

The kettle clicked itself off and I filled the cups first and then the pot, took some biscuits from the press. The scent of mint wafted in the air. I didn't know why it bothered me so much, her age. Mum was happier than she'd been all day, all week maybe, since Lily-Anne had arrived. Why couldn't I let her have that?

When I came back in with the tray they were reminiscing about some trip they'd taken together to the Aran Islands.

'Weren't they re-thatching the roof of the B&B next door?' Mum said.

'That's right!' Lily-Anne nodded, sitting back, her fingers touching in an arc. 'That was the time they had the market and I bought that necklace, the one with the orange and brown beads.'

'You wore that for years! In every photo you've got it on.'

'I'd be still wearing it if that little fecker in India hadn't got it caught in his handlebars. I thought I was going to cry when I saw all my little beads spilling away down the road.'

I put the tray on the table and went to get a wicker chair from the conservatory.

'Thanks, love,' Mum said.

'Mm, chocolate biscuits.' Lily-Anne reached over and took one. 'Joe – my husband – is on a diet and it's killing me not having sweet things in the house. I almost bought a Moro on the way over, but I knew you'd have something.'

'People who meet Lily-Anne for the first time assume she eats like a bird, but she's a huge appetite, don't you?' Mum smiled at her friend. 'And a real sweet tooth.'

Lily-Anne nodded, and started a story about some time they'd been in India, some food they'd eaten off a truck. It was a convoluted tale, involving people with the same name. I held my coffee and smiled at the punch line. She obviously liked to talk about herself. For some reason I was surprised that she was married. I pictured her husband, Joe. In my head he was quiet, absent, taking refuge behind a copy of the *Irish Times*.

'We have to go back soon,' Mum said.

Lily-Anne brushed crumbs from her top on to the floor,

causing Chips to lick the carpet. 'We will, Coll, we will.'

They weren't going to India, Lily-Anne knew that, even Mum probably knew it. I picked my book up from the floor and held it in my lap. Only twenty minutes ago the atmosphere had been easy, calm. Now I felt out of synch with them, irritable and exhausted. It was time to escape.

'Did you show Carla any of the India photos?' Lily-Anne said.

Mum screwed up her face, trying to remember. 'I don't think so, did I, love?'

A thought crossed my mind; I could pretend I'd seen them and she wouldn't remember. But I couldn't do that, even if it meant being stuck there for longer. 'No,' I said. 'I don't think you did.'

'Oh, show her,' Lily-Anne said. 'Get the ones of you and the elephant.'

Mum put her hand to her mouth. 'Oh, God, that elephant! I was terrified.'

'So was she, all your screeching!'

Mum put down her peppermint tea and stood up. 'You'd get a kick out of that one, Carla. I'll just run upstairs and get them.'

'You know where they are, Coll?'

'Do you need a hand, Mum?'

'Yes, yes, I know where they are. Stop fussing.' Mum waved her hands at us to stay sitting down. 'I'll be one minute.'

As Mum walked out I knew she might be gone for ten minutes, longer, that she might even forget what she was looking for. The CD had come to an end and in the silence we listened to her footsteps on the stairs, the landing. Sensing something change, Chips looked up. Lily-Anne reached down and rubbed the top of his head till he laid it on his paws again.

'What kind of dog is he?'

'Welsh terrier, or half, anyway. His mother was pure bred but then some mongrel got at her, we never did find out what type.'

There might have been a good response to that but I couldn't find it so we sat there listening to Mum dithering upstairs, going across her bedroom and back again.

'How are you finding things, being back? You must see a big change in her.'

Lily-Anne's voice was different when she asked that, lower, and I wasn't sure if there was a barb twisted under the words, about how long I'd been away.

'Not really. She's grand most of the time,' I said. Lily-Anne nodded, and I saw she was waiting for me to say more. For the first time I noticed her feet, in Converse, just like mine. I pushed my own under the chair. 'She was quiet earlier, but she's perked up since you got here.'

She combed the tassels of her scarf. 'She loves to reminisce — holidays, trips. We spend more time talking about the places we went than we ever spent there.'

When she looked up her laugh was gentle, not the crazy laugh like before. Her eyes were an unusual blue, pale and watery. I wondered how many times she and Mum had told the stories they'd just told me.

'Tangible things seem to work. Little props — a piece of jewellery, a photo — seem to help her really participate, to be present in the conversation,' she said. 'And that gives her a lift, which seems to be half the battle right now.'

I didn't like what she was saying, what she wasn't saying. 'I find her pretty chatty,' I said. 'You know, she's herself, most of the time.'

Lily-Anne smiled. 'Well, I suppose she can't be anyone else, can she? The problem comes when the self she is today isn't the one we remember, the one we want her to be.'

It was a real therapist thing to say, like something Mum would say. I wasn't sure where she was going with it, but it felt safer to head it off at the pass.

'I know she's changing,' I said. 'I'm preparing for it, reading about it.'

I held up my book, one that Suzanne had given me about the stages of the disease, closing it on my lap.

'Do you find that helpful?' Lily-Anne said.

'Yes and no.' I shrugged. 'I mean, I suppose it's good to know what's coming, but it's kind of depressing. And it's confusing too, trying to pinpoint what stage Mum is at.'

Upstairs I heard drawers opening, closing. Lily-Anne reached down and ruffled Chips's fur. 'I tried reading some of those books. Your mum did too.'

'And?'

She shook her head. 'I don't want to put you off but I ended up being very focused on the future, what was coming next, instead of what was happening right now.'

I hit my leg with the book. 'That's exactly what I said to Suzanne! That we should focus on today, the fact that Mum is fine today. Do you know what she said? That I was in denial!'

I beamed at Lily-Anne. Already, in my head, I was telling Suzanne that Lily-Anne agreed with me, but when her head wobbled a little from side to side I wasn't sure, suddenly, that she did.

'It's a tricky one, isn't it?' she said. 'The space between getting tangled up in the future and denying it entirely. Denial is somewhere we all go, isn't it? The most natural place in the world to go.'

'So you don't think reading these books helps?' I said, trying to clarify.

'They might help some people. The books that help me are the ones that help me through everything – meditation books, mindfulness. The ones I always have in my toolbox, you know.'

I nodded. I didn't know.

'A lot of people sneer at self-help books but the simplest things in life are usually the hardest – that's why people keep writing books about them. I'm sure you've seen them all in your mum's office.'

I felt redness creep into my face. It was as if she knew I'd already read one and that it was still upstairs by my bed. Before I could answer her, the door opened and Mum was back, a shoebox in her hands. 'Finally!' she said, sitting down. 'I must've been through every box of photos before I got to these ones.'

169

Lily-Anne got up, walked around the back of her chair and sat on the arm. Mum passed me a photo of herself, in a yellow and green shawl, next to the leg of an elephant. She turned to Lily-Anne. 'You're a brutal photographer. You didn't even get its face in. I could be standing next to anything!'

I wasn't looking at the elephant, I was looking at Mum, her smile, the colours of her shawl fixed for ever in a flattened image in time. When was it taken? Had the disease started to make inroads in her brain even then?

They passed me more photos and I put my book – Suzanne's book – on the floor, the cover facing down. As I did I felt a flash of anger for the time I'd wasted reading those pages when, according to Lily-Anne, I should've been reading other pages in other books.

Watching her as she leaned in to point at another photo, I wondered why I felt such a build-up of resentment towards a woman I'd only just met, who was such a big part of Mum's life. What she'd said about the books, she was only trying to help, I knew that. But I couldn't shake the feeling that, no matter what I did to try and understand what was happening with Mum, to try and help her, that it would always turn out to be wrong.

SEVEN

I pushed myself back in the chair, liking the way it bounced a little. It had become my spot, Mum's therapy room, my little quiet corner of the house. Tonight I was in her chair, not the client one. In my lap the cordless phone was silent and I checked my watch. After our last attempted conversation, screaming over New York City sirens, Eddie and I had decided to plan our calls, the way I used to with Mum.

The phone rang.

'Hello?'

'Hi, can I speak to Carla, please?'

'Eddie! It's me!'

'Hey! I wasn't totally sure – you sounded different. You sound different over there.'

'Do I?'

'Sure. More Irish, like you've been brushing up that brogue.'

It was a joke, an old one, from the days I used to work in O'Callaghan's. Rhonda always said I put it on to get better tips. I laughed, relaxed into the chair.

'Well, seven days over here and it's all bound to come back,' I said. 'How are you? What's going on?'

'The Terminal 5 shows were great,' he said, 'really awesome.'

I started to tell him that he'd already told me about that, in the last call, but between the delay and the way my words seemed to echo back it was easier to stay silent and let him talk. I listened as he told me they'd be playing support for the same band in the Brooklyn Bowl, that there was more talk of a national tour.

'Our Myspace has gone crazy!' he said. 'Have you seen it? We've, like, a few hundred more fans. Dawn's little sister is helping us answer the messages because we don't have enough time to get to everybody.'

I hadn't looked at it since I arrived, hadn't even thought about it. I asked him a question to sidestep my pang of guilt. 'How's Dawn?'

'She's OK, I guess,' he said. A pause. 'She broke up with Chris.'

'They broke up?' I moved the phone to my other ear. 'What happened?'

'I don't know. It'd been coming for a while. I think he was pissed she was spending so much time with the band. He wasn't very supportive.'

'Really? He always seemed like a nice guy.'

'I don't know, really. I think he wanted kids and stuff. He's pretty traditional. I'll find out more tonight. We're going for Chinese.'

'With Nick?'

'No. Would you believe he's on his third date with that Belgian girl?'

'Wow!' I said. 'It must be serious.'

'Yeah,' he said, 'for him.'

He laughed and I joined in. It didn't sound fake, exactly, my laughter, but scripted maybe, like we were both following lines that were so well rehearsed we thought they were our own. So Dawn was single. I thought about what Rhonda had said, how she wouldn't trust Michael around her. I checked to see if I was feeling jealous, but I didn't seem to be feeling anything at all.

'So what's up with you?' he said. 'You and Ange setting the Dublin party scene alight? Making up for lost time?'

I stood up and walked to the other side of the room. 'You've got to be kidding? I haven't even seen her. I'm supposed to be calling over to her house next week to meet the kids.'

'That sounds like fun,' he said. 'Tell her I said hi.'

Saying it out loud, it didn't sound like fun at all.

'I will.'

There was silence on the line then, except for his breath. I paced to the corner of the room, towards a white door built into the wall I hadn't noticed before. I opened it to find shelves of books, shelf-help books. Lily-Anne's toolbox. I closed it again. He was going to ask me about Mum. He'd better ask me about Mum.

'How's your mom doing?'

'Great,' I said. 'She's good. Fine.'

From great to fine in only a few seconds. Now that he'd asked it seemed I didn't have an answer, like I didn't know how she was. 'It's nice spending time with her,' I said. 'We go for walks, lunch. We got our nails done last week.'

'Nice. I could use a vacation like that, some downtime.'

'It's not a vacation, Eddie! I have to cook for her, clean the house.' Even as I heard the irritation flare in my voice I knew it was irrational, that he was only responding to what I'd said.

'Sure,' he said. 'I know.'

I walked to the other chair, the client chair, sat down in it, hard. 'I'm sorry, it's just that it's late and I'm tired.'

'No problem, Carls. I'll let you go.'

I didn't want him to go, not yet, but what could I tell him? How everything was the same and somehow different? He'd never been here, it wouldn't mean anything to him. It was like he was someone from another world, a world I wasn't part of anymore, maybe I never had been. I unfolded my legs from under me, stretched them out so my toes touched the edge of the rug. 'I didn't mean for you to go yet,' I said. 'I'm just tired because I was up early for a run this morning.'

'Wow,' he said. 'No nights out, runs at daybreak. I won't recognise you when you come home.'

'Well, it's only been a week. Let's see if I can keep it up for five more.'

He laughed but it didn't sound like his laugh, some far-away noise. I stood up and walked over to the window. I needed to tell him something real, something that mattered.

I pushed the slats of the blinds apart, looked out into the darkness. On the other side of the glass there was a sudden dazzle, the glare of a spotlight, a cat, frozen on the gravel of the driveway, its eyes a reflection before it ran away into the night. From three thousand miles away Eddie heard my intake of breath. 'You OK?' he asked.

'Yeah, the spotlight just came on. It gave me a shock but it was only a cat.'

'Damn cats,' he said.

'I've seen it in the garden before. One of Mum's friends has a dog and it drives him wild.'

Another silence on the line, a gap where words should have been instead of dead air, the sound of all those miles between us.

'Do you think there's an actual phone line connecting us right now?' I asked.

'What?' he said.

'You know, the line. Would you say it's real? Something that runs under the land and under water all the way to New York.'

'I don't know,' he said. 'Probably not. It's got to be wireless. Or satellite. I never thought about it. It's not like it matters.'

'No,' I said. 'I guess it doesn't.'

I let the blinds fall back against the glass. He was right. It didn't matter – of course it didn't matter – but somehow it did. I reached out and touched the radiator but it was off, the echo of fading heat in the metal. I pulled my cardigan closer around me.

'You'd better go if you're getting up for a run in the morning,' he said. 'Isn't it after midnight there?'

'Yep,' I said. 'You're right, ten after.'

As I said it, I noticed how easily I'd adapted to his way of talking, to make it easier for him. Nearly ten past twelve here, ten past seven in New York. Maybe it was the hours and minutes that made it feel really far away, not the miles at all.

'Hey,' I said, 'we should Skype next time. That way we get to see each other.'

'Yeah, good idea, we'll do that.'

'And have a good night with Dawn. Tell her sorry. You know, about Chris.'

'I will,' he said. 'Good night, Carls. I love you.'

It caught me by surprise. We'd never been the kind of couple who said that at the end of every call.

'I love you too.'

He said goodbye again and I did too. I'd picked up the Dublin habit of saying too many of them, and he hung up somewhere in the middle. In my hand the phone was hot. I thought of Mum, hanging up from conversations with me, the silence afterwards. Now here I was hanging up after a conversation with Eddie.

Immediately I was struck with an urge to call him back, but to say what? I reached over to turn out the lamp, standing, for a second, in the dark, before I left the room.

EIGHT

The raindrops on the windscreen were running sideways, like little sperm.

'I can't believe it's still raining,' I said. 'It's rained every day since I got here.'

'You can't tell me it never rains in New York,' Suzanne said. 'I've never seen anything like the downpour the night I was there.'

She didn't look at me, kept staring out the window even though the traffic wasn't moving. She looked uncomfortable in her work suit, squashed up too close to the steering wheel.

'Oh, yeah, that rain was crazy. We must have been an hour late for you and Ian.'

'An hour and a half,' she said. 'We were beginning to think something had happened to you.'

I'd been going to ask her about Ian, if they were ever in touch, but her tone suggested there was no room for reminiscence. The wipers swished. The car in front moved and then the lights changed, making speckles of red from the rain.

'Fuck!' Suzanne smacked her palm on the steering wheel.

I checked my watch. Ten minutes till the start of class.

Her head snapped around. 'I'll get you there, OK? I don't know what's going on with this traffic.'

'I didn't say anything.'

'Usually if we left at a quarter past we'd have loads of time.'

'Suzanne, I didn't say anything.' I looked out the window, wondering if other sisters were like this, able to have a row even without words. Especially without words. For some reason I didn't understand, part of me didn't want the light to change, wanted to be late for the yoga class, like it would be enough to say that I'd tried to get there, that it wasn't my fault I'd missed it.

'Finally,' Suzanne said, edging around the corner.

I watched the wet hedges pass, the pillars and driveways. A piece of road opened up and she sat back, increasing her speed a little.

'It'll be great when you can drive,' she said. 'Remind me later to give you the number of a driving instructor a girl from work recommended, Sean someone, from Monkstown. He's meant to be very good.'

I wasn't getting driving lessons. I'd told her there was no point this time, that I wasn't here long enough. She'd ignored me, of course, acted like I'd never said anything at all, as if talking like I was staying would, in some way, make me stay.

She glanced over to see my reaction, her earrings making a shadow on her neck as she turned her head. I wasn't going to say anything. Another red light. We were making another turn and it seemed like this whole wet journey was going to bring us right back to where we'd started.

'It'll be nice in the summer too, when you can take Mammy further afield,' she said. 'To Greystones or maybe as far as Wicklow.'

Did she really think I could afford to make this trip again in the summer? Or did she think I could stay until then? I shifted in my seat, counted the tick of the indicator. She'd been itching for a fight ever since she'd got in from work, and I could feel the anger she'd created in the clench of my shoulders, the spit that sealed my lips. If she wanted a fight, I knew how to give her one.

'I might take Mum to this yoga class next week, if it's any good.' I paused. Silence. 'It's unlikely I'll have mastered driving by then, but I'm sure you wouldn't mind dropping the two of us down.'

She did something on the dashboard and warm air blasted into the car, chasing the steam from the windows. 'No,' she said, over the noise. 'That's not a good idea.'

'Why not?'

She made a right into a narrow street, houses on one side, shops on the other. 'It'd be too stressful for her, an hour and a half long class, people she doesn't know. She might not be able to follow it.'

'Mum's done yoga for years. She practises with me every morning. I think she'd enjoy it.'

'Mammy's not going to yoga. End of discussion.'

Looking at the jut of her chin, the hunch of her shoulders, I wanted to hit her. She was so definite, as if her word was the final say, as if I had no input at all. I forgot that I'd brought up the yoga class to annoy her, that I wasn't sure about Mum going either, because by then it wasn't about Mum.

'You can't just shake your head and say, "End of discussion", Suzanne. What Mum does and doesn't do isn't all up to you. What about what *she* wants? What *I* want?'

A car in front of us stopped in the middle of the road and she braked sharply.

'Give me one good reason why Mum couldn't at least try this yoga class.'

'I'll give you three,' she said. The yellow lights from the car in front flashed, lighting up her face. 'When you do yoga with her it's in the morning, she's fresh. It's not half seven at night. Second, it's a sequence she's been doing for years. And third, if I'm looking after Mammy on my own, like it seems I'm going to be, I'm not going to be rushing home from work every Thursday to go to yoga with her. I don't even like yoga.'

She straightened a finger with each reason, watching for my reaction. It was only when she heard a beep from behind that she noticed the car in front had moved on and she pulled in to park.

I undid my seatbelt, clicked the door open. 'So, that's what this is about. You. This has nothing to do with Mum, whether she'd like it or whether it'd be good for her.'

I pushed the door open further, the rain on my hand and face.

She looked at me and back to the dashboard where she turned the fan off. The silence was loud. I thought she might slam her hand down again, curse, drive off with me half out of the car, but she didn't do any of those things.

'You're right,' she said, lifting her eyes to me. Without the anger she sounded tired. 'I'm not going to deny that. I have to think about me. Because if I don't, Carla, who else is going to?'

A strand of hair fell across her face and she let it hang there. The inside of the car was wet, the seat, the door. I'd wanted to hurt her, like she'd hurt me, and now I had. 'I've got to go. I don't want to miss this class.' I climbed out on to the wet street and slammed the door.

★

From outside, the studio looked like an office, but inside it was better: the smell of sandalwood incense, fresh flowers on a low table. A woman with short red hair was behind the wooden reception desk. She smiled when she saw me. 'Hello! I was just about to lock the door,' she said. 'I'm Audrey.'

'Carla.'

She held out a hand and I shook it.

'Welcome, Carla, nice to meet you. Is this your first class?'

'Here it is,' I said. 'I live in New York and practise there.'

'Oh, gosh,' she said. 'I hope our little studio can live up to that.' She smiled again and handed me a form. I filled it out. When I'd finished she glanced over it, waved my money away. 'The first class is free. We think it's a good investment, because we hope you'll come back.'

After the row with Suzanne, this might be my first and last time but there was no point in telling her that. Following her upstairs, I noticed her wide hips, legs short in green leggings. She didn't look like a yoga teacher, not like Jan who used to be a dancer. At the start I'd felt clumsy next to her, all tightness and angles until I realised that that didn't matter, that it wasn't what she saw when she looked at me.

The studio was small and I took a spot by the wall, sat cross-legged. Audrey sat at the top of the room and welcomed their New York visitor. I opened my eyes and smiled, closed them again. Audrey was talking, something about yoga being training for life, on and off the mat. Inhale, exhale. The echo of Suzanne's voice was still in my head, too vivid for the breathing to push away. My back was sore – Audrey was talking too long. Jan always got us into poses straight away.

Eventually we started and I took in the studio properly – bare cream walls, net curtains, nothing like Jan's room in the Brooklyn Heights' brownstone, all wood and light. I knew I shouldn't compare but it was hard not to. I loved that room: the tall plants by the window that I focused on when I needed to balance, the smell from the bakery downstairs.

Class was in full flow and I was miles away, thousands of miles in another class in another country. In five weeks, I'd be back there. For now I was here, tuning into Audrey's voice, leaning into a forward bend. I grabbed my ankles, made my tattoo disappear. Her voice was loud, competing with the music. Jan's voice was so lyrical it almost *was* music. If I was going to keep comparing every little thing I might as well go home.

I focused on the movement. Raised my arms, looked up at the speckled ceiling tiles. The woman in front of me was overweight. Every time she moved forward I could see the top of her knickers, a grey line edging above the tight navy band of her tracksuit. I tried to watch Audrey instead.

The class trundled on too slowly, holding poses for ever, it felt like. The movement wasn't enough to get inside my head, so the fight with Suzanne swilled around, a mix of guilt and anger. I ground my feet into the mat. It wasn't my fault – none of it was my fault.

Audrey had us in a standing twist, hands in prayer. My elbow pushed hard into my thigh. I hated this pose, always had. Next to me a skinny blonde woman was doing it perfectly. My mind moved on to Eddie, our phone call earlier. I'd called him on the spur of the moment and he was at work, sounded irritated, impatient at the interruption. He didn't say, 'I love you,' at the end of the call this time, but I didn't either and it wasn't like we needed to say it all the time. My hamstrings ached and I was about to get out of the pose before she made us switch sides. We'd only been on to each other for five minutes and he'd spent most of the time bitching about some client. Twisting to my left, I realised I was angry with him too, as if the pose was wringing it out of me, like water from a J-cloth.

I pushed my hands into the mat, my hips high in downward dog. Plank, cobra, downward dog again. The class was speeding up. The woman next to me was in child's pose, but I didn't need it, could hold for as many breaths as Audrey asked us to. It didn't make any sense to be angry with Eddie, he hadn't done anything. When we were together we never fought, hardly ever, but since we'd been apart he seemed to irritate me all the time. Only yesterday, when a shopping bag split open and a jar of pasta sauce shattered on Mum's front step, I'd found my mind flicking to Eddie, as if he could somehow be responsible from thousands of miles away.

We were near the end of class, time for backbends. Audrey used the English names for the poses – I wondered if she even knew the Sanskrit, if she'd ever been to India. Pushing myself up into wheel, I thought about Mum, about all those times she'd said she'd love us to go to India together. It should've been me with her there, not Lily-Anne. Audrey was coming around again and I saw her behind me, her hands reaching in to cup my shoulder-blades. Jan had never done that.

'Soften, Carla,' she said. 'Just let go, let everything go.'

When it was time for relaxation and Audrey brought me a blanket. I took it, even though I didn't usually. Now that the music was lower I heard the rain, the wind hurling snatches of it against the window. Would Suzanne come down and get me? She'd hardly leave me here on a night like this.

Lying under the blanket, I let myself relax, grateful for the floor. I loved this bit. Jan used to come around to everyone and massage lavender oil into our temples. Audrey stayed put at the front of the room, talking us through each part of our bodies, her voice softer than before.

My feet were relaxed, my toes, my ankles, my shins, my kneecaps. I was enjoying this now, glad I'd come. My thighs and hips relaxed, my stomach, my waist. Feeling the rest of my body made me see how tied up in my head I'd been. Maybe I'd bring some of the poses into practice with Mum tomorrow, tree pose, maybe. But what if Suzanne was right, what if she wasn't able for them? Did I really want to find out?

That was what I was doing when I was supposed to be relaxing, imagining the scene where Mum didn't know where to place her feet on the mat, her hands. Audrey's voice drifted in, urging us to let go of thoughts, to see them as clouds passing, but the more I tried to, the more tightly the image held. We rolled on to our sides, sat up cross-legged, eyes closed. There was a gap of silence before Audrey spoke again, saying how yoga was about being present in the moment, whatever it held, not trying to change it. I thought about what Lily-Anne had said about Mum. For the whole class my mind had been a revolving door of thoughts – Suzanne, Mum, Eddie, now Mum again. If I couldn't manage to stay present for ninety minutes how was I supposed to try for any longer?

I packed my stuff away, left my phone switched off. There was no point in turning it on to find some message from Suzanne telling me to make my own way home. The other women stood around chatting and I was first downstairs to open the door. Rain dripped off the porch. I zipped up my tracksuit as far as it would go. There were no buses, no cabs. I'd make sure she saw me when I got home, how wet I was. Then she'd feel guilty.

On the road a car was slowing down, stopping. I closed the door and stepped out into the wind. It was black, like Suzanne's. The headlights flashed, lit up the rain. I heard the sound of doors unlocking. A light went on inside and I saw her. She wasn't smiling. She didn't wave. But she was there.

She'd come back.

NINE

My bedroom door was open, that was what I noticed first, a rectangle of grey, lighter than the rest. In the darkness, there was a shape, a person, by my bed. I sat up hard, kicking my foot against the radiator.

'Who's there?'

'Carla!'

'Mum?' I reached for the lamp, fumbled for the switch. 'Mum?'

Even with the light on, when I could see it was her, there was still a question in my voice because somehow she didn't look like herself. I pushed the duvet back, swung my feet to the carpet. 'Mum? What is it? What's happened?'

'Sssh!' She leaned down to whisper in my ear, her hand on my shoulder surprisingly heavy. 'He'll hear you. We don't want him to hear you.' She turned and pointed towards the door, her finger over her lips. My heart pounded. I tried to stand up but her grip was too strong, pushing me back into the mattress. 'He's been knocking again,' she said. 'All night, he's been knocking.'

In the lamplight I saw then what was making her look like someone else, the terror in her face as her eyes slid back to the open door and the landing beyond. I put my hand on hers, loosened her grip and stood up so we were side by side. I felt as if I was moving in slow motion. 'Who is it, Mum? Who's knocking?'

I knew, I thought I knew, that no one was knocking, that the

184

thing to be afraid of wasn't someone else, but Mum, her fear.

'Did you not hear him? He's been doing that all night – all night! It's coming from the thing in my room, the fireplace.'

She didn't have a fireplace in her room, but maybe she meant the chimney breast. Maybe a bird was caught behind it or there had been a noise from next door. I reached out and took her hand. It was freezing, like she'd been outside – but she couldn't have been. I felt a wave of relief then, for Suzanne, her locks.

'Come on, let's go and see what it is.'

'No!' She sat down on the bed, her grasp strong on my arm. 'No! I'm not going back there. He'll kill me.'

There was certainty in her fear, something solid and hard to ignore. I tried to remember all the things I'd read about what to do in a situation like this. Only I'd never read about a situation like this.

'Please,' Mum said, tears on her face, 'please, don't go out there, love.'

'I won't, Mum,' I said. 'I'm not.'

I closed the door firmly. There was a sweatshirt on the chair by my desk and I grabbed it, put it around her shoulders. I pulled the duvet back, the sheet underneath still warm. 'It's OK, Mum,' I said. 'I'm here now. Everything's going to be OK. Why don't you lie down?'

Under the sweatshirt she seemed to soften, and I rolled her over a little, folding her legs in, pulling the covers up around her. I dropped down on to my hunkers next to the bed so I could stroke her hair, smooth it down with my palm. 'You're safe now. No one can hurt you. I'm here. I'm here.'

She started to cry, soft breathy cries, half swallowed by the pillow. I wanted to get a tissue but I didn't want to move, afraid to take away my hand and whatever comfort it was giving her. Where was Suzanne? How had she not heard all of this?

Time passed in the darkness, marked by the rhythm of my words, the stroking, longer gaps between her sobs. Over and over I told her she was safe, that it had been a bad dream, that I was there. As her panic receded I felt an ache in my knees and swivelled my legs around so I could sit down.

I didn't know I'd had those words inside me but sitting there on the carpet I remembered where I'd heard them: from Dad, one night when he woke me from a nightmare, scooping me away from it and into his arms. It was harder in the dark to fight off the memory and I let myself hear his voice, feel my legs and arms fastened around him as he carried me across the landing before placing me gently in their bed, whispering that I must be quiet, that Mammy was tired from her work away, that we were going to have a sleep sandwich.

Back in my bed, Mum's breathing had changed, the sobs gone, replaced by sleep. I lifted my hand away, feeling for the first time how cold I was. I pulled the duvet around her neck and took one last look at her as I eased my way on to the landing. Suzanne's door was closed. All these years later I was going to have to sleep in their room again.

The light was off and when I turned on the lamp a chair was pulled up to the chimney breast, the clothes that had been on it in a pool in the corner. Two drawers were open. A bra hung out of one. I paused to listen, my ear flat against the cold wallpaper. Only the swoosh of air. Maybe though there had been something, the beating of a bird wing, trapped in the soot. Tomorrow I'd call the chimney sweep, that was something I could do.

I carried the chair back to its proper place, folded the jeans and jumpers back on it. Her dressing-gown was there too and I opened the wardrobe door to find a space. The clothes were packed tight, organised by colour, texture. She had the whole thing now, Dad's half too. Before I could stop it another memory came of the last time I'd opened that wardrobe, the smell of him. I hadn't realised he'd had a smell until that moment emptying the hangers of shirts, trousers, jeans with a belt still on them. I did it quickly, pulling cloth from metal, everything going in the black bag, his green corduroy jacket that he said made him look like a fake professor, his shoes, a cartoon character tie that Suzanne and

186

I had bought him some Christmas.

I closed the door on the memory, picked the bra up and pushed it back into the drawer.

Afterwards I'd worried that the charity shop would complain because the bags weren't sorted properly. I'd shoved everything in together, pens, a dictionary, Dad's Dylan tapes, a pair of swimming togs I'd never seen him wear. For weeks afterwards, when the phone rang, I was sure it was going to be that shop, calling to complain, but it never was.

I sat down on Mum's side of the bed, pulled my legs in. On the locker beside me lay a journal, red, with 'Keep Calm and Carry On' in white. She'd had that in Montauk, wrote in it all the time. I thought about opening it, about reading what she had said, but before the thought could become action I turned away and closed my eyes.

★

'It's the Aricept,' Suzanne said, the next morning. 'They put her up to the heavier dosage. Dr Glavin said there was a higher chance of side effects. Nightmares.'

She was eating toast without a plate. Crumbs fell on the counter. She picked one up on her index finger, licked it off.

'This was more than a nightmare, Suzanne. She was in such a panic. She was terrified. I think she'd been up for ages before she came in to me.'

Outside the morning was beautiful, the sky in stripes of pink and yellow. I should have been out for my run now, down by the sea, but I hadn't woken on time. Mum must have slept through the alarm I'd set, or turned it off, because she was still asleep in my bed.

'She's been having restless and broken sleep for ages,' Suzanne said. 'Dr Glavin said to keep an eye on it, to keep her posted if it got worse. I'll call her later, tell her about it.'

She took another bite of toast. A flicker of something in my stomach. Resentment? Jealousy?

'You'll tell her how scared she was? That she was really in a panic?'

She nodded.

'Terrified. Like a child.'

She swallowed. 'You said. I'll tell her.'

'I'll call the chimney sweep,' I said. 'See if they can come over today.'

Suzanne brushed crumbs from the front of her blouse, catching them in one hand. 'We had him over only a few months ago. We don't need him again.'

I stood up too, my hands on my hips. 'Look, I want to make sure there's nothing stuck there, nothing frightening her.'

'Carla, there was no one knocking.'

'Jesus, Suzanne, I know that. I just want to make sure we get rid of anything that might have triggered the nightmare in the first place.'

She shrugged and poured the rest of her tea down the sink, picked her suit jacket up from the back of the chair. She could only be so matter-of-fact because she hadn't seen Mum, how scared she was. If she'd seen her, she'd understand.

'Fine, do whatever you want. The number's on the fridge. Just make sure to put papers and sheets down. He makes a mess.' She picked up a folder from the table, checked her phone, then dropped it into her bag. 'And don't be tempted to let Mum sleep in or she'll be up again tonight. That's how it starts.'

She was gone before I could respond to that, footsteps in the hall, the sound of the top bolt, the middle lock, the lower one, the swoosh of the porch door as it closed. As a teenager I'd loved that sound, the sound of them all leaving, knowing I had the house to myself. This morning I didn't have it to myself. I filled the kettle again, watched a line of birds flying low over the trees, black against the sky.

I was going to have another coffee before I woke Mum. Give her an extra half-hour in bed. Screw Suzanne and her regimented schedule. She hadn't been there last night, she hadn't seen Mum's panic, her fear, her confusion. And despite everything that had happened, one thought stood out from all the others. Last night Mum had needed someone and she hadn't chosen Suzanne.

She had come to me.

Ten

As the bus crawled up the hill I saw the new estates ahead, clusters of light that climbed higher up the mountain, then finally the mountain itself, black against the darkening sky. The journey had taken much longer than I'd thought, waiting on the second bus for twenty-five minutes, but it was worth it to get there without having to rely on Suzanne.

The road names were versions of each other: Valley Hill Avenue, Valley Hill Park. I checked the piece of paper in my pocket. Ange's was Valley Hill Glen. A contradiction, surely. Each of these roads was a newer version of the one we'd grown up on, each house just like the one before.

Number sixty-three had a silver car on a driveway made for two, a red scooter propped against the wall under the window. When I rang the bell it was a child's voice I heard first. Then I saw a small shape through the glass before an Ange-shaped one. When she opened the door it was her hair I noticed, her curls pulled into two tight ponytails on either side.

'Oh, my God!' She pulled the door back and I saw she had the baby on her hip. 'Come in, come in! Oh, wow, your hair is fab that colour. It suits you dark.'

She gave me a one-armed hug, a kiss on the cheek. We never used to kiss. One of the boys was hanging behind her legs. I thought it was Ben, but I wasn't sure enough to say his name.

'I love your bag! Let me see it.'

'Thanks,' I said, holding it up. 'I picked it up at some market. It was only ten bucks.'

'Ten bucks! Listen to you, you're so American! Look, Mikey, it's Auntie Carla. She's home from America. Aren't you going to say hello?'

Mikey. Thank God I hadn't said Ben. He sucked his thumb, staring at me. Too late, I realised I should have brought something for the kids instead of the bottle of wine that was in the bag Ange had been so busy admiring.

'Hi, Mikey!'

'And this is Emily,' Ange said, holding out a pudgy hand.

'Hello, Emily,' I said, as she grabbed my finger, sticky and tight.

'Ben, come down and say hello to Auntie Carla. I'm going to put a DVD on for the boys, so we can get some peace.'

Auntie Carla? When had that started? Ben came down the stairs looking as unsure of me as I was of him. He was a bigger version of Mikey, in a matching sweatshirt but without the thumb-sucking.

'Can we watch *Spiderman*?' he said, leaning into the banisters.

'Don't you want to watch *Shrek*? Mikey likes that.'

'*Shrek*'s boring! I want to watch *Spiderman*!'

'OK, then, so long as you're quiet. And if you're really good boys you can have strawberry ice cream afterwards.'

'Can we have it now?'

'No, I said after. And remember, you have to be very quiet. Auntie Carla and I have lots to talk about.' She turned to me, rolled her eyes. 'You go on into the kitchen, excuse the mess.'

She wasn't joking, the kitchen really was a mess. I picked my way around the toy cars on the floor, a stray runner. One of the chairs had a pile of clothes on it and I took the one next to it. I reached across the table to pick up the paper. Underneath it, green and red Plasticine was squashed into the table. I put the paper back.

'I wanted to feed them early,' Ange said, coming in. 'Get dinner out of the way before you came. I didn't have time to clear up.'

She went to the sink, holding Emily in one arm, taking plates out and putting them into the dishwasher with the other hand.

'What are they?' I asked, gesturing towards what looked like a pile of plastic clogs by the back door.

She followed my gaze and laughed. 'Crocs! You've never seen them? So handy. Blue for the boys, pink for the girls. Although Emily's a little small yet, aren't you, Em?'

She grabbed Emily's little foot and pretended to eat it. One of the blue pairs was man-sized, Pete's. I'd always liked Pete, his neurosis, his black sense of humour. I tried to imagine him wearing blue plastic shoes.

'Tea or coffee?' she said, her back to me at the counter.

'I brought wine,' I said, taking the bottle out.

'Oh, you want wine?'

Of course I wanted wine but it was clear from her tone that she didn't. 'No, coffee's fine. You and Pete have it another time.'

I put the bottle down, wishing again that I'd brought something for the kids. On the counter there was a boxy stainless-steel coffee-maker and I waited for Ange to turn it on. Instead she took a jar of instant from the cupboard. 'I don't know how to use that thing,' she said, nodding towards it, as if she'd heard what I was thinking. 'It's one of Pete's toys, that and the breadmaker. You know how he loves his gadgets.'

'I remember,' I said. 'How's he doing? I thought he might be home by now.'

She glanced at the clock. 'He doesn't get home till eight or so, usually.'

'That's late.'

'I think so too, but he says it's normal. He says that's what's expected, these days, that everyone does it.'

'Well, Suzanne's the same, and she takes her laptop home to work in the evenings.'

'Really?' Ange lifted Emily into a high chair. The baby stared at me with Ange's eyes, grey blue and serious. I made a smiley face and she kept staring, her bottom lip oozing drool.

'Hey, you never told me Damien had a baby. That he has another one on the way.'

'Did I not?' Ange emptied a packet of biscuits on to a plate.

'No. I found out from Nosy Rosie, of all people! I met her on the pier with Mum.' I repeated what Mum had said to her as Ange opened the fridge, took out juice and milk, then filled the cups with boiling water. When it came to the punch line she was rinsing a beaker under the tap, and although she laughed, I knew she hadn't been listening properly.

'Here you go,' she said, putting two mugs on the table, far away from Emily's reach. She went back for the beaker, filled it with orange juice. 'Imagine having her as a mother-in-law. You'd a narrow escape.'

She sat down then and faced me, before turning to Emily, holding out the beaker. The coffee was horrible. I stirred in some sugar. 'Are they still as friendly, Pete and Damien?'

She shrugged. 'They are, but you know what guys are like. They rely on me and Rebecca to make the arrangements to meet up.'

I hadn't known Ange was that friendly with Rebecca. I remembered the summer of fifth year, me and Damien, Ange and Pete, always together. We'd planned it all out, Ange and I, a lifetime of kids the same age, dinner parties, holidays together.

'Anyway, enough about Damien. Why are we even talking about him? How's Eddie? I can't believe you finally got married! Let's see the ring.'

I held out my fingers, bare except for the rings I'd always worn. 'I don't have one.'

'Not even an engagement ring?' she said.

'No. Way too expensive. I've never been into that stuff. I wouldn't know a solitaire if I fell over one.'

On Ange's hand, the engagement and wedding rings fitted perfectly together. When they'd got engaged she'd emailed me a photo of that ring, as well as describing it in detail over the phone. I thought about telling her about the ring disaster in the register office and decided against it.

'Well, you and Eddie were never exactly conventional,' Ange

193

said, making a kissy face at Emily. 'You always like to do the opposite to everyone else.' She picked up Emily's beaker so the baby could drink and some orange juice leaked down her chin. Hearing Ange describe me and Eddie like that made us sound a little lame, surely at some stage doing the opposite became just another form of convention.

I rolled the mug of coffee between my hands. Ange broke off a corner of a biscuit and held it up to Emily, who smiled a gummy smile. I watched them, smiling too. Emily opened her mouth to show us the sludge the biscuit made on her tongue and we laughed. I wanted to ask Ange about her mum, how she'd been doing since the funeral, but it didn't seem like the right time. I got the impression that she was mad at me because I'd missed it. Or maybe she was used to it by now, me missing out on all the big parts of her life, just like she'd missed out on so many of mine.

'Hey, guess who was asking for you the other day?' she said, wiping Emily's mouth with a tissue. Emily pulled away, made a noise like she was going to start crying.

'Chrissy Daly!'

'Chrissy Daly?'

'Yep. I ran into her in the supermarket – she was all chat.'

'Is she not too cool for the supermarket?'

'I know, right? It's funny, she seemed totally normal, has two kids, looked like a typical mum. I was laughing to myself afterwards, thinking how in awe we used to be of her and Sophie Cox. Do you remember the time she asked us to go with her and Sophie to the pictures? How thrilled we were?'

From down the hall the TV was suddenly audible, then louder, then blaring. Something crashed.

'Ben? Mikey? What's going on in there?'

Ange popped a soother in Emily's mouth before jumping up and running into the hall. After a second the volume was lowered and I heard someone crying. Emily spat her soother on to the floor. I bent down to pick it up and walked over to the sink.

Chrissy Daly and Sophie Cox, I hadn't thought about that in years, the four of us going to see *Ferris Bueller's Day Off* at the Adelphi. 'Here you go,' I said to Emily, putting the soother back into her mouth. She spat it out on to the floor again.

'Sorry about that,' Ange said, as she came back in. 'Mikey and Ben are going through some phase at the moment. One minute they're thick as thieves, the next they're killing each other.' She picked up the soother, sucked it, then gave it back to Emily.

'That's what Mum used to say about me and Suzanne, but I only ever remember us killing each other.'

'How *is* Suzanne?'

'Bossy. Controlling. She hasn't changed much.'

Ange giggled. 'Stop it! She can't be that bad.'

'She is, Ange, I'm telling you. Everything is her way or no way. She knows everything about this disease, what's right for Mum. What to do in every situation. I, of course, have no clue.'

A curl had escaped from one of her ponytails and she twisted it around her finger. 'Maybe she's just getting used to having you around again. For so long, it's been just the two of them. It has to be a change.'

I helped myself to another biscuit.

'I presume she's still playing hockey?'

I shook my head and swallowed. 'No, not for ages, since she did in her knee.'

'Her knee?'

'I didn't tell you about that? She'd an accident playing, a couple of years ago. Don't ask me the details. She had keyhole surgery but it mustn't have worked because she hasn't played since.'

'Oh, poor Suzanne.' Ange looked genuinely upset and I wished then that it was her I'd told when it happened, instead of Eddie and Rhonda who didn't really know Suzanne at all.

She started to say something else but Emily let out a sharp cry that gave way to a ragged whine. She held out her arms to Ange, who plucked her from her chair and sniffed her butt, oversized in baby jeans. 'I thought I smelt something,' she said, in a funny lilting voice. 'Someone needs a nappy change, don't they? Don't they?'

I fixed a smile to my face.

'Do you mind if I go up and change her quickly?' she said, in her normal voice. 'I'll be five minutes.'

'It's fine,' I said. 'Take your time.'

'Make more coffee if you want.'

I took another biscuit, a custard cream. I used to love them. I swivelled the top off, scraped at the cream with my front teeth. The clock said seven-twenty. I stood up and walked over to the fridge to look at the photos, stuck there with magnets. There was Pete holding Emily, a man version of Pete with the same smile but less hair. Next to it was one of the two boys, cheeks squashed together for the camera. Hanging underneath there was a drawing, four stick figures with arms coming from their waists, a tree, a yellow marker sun.

In New York I didn't know anyone our age who had kids but over here everyone was at it – Damien, Ange, even Chrissy Daly. When I thought about Chrissy Daly I imagined her still in her school uniform, her tie in a tight knot, her hair shaved on one side. Of course I remembered the day she'd asked us to go to the cinema. I'd wanted to kill Ange – she'd told Chrissy I was never around on Sundays because I spent them in Trinity with Dad. I could still picture the scorn in Chrissy's face, hear the words she'd spat at me. 'Sounds like school, only worse. You must be a right little daddy's girl.'

I put the drawing back, hanging it up with a magnet shaped like a rugby ball. The memory was nearly twenty years old but it could still make my cheeks burn. In the hall, the phone rang and I heard Ange answer it upstairs. There was so much I wanted to talk to her about: the weird irritation with Eddie, the way I found myself testing Mum all the time, laying traps for her sometimes, asking if she remembered things from New York, some things we'd never done together, at all.

Seven–thirty. Ben's head came around the door and disappeared again. Footsteps on the stairs, a whine for the promised ice cream. The conversations I wanted to have with Ange were conversations that needed to come out in more than five words at a time. That would be the only thing worse than not having them at all. I put my jacket on, picked up my bag.

'Sorry,' Ange said, wiping her hands on her jeans as she came back in. 'I just thought I'd put Emily down while I was up there. I'm going to get the boys some ice cream and then I'm all yours.'

She stopped when she saw me zipping up my jacket. 'You're not going?'

'Sorry, Ange, I don't want to be back too late. Those buses take for ever.'

She nodded. 'I feel bad. I'd drop you home only that was Pete, he's stuck late in the office.'

'It's fine.' I smiled. 'The bus is fine.'

'Sorry it's been such a madhouse. We'll meet up again, one night for dinner, before you go back.'

I had four weeks left, surely time for more than one night out.

'Great,' I said. 'We can go to some of our old haunts. Do people still go to Bruxelles?'

She laughed. 'You're asking the wrong person. When we go into town now, it's with Pete's work to some fancy restaurant. The last time I was in Bruxelles was probably with you.'

We walked together into the hall. I couldn't leave without mentioning her mum.

'I wanted to ask you how you were doing, you know, after your mum . . .'

In the doorway of the living room Mikey was on his hands and knees, grinding a toy car over the wood floor. Without warning he rammed it into my heel.

'Ah, you know,' she said. 'A day at a time and all that. What about yours?'

She bit her bottom lip, something I hadn't seen her do in years but I knew what it meant. In the bright light of the hall she looked tired. Just because she'd asked, it didn't mean she wanted to know, really wanted to know.

'She's grand,' I said. 'In good form mostly.'

'Would you notice it? Like, if you didn't know?'

I hesitated. I wanted to say something true but something that would end the evening in a place we both wanted to end it. 'Well, the garden looks a wreck,' I said. 'She still loves working on it but she starts one thing, then forgets about it and goes to do something else. Of course, Green Fingers here has to follow her around, try and finish it.'

Ange laughed, as I'd known she would.

'And then she ends up giving out hell to me because I don't know what I'm doing, pruning things the wrong way, digging up plants, leaving the weeds!'

The story had carried us to the front door and on to the step outside. Mikey was standing by her legs again and she took his arm and waved it at me. 'It was so good to see you. We have to do that dinner definitely before you go back.'

'Yeah, that'd be great.'

She hugged me, kissing my cheek again. 'It's so nice to have you home.'

Her words floated around my head as I went down the driveway, past the houses with their lights on and curtains pulled, the families safe indoors. The night was colder now and I pulled my scarf higher, breathed back in my hot breath. Chrissy Daly probably lived in a house like this now, Sophie Cox too.

We'd gone to see *Ferris Bueller's Day Off* with them, Ange and I, of course we had – we were always going to take our brief chance at being cool. And it would've been fine if I'd just told Dad beforehand, rather than running out that morning without even saying goodbye. I'd felt so guilty afterwards that I could hardly concentrate on the film, timed my laughter around Chrissy's, glancing around now and then to see her next to me in the dark.

Out of the maze of the estate the road was narrow with high walls. Headlights swept around the bend and the cars felt very close suddenly, very fast. Dad had made a joke of it over dinner, how I'd abandoned him, leaving him to go to Trinity on his own.

'God, Dad, you don't expect me to go to Trinity with you every Sunday for the rest of my life, do you?'

That's what I'd said, something like that, and he'd smiled at me. I remembered that smile, the way he held it as he cut his roast beef, the look Mum gave him as if she wanted to touch him, but she didn't. He'd laughed, then said something about me being a teenager now, with better things to do than hang out with an old bugger like him.

At the bus stop the timetable had been ripped off. I pushed my hands deep into my pockets, ready for a long wait, but there it was already, coming around the corner, a double-decker of lights in the dark. I took my ticket from my back pocket and climbed on. It was nearly empty and I found a seat at the back.

We'd never hung out with Chrissy and Sophie again, after that one time, but I'd never gone back to Trinity with Dad either. I'd wanted him to ask me to go with him, but he never did. Instead he asked me, every Sunday night over dinner, how my day was and I always made it sound like fun. Going down the hill, the bus picked up speed so I could feel the tremor of the engine through the soles of my runners. Tonight when I got home Suzanne and Mum would ask me about Ange's, how the night had been, and I'd make it sound like fun. I wondered what it would be like to tell them — really tell them — about it but even as the thought formed I knew I wouldn't. It was just like Ange, asking about Mum; people asked, but that didn't mean they always wanted to know.

And it was just easier, sometimes, to tell them the other thing, the thing they wanted to hear.

ELEVEN

It was the first time I'd made soup from scratch and it seemed like a lot of effort – shopping for lentils, celery, onions, carrots. All that chopping. Now that it was ready, though, and I was filling the two bowls, I was glad I'd bothered – you could practically taste the health in it.

'You like the soup, Mum?'

She hesitated, holding her spoon in mid-air. 'Mm. It's good,' she said. Two lines appeared between her eyebrows. 'Did you put the cumin in?'

'I put everything in, I followed the recipe exactly.'

'Ah.' She nodded. 'I always add a bit of cumin. It's not in the recipe but it helps to bring out the taste.'

My shoulders tensed. Of course my soup wasn't as good as hers. 'I'll remember for next time,' I said. 'Or, better still, I'll find my own recipe.'

She didn't respond, only dunked her bread in the soup and ate some more. I stirred mine and steam rose from the bowl. Suddenly I didn't want it any more.

She glanced up over her spoon. 'I didn't mean I don't like it, Carla. It's tasty. Very tasty.'

She smiled and I managed a smile back. I put myself in her shoes, what it must be like not to be able to cook the food you want any more, to rely on others to cook for you.

'You know Roisin's coming over later?' I said.

Her smile froze, turned to a glare, and she dropped her spoon into the bowl. 'Yes, I know she's coming over. You've told me

200

twenty times already. Now you're telling me again.'

'Sorry,' I said. 'I didn't realise I'd said it so often.'

'Well, you have. And I don't like it. Yes, my memory lets me down. Yes, I have my cloudy days, but I still remember who my oldest friend is, that she's coming over for coffee.'

Her 'cloudy days' was what she'd been calling them lately, something outside her control, like the weather.

'You're getting as bad as your sister, jumping ahead to some place when I won't know who my friends are any more. I do today. Is that not enough?'

My cheeks flushed. She was right, of course. I didn't want to see a day when she mightn't remember Roisin, when she mightn't remember me. 'I'm sorry,' I said again.

We ate in silence and I could feel her anger radiating towards me, as real as the heat from the soup. Yet even as I felt guilty, and sad, I realised that part of me had enjoyed seeing Mum get angry and put me in my place in the way she always used to. As the thought formed, another tailgated it – who was going to do that for me when she wasn't able to any more?

★

I was in my room when I heard the bell. By the time I got to the stairs, Roisin was in the hall, she and Mum hugging each other.

'Well, would you look what the cat dragged in?' Roisin said, when she saw me. Her hair was as blonde as ever, her lipstick still bright red. She held out her arms and I was fourteen again, ten. I jumped the last few stairs.

'It's so good to see you,' I said, squeezing her as tightly as she squeezed me. I remembered hugging her when my head only reached the softness of her belly. Now I had to reach down. 'I've missed your hugs.'

'In the city that has everything you're missing my hugs? Go on out of that!' She laughed and held me away from her. 'Look at you, all grown-up. Love the hair. Although, even with it, you're still the image of your father.'

She let go of me and turned to Mum, telling her how great she looked too, as they headed into the sitting room. I'd planned to leave them to it but somehow I found myself following them, sitting down on the couch. Being in the same room as Roisin was like stepping back in time to when she and Noel came round every week to play cards and I didn't want it to end just yet.

'How's Noel?' Mum said. 'And Caroline and Stephen? Are they doing well?'

I noticed how she said the names, listing them. She was getting worse with names, and I'd been ready to prompt her but she hadn't needed it. I settled back further into the cushions.

'Noel is Noel,' Roisin said, taking off her coat and swinging it over the arm of the chair. 'Wouldn't be happy without a crisis. Last year it was the dean – he couldn't stand the man until the Christmas party and now they're best buddies. The year before it was the building on campus, how it was going to destroy the atmosphere. Now it's the fact that fees might come back in. Take your pick.'

'He was always a worrier,' Mum said.

'That's why he and Nat rubbed along so well,' said Roisin. 'He calmed him down.'

'Nat?' Mum said. 'Calm?'

'He was practically horizontal, compared to Noel,' she said, smoothing her skirt over her knees. 'I always thought Noel would be the one to take a heart attack, not Nat.'

She threw the words out casually, laughing as she said them. *Take a heart attack* – as if Dad had had a choice. If he had, would he have taken a heart attack rather than Alzheimer's? Would I?

'Still, I shouldn't say that.' Roisin touched the wooden shelf next to her. 'You never know what's around the corner.'

'Do you remember the night you first met Nat?' Mum said. 'You met him before me, the night you and Noel had that fierce row in O'Neill's.'

'Was it not Mulligan's?' Roisin wondered. Her face cleared. 'No, you're right. O'Neill's. We were supposed to be going to the pictures, to see *Love Story*, if you don't mind. He was late and I'd a suspicion where I might find him.'

'Was he drunk?' I said.

'Oh, yes, three sheets to the wind and laughing at everything that came out of your father's mouth, just like all of them around the table. He wasn't laughing when he turned and saw me.' She made a fist with her hand.

'You were raging when you came back to the flat,' Mum said, giggling. 'You said you'd told Noel that he may as well take that English upstart up the aisle with him, if he was going to carry on like that, because he certainly wasn't going to marry you!'

Roisin tipped her head back, her laughter joining in with Mum's. 'That's right, and I meant it,' she said. 'I couldn't stand Nat back then. I thought you were half cracked when you said you were going out with him.'

'You were never behind the door in letting me know either,' Mum said, wiping her eyes with a tissue.

Roisin turned to me. 'She could have had anyone, your Mam. Half of Dublin was after her and she went for this English fella with funny glasses. I didn't get it.'

'I liked him, he made me laugh,' Mum said. 'Not to mention he was a younger man.'

'He pursued your mother like a bloodhound, like a missile. He showed up at the flat every Saturday with flowers. And he wrote her poems. Poems, if you don't mind! You heard about the time he appeared on her doorstep in Sligo, the day after Stephen's Day?'

'Yeah,' I said, 'but tell me again.'

Roisin clasped her hands. 'It was like *Planes, Trains and Automobiles*. He'd got himself from Brighton to Holyhead, taken the mailboat, hitched a lift from Dublin and walked the rest of the way. Noel was only down the road and we didn't see each other for three days that Christmas because the bus wasn't running.'

I knew the story well, every beat of it. Roisin's stories were easy and comfortable, always with the same theme: her and Noel bickering at every turn, Mum and Dad like Romeo and Juliet.

Even as a child I couldn't picture them like that, Mum and Dad, but I was glad that Roisin could. 'Let me put the kettle on, make us some coffee,' I said.

'Good girl,' Roisin said. 'I'm dying for a cup. And where's my head gone to? I can't believe I forgot to say congratulations.'

There was a split second's pause. I put my hands into the back pockets of my jeans.

'About you and Eddie! I have a card for you in my bag somewhere.'

'Oh!' I said. 'Thanks, sorry, I keep forgetting it's still news over here.'

She pulled an envelope from her bag and handed it to me. 'What made you finally give up living in sin?' Her face was open, smiling. She didn't mean anything by it, wasn't trying to dig.

'It was about time, really,' I said. 'We'd always planned to, you know.'

Compared with Dad's pursuit of Mum, it sounded lame. I turned the card over in my hands.

'I'll let you in on a secret, Carla,' Roisin said, dropping her voice. 'Most men need a good kick up the arse. Nothing wrong with that. Not all like your father. Noel now, he needed a bit of prodding. And look at us, nearly forty years of wedded bliss! Isn't that right, Coll?'

She laughed, sitting back a little in her chair.

'Yes,' Mum nodded, 'that's true.'

'Forty years,' Roisin said, shaking her head again. 'You wouldn't get that for murder.'

★

From the kitchen I could still hear them, talking over each other, bursts of laughter.

A word came into my mind that I never used: a tonic. That was what Roisin was for Mum. Suzanne had said it was ages since she'd been over. I must tell her to come more often, that it'd do Mum good. Roisin got everyone laughing, all her stories, and whatever she said about Noel they must be happy, something had to keep people together for forty years.

The kettle clicked off and I filled the coffee pot. That shelf-help book was confusing, it had kept coming into my head ever since I'd read it. It was hard to figure out where love stopped and this co-dependency stuff began. If Dad hadn't died, I wondered, would he and Mum have lasted as long as Roisin and Noel? Would Eddie and I?

Behind me, the door opened, and when I looked around, Roisin was there, her hand hovering over the scones I'd laid out. She snatched it away. 'Just checking if you needed help. Your Mam's gone to the little girls' room.'

'Help eating the scones?'

She grinned. 'She's in great form, isn't she? And she looks fantastic.'

'She is today,' I said. 'I was just thinking how much she's enjoying your company. I haven't seen her laugh so much since I got back.'

'Don't be silly. I'd say it's you being home that's got her on a high. How long will she have you for?'

I took the milk from the fridge, filled the jug. 'I'm supposed to be going back in three weeks.'

'Supposed to?'

'Suzanne's got me on some guilt trip. She thinks I should stay longer. That I should move home or something.'

'Carla,' she said, 'it's great you came over, but you have your own life in New York. You're a young woman, you'll be wanting to start a family. Collette wouldn't want you to stay here because of her.'

All this stuff about kids, everyone assumed it was next. I tried to imagine us with a kid, a baby, taking it on tour. Eddie and I had never talked about kids. Not properly. How had we managed to go eleven years and never talk about it?

'This thing can go on for years before there's any real problem. Your Mam seems fine to me, better, if anything.'

'Really?'

'Ah, yeah! She forgets the odd thing, but who doesn't when you get to our age? You heard her, remembering things from years ago, things I'd forgotten. I think the drugs she's on are working.'

Suzanne said the doctor had talked about taking Mum off the medication if the nightmares got worse. Delusions, she'd called them. But how did she know for sure it was working or not?

Roisin reached out and held my arm. 'You're a good daughter, Carla. I'm not saying you should disappear for another ten years but you're not stuck here. Now you have the visa, can't you come and go as often as you like?'

Before I could answer her we both heard the door open and Mum came in. If she knew by the silence that we'd been talking about her she didn't say anything. She put the back of her hand on the scones. 'Turn on the oven, Carla, will you?' she said. 'They're much nicer heated up.'

★

Outside it was nearly dark and I stood up to pull the curtains.

'I'd better be making tracks,' Roisin said, looking at her watch. 'The traffic is always desperate these days.'

'It's been great seeing you,' I said. 'You should come over again before I leave.'

Roisin smiled as she put on her coat. 'I'd love to. Maybe I will. I'll try.'

'Do,' I said, even though I knew she wouldn't.

She did up her buttons, tied the belt around her middle.

'Roisin,' Mum said, 'do you remember the night you first met Nat? The night you and Noel had that fierce row in O'Neill's?'

Roisin looked at Mum and then at me. 'That's right, Coll,' she said, patting Mum's arm. 'It was O'Neill's, not Mulligan's.'

Mum turned to me. 'She was raging when she got back to the flat. She'd told Noel that he could walk down the aisle with that English upstart because he wasn't going to be marrying her.'

Mum's laugh was a real one, but Roisin's was a beat off cue.

She adapted quickly. 'That's right,' she said. 'Nat was there, making them all laugh. As usual.'

The story was flat now, all of the life sucked out of it. Mum heard it too, looking from Roisin to me. I felt as if I was watching something on stage, something I wasn't part of.

'What?' Mum said. 'What is it?'

'Nothing, Coll!' Roisin smiled wider, talking more now, filling up the space between us all. 'We'd a humdinger that night, me and Noel. I told him what he could do with his engagement ring.'

Mum was still looking at me and I tried to make myself laugh, even smile, but I couldn't. A new stage. That was the thought, like a tickertape in my mind. This was the start of a new stage.

'Did we have this conversation already?' she said. 'We did, didn't we? Tell me, Carla, am I repeating myself?' Her eyes, holding mine, were still her eyes.

I didn't answer her. I didn't have to. I watched as she swallowed, then clamped her hand over her mouth.

'Mum?' I didn't know what I was going to say but I didn't get a chance to say anything because she ran past me and out the door. For a second, we just stood there, Roisin's hand over her mouth too, as we listened to Mum's footsteps in the hall, on the stairs.

'She's grand,' she said, 'just leave her.'

I wanted to believe her, but I couldn't. Before she could say anything else I was in the hall, on the stairs, taking them two at a time. Mum's bedroom door was closed.

'Mum?' I knocked. 'Mum?'

I turned the handle. It was locked. Her voice, when she answered, was muffled. 'I want to be on my own,' she said.

'Mum, are you OK?'

'I'm just tired.'

I tried the handle again. What was I supposed to do? What was in her room? Could she hurt herself? Should I call Suzanne? Lily-Anne? But what could they do that I couldn't?

'Is everything OK?' Roisin's voice drifted up from downstairs. I looked over the banisters and she had her coat buttoned, her handbag strap across her shoulders. I came slowly down the stairs.

'I would stay,' she said, jangling her keys, 'but if I'm not back by six Noel will send out a search party.'

'It's fine,' I said. 'You go on.'

'I think she's overreacting a bit, Carla. Sure, I repeat myself all the time, the kids are always telling me that.' Her hug was quick this time and she had the hall door open before I had a chance to reach for it. The smile on her face was fixed, a photograph smile, but I knew what hid behind it. 'I'll give you a ring tomorrow,' she said, opening the porch door and stepping out, 'to see how she is.'

'OK.'

'And have a safe trip back to New York, now, won't you?'

'I will.'

I watched her walk across the gravel, her footsteps quick in high heels. I tried to process what had happened in the last five minutes, how the afternoon had become such a disaster. When she got to the gate I waited for her to turn and wave the way she always did, but instead she rushed out of sight to where her car must have been parked, on the other side of the hedge.

★

I washed up the cups and plates and put the tray away. I left the radio off so I could hear any noise from upstairs, but it was quiet. I took the potatoes from the cupboard, rinsed them in the sink, scraped off the bad bits. The light came on when I turned on the oven. I dried them with kitchen paper before I put on the oil, spiking them with a fork the way Dad had shown me.

There was nothing on TV and I didn't feel like reading. I wandered into Mum's therapy room, sat in the chair, closed the blinds. Suzanne rang. Eddie texted and I texted him back. I put the chicken Kievs in to join the potatoes. No sign of Mum.

I made a noise going up the stairs and turned the landing light on. My knock on her door was authoritative, cheery. 'Mum? Dinner will be ready soon.' I turned the handle and this time the door opened. 'It's chicken Kiev.'

The light from the landing lit the bed. She was lying on it with her back to me. When she sat up I saw she was holding a cushion to her stomach. 'Are you OK, Mum?' I asked, in a way that meant I wanted her to be OK. I turned the lamp on. Her eyes were red, her mascara a mess on her face.

'The state of me,' she said, reaching for a tissue.

'You're grand,' I said. 'Roisin went.'

She nodded, blowing her nose.

'Dinner's nearly ready. Suzanne called, she's on her way.'

She nodded, tucked the tissue inside her sleeve and swung her feet to the floor. She sat there, her elbows on her knees, her hands covering her face. She was crying – she wasn't making any noise but I could tell by her shoulders. I didn't want to see her crying. I sat down next to her on the bed. 'Mum, I know you're upset but you just made a mistake. Anyone could. Roisin was just saying she repeats herself all the time. And it was only that one story. The rest of the afternoon was grand. You remembered loads of things she didn't – you didn't forget anyone's name, even.'

My words rattled out of me, one pulling the next. She opened the drawer of the bedside locker, took something out and passed it to me. It was a photograph, an old one with a white border. It took me a second to recognise the riverbank, the boat behind, Roisin in big sunglasses holding hands with two little girls on either side. One of them was me. Sitting in front of us on the grass, a little boy was clutching a beach ball.

Mum was watching me, waiting for me to get it. I turned the photograph over and on the back there was a date. Mum's writing: '1986, Carrick-on-Shannon. Roisin, Caroline, Carla and Stephen.' I turned it back and stared at the fixed blurry smiles.

'I keep thinking I've found a way to beat it,' she said. 'Remember the children's names, say them early. And it works, for now. Or it will, until I forget that there's a photo, or until I forget the people in it.' Her voice cracked.

'Mum.' I reached my hand out, put it on her knee. She covered it with hers. 'You don't know that's going to happen.'

'Don't I?'

Our feet lined up next to each other on the beige carpet, hers in stripy socks, mine in runners.

She took her hand away from mine and reached for another tissue. Before she could reach her face with it she crumpled it up. When she spoke her voice was tiny, a whisper, like it was only half her voice. 'I'm scared, Carla,' she said. 'I'm so fucking scared.'

She never cursed. Our feet were the same size, the same shape, our big toes smaller than the rest. I'd noticed that in yoga. 'I know,' I said. 'I know you are.' I reached for her hand again and she clasped mine hard. I ransacked every brain cell, every thought, for something to say that would make things better. I had to make things better. 'You don't know how things are going to pan out, Mum. You're doing so well. Even Roisin was saying she thought the drugs were working. They might even find a cure.'

As I spoke, I knew the sound in my voice had been desperation, not hope. Her eyes filled again. I don't know if she would have answered me or not because right then we heard the front door opening and Suzanne calling hello.

'Don't say anything,' Mum said, blowing her nose properly, wiping the mascara from under her eyes. 'She'll only worry.' She nodded, like I'd already agreed, all businesslike now, up on her feet, pushing her blouse back into her trousers, fixing her collar. It seemed like that was it, that it was over, only it couldn't be over. I stood by the door, my hands in my pockets. As she put on fresh mascara she caught my eye in the mirror. 'I'm fine,' she said. 'Everything's going to be fine.'

Coming downstairs, the house was full of the scent of chicken Kiev and potatoes but I didn't feel like it by then. I didn't feel like anything at all.

TWELVE

For the first time I was grateful for the neat list of numbers Suzanne had left on the fridge. They were in alphabetical order by last name: Billy Cassins, Dr Mairead Glavin, Patrick Kilfeather, Lily-Anne McDermott, Olga Nugent – I couldn't remember who half of them were.

Lily-Anne had two numbers listed, home and mobile. I dialled her mobile, half hoping that she wouldn't answer. The phone rang on. She was probably in a session with a client, or doing yoga, or walking Chips. She wasn't going to pick up.

She picked up. 'Hello?'

It was a bright hello, cheery, like she expected good news.

'Hi, Lily-Anne, it's Carla here.'

'Hello? Hello? Hang on, I can't hear you...'

There was a thump, a muffled noise, a dog barking. I heard her call out to Chips to relax and then louder, presumably to me: 'Just a minute, hold on a minute, I'm pulling over!'

I walked down the steps of the conservatory, sat in one of the wicker chairs. I hadn't done any yoga this morning, it wasn't the same without Mum. What if yesterday had been our last time? I took a deep breath.

'Sorry about that.' Lily-Anne's voice was on the line, clearer now. 'Hello, are you there? Hello?'

I'd hoped she'd see the number come up, save me the introduction, but it didn't seem that she had.

'Lily-Anne, it's Carla. Collette's daughter.'

'Carla! How are you? I was only just thinking about you. I was listening to the radio earlier and they advertised a lunchtime concert in the National Concert Hall. I was thinking the three of us could go.'

I hadn't expected that. I'd thought that once she'd heard me on the phone she'd know something was wrong. 'Oh,' I said, 'sure.'

'Excellent. I'll get the tickets. I think those concerts are on Thursdays. You're here for a few more Thursdays?'

I switched the phone to the other hand. 'Listen, Lily-Anne, I don't mean to cut across you but the reason I'm calling? It's Mum. She's not – she's not great today.'

'What's the matter? Has something happened?'

'She's still in bed,' I said. 'Usually she's played the piano by now and we've done some yoga, but she won't budge.'

'Will she eat?'

'I brought her up some tea and toast but she wouldn't touch them.'

'Is she talking? Crying?'

Her tone was totally different now, businesslike, efficient. I could almost see her sitting up straighter.

'She's not crying but she won't speak to me, just lies there, her face turned to the wall.'

A robin landed on the bird table in the back garden, pecked and flew away again. I wondered when anyone had last put out some seed.

'Did something happen to trigger it?'

I stood up and walked to the wall, stood next to the framed poster of the flamenco dancers. I loved that poster, the colours, the shape of their movement. 'I don't know if you know her friend Roisin. She came over yesterday.'

The pause was slight. 'Roisin, yes, of course.'

'Mum told her the same story twice. She got upset, confused. It'd been a few months since she'd seen her.'

'It's over a year I'd say,' Lily-Anne said.

Roisin had made out like it was just before Christmas but Lily-Anne sounded definite and something made me believe her.

Roisin had said she'd call this morning, and she hadn't yet. Then again, it wasn't even lunchtime.

'Anyway, Mum was upset afterwards, quiet over dinner. And now this. I thought – I thought you might know what to do.' I wanted her to come over but somehow I couldn't just come out and say it. Just like I couldn't tell her how panicked I was, that I'd tried Suzanne at the office too. Twice. That Lily-Anne was my last resort, that I'd no plan after that.

'You were right to ring me,' she said. 'I'm only down the road in Blackrock. I'll come over.'

I smiled. 'You're sure? It's not a problem?'

'Of course not. I'll be there in ten minutes.'

I started to tell her how much I appreciated it but she'd already hung up. The relief that she was coming, that I wasn't on my own, flooded my body. I tilted my head and stared at the ceiling. Upstairs Mum was lying there, staring at another one.

The echo of her voice from last night ran through my head. *I'm so fucking scared, Carla.* She wasn't the only one.

★

There was a smell in the hall of something frying. Sausages. The sound of the radio. It had been Lily-Anne's idea that I should get out in the air, go for a run, and at first I'd said no. I'd felt guilty, leaving Mum, ashamed at how good it felt to close the door behind me, but now that I'd been out I felt so much better coming back.

Upstairs, I could hear the shower.

'Hi,' I said, as I opened the kitchen door.

Lily-Anne was standing at the cooker, her back to me. When she turned I saw she was wearing an apron I'd sent Mum from New York, the one with the subway map on it.

'What do you think?' she said, holding it out so I could see it properly. 'I was just trying to figure out the quickest way from Times Square to 42nd Street.'

Chips came out from under the table, sniffing at my runners, my knees.

I laughed. 'Times Square *is* 42nd Street!'

She turned back to the frying pan. I saw there were tomatoes as well as sausages, mushrooms, potato cakes, black pudding. It was comforting to see her at the cooker, her long white ponytail straight down her back. 'Where did all this come from?'

'When you phoned I'd just been to Superquinn. Joe loves his fries.'

'Sorry – you should have said. I'll go down to the shop now, pick up some more stuff.'

She waved a spatula in my direction. 'Don't talk nonsense. Sure I'll just swing by again on my way home.'

I filled a glass from the tap, drank it quickly. I wondered if I should offer to give her the money but it was for Mum to do that, really, not me. Chips wandered around my legs and went back to his vigil by Lily-Anne, his neck craned upwards towards the food.

'I heard the shower on – you got her up. Well done.' I sat down in the chair that was always *my* chair.

'She got herself up,' she said, without turning.

'She wouldn't move for me. You must've done something right. What's your secret?'

She lowered the heat under the frying pan and turned around. 'No secret. I asked her to talk to me, to tell me what was going on, and she did. I listened, that's all.' She bent to take a box of eggs from the fridge, holding Chips's head away with her knee. She cracked them straight on the edge of the pan, the oil sizzling as they landed. Dad always did the eggs like that when he made a fry. Mum always broke them into a bowl first.

I pushed back in my chair. 'You must have done more than that. I tried to talk to her last night, this morning. Nothing I said made it any better.'

There was silence when I said that, the sound of the food frying, the spatula in the pan.

'I found that one of the hardest things in my training was learning to just listen, to let go of trying to make things better for people. It sounds easy, but it isn't.'

I stood up to get some more water. Mum used to do that too, pretend to talk about herself when really she was talking about me. It must've been one of those tricks they taught them in college.

I glugged the water, refilled the glass. 'Well, I'm just glad she's feeling better. I'll set the table.'

Chips followed me across the room to the press. I took out the plates, cups with matching saucers.

'I don't know if she is feeling better,' Lily-Anne said, from across the room. 'I suspect she's feeling the same. Depression is such a big part of this disease but, like anyone suffering from depression, it's sometimes easier for her not to let us see it. You know how good she is at putting on a mask.'

I put a plate down in my place, then Mum's. The hand holding Lily-Anne's hovered between Dad's place and Suzanne's before choosing Suzanne's. I hadn't known that, about the mask. *I'm so fucking scared, Carla.* The mask had slipped to show me her fear and I'd wanted her to put it straight back on. I hadn't wanted to see the truth.

I opened the drawer next to Lily-Anne, took out knives and forks. 'I can't stay here,' I said. 'You know I can't.'

She turned to me, her face red from the heat. I felt something at my foot and looked down. Chips was sniffing my laces.

'Do you think that's what I meant, that I think you should?'

'Suzanne's stopped saying it, but I know she does.'

Lily-Anne walked over to the oven, took out some warm plates. We weren't going to need the ones I'd put out.

'Your sister's scared of dealing with this on her own. That's all. Maybe she just needs to know you're there for her.'

Suzanne was scared. So was Mum. And so was I. Was that what fear did? Split everyone apart?

'I'm going at the end of March but I'll come back again soon, maybe September. That's what I've decided.' I laid out the knives and forks, collected the plates we didn't need.

'You know you have to do what *you* want, Carla, not what

Suzanne wants, or your mum, or Eddie. "To thine own self be true" and all that.'

'*Hamlet*,' I said. 'One of the only quotes I remember.'

She smiled as she dished up the tomatoes, the triangles of potato cakes, the eggs. 'I forget to give Shakespeare credit for that sometimes. I've read so much of what Melody Beattie's written about co-dependency that I've started to think she came up with it.'

I took a second glance at her, to see if she was making a point, if she knew somehow that of all the books in Mum's office that was the one I'd read. 'I hadn't pegged you for such a Philistine, Lily-Anne,' I said. 'There were books before self-help ones, you know.'

Lily-Anne laughed her big laugh. 'Sometimes I need to be reminded about that.'

When she put the sausages on the plates they were split down the middle so their insides seeped out, the way Dad always used to cook them. One rolled off the spatula and Chips caught it between his teeth. He ran to the corner by the back door where he held it between his paws, nipping off the top and chewing fast.

'Would you look at that?' she said. 'Would you not always drop something on purpose, just to see that face? Just watch. He'll be back in a minute to lick the floor.'

I reached over for the plates. 'Well, let me put these out before he gets any more of our lunch.' I smiled so she'd know it was a joke. Her hand found my arm, squeezed it. Close up her face had hardly any wrinkles. 'You can handle this, Carla,' she said. 'Whatever you decide, you'll handle it.'

Her grip was tight as if she wanted to impart her knowledge through her fingertips. I'd already decided, I'd told her that, and I wondered then if she'd been listening to me at all. Below us, Chips was licking the floor now, just like she'd said he would. I stepped around him and went to the hall to call Mum.

THIRTEEN

Walking up the steps towards the heavy double doors I knew it was going to be the kind of bar I hated. Inside, it was purposely dark, the lighting barely enough to see the empty tables and chairs where people should have been. From behind the swirling counter the bottles glowed on brightly lit shelves.

'What are you having?' Suzanne said, reaching into her bag.

'I'll get it.'

She waved my hand away, leaned against the bar. 'You find us a table.'

'Thanks. A bottle of Miller, please.'

I walked up the shallow steps towards a row of booths by the window, choosing one in the middle. The leather felt fake and there was some weird patterned trim along the edge. Coming here had been Suzanne's idea – the whole night, in fact, had been her idea. I'd been shocked when she'd suggested it, had tried to remember another time that we'd been out like this, for a drink, just the two of us, and I couldn't. I pushed closer to the window, trying to make out the view. Suzanne said on a summer evening you could see the whole harbour from here. On this rainy Tuesday I could see just my face, reflected in the darkness.

'Here you go.'

Suzanne slid the beer and a glass filled with ice cubes towards me. She'd got a little bottle of red wine for herself.

'Thanks,' I said, wiping the top of the bottle with the little white napkin she'd handed me. 'Cheers.'

She poured the wine into her glass. 'Cheers.'

The beer was lovely and cold. I couldn't believe it was my first in over a month, my only night out in Dublin so far, a mid-week drink in Dun Laoghaire with my sister.

'I'm not sure what I think of this place,' she said. 'Maybe it tries a bit too hard.' She smiled, and in the dim light she looked softer than she usually did. She'd changed after work into an olive green jumper with long beads. The colour was nice against her skin.

'Looks like they've invested a lot of money in it,' I said, looking at the low chandeliers. 'We're going to need to drink a lot to keep them in business.'

Suzanne laughed. 'Don't worry, it gets packed at weekends.'

'This is where you come at weekends?'

She shook her head. 'Not really. It's hard to get out, you know, with Mum.'

She could've gone out any of the last five Saturday nights I'd been there and she had just once, to some birthday party. On Friday nights she had drinks after work, but she was home by nine. I wondered if Mum could almost be an excuse.

A couple walked past us and I watched as they hovered between two tables, choosing the one furthest away.

'First date,' I said. 'I bet you anything.'

Suzanne glanced around. 'You think?'

'Oh, yeah – you can tell by the body language.'

'It's been so long since I've been on a date I've probably forgotten.' She filled her glass with the rest of the wine.

'Knowing you, it can't have been that long.'

'Really,' she said, swivelling the glass on the white napkin. 'You don't want to know.'

'Well, me too. In fact I don't know if me and Eddie actually ever went on a formal date. Or me and Damien. How sad is that? To have never gone on a date!' I smiled and drank some beer.

'Lucky you,' she said. 'I'd have loved to avoid the dating game entirely.'

'Ah, I don't know.'

Suzanne looked out the window and back to me. 'Seriously, you are lucky, what you and Eddie have. Very lucky.'

I picked at the label on my beer bottle. 'Things aren't always perfect, you know.'

She took another sip of wine. It seemed to be going fast. Her car was in the car park downstairs, I was surprised she'd had anything at all.

'Since when is any relationship perfect? You've been together for ever, you love each other, you never seem to fight. What more do you want?'

I thought of the conversation we'd had on the phone earlier, the one that hadn't quite been a fight. It looked like the tour was coming through, that Eddie might be on the road as soon as I got home. He'd been excited, couldn't understand why I wasn't, why I might not want to pick up and go straight away. It hadn't been the right time to ask him if he'd ever consider living in Ireland but I'd asked anyway. He'd assumed I was joking.

'I know,' I said. 'I *am* lucky. Being here, though, away from him, has made me see how wrapped up I can get in his stuff, the band and that.'

She nodded, waiting.

'I was thinking that when I get back I might look for a new job. Now that I have a visa I can get something different, a proper job.'

Eddie didn't get it when I'd said that about a job. He'd kept saying we'd have enough money from the tour for us both, that he thought I'd be happy to jack in waiting tables for a while.

'What kind of job?' she said.

'Anything, except waitressing!' I laughed. 'I don't know. You seem to like yours.'

She stuck out her bottom lip, nodded. 'Yeah, it's fine. A lot of responsibility, good money.'

I took another slug of beer. The bottle was nearly empty now. 'It's funny,' I said, 'but growing up I'd never have pictured you in an office job. Remember you always wanted to coach hockey for Ireland?'

She peered at her fingers, turning her glass full circle. 'God, I'd forgotten that.'

'Did you ever think about it? Not for Ireland, I mean, but a club or a school or something?'

'Yeah, right, like coaching hockey's going to pay my mortgage.'

'It must pay something. Anyway, don't your tenants pay the mortgage?'

'Even if I wanted to, I couldn't with my knee. I can barely run any more.'

I rolled the bottle from side to side, thinking about it. It was warm between my hands. 'I don't remember the coaches at school running much. Could you just—'

She was shaking her head as I spoke. She wasn't going to let me finish. 'No! I couldn't.'

'You don't even know what I was going to say.'

'It doesn't matter, Carla. You can't just be whoever you want to be, do whatever you want.'

'Why not?'

'Because . . .' She drank some more wine. 'Because it's not the way it works. You make compromises, choices. People have responsibilities, Carla.'

I didn't say anything; there was no point. For once I wasn't trying to annoy her, I was trying to help, but it had had the same effect. 'Fine,' I said. 'Whatever. Do you want another drink?'

'I'll have a sparkling water and cranberry juice. And then I want to talk about Mammy. They'll be back from the meditation session at ten and we don't want Lily-Anne to have to hang around for us.'

She had her preachy voice on again, the one I hated. 'Fine by me,' I said, and pushed my way out of the booth towards the bar.

★

I went via the toilets even though I didn't need to. At the bar, the guy from the couple I thought were first-daters was being served two pints of Guinness. I took some money from my purse and waited.

Suzanne was scared, Lily-Anne had said, and maybe she was right. I needed to show her that I wasn't running away from this, like she thought I was going to. I gave my order to the girl behind the bar and paid her. The trick was to be assertive, not to end up on the back foot. There was something about the way Suzanne had started talking that made me feel seven years old again.

I carried the drinks back on a tray. Suzanne's shoulders were hunched. She turned when she heard me coming.

'Here,' I said. 'I got Pringles too. Take whichever flavour you want.'

'Thanks.'

She took the ready-salted, leaving me sour cream and onion. I dumped the tray on an empty table and started talking before I was even back in my seat. 'Look,' I said. 'I just want to say something before we get into the nitty-gritty. I know you're right that Mum's sicker than I first thought she was. I see that now.'

She mixed the juice with the water, then opened the tub of Pringles.

'And I want you to know that I'm not just going to disappear back to New York and not give you support. I'll be on the phone, Skype, all the time. The flights are crazy money in the summer but I'll be back in September. Maybe for six weeks again, longer even. You could go on holidays, get away.'

I waited for her to say something, but she only nodded slightly. I wiped the top of the new Miller, drank some.

'What about your new job?' she said.

'What?'

'The job we were just talking about you looking for when you go back. How are you going to get all that time off from a new job?'

'Come on, Suzanne, there is no new job yet. I was only saying I might look for one—'

'And I'm only saying that I don't want you to make half-commitments, promises you can't keep.'

Behind her, the double doors opened and a group of guys in football shirts came down the steps. She took another handful of Pringles. Her earlier softness was gone, her jaw crunching through the crisps. 'Once you pop, you can't stop,' she said.

'Suzanne, I know you're angry, I know you think it's selfish, but I can't stay. I can't.' I made my voice sound reasonable, flattened my palms on the table. 'But tell me what else you want – financial support, visits, whatever – and I'll see what I can do.'

'Financial support?'

'Yes. You said something about that before and I'd be in a better position to pay my share if I get a decent job.'

She took some more crisps and ate them slowly this time, picking one after another from her palm. 'That's not what I meant. We need to plan for Mammy's savings, her investments, the insurance from Daddy, the house – make sure it's all set up for the long haul.'

I didn't get it. 'What do you mean? Mum's never had money worries. Won't those things just tick along?'

She rubbed her hair off her face so it stood up at an angle until she flattened it again. 'We need to make sure the money is invested safely, not high-risk stuff. We want it to give long-term returns.'

'Investments and returns? Come on, that's your area, not mine. I wouldn't have a clue.' I swallowed some more beer. Until six months ago I hadn't been able to open a bank account and I still hadn't got around to it. Not that she needed to know that.

'I'm not talking about where to invest it, Carla, we can get a financial adviser to help with that. But there are other decisions we need to make, about nursing homes, the house. We could sell it or rent it out, only I don't think the rent would cover the nursing-home fees.'

She was so matter-of-fact, sitting there across the table with her hand around her glass. She could've been talking about

222

anything, but she was talking about putting our mother in some institution and selling our home.

'Sell the house? Suzanne, come on, you're jumping way into the future now. Mum's a long way off a nursing home.'

'Is she, Carla? How do you know? I don't. Something new seems to be happening every week now, every day. Even in the time you've been here.'

I could feel the effects of the beer already, a tingling in my legs. I had to keep my head clear. 'We have to stay in the day with this stuff – we can't go flying off into the future—'

She held her hand up. 'The last thing I'd want is for Mammy to leave her house but some day she'll have to. It mightn't be today or tomorrow but it's something we have to plan for.'

Planning, planning, it was all about the plan. I pushed back hard into the booth, folded my arms. I was about to say that Mum's illness wasn't some IT project, that she couldn't work it out on flipcharts and whiteboards, when I noticed that her eyes were shiny. The tears were holding on, just about, and I didn't want to make them fall.

I kept quiet, let her talk about something called 'power of attorney', something that meant Mum would sign over decision-making to us. It needed to be done when she was still well, apparently, still of sound mind. Suzanne wanted to make an appointment with the solicitor, for the three of us, before I went back.

The girl from the couple behind her got up. She was off to the bar again. The date must be going well. She looked a good bit older than him.

'Carla? Are you even listening to me?'

I looked at her. 'I'm listening,' I said. 'I'm sorry, but I'm struggling with this.'

'Look, it's only legal jargon, it means—'

'No, not that.' I shook my head. 'I get that.'

Two little lines of frown formed between Suzanne's eyebrows, the same two lines that Mum had.

'What, then?'

I took a breath. 'All of it, I suppose. I'm struggling with all of it.'

She sighed, pushed her glass away, brushed some Pringles crumbs from the table into her napkin. 'I know I might sound detached,' she said. 'Even cold. But this is the only way I can deal with it, Carla. If I start to let my emotions in, or out, or wherever they need to go, I'll never be able to turn them off again. And that won't help anyone. It won't help Mammy.' She looked out the window and then back to me. 'Do you understand?'

There was something about the way she held my eyes that made me think about those long nights after Dad died. Lying awake and listening to her through the wall between our bedrooms – pacing, crying, Mum's voice low as she tried to comfort her.

'I understand,' I said. I lifted my bottle but put it down without drinking. I'd never asked her about all that, the counselling, if it had helped. But it wasn't the time now.

Across the table she nodded, gave a half-smile.

'I understand,' I said again.

FOURTEEN

Outside, I heard an engine stopping. When I looked out my bedroom window, Lily-Anne's car was pulled across the driveway. 'Shit.' I took off the silver necklace, put on the beads instead. Too long. My pendant would go, the one with the navy blue stone. I turned my little jewellery box upside down on the dresser. It wasn't there. Downstairs, the doorbell rang. I checked my desk, my bag. It wasn't there either.

'Carla! Lily-Anne's here!'

'Coming, Mum!'

The silver necklace would have to do. When I went back to the dresser, the navy pendant was on top of the pile where it must have been all along.

'Carla, are you ready?'

'I'm coming!'

The clasp was stuck and I forced it, bending the metal. Mum needn't have sounded so impatient – if it hadn't been for her I'd've been ready ages ago.

In the mirror I saw a line of foundation on my jaw and rubbed at it hard. My hair was horrible, that in-between length with the colour growing out, a line of light brown at the roots. I pulled it back in a ponytail. It'd have to do.

'Carla, we don't want to be late!'

Lily-Anne's voice now. Dithering by the wardrobe I pulled out my leather jacket. 'Coming! I'm ready!'

At the bottom of the stairs Mum was chatting to Lily-Anne as if nothing had happened, her hands in black velvet gloves, holding her silver bag.

'Sorry,' I said. 'I wasn't quite sure what to wear to the National Concert Hall.'

'Anything goes, really,' Lily-Anne said. 'As you can see, I took hours to get ready myself.'

She laughed her big laugh, twirling to give me a full view of her long purple skirt and the matching velvet bow at the end of her white plait. Over the skirt, something wasn't quite right and I saw it was a fanny pack, poking out just below her jumper.

'I know, I know. Who wears a bum bag to the concert hall?' she said, patting it. 'But I've never been one for handbags and this is so handy. I'd wear it anywhere, wouldn't I, Coll?'

'She would,' Mum said, nodding.

'At least one of us scrubs up well, though,' Lily-Anne said. 'Doesn't she look nice?'

Mum smiled at me and I wondered if she remembered that I'd dressed her, that I knew every stitch she was wearing under her long grey coat, the hooks of her bra, the twist of her tights, things I shouldn't know. I didn't know what had panicked me more: finding her on her hunkers in front of the wardrobe, insisting there were people in there, or the fact that she was naked.

She didn't remember, I could tell, and I was glad. She'd done her makeup herself, and she'd picked out a scarf too, a silver and black one that she'd tied off to the side in a way I could never tie scarves. 'You look lovely, Mum,' I said. 'I'll be proud to be seen at the concert hall with you.'

'And with me too, I hope,' Lily-Anne said, with a wink.

As I locked the front door, I wondered if Lily-Anne knew what I was thinking – that she was the one who looked like the Alzheimer's patient, not Mum. Hurrying down the driveway after them towards the navy blue Volvo I pushed the thought away. The car's back door opened with a clank and I shoved a dog-haired blanket over to make room.

'No Chips today?' I said.

'Ah, no,' she said. 'I couldn't leave him in the car for that long.

He's at home, with his daddy.'

She yanked at the steering wheel, pulling it around three times before she got the car away from the kerb. My mind only then registered the two long scratches I'd seen along the side. I wound the window down to let in a line of air.

Lily-Anne stopped suddenly at the entrance to the main road. The blanket slid from the seat and on to the floor. In the front, Mum jerked against her seatbelt. At least she had one. In the rear-view mirror Lily-Anne's eyes sought mine. 'Do you like classical music, Carla?' she said. 'Who's your favourite composer?'

We picked up speed down the hill and drove towards the coast road.

'I wouldn't have a clue. It's not really my thing.'

As soon as I said it I felt like a sulky teenager, that the next words out of my mouth would be that I only liked groups on *Top of the Pops*. She was the one who'd bought the tickets and I'd been looking forward to it, genuinely, until earlier. Maybe I should've called her. Maybe we should have cancelled. Mum turned to me.

'You like what I play for you in the mornings,' she said, 'and I've heard you humming to my station on the radio.' She smiled her wide smile and I was glad then that I hadn't said anything.

The car came to a sudden stop at the lights.

'Ha-ha!' Lily-Anne said. 'A closet Lyric FM fan. I'd put it on to get you in the mood, if only the radio worked.' She laughed her laugh again. It had been growing on me, or I'd been becoming immune to it, but in the confines of the car it grated again. I pushed myself back in the seat, remembered to breathe. Audrey had shown us an easy meditation last week, using one nostril first, then the other. Mum and Lily-Anne were talking about some other concert they'd been to, chamber music.

Outside the window the sea skimmed alongside us, clouds hanging just over the surface. Looking at the lines of colour a memory came and I didn't push it away. The game Dad and I always played, naming the colours in the sky, the water. Whoever ran out of colours first lost.

Lily-Anne slowed down and I could see the railings, the steps, the Martello tower below. They looked like the same railings that were there when I was too young to sit in the front seat, and Dad had let me anyway, when I'd learned the words 'violet' and 'indigo' and 'russet'. I remembered the time I beat him by saying 'ochre', the surprise in his smile as he looked at me sideways from behind the steering wheel. I won an ice cream that day, a 99 from Teddy's, for my trouble. I didn't tell him I didn't know what colour it was at all, that I'd heard it in one of the songs from *Joseph and the Amazing Technicolor Dreamcoat*, that there were so many colours in the sky I'd only been guessing it must be one of them.

We picked up speed again, turning into more traffic on the main road. Over my shoulder all I could see were anoraks and umbrellas on the back window ledge, for now the sea was gone, just like the memory.

*

Lily-Anne somehow found parking on Stephen's Green, jutting the car between two smaller ones so the boxy boot stuck out, as if it was waiting for the passing traffic to clip it off. While she ran to pay for parking, Mum and I waited, the only two people standing still, it seemed, in the swarm of Dublin's Thursday lunchtime crowd. Everyone seemed to be smartly dressed in office clothes, stepping around each other like some complicated dance, never missing a beat of conversation on their mobile phones, never spilling a drop of coffee.

Lily-Anne reappeared, waving a white ticket that she put on the dashboard. 'It's ten to! Come on, girls!' She linked both our arms, her grip tight, steering us across the road and into the Green. I was conscious of how we must look, the three of us. We seemed to be walking in the opposite direction to everyone else and they parted to let us through, stepping on to the grass. Watching them as they passed was mesmerising, their certainty, their sense of purpose. Mostly they were my age, younger. How had they got to be so sure of their place in the world? Or were they only pretending?

We got there in time and Lily-Anne led the way through the foyer and to our row, thanking the people who stood to let us through. As we sat down in the felt seats, Mum turned to me and smiled, the last thing I saw before the lights dimmed, leaving only a single spotlight on stage, a circle of light that fell on a woman, dressed in black. She started to sing, alongside a single violin. I wondered if Eddie would like it, and realised I had no idea.

I didn't know the music, but that didn't matter. It was intricate, delicate and strong at the same time, layers of cello, double bass and piano that wrapped around the audience, holding us tight until they let us go and suddenly the lights came on. Mum and Lily-Anne were on their feet and I stood up and joined them, clapping until my palms buzzed.

I leaned over to Lily-Anne. 'That was amazing. Thanks so much.'

'Wasn't it breathtaking?' she said. 'I'm so glad you came.'

We shuffled out with the rest of the crowd, and as we made our way up the narrow steps, I spotted a sign for the toilet. 'I'm going to run to the loo,' I said. 'I'll see you in the café.'

Lily-Anne stopped. 'Coll, do you need to go to the toilet?' she said. 'Carla's going now – might be good to go before lunch.'

People squeezed past and I could sense their eyes on us but Lily-Anne was oblivious. I wished she'd notice, that she'd stop talking to Mum as if she was a child where everyone could hear.

'OK,' Mum said. 'I'll go with Carla.'

Lily-Anne took my hand and put it on Mum's arm. 'Make sure you hang on to her,' she whispered. 'She's not great in crowds.'

Mum didn't say anything and I pulled her behind me until we joined a queue of women that edged out of the cloakroom door, all of them Mum's age or older. She looked better than any of them I decided, her skin clearer, her figure slimmer. No one would ever know that she was the one who was sick.

'Carla Matthews!'

I heard the voice before I saw her, the roundish woman with the blonde hair and the brown coat who stopped in front of me.

'It's you, isn't it? I'd know you anywhere!'

She smiled and I recognised her then, the shape of her eyes, the curve of her mouth. I could see that face, above the collar and tie of a school uniform. 'Celia?' I said. 'Celia Clarke?'

'Celia O'Riada now,' she said. 'A bit of a mouthful, Tomás is from the west, Mayo, near Geesala.'

She said it like I might know it so I nodded, in case I should. 'Oh, right. You live in Mayo?'

'God, no!' She laughed, flicking her hair back. 'We're out in Glasnevin.'

The queue shuffled along, three people ahead of Mum. Celia shuffled with us and I thought about introducing her but Mum wasn't paying attention and, anyway, it was easier not to, just in case.

'The last I heard of you was that you did a bunk to America, ran off with some fella and joined a band,' she said. 'Imagine you dropping out of college, with all your brains.'

I laughed. 'You're half right. Where did you hear that?'

'Sure Dublin's only a village.' She winked. 'Tell me, anyway, did it work out?'

The question surprised me, and before I could think of another way to answer it, I found myself telling her that it had, that we'd got married a few months ago. I glanced at Mum, who was next in line. A cubicle opened and Mum smiled at me before she went in. Celia was still talking, rattling on about her children, that one of them would be starting in secondary school next year. She laughed, showing lipstick on her teeth.

Another cubicle opened and I excused myself, nodding at whatever she was saying about a reunion. Relief mixed with irritation. Had Dublin always been full of people like her, people who seemed to know your business before you even knew it yourself?

I thought Mum would be there when I came out but her cubicle was still closed. The water was too hot as I washed my hands. There was still a queue. A woman was putting on lipstick, getting in everyone's way. I waited for the hand-dryer. From the corner of my eye I saw the door to Mum's cubicle open. A woman came out, small, in a red coat. Maybe I'd got it wrong. Mum must've been in the other one.

When my hands were dry I went to the door in case Mum was outside. The last of the queue snaked around the corner. I walked the length of it. No sign of her. When I came back into the cloakroom another door closed, next to the one I thought she'd been in. Two women washed their hands, the one with the lipstick dabbed her mouth with a tissue.

Maybe I'd missed her outside. Maybe she'd gone to the end of the corridor. I walked as far as the corner, down the queue and back again. It was shorter now, hardly a queue at all. Back in the cloakroom I washed my hands again, watching as each toilet emptied in turn, a different person coming out each time. None of them was Mum. There was no queue now, only one woman, on her phone.

Mum must have gone back to meet Lily-Anne. They were probably eating lunch already, wondering where I was. An image formed in my mind of earlier that morning, Mum on her hands and knees by the wardrobe, seeing something I couldn't see. The memory of her nakedness still shocked me, the knobbles of her spine, a long green vein snaking down the back of her thigh. When she stood up to face me, water from her hair had made little puddles in the hollows of her collar bones.

A woman in a navy uniform came towards me in the corridor. I thought about stopping her, asking for help, but she'd already passed me by the time I'd decided what to say. In the lobby the crowds were dwindling. I locked my gaze on every person, homing in so the detail of them was razor sharp before I moved on. A man helping his wife put her coat on. Two women laughing by the door, one with a purple bag over her shoulder. The sounds of a restaurant: laughter, voices, cutlery on plates. That was where she was, with Lily-Anne. I was sure, I was absolutely sure.

The first person I saw when I walked in was Celia, with three other women at a table by the window. She waved, looked like she was trying to call me over, but I kept going. I scanned the tables, all women, nearly all. No Mum, no Lily-Anne. At the back, steps, another room. Maybe I'd got the arrangement wrong, maybe we were meeting somewhere else – but no, there she was, Lily-Anne, all in purple, waving. She was alone.

I stopped dead. Behind me a waiter clipped my heel with his foot and sidestepped. For a second I thought I might be sick, right there in the middle of the restaurant. Lily-Anne was half standing now, craning her neck to see if Mum was behind me. I turned, as if somehow she might be there, but of course she wasn't.

I couldn't seem to make my feet move and Lily-Anne was up now, coming towards me. I felt an urge to turn away from her, to run back the way I'd come. I didn't want her to reach me, because when she reached me I'd have to know the truth – that I'd let my mother go missing.

FIFTEEN

Lily-Anne put her hand on my back, pulled out one of the three chairs at the table. 'What happened?'

My voice didn't sound like my voice as I told her the story, focusing too long on meeting Celia when this wasn't about Celia at all. As I came to the part in the toilets, my voice edged higher as the fear became fact: Mum was missing. 'I'm sorry,' I said. 'I'm so sorry. You said to watch her and I thought I was.'

She put her hand on my shoulder, the way I'd seen her do so many times with Mum. For someone with such small hands her grip was firm.

'It's OK,' she said. 'We'll find her. She's not missing, only lost. We'll find her. The important thing is not to panic.'

At the table next to us there were four women, younger than Lily-Anne, older than me. One of them was telling a story and the other three listening, soup spoons in mid-air. We should have been eating soup.

'Did you tell anyone? Anyone who works here?'

I thought of the woman in navy. 'No.'

'Did you try calling her on her mobile?'

I looked at her, took a breath. It was so obvious. 'No, I didn't even think of that. I'll do it now.'

'Good,' she said, standing up. 'If you get her, tell her to stay where she is, ask her to describe what she sees.'

'Where are you going?'

'I'm going to find the manager first, see if we can get all the staff looking for her while she's probably still in the building.'

My mind hadn't got to that place yet, the place where she was outside, crossing the road, somewhere in the crowds of Stephen's Green, Grafton Street.

'Don't worry, Carla, it'll be fine.'

She smiled but it didn't reach her eyes. I nodded, smiled too.

'Keep trying her on the phone, and if you reach her, call me. I'll switch my mobile on.'

She was halfway across the restaurant when I realised it didn't matter if her mobile was on or off – I didn't have her number, hadn't saved it into my phone. Suzanne would have it, though. Fuck. I was going to have to tell Suzanne.

My phone had been off and it took for ever to come on, the little icon connecting to find a network. My hand clenched around it, willing it to connect faster. When I looked up a waiter in black and white was standing beside me, his hand poised over a notepad. 'Are you ready to order?'

I looked at him, unable to understand what he was saying at first. 'No,' I said, 'not yet.'

There was a pause and he looked at the empty table, the three menus, and back towards the knot of people standing by the door.

'I'm waiting for someone.'

I waited for him to tell me I had to move, that I couldn't hold the table. I almost wanted him to. One word, that was all it would take, just one word.

He nodded, put the pad away. 'Call me over when you're ready.'

In my hand the phone beeped. A text from Eddie. I found Mum's number. Dialled it. She had to answer, she was going to answer.

'*Hi, you've reached Collette Matthews. I'm not able to take your call at the moment but if you leave your name and number I'll ring you back as soon as I can.*'

It was a long time since I'd heard that message. I hadn't called her since I'd come home. Was it my imagination or did she sound different now from the woman on the recording? I hit the redial button.

The wave of panicky sickness had been replaced by an absence of any feeling at all. I didn't wait for the whole message before hanging up. Sitting there, listening to the same snippet of Mum's voice, I felt almost invisible, somehow insulated from the other diners. I hit redial. Through the window I could see a tree blowing, sun on bare branches. Breath came, in and out.

'*Hi, you've reached Collette—*'

Lily-Anne had said to call Mum. I was doing that. I was doing the only thing I could do. I hit the green button again.

Lily-Anne had said not to panic and I wasn't going to, just like I hadn't panicked that Saturday morning in March. I hadn't panicked when I saw him from their bedroom window, crumpled over in the daffodils. I'd run downstairs, fast, but I kept my hand on the banisters all the way, I didn't panic. As I got close to where he lay, felt the grass, damp, cold on bare feet, wetting the ends of my pyjamas, I didn't scream.

Green button. '*Hi, you've reached—*'

I didn't want to remember that Saturday morning, not then, but suddenly it was all around me: Suzanne's footsteps in the side passage before I'd had a chance to do anything, her scream as she dropped to her knees, pulling at the neck of his polo shirt so it stretched out of shape and his glasses fell off. I hit the green button again, clenched the edge of the table, pushing the corner into my skin but it didn't work – I could still feel the grass, see the three tea-towels on the line. It was my own fault, earlier, for letting myself remember the game. That was the thing with memories: you didn't get to pick the ones you wanted to remember and the ones you wanted to forget.

'*Hi, you've—*'

Red button. The waiter cleared the next table, getting the diners ready for their main course. He didn't talk to them. I would've talked to them, customers loved chat and banter.

My fingers moved on the phone, one button to the next, red,

green. In my head I was calling another number, 999, talking to a man first, then a woman. I told her that I was getting up to help him, that I'd been on my way down, but she cut across me, asking me to describe his position, whether he had a pulse, if I knew CPR. We didn't have a cordless phone then but I didn't need to go out the back to describe the angle of his neck, his knee, the daffodil stalks broken and flattened under his arm. The picture in my mind was clearer than my own image, reflected in the mirror in the hall.

Red button, green button. I should call Suzanne. I couldn't call Suzanne. What could I tell her? I didn't have any more answers for her than I'd had that Saturday morning in March. The only thing I knew was that it was my fault, what had happened, just like before.

It was all my fault.

★

Lily-Anne came back with a man in a grey suit, the manager, Peter. He seemed young to be the manager, frightened. He asked me which cloakroom I'd used, what she'd been wearing, even though Lily-Anne must already have told him that.

He'd called the police, he said. We didn't need to wait here in the restaurant. He had somewhere better for us. I picked up my bag and followed Lily-Anne across the dining room. Her plait swung, the purple bow like a pendulum. I stepped around a waitress with a dripping bottle of water, passed people laughing, chatting, having lunch as if nothing had happened.

We waited in an office and a girl brought us coffee and sandwiches that we didn't eat. Lily-Anne called Suzanne, but her phone went to voicemail.

When the police arrived there were two of them, just like on TV, a woman and a man. They asked me the same questions. When had I last seen her? Might she have gone home? What was her mood like earlier today? Fine, I told them, glancing at Lily-Anne, who nodded, agreeing, yes, she was fine.

They told us to go home and wait for her, that they'd have people on alert here, in case she came back, but it felt wrong somehow, leaving. Outside the air was colder, carrying the yellowish tinge of evening. Ochre. We crossed at the lights, so many cars, buses, mopeds. People. We didn't talk. When we got to Lily-Anne's car it had been clamped – a flash of yellow on the wheel, a big white sticker on the window.

'Fuckers!' Lily-Anne said. 'Excuse my French but, really, they're fuckers.' She smacked the roof with the flat of her hand.

'I'm sorry, Lily-Anne, this is my fault—'

'Your fault? I must've missed that, when you ducked out to put the clamp on.'

At first I didn't get it, but then I did. It wasn't funny enough for a smile.

'It can damn well stay here. We're getting a taxi.'

The driver tried to talk at first, then stopped. Lily-Anne rang Joe and reached across the back seat to hold my fingers. I didn't pull away even after she'd hung up. My phone rang and we both jumped. It was Mum, it had to be. I fumbled for it in my bag, and when I took it out I saw it was Suzanne. I held it for a second before Lily-Anne took it from me.

'Will I tell her?' she said.

I nodded.

Outside the window there was concrete and cars, more concrete, more cars. I named the colours, wishing the taxi driver had taken the coast road.

'She took her eye off her while she used the loo,' Lily-Anne said. 'Just for one minute. I should've been there with them.'

Lily-Anne's fingers tightened around mine. She handed the phone to me. 'She wants to talk to you.'

Suzanne's voice was high, breathy. 'What happened?'

'I don't know Suzanne, one minute we were in the queue and the next—'

'You should've waited outside. I always wait outside for her.'

'I didn't know, I thought—'

237

'Did she seem OK before that? Did you notice anything this morning?'

I hesitated, swallowed. 'No, she was fine. She was in good form, enjoying the concert.'

Lily-Anne was nodding, agreeing, but she hadn't seen her that morning. I should've told her, even if it had meant rearranging the day, even if Mum had been annoyed. I should've told her.

Suzanne was going through lists of people we should call. Roisin, Olga Nugent, Dr Glavin. The taxi pulled into the estate, drove up the hill. The house was dark, no lights on.

'We're just home, Suzanne. Let me call you back when we get inside,' I said.

'She could be anywhere and it's getting dark. I can't believe you let this happen! I can't believe—'

I hung up. Lily-Anne was paying the driver. He was parked in the same spot as she'd parked four and a half hours earlier. Was that really all it had been? I wanted it to be then, to be rushing down the stairs again, I wanted Superman to come and twist the world back to when Lily-Anne had just arrived.

A light rain was falling. Lily-Anne put her hand on my shoulder as we went up the drive, past Mum's car that wasn't Mum's car any more. In the dark I couldn't see which key was which, and as I held them up, I saw that my hands were shaking.

'Come here, let me do that.'

Lily-Anne took them from me and I watched her open the locks, bottom, middle, top. The door swung open and I followed her into the hall. It was warm, the heating on and somehow it seemed to make it all the worse.

Lily-Anne turned to me. 'Suzanne's just scared. She didn't mean what she said – she knows it wasn't your fault.'

In the hall mirror I saw my face, the same face as I had seen all those years ago on that Saturday in March, older now. I saw it crumple and the tears I'd been holding back all day finally came.

★

The police who called up were different police but they asked the same questions. Closing the door after them, I saw another car pass them on the hill and something made me wait. The headlights were coming straight for our house. A black car. Suzanne's. My stomach sank. Tyres bounced over the kerb and crunched on to the gravel. There was someone with her in the passenger seat. A woman. Mum.

I was in the garden before I had time to call Lily-Anne. Mum took ages to get out but when she did she was smiling. She looked fine, her grey coat, her scarf, the silver handbag.

'Mum, where were you? We were so worried.'

Her hands were freezing and I realised her gloves were gone. 'I took the bus. Carla, why are you crying?'

Lily-Anne was beside me now, her hands feeling Mum's shoulders, sliding down her arms, checking maybe for broken bones, or to see if she was real. 'Are you all right, Coll? Are you sure you're all right?'

'Let's get her inside,' Suzanne said. 'She's freezing. Carla, get a blanket from upstairs. And a hot-water bottle.'

I took the stairs two at a time. On the landing I paused, lost for a few seconds, till I remembered what I needed, found them and bounded downstairs again. They were in the kitchen, Suzanne telling Lily-Anne over the sound of the kettle that she'd been on the way up the hill and had just seen her, walking, that she'd know her walk anywhere.

'I think she might have walked all the way,' she said. 'I didn't pass any bus, and she was freezing.'

'She'd hardly have walked from town,' Lily-Anne said, picking up Mum's bag and opening her purse. 'Then again there's twenty euro in here. If she'd bought a bus ticket, there'd be change.'

In the middle of them Mum yawned without covering her mouth. I wrapped the blanket around her, holding her shoulders. 'Do you want to go up to bed, Mum?'

Suzanne turned around. 'It's too early – she'll be up all night – and she hasn't eaten.' Seeing Mum's eyes were closed, she stopped, put the teapot down. 'OK, I'll take her up,' she said.

★

In the bright lights of the living room, Lily-Anne looked exhausted. She had her coat on, waiting for Joe. Upstairs we could hear footsteps, Suzanne's, Mum's.

'Would you say Suzanne's right, that she really walked out of town?' I asked.

She shrugged. 'Maybe. There was no sign of a bus ticket. But then again, I can imagine Coll just getting on the bus, swanning past the driver without a bother on her.'

We both smiled.

'I keep thinking, you know, what might have happened.'

She pulled her plait over her shoulder. 'Don't go there, Carla. She's home, she's safe. That's what matters.'

She was right. Outside we heard a car. Lily-Anne stood up, looked through the blinds. 'Here he is.'

I stood up. 'She wasn't herself this morning, Mum wasn't. I should've told you, said something, but I thought she'd be OK.' The words came out in a rush, directed at her Converse on the rug. 'Maybe we shouldn't have gone to the concert. Maybe we should've just stayed at home.'

The doorbell rang. When I looked up, I thought she might be angry, shocked, but her face was kind. 'Carla, your mum's OK. It wasn't your fault. Go easy on those "shoulds".'

The day, everything, was a blur of images, still too real to be a memory yet. As we walked into the hall I wanted to tell her how much it meant to me she was there, to thank her properly, but somehow the words wouldn't come and then Joe was there – a stocky man with a beard, nothing like I'd pictured – and it was too late anyway. I didn't say anything as I leaned down to hug her, or as I shook Joe's big hand. I didn't call after them as they walked, arm in arm, down the driveway.

240

But at the pillar, just before I slid the porch door closed, she turned back and waved and I thought that maybe I didn't need to say anything else. Maybe she already knew.

Sixteen

Suzanne was sitting in Mum's chair, her face lit by the silvery glow from the TV. On the table next to her was an empty crisps bowl, a bottle of wine with less than a quarter left. She looked up when she saw me. 'You're home early.' she said. 'Didn't expect to see you tonight.'

The glass in her hand was nearly empty.

I leaned against the wall. 'We were both kind of wrecked. We had a nice meal. It was time to call it a night.'

She looked at me for long enough so I knew she didn't believe me, but I didn't want to get into it all – how Ange had shown up half an hour late for dinner and yawned all the way through, the snippy conversation I'd had with Eddie on the phone on the way home.

She pushed herself up and refilled her glass.

'Can I talk to you for a minute?'

I hesitated, glanced at the TV. Some lame chat show, fake laughter from the studio audience. 'I'm pretty exhausted.'

'Just five minutes,' she said.

I walked across the room and sat in Dad's chair, kept my coat on. I wondered if she had any more wine.

'I'll turn this off.'

The room went dark, the afterglow from the TV, the sound of static. Suzanne turned the lamp on, and in its glow I saw her lips were wine-stained.

'Patrick Kilfeather got back to me today about the power of attorney,' she said, leaning forward, holding the glass between her knees. 'He'd been away. Lanzarote.'

An image surfaced of the three of us crammed into a tiny office in one of the Georgian houses on Fitzwilliam Square while a man with a country accent read Dad's will. He was older than Dad, with hair so thick it must've been a wig. 'I hadn't realised he was the one who'd do it,' I said. 'He never struck me as being the sharpest.'

'Me neither,' she said, 'but he's the one who sorted everything for Mammy, after Daddy died. And it seems she's already been in touch with him.'

She filled up her glass again, nearly emptied the bottle. I needed to pee.

'So? Were you able to get an appointment before Wednesday?'

'It looks like we don't need to come in. Mammy's already done it. It's all sorted.' She lifted her glass and drank the rest of the wine.

'That's great. She's saved us some work.'

I stood up and walked to the door. I had my hand on the handle before I saw her face and I knew I was missing something – something big.

'What?' I said. 'It's good news, isn't it?'

'No, it's not.' There was a drop of wine on her top lip and she licked it off. 'Because Mammy didn't sign power of attorney over to you or me. She signed it over to someone else.'

'Who?' I said.

'Guess.'

'I give up! Tell me.'

'Lily-Anne,' Suzanne said. 'Who else?'

I had my hand on the handle of the door and let it come up with a squeal. 'Lily-Anne?'

'He said it in passing, like he assumed I knew. I think Mammy'd told him we knew.'

'You'd think Lily-Anne would have said something. Maybe she thought Mum already had. Maybe she forgot.'

I sat down on the arm of the couch. People forgot things. I'd forgotten to call Eddie on Thursday night after Mum had gone missing. Once I'd have called him before anyone else.

'My guess is Lily-Anne didn't tell us because she didn't want to upset us,' Suzanne said.

'Maybe.' I thought it over. 'I don't think I'd have been upset, though, would you? Lily-Anne and Mum are so close. Thinking about it, it's not such a big deal, really.' Even as I said it, I felt that maybe it was a very big deal, that maybe I just hadn't got it yet. 'Well, is it? Am I missing something?'

She put her empty glass down, pulled her hairband out and pushed it back into her hair. 'That wasn't all he said, there was something else.'

She cleared her throat. I waited.

'I asked him when they got the paperwork made up. He wasn't supposed to tell me but I pushed him. This wasn't recent, Carla. Mammy signed her power of attorney over to Lily-Anne two and a half years ago. Two and a half years! That's almost two whole years before she told either of us that she was even sick.'

★

Lily-Anne sat on the arm of Mum's chair, even though there was room on the couch, where I was. Suzanne had been sitting down too, but now she was pacing, cutting a line on the floor between the two of them and me.

'The important thing,' she was saying, 'is that you haven't registered it yet. Once it's registered it's hard to revoke. You have to go to court. According to Patrick Kilfeather, changing the attorney before then is relatively straightforward.'

Kilfeather was such a ridiculous name. I wished we had another solicitor. Suzanne arrived at the window and turned back. I looked at Mum and Lily-Anne. The way they were sitting was deceptive, Lily-Anne on the arm of the chair, raised up like she was taller, Mum shrinking into her seat. Lily-Anne's eyes followed Suzanne. Mum's were fixed on her fingers, which were shredding a tissue on her lap.

'The four of us need to go in together and redo the paperwork. He has a slot on Monday afternoon.'

'Suzanne, would you mind sitting down?' Lily-Anne said. 'All this pacing is making me nervous.' She laughed a little but no one joined in, not even Mum. Suzanne sat down in Dad's chair and leaned forward.

'There are pros and cons to Mammy having Carla and me as joint attorneys but it seems the most logical thing to do. If a decision needs to be made when Carla's not here, I can call her and we can agree it.' She looked to me for approval and I nodded. The other day she'd told me she was getting a plasma-screen TV for Mum's therapy room, mentioned casually over breakfast how she was turning it into a second TV room. If she didn't ask me about things like that when I was here, how much input would I have from three thousand miles away?

Lily-Anne reached for Mum's shoulder. She kneaded it under her fingers. 'Can I say something?'

Suzanne waved a hand at her, and I had a sudden sharp image of her in a board meeting, giving a colleague just enough rope to hang himself.

'I know you're angry with your mother and me,' she looked from Suzanne to me, 'but, much as giving me power of attorney is an unpopular and in some ways impractical choice, given my age, you have to acknowledge that it's what she wants.'

Mum looked up at Lily-Anne and nodded.

'It's what she *did* want,' Suzanne said, 'not necessarily what she wants now, do you, Mammy?'

Mum turned to Suzanne, her eyes clear. 'Yes, I do.'

'You want Lily-Anne to act as your enduring power of attorney? To register her with a court of law when the time comes?'

Suzanne spoke fast, her eyebrows raised. Mum looked back to Lily-Anne.

'Would you stop coaxing her?' Suzanne burst out. 'Just let her speak for herself.'

Lily-Anne held her arms out wide. 'I didn't say a word. I'm just sitting here.'

'Why don't you sit over there, next to Carla?' Suzanne said. 'Give Mammy some space. She's not a puppet.'

An expression passed over Lily-Anne's face then that I hadn't seen before. It hardened her features, her jaw. I thought she was going to say something but she didn't. She got up slowly and came and sat at the other end of the couch from me. Alone, Mum seemed even smaller.

'So, Mammy,' Suzanne said, 'go on.'

Mum smiled at Suzanne, her face blank.

'You were about to tell us what exactly it is you want.'

'Did you hear me, love?' Mum said.

'You have to clearly state—' Suzanne's voice was bullying.

'Suzanne,' I broke in, 'come on.'

'She's told you several times what she wants,' Lily-Anne said, 'if you'd only listen to her.'

'I want her to tell me, clearly, that she wants you as her power of attorney, rather than us, her daughters,' Suzanne said. A patch of red was growing on her chest, snaking its way up her neck. 'And I want her to explain why.'

'For Pete's sake, I told you that already!' Lily-Anne hit the arm of the couch. 'It's because she loves you both so much! She didn't want to saddle you with the decisions she knew would have to be made. She wanted to give you whatever kind of freedom she could to live your own lives. That's why she nominated me. That's right, isn't it, Coll?'

Mum smiled again, and nodded, but she didn't seem to be following what Lily-Anne was saying any more than she'd followed Suzanne. She stood up and walked over to the window, leaving a trail of tissue on the carpet.

We watched her, all three of us, waiting for her to speak.

'That hedge needs a trim,' she said. 'I might go out and do it now.'

'Mammy, would you ever sit down,' Suzanne said. 'Now's not the time for trimming hedges.'

'She's getting agitated,' Lily-Anne said. 'This is all too much for her. Why doesn't she go and potter around in the back garden and we can get this sorted out between us?'

246

That was a good idea. I was about to offer to take her outside, to get some air, but Suzanne was shaking her head, her arms folded. 'Now *you're* not listening, Lily-Anne. Mammy's the one who needs to sort this out, who needs to set Patrick Kilfeather straight about what she wants—'

'Suzanne, she's told him what she wants.'

'No!' Suzanne stamped her foot, actually stamped it, there on the carpet. 'She wasn't thinking then, she can't have been. Otherwise she would have talked to us about it, wouldn't she, Carla?'

Having Suzanne say my name jerked me back into the room. I didn't want to be part of this, any part, but it seemed I already was.

'She should have told us, Lily-Anne,' I said, without looking at her. 'You have to understand where we're coming from.'

'I know, I said that to her at the time. She told me she'd discussed it with you. I don't know why she didn't.'

'And you never thought to ask one of us about it?' Suzanne's whole neck was red now. She went to say more but I got there first.

'Look, Lily-Anne, no one's blaming you for Mum's decision, it's not your fault she didn't tell us in the beginning,' I said, 'but we need to decide what's best for her now and in the future.'

Suzanne smiled a tight smile, nodded hard. Mum glanced at me and back to the garden. I wanted to pick the tissue up off the floor, to hide it, to take Mum's arm and sit her back in her chair. Six weeks ago I'd sat in this seat and she'd been fine. How had we gone from that to this?

'Don't you want to honour what your mother wants, Carla? Do you think I wouldn't do the very best for her? That I wouldn't always talk to you and Suzanne about any decision, even the smallest one?'

Lily-Anne was gazing at me, her blue eyes more watery than ever. Her voice was gentle, kind, the one she put on when she wanted you to do something. All those conversations we'd had and she'd never said anything, not a word. Two and a half years. Between my knees my hands were fists.

'As you said yourself, you're older, something could happen to you—'

'We can make provision for that, put in that it reverts to you,' she said, holding her palms out. 'It might already be in the agreement.'

I rubbed my palms on my jeans. 'Lily-Anne, for me your age isn't the biggest thing. It's not even that Mum chose you over us. I understand that she might have stuff she can talk to you about and not us. I get that.'

Suzanne was shaking her head as Lily-Anne nodded.

'But what I don't get is that you didn't tell us how bad things were, that neither of you did.' My voice cracked a little, but I kept going. 'And whatever about the decisions Mum makes, you don't have an excuse. I trusted you – we both did.'

'I'm sorry,' Lily-Anne said. 'I'm so very sorry.' She was crying now, shiny tracks on her pale skin. I was making her cry. By the window Mum was statue still, a sentinel. Suzanne covered her face with her hands.

'And that's the thing I can't get over. For you to act as Mum's power of attorney – to make those kind of decisions – we need to know we can trust you. And to know that you knew how much sicker Mum was? That you didn't tell me, tell us? I don't trust you Lily-Anne. I can't. Not anymore.'

I'd no tissue and wiped my nose on the corner of my sleeve, shiny ooze, like a snail's trail. I had to keep talking, to finish it.

'So I'm asking you – pleading with you – to use whatever influence you have over our mother to undo this, to help us to help her, in whatever way we can.'

By the window Mum had found another tissue and was shredding it on to the floor. I turned back to Lily-Anne, held her gaze. She looked sad, tired.

'OK,' she said. 'If that's what you think is best. OK.'

Seventeen

I was in my room, packing but not really packing. The backpack lay on the floor, and around me on the bed there were piles of clothes, some dirty, some clean. My grey hoody was missing and so was my stripy dress.

The knock on the door was light.

'Carla? It's me.'

Lily-Anne. We hadn't spoken since the meeting in Patrick Kilfeather's office. It was bigger than his old one, in a new glass building that overlooked the river. I'd heard her earlier, downstairs with Mum. Packing had been a good excuse to avoid her. There was nothing to say.

The knock knocked a second time.

On the white-painted door I thought I could still see the traces of four pieces of Blu-tack from where my poster of Dylan's *The Freewheelin'* album cover used to be. I remembered the day I'd ripped it down.

'Yes! What?'

She opened the door slowly and stood there, half in my room, half on the landing. She was wearing her purple Converse and rubbed one on top of the other. 'I see you're packing.'

I threw the vest top in my hands on to the bed next to me. 'I'm supposed to be, but honestly I don't know what I'm doing.'

'Can I sit down?'

'It's a free country.'

She picked her way around the albums on the floor by the record player. One of them was out of its cover, a circle of vinyl lying on the carpet. She picked it up and blew off the dust, then carefully slid it back into its sleeve. 'John Denver?' she said. 'He's more my era than yours.'

'The records were my dad's,' I said. 'They're mine now.'

I sounded like a surly teenager, but somehow I couldn't find any other way to talk to her. She took the clothes from the chair, lifted them on to the desk and sat down. The drawer was still slightly open from earlier when I'd been looking through some of the photos I'd put away all those years before. The one in the frame was face down so she didn't see me and Dad leaning on the railings at Brighton, our giant ice cream cones, our smiles. I hadn't decided yet if I was going to take it.

'I wanted to say goodbye to you,' she said, 'and that I'm sorry again for everything that happened.'

I picked up a T-shirt, started to roll it up.

'I understand why you and Suzanne had to do what you did. I respect that.'

I shoved the T-shirt into the bottom of the backpack and reached for another. I didn't look at her, it was easier not to. She kept talking.

'I've enjoyed getting to know you, Carla. I felt like we were developing a friendship, you and I. I hope we can get that back, even if you feel betrayed by me.'

If I felt betrayed? Sitting there, surrounded by my stuff, she looked so innocent, like she'd played no part in this at all.

'There are no ifs here, Lily-Anne. You betrayed my trust, plain and simple. You were the one person I confided in about how I was struggling with the decision to stay or go and you never said anything. Not one word.' In the winter light her skin was paler than ever. 'How are we supposed to be friends when I can't trust you?'

I threw the T-shirt in my hand on to the floor. It landed on my foot and I kicked it away.

'You're angry, Carla,' she said.

'Of course I'm fucking angry!' I looked right at her and

shouted the words. It felt good. 'Things were bad enough, but I was coping. I was.'

She nodded. I didn't need her to agree with me.

'But now this—' I ran out of words. 'I don't know.'

She had the decency to look down and I was glad I'd hurt her, like all this was hurting me. I watched her as she played with her necklace, her fingers stepping from the big purple beads to the smaller pearly ones as if she was saying the rosary. When she looked up her eyes had tears in them. 'I'm sorry I've made it harder for you. I am, truly. It's the last thing I wanted.'

I pulled the band from my hair and shook it loose, then pulled it back again.

'If you want to know the truth, I've struggled with it myself. I didn't want to be in this position. On one hand, I wanted your mother to keep her independence as long as she could and to respect her decisions. But then I wondered if it was a decision she'd have made if she wasn't sick.'

On the floor I counted the album covers, seven, eight, nine. I wondered was there any way to fit them into my backpack. I had to ask the obvious question. 'Why didn't Mum want us to know? Why did she want to keep it a secret?'

Lily-Anne dropped her necklace and rested her hands on her knees. 'I don't think it was so much that she wanted it to be secret . . .'

'Well, what, then?'

She shook her head. 'You know what she's like, how independent she is. She didn't want to be a burden on you and Suzanne. She didn't want you to feel you had to take care of her. She thought if she sorted some things out first, it would be easier.'

I couldn't believe what I was hearing. 'This is easier? Tell me, how is this fucking easy?'

I punched the mattress but it was too soft, silent. I wanted to hit something real, something hard.

Lily-Anne shifted in her chair. I thought she was going to get up and come to sit next to me on the bed, but she didn't. 'I know it's not easy. I don't think she meant this to happen. It was supposed to be for a while, so she could get used to it herself.'

'A while? Two and a half years? It's gone on longer probably, hasn't it? It could be three years, four.'

Lily-Anne kneaded her knees. 'Carla, I don't think she realised how much time was passing.'

'Exactly!' I punched the bed again. 'That's why you needed to step in. What am I supposed to do now? Go down to her room and blast her out of it for something she doesn't even remember? Will that make me feel better?'

'I don't know,' she said. 'What do you think?'

'Oh, Jesus Christ!' I stood up, wanting to pace, but there was no room. I kicked at the nearest thing to me, the pile of stupid self-help books by the bed. Lily-Anne's so-called toolbox. They tumbled over each other on to the carpet. 'Stop acting like my fucking shrink, Lily-Anne. I'm going back to New York tomorrow, a city full of shrinks. I can find one of my own.'

I scuffed at two remaining books so they skidded under the bed. I was raging at the people who had written them, Lily-Anne for making me read them and for not being the one with Alzheimer's. She was an old lady. She'd no kids. She should be the one with this horrible disease, not Mum. It wasn't fair. The thought nearly became words but I stopped them just in time. As quickly as the anger flashed it dropped away again, taking my energy with it. Suddenly I was tired, heavy. I sank down on to the bed.

'It's OK' she said. 'It's only anger. Just feel it, let it out.'

Her voice was gentle, tugging at something inside. I took a breath and swallowed, but it wasn't enough. I could feel the tears coming. I couldn't stop them this time, and I didn't want to. I covered my face with my hands, felt my elbows dig into my thighs. I was so tired of fighting them, of holding it together.

I started to cry. Whatever was coming was going to come and there was nothing I could do except let it flow through me and out the other side. I cried for Mum on her own downstairs, locked into her own house. I cried for Suzanne, at work, the look in her eyes this morning when she thanked me for making the coffee – she'd never thanked me before. And I cried for me. Most of all I cried for me.

When it was over, I felt freezing and rubbed my hands on my arms.

'Here,' Lily-Anne said, passing me a pack of tissues.

I took them from her and nearly made a joke about therapists always being prepared but I didn't. I was glad she hadn't moved to sit next to me. There was something else I needed to ask her. 'How long have you known, Lily-Anne? When did Mum find out?'

She sighed, played with her necklace. 'I first noticed something around the time your aunt died. I don't know if Collette had noticed before that.'

Olivia had died five years ago; no, longer. It was six years since that Christmas when Mum had come over, the time she'd brought the wine for Bonnie. Six years.

'One of the first real symptoms I noticed was her spelling,' she said. 'Your mum was a fantastic speller so I knew when I noticed her mistakes, they must have been bad.'

She smiled, like it was funny. In my mind I was racing over addresses on envelopes, Christmas cards, birthdays. I'd never noticed. Why hadn't I noticed? But there had been something.

'When we were in Montauk I got her the *Irish Times* and she did a bit of the Simplex crossword, not the hard one she always used to do. I remember noticing that.'

Lily-Anne nodded. 'Funny you should say that. I started to find her crosswords half finished around the house. I found myself checking to see how far she'd got, how much was filled in.'

I could picture the half-completed crosswords, a third done, less, the empty boxes like the cells in Mum's brain going missing.

Lily-Anne plucked at her necklace again, her eyes on the beads. 'Her GP said she was fine, that it was stress. She was still worried, though. She felt she wasn't present enough for her clients so she went to my doctor for a second opinion. I knew Olga'd take it seriously, even though I hoped against hope it wasn't what we were both afraid of.'

Downstairs the washing-machine jolted on to a spin cycle. I knew, I knew when Mum had said she was giving up her practice. Some part of me had known.

'She could've kept working. The results at that stage were inconclusive but a few things happened around the same time. She missed an appointment, she misplaced someone's notes. Before she got sick she hardly ever needed to take a note. I used to envy her that.'

Lily-Anne was telling me too much. I didn't want to picture Mum in tears, ransacking her office, the car, for missing notes. Confessing to some faceless client. Over her shoulder I could see the tickets for every gig I'd ever been to, a map of my teens pinned up on my notice board – Hothouse Flowers, U2, INXS, The Stunning. I'd forgotten I'd been to see The Stunning.

'When she asked me about the power of attorney thing she said she didn't want to choose between you and Suzanne, that she knew a shared one would only lead to strife.'

Strife. It was a good word to apply to me and Suzanne. Even now, even after I'd taken her side, there was tension between us. She still didn't think I should leave. She'd stopped saying it but I knew. And I had to leave. I couldn't stay.

'You still should have told us,' I said, 'especially when you saw Mum getting sicker. It wasn't your decision, Lily-Anne.'

She smiled a sad smile. A strand of her white hair had come loose, falling into her eyes, and she shook it away. 'You're right,' she said. 'Joe said the same.'

'You should have listened to him.'

'I did,' she said. 'And then I'd talk to Collette about it, argue with her. But there was one thing she said that I could never argue with. She said that the minute she told you neither of you would see her any more. You wouldn't see your mother, you'd only see the disease.'

The sweatshirt I'd wrapped around Mum, the night she'd slept in this bed, lay beside the backpack. Had it been her that night or the disease? Of all the hard things, that was the hardest of all: to know where Mum stopped and the disease began.

'You have to tell Suzanne this,' I said. 'She won't ask but you have to tell her.'

Lily-Anne nodded. I wanted her to laugh her big silly laugh, to tell me a story about Chips. 'I'll tell her,' she said. 'Does that mean you're beginning to understand why I didn't tell you? Why I couldn't?'

I kicked at the discarded books. 'I think so,' I said. 'But I don't know if it matters. The point is that I missed out on all this time with Mum, all these years.'

Lily-Anne kept looking at me, her blue stare steady. 'You're talking as if she's gone but Collette is still here, Carla. Your mother is still here.'

For a minute I thought the tears might come back, but I kept them in check. 'She's not, though, is she? Not really. She might be here today, part of her, but she could be gone tomorrow. Never mind next September.' I turned to face her fully. 'So, yes, I think I understand why you did what you did, Lily-Anne. But that doesn't mean I forgive you.'

She hesitated for a second before she spoke. 'That's OK,' she said. 'I can accept that. But, Carla, maybe I'm not the one you need to forgive.'

Eighteen

The mug was at the very back of the cupboard and I reached over the others to pick it out. It was a silly thing to take, really, when you couldn't even see their faces any more, but it would be nice to have something from home.

Suzanne looked up from the magazine she was reading. 'Are you making tea?'

'I wasn't planning to. I was getting my Take That mug,' I said. 'I'm taking it with me.' I started to wrap it in kitchen roll. 'You don't think Mum will miss it, do you?' It was supposed to be a joke and I laughed but Suzanne didn't.

'Oh, right,' she said. 'No, she won't.'

She turned back to her magazine but I'd already seen her expression change, the red blotches on her face, her neck. Something was up. I didn't want to know. I knew I shouldn't ask, but I did anyway. 'What?'

She ignored me, turned a page.

'You're not pissed off at me taking the mug? Did you want it?'

When she looked up her eyes were red and I really wished then that I hadn't asked. I thought she was angry but then I saw it was worse than that.

'Nothing,' she said, taking a tissue from her sleeve. 'It's stupid. Just seeing you taking stuff like that, it makes me realise—'

'Realise what?'

She sniffed. 'That you're not coming back.'

I put the mug on the counter. 'What's that supposed to mean? Of course I'm coming back.'

She raised her eyebrows, half smiled.

'What? I am! How many times do I have to tell you?'

She pushed her hair off her face. 'That's what you say now and you probably even mean it. But once you get back there, you'll be in another world. Eddie's world.'

'Suzanne, that's not fair.'

'No, Carla, what's not fair is me having to deal with this on my own. Mammy is just as much your responsibility as she is mine. You should be here, at home, not running away to New York.'

The clock on the wall showed it was almost midnight. We'd nearly made it through this whole day, this whole week, keeping the argument under the surface where it belonged. I picked up the mug and headed towards the door. I wasn't going to let her drag me into it. 'Suzanne, I know you're upset but all I can say is that I'll be back, I'm not running away.'

'Yes, you are, even if you don't know it. Just like you did after Daddy died.'

I had my hand on the door handle, had almost made it into the hall. She knew the words to draw me back in, the words I couldn't let go. 'What are you talking about?'

'You couldn't wait to get out of here, Carla.'

'That's not true!'

'Come on, you're not going to deny it. Even on the day of the funeral you were barely here. You went off with Damien and your friends.' She waved her hands in the air, like the funeral was still going on around us.

A fleeting memory, every room of the house, packed. Male voices laughing. Smoke hanging low in the March sun. Hands on my shoulders. My arms. *You're the spitting image of your daddy.*

'What the fuck, Suzanne? Dad was dead well over a year before I left.' It was hard to hear my words over the drumming of my heart but I kept talking. 'And who was it who did everything during that year? Cleared out his clothes? His shoes? Collected his death cert? I even painted that fucking wall where the paramedics took a gouge out of it with the stretcher.' I was shouting by then, banging my mug off the table with every word, the stupid mug that had started all this.

She let the tears slide down her face. 'But you'd never talk about it to me or to Mum. You went around as if nothing had happened. As if you didn't know he was dead.'

I was shaking. I'd walked in on Mum saying something like that to Olivia, years before, in this very kitchen. It hurt like a blade, knowing that she thought that. As if I didn't know Dad was dead. As if I didn't know it in every single cell of my body, every single second of every horrible day. I longed to forget it, for even one of those seconds, until I did and then I discovered it was worse to have to find out all over again.

'Denial was your way of coping, Carla, I know that but it doesn't work.'

She'd made her voice soft, like she cared, like she could salve the wound she'd just ripped open. So what if she was scared, upset, angry? What about me?

'I don't think you're really one to talk about coping mechanisms, are you, Suzanne? At least I didn't fuck up my finals.' I knew as I said it that it wasn't fair, but right then I didn't care. 'Not everyone needs a shrink to get through shit in life. Some of us are strong enough on our own.'

She opened her mouth to say something, but I didn't want to hear it. I got in first. 'I've told you I'm coming back and that means I'm coming back. You can dredge up all the shit you want, you can act like a martyr about it, but nothing you say is going to stop me getting on that plane tomorrow.'

We stared at each other across a table that we'd both grown up around, eaten hundreds of meals from. The silence was loud, and before she could fill it, I picked up my mug and opened the door. I closed it gently behind me, before I went upstairs.

*

The airport was packed, queues snaking around and back on themselves so you didn't know which was the beginning and which was the end. I watched as one group of backpackers stood behind another, only to find, after a while, that it wasn't a queue at all.

I hadn't expected it to be so full so early. For all the changes in the city, the airport was still the same, the same check-in desks, the big board hanging from the ceiling listing each flight. Dad always stopped to check the board but Mum hurried past it, she'd always known where to go. I remembered my hand in his as we followed her gliding through the crowds, all of us dressed up as if we were going to mass. No matter how busy it was we never had to queue, had a check-in desk to ourselves, it seemed. People greeted her by name, men and women in uniforms, who leaned down to say hello to me and Suzanne. I felt special then, special and proud to be Mum's daughter. Today I was just me, waiting in line like everyone else.

My backpack dug into my shoulders and I adjusted the straps. The taxi driver had winced when he picked it up to put it in the boot, asked me if I had rocks in it. Suzanne had been supposed to give me a lift but last night I'd called a taxi instead. I didn't mind the money, it was the talking I'd hated – as we'd sped along the empty Dublin streets, he wouldn't shut up about the price of houses, holidays, decking, gym membership, a meal out, a pint. I murmured agreement as I looked out at the stripes of lavender in the sky, thinking about the Oscar Wilde quotes Dad used to have up in his office, wondering what had happened to them.

This queue was taking for ever, only one man checking everyone in. At the top, a couple had a suitcase open between them and were pulling six packs of Tayto crisps out on to the floor.

The lady in front of me turned, smiling. 'That's not going to do them much good,' she said. She saw from my expression that I didn't get it.

'You know, to get the weight down.'

'Oh, yeah. True.' I smiled and took my phone out of my pocket. She was obviously a talker and the last thing I needed was to be stuck next to her on the flight. She turned away and I checked my texts. No new ones, only Eddie's from yesterday: *What time r u getting home tomorrow? Have a gud flight. E x*

Home. Everyone used that word all the time, what did it even mean? Suzanne's words from last night bounced around my mind, about my responsibilities being at home. Where was home anyway? Where you'd grown up? Where you lived? I thought of the Billy Joel song, the one I'd always loved, that Eddie and I used to dance to in our first apartment. Billy Joel thought home was another person, but maybe he was wrong; maybe home had to be yourself.

At the check-in desk the couple walked away, the wife stuffing a hairdryer into her handbag. I hadn't slept at all last night, had been up and down checking the clock, drinking water, going to the loo, Suzanne's stupid words about running away in my head the whole time. I saw a line of light under her door at one stage and thought about knocking and going in, but there was nothing to say.

The queue inched forward. Only two more people in front of the woman in front of me. It wasn't fair, what she'd said about running away, and it wasn't true. Maybe it hurt more because I'd tried, really tried, to be on the same side as her for once. I knew I'd hurt her, with what I'd said about the shrink, but she'd hurt me first. And if I'd run away before, that was eleven years ago and it certainly wasn't what I was doing now.

Two people between me and check-in. The guy at the top of the queue was a New Yorker, definitely, probably from Brooklyn. I could tell by his jacket, his jeans, his runners. I could picture him at the bar in Union or drinking coffee in Mitchell's. I might even have served him. There was something about seeing him there, in dingy Dublin airport, that made me realise those places were real, not just memories; the Brooklyn sidewalks they were on really existed, and in a few hours I'd be walking along them. As the thought formed, the need to be there was urgent, physical, and I felt like pushing everyone out of the way, everyone who stood between me and New York. Wherever Eddie's tour might take him I was staying there. It was my city now, just as much as it was his. Maybe it always had been.

The Brooklyn guy was called to the check-in desk. Not much longer. My shoulders ached but there was no point in taking the backpack off, not now that I was nearly there. I tilted my head back. The mezzanine level was all restaurants these days. Once there had been the cockpit of a plane up there, a real one that you could play in. Dad had taken us to the airport to meet Mum off a flight and Suzanne and I had gone into it. We'd waited ages for our turn to be pilot, shoving our bums against each other on the hard plastic seat. The windows had been tiny – I remembered waving out of one at Mum and Dad. Dad hadn't seen us – he'd met someone he knew – but Mum had. I could still picture her, in her green uniform, her hair a dark roll at her neck, smiling, waving back. The same wave she'd waved from the porch this morning, in her dressing-gown. She was the same woman, almost the same woman.

'Next, please.'

The lady in front of me went to the desk. Only empty space now between me and it. Fuck it. I wasn't running away. I'd be back in six months, less. How much worse could she get in six months? It wasn't that long, she'd be fine. But what if she wasn't? What if I came back and she wasn't fine at all?

The lady was smiling, taking something, putting her passport away. She was too quick. How had she been so quick?

From behind the desk, the man in uniform leaned forward slightly. 'Next please.'

Fuck Suzanne. I'd run away before, maybe I had, but that wasn't what I was doing now. I didn't want to do it now.

'Next, please!'

I felt the person behind me inch forward, knew they were about to say something.

I wasn't running away. I didn't want to run away. Not this time.

'Next!'

I hitched my backpack higher on my shoulders, turned away from the queue and headed for the door.

NINETEEN

The computer screen was black, except for a swirl of grey, an arrow making a circle. I heard Eddie before I saw him or, at least, half of him, his forehead, his eyebrows, his eyes.

'Carla?' he said. 'Can you see me?'

'Pull the screen back – there you go. That's perfect.'

It was weird, him sitting at the table in our apartment, a bit of the couch in the background. He looked different, more tanned, but he couldn't be. His hair was longer.

'Hey,' he said, waving. 'It's good to see you.'

I started to reply but then he froze on the screen, his mouth half open, his skin a mosaic of colour. 'Eddie? Eddie? Can you hear me?'

The call dropped and I was alone in the room that used to be the dining room. I reached for some water, glad of the unscheduled break. I waited for him to call again. He did.

'Hey,' he said. 'I don't know what happened there.'

'There's probably five billion people online or something.'

'So what's going on? Did something happen with your mom? Did you miss the flight or what?' His eyebrow piercing rose.

Already my heart was galloping. 'I didn't miss the flight,' I said. 'I decided – I just decided to stay a bit longer.'

On the screen I could see him hesitating, trying to read me. It was too soon to tell him but I had to.

'How much longer?'

'I don't know exactly. We found out – me and Suzanne – that Mum is sicker than we thought. I didn't think it was the right time to leave, before we'd figured it all out.'

It was true, part of the truth.

'Oh, OK,' he said.

'And I figured that – you know – since it looks like you might be on tour soon anyway, there's no point me coming home for you to be away all summer.'

'Turns out the tour might not be till August now,' he said. 'There's some problem with the San Diego venue, and if we wait till later, we might get Portland too. And guess what?' He couldn't hide the excitement in his face, his voice.

'What?'

'They're talking about going international. Europe, maybe even Asia! Can you believe that?'

I smiled for him. 'That's cool. Congratulations.'

'I know you weren't so keen on tagging along all over the country, but the European tour would be awesome. We might even play in Dublin.'

I pressed my fingers into the table so the skin went white under my nails. I tried to keep smiling but I couldn't, and when I glanced up, his smile had faded too. A metallic noise came from nowhere, grinding over the line. On the screen I saw Eddie's lips move. 'Eddie? What did you say? I can't hear you.'

He leaned towards the computer and he was back then, half a sentence chopped off.

I hated having a conversation like this – having *this* conversation like this.

'I was just asking what's up. You looked upset.'

The metallic noise got louder and then faded.

'Eddie, this thing with Mum. It's really serious – every day now, something seems to happen.' My voice had gone all high-pitched. I dug in my pocket for a tissue. Eddie was leaning in close to the computer. 'I might need to stay a long time, Eddie.'

'How long?'

I crossed my leg over my thigh, pulling my foot in close. On the gap of skin under my tracksuit I saw the black curve of my tattoo. I pulled my sock over it. 'I don't know. It feels like I'm losing her and I want to spend whatever time we have left together.' I reached for another tissue. For someone who never cried, since I'd started with Lily-Anne the other day I hadn't stopped.

On screen Eddie had frozen again, but his voice was clear over the line. 'So you're staying, like, indefinitely?'

'I don't know. I just don't want to get back here when it's too late, when she doesn't know who I am.'

I blew my nose again. 'What about the visa? Remember what the lawyer said about the six-month thing?'

'I know, I know. It's such a mess, all of it.'

The enormity of what I wanted to do suddenly hit me, winding me. Eddie kept talking. 'Hey, it's OK, it's OK.' He was back again, moving. 'You need to stay with your mom. We can talk to the lawyer, see if we can work something out. There's got to be a way to extend it when someone's really sick.'

I clamped my lips together. He was being so nice, so supportive. How could I even be thinking what I was thinking?

'The timing's not really that bad. Like you say, I'm going to be on tour anyway, most likely. Fingers crossed.' The smile crept back on to his face as he talked about the tour. I felt a twitch of irritation that we'd skimmed over Mum, over me and back to him.

'I can pack up the apartment, put some stuff into storage, get rid of the junk we don't need. We can figure out what to do when I get back from the tour.'

This was going to be the last apartment we'd ever have together. The thought, when it came, was fast and certain. It was too much.

'Christ, Eddie, can you not talk about your fucking tour for five minutes?'

'What?'

'You're so damn matter-of-fact about everything. Are you going to miss me at all?'

Even as I was saying it I knew it wasn't fair, that what he was saying made sense. But somehow I didn't care, right then, about fairness, only about the hurt that was ballooning inside me, like a tumour, and this was the only way I knew to get it out.

He ran his hands over his hair, pushed it down on his forehead. 'What kind of crazy question is that? Of course I miss you.'

'Really? Because it doesn't sound like it. We could be talking about months apart here, a year. Longer. There was a time when we couldn't spend a night apart.'

'Carla——'

'What, Eddie? You don't remember that?'

He looked away. A strange noise came through the speaker and I realised he was drumming his fingers. I could picture him doing it, the way he always did. When he looked back at me, his eyes were sad. 'What do you want me to say?'

'The truth,' I said. 'I want you to tell me the truth.'

The hum was back on the line, an aeroplane cutting through our conversation. I was putting this on him, making him say it, and suddenly I wanted the call to drop again, to stop this conversation going where the words were taking us.

He shrugged. 'I don't know what you want me to say. Things change, relationships change.'

I looked straight into the camera so he could see into my eyes. As I did I realised it wasn't possible, with this stupid technology, to look and see at the same time.

'What?' he said.

I pushed harder into the table. I couldn't say the thing that had been so clear to me that morning. Running by the sea, I could see that this was what we needed, what both of us needed. It had brought relief, a sense of space in my head, but now, looking at him, the space was filled with images as vivid as those in a photo album: Eddie and me side by side on the drive to Washington DC, my feet on the dashboard; sitting on the steps of our first apartment eating pizza; standing on tiptoe to see over the crowd in Penn station to welcome him home.

On the screen he looked the same as if he hadn't aged at all. His voice still sounded the same. And yet he was right, of course he was: something had changed. Something big. I took a deep breath. 'You know I've been doing a lot of thinking lately and things with us, well, they're not perfect, are they? I mean, they haven't been. I thought it might be a good time – if there's ever a good time – to take a break.'

The words came out in a jumble, one hooked on to the next. As soon as I'd finished I wanted him to shake his head, to say no, that he couldn't believe I was even suggesting it, but he didn't say anything, just kept looking at me through the screen. I couldn't bear the silence that wasn't even silence so my mouth opened and I kept talking, talking, talking, saying all these words I hadn't planned to say.

'I mean, I'm not talking about splitting up, just, you know, taking some time apart, to reflect on where we're at, what we both want.'

I didn't even sound like me. I sounded like that damn book on my bedside locker.

He still didn't say anything. His expression hadn't changed.

'I mean, we've been together such a long time,' I said.

'Eleven years,' he said.

'Eleven years.' Something about hearing that made me start to giggle. I giggled my way into a full-blown laugh.

Now he looked angry. 'What's funny? Why are you laughing?'

'I don't know. Maybe I'm having some kind of breakdown over everything that's happening with Mum. You probably think I've gone crazy, that this is a terrible idea.'

He shook his head. 'No,' he said. 'I don't.'

Inside I felt something sink. His fingers were drumming again and he was watching them, not me. When he looked up, he was nodding slightly. 'You're right, I've been thinking about it too. Things have been horrible lately. Some time out, some time apart, makes sense.'

I nodded, swallowed. Horrible. That was the word he'd used. Somehow the fact he'd been thinking it too made it worse, so much worse.

'People take time apart all the time,' I heard myself saying. 'And then they get back together.'

'Yeah,' he said. 'They do.'

And some of them don't. The unsaid words were loud on the line. Something made me look over at the piano, the photo of us smiling at Coney Island, the lights of the Cyclone in the background. I remembered another day at Coney Island, the day he'd asked me to stay.

'I was talking to Dawn about it and she said not to do anything while your mom is sick, that maybe that was making things so crazy.' He said it casually. His hands were behind his head so I could see little lines of sweat in his armpits.

'You were talking to Dawn about us?' His face changed as he realised he'd said the wrong thing. 'Who else have you consulted?'

He ran a hand over his hair. 'Jesus, Carla, I haven't talked to anyone else. It came out that night when we were out, after she broke up with Chris.'

'I bet it did.' I folded my arms across my stomach, pushed in under my ribcage. It felt like there was a gap there, a hole I needed urgently to fill.

Eddie was leaning close to the screen again, his arms disappearing alongside the keyboard. 'Carla, don't get crazy. Nothing's going on, if that's what you think.'

'I don't know what to think.'

'Dawn's my friend, Carla, that's all. You're the one who brought this up. You're the one who's staying in Ireland. This is what you want, remember?'

Right then I didn't know what I wanted, other than for this conversation to end. For it never to have started in the first place.

'It just seems so easy for you,' I said, 'so matter of fact. You haven't even asked what it means, what kind of contact we can have.'

'What type of contact?' More drumming. 'Fuck! I hadn't even thought about that. Can't we just play it by ear?'

I must have heard that expression a million times but it was the first time I'd ever understood what it meant. I pictured Eddie listening to music in his head, picking out the notes. The songs he'd written for me. I gripped the edge of the table. 'Fine,' I said. 'We'll play it by ear.'

It was late by then and cold in the room, but somehow I didn't want to finish up. Neither, it seemed, did he, and we dawdled over the call, telling stories, jokes. Seconds could pass when I'd forget what we'd decided and then it would come back again, cutting through the conversation like an iceberg. How could it be that just when we'd decided to break up, or whatever we'd decided, we were getting on better than we had in a long time? A voice in my head kept saying that this was a bad idea, a terrible idea, but even as I listened to it some other part of me knew it wasn't, knew it was the only thing to do.

'I'd better go,' I said eventually. 'It's nearly one and I've to be up early in the morning.'

'Running?' he said.

'No, yoga. I've found a nice class over here.'

'An Irish Jan?'

I smiled, thought of Audrey. 'Actually, she's nothing like Jan. But I like her.'

'Well,' he said, 'enjoy it.'

Neither of us spoke and I almost wished Skype would make its crazy noises then, but there was only silence. When would we speak again? See each other? What if this was the last time? Each thought was laced with more panic than the last.

'Let me know, won't you, when you find out about the tour dates?'

'Sure,' he said, arms folded again. 'Sure, I will. Say hi to your mom. And Suzanne.'

'I will. And you say hi to Bonnie. And to Nick.' I couldn't mention Dawn. 'Tell him to straighten up and fly right.'

It was an old joke and it made him laugh, as I'd known it would. That was what I wanted to remember, for him to remember, the two of us laughing.

'You take care out there,' he said, 'and if you want to call me, call me. OK?'

'You too. Call me. Whenever you want.'

'I'll call you.'

We'd talked our way to the end of something but we were both still there on screen.

'I love you,' I said. I knew it wasn't the right thing to say, the right time, but more than anything I wanted to say it. 'You know I love you.'

'I know,' he said. 'I love you too.'

Somehow the words sounded sad, as if they were true but, for some reason I didn't understand yet, they weren't enough.

I waved at the screen, he was waving too. For a few seconds we stayed like that, smiling and waving, until I hit the red button and he was gone.

PART FOUR

ONE

The December morning was still dark, the dawn only an edge of light at the corners of the sky. In front of me the path swept up around the Martello tower. I used to hate this part of the run, but nine months of doing it nearly every day meant I could power up it where I used to have to slow down. My playlist was on The Killers song, one of my favourites, 'Why Do I Keep Counting?' Sometimes it seemed like it was all I could do, keep running, keep counting, keep putting distance between me and everything that had happened.

Down near the water's edge the path was scattered with seaweed, mounds of it that oozed water into little puddles. I stepped around them easily. The sea was calm now, glassy, and if it wasn't for the seaweed it'd be easy to forget last night's storm had happened at all.

The song faded, then ended. I heard my feet pound on concrete, my breathing. In the gap of silence before Eminem started, the dream snuck in, clinging to me, like the seaweed on the rocks. I hated that I still dreamed about him. When we were together I never did, or hardly ever, but since we'd split up he seemed to pop up all the time, whenever he felt like it. Last night we were going to someone's wedding, him in a weird blue suit.

Back on the road and around the corner, past the house with the Christmas lights up since October. My breath in front of me was clouds of steam. Eddie and I had been to just one wedding together, down in South Carolina, his cousin Gina. I was the only one wearing black. Eddie had liked that dress. I remembered that, and how when everyone else was listening to the best man's speech we were upstairs in our hotel room having urgent, half-undressed sex.

Over the wall of the harbour I saw the boats were high, the sleek line of a seal under the water. I almost didn't notice the man coming towards me with the spaniel on the stretchy lead and ran around him at the last minute on to the road.

I'd forgotten about that wedding and wished I hadn't remembered it then either. I'd noticed lately that every day some new memory surfaced, something we'd done together, years before, as if I needed to remember every little thing before I could forget. It was four months, longer, since we'd spoken, since those last emails about the security deposit for the flat. They'd annoyed me, those emails, how happy he sounded with his exclamation marks and smiley faces, his excitement about the tour, like us being apart wasn't bothering him at all. When I'd said I didn't want any more contact, he'd obviously taken it at face value, assumed I actually meant it. As the months had passed I'd thought about getting in touch again but the longer it went the harder it was and it was easier, in a way, this silence, being able to pretend that he didn't exist, that none of it had ever happened at all.

I was getting towards my favourite part of the run, and even though my breath snagged in my chest, I didn't slow down, powered up my body. Up the hill, around the corner, and the sea was stretched out in front again, the edges of the waves clipping the rocks. I could see the shoulder of the island, a slope of green. In less than a minute, I'd see the whole thing.

Here, next to the sea, there was only me, the air and my breath. And the faster I ran the easier it became to believe that Eddie had never existed at all.

★

When I came into the kitchen Suzanne was singing along to the radio. 'You're going to turn into a streak of sweat on the road if you do any more running,' she said. When she turned around she had two bowls of oatmeal in her hands. 'Didn't you go for a run last night as well?'

'Yeah – so?' I peeled off my jacket, filled a glass of water.

'Are you training for a marathon or what?'

'Maybe,' I said. I refilled my glass. Maybe I would train for a marathon. Maybe that was what I needed. Focus, a goal.

She put the bowls down and I watched as she stirred the oatmeal so the blueberries disappeared into the milk. We'd started to take turns making it for each other every day. On the mornings I was looking after Mum I made it for her too, but I had to remember to call it porridge. I took my place opposite her.

'You know I'm going to be late tonight,' Suzanne said.

'You told me. How many Christmas parties can one company have?'

She swallowed before she spoke. 'I know, it's a bit crazy. This should be the last. It's the team one.'

'Was that not last week?'

'That was the department one.'

I shook my head. 'While you're enjoying all your parties, I'm busy working at everyone else's. The restaurant's fully booked for lunch and dinner until Christmas Eve.'

Suzanne smiled. 'You're making loads of cash, though, and you seem to like it there.'

'Not loads, nothing like I'd make waiting tables in New York. But it's OK.'

I took a mouthful of oatmeal. It tasted good. The money was much better than I'd expected and it was nice being back at work, having a routine.

Suzanne had finished, scraping her bowl. 'So,' she said, 'what's your plan for your day off?'

'Lily-Anne wants to take Mum Christmas shopping in Dun Laoghaire,' I said. 'I might tag along, I haven't got anything yet. I don't feel Christmassy in the slightest.'

'So long as she doesn't start her off on all that Christmas-cake business,' she said. 'It was a nightmare last year.'

'What happened?'

She shuddered. 'Did I not tell you? It was a disaster. Mammy insisted that she'd make all the cakes, as usual. Refused any help from me whatsoever.'

'And?'

She sighed and pushed the bowl away. 'It was a nightmare. She wouldn't even let me into the kitchen. She was at it until three in the morning, me lying awake upstairs, listening to things banging around, stuff being dropped.'

I giggled. 'What did they turn out like?'

'The next morning she was still asleep and I saw them. I don't know what the heck she put in them, but they were like two tyres, burned around the edges, big saggy holes in the middle.'

The giggle turned into a laugh. I couldn't help it.

'Stop it! We shouldn't laugh!' Suzanne covered her mouth too.

'Did you have to eat them?'

'God, no! And I couldn't let her give them to anyone else. I went out and bought two from the bakery in Dalkey and brought the other ones to work to throw them out so she wouldn't find them.'

'Did she not notice the difference?'

'No!' Suzanne laughed harder. 'We iced them together and she was so proud of them. Everyone kept saying they were her best cakes ever, and she got great pleasure out of telling them that if I'd had my way she wouldn't have been able to make them at all.'

Just as she reached the punch line the door opened behind me. I looked around to see Mum in her dressing-gown, her hair wet. 'This is nice, coming down to find you two laughing together. What's funny?'

I caught Suzanne's eye. I was nine years old again, in school, in mass, where not being allowed to make a sound made the sniggers expand into full-blown laughter. I let it out now in a howl that made Suzanne laugh even more. Mum sat down between us and joined in, her breathy laugh. She didn't know what was funny and for a second that mattered, until it didn't. Because right then, at that moment, the joke itself was forgotten.

Just laughing, really laughing, was enough.

★

We'd been in Shaw's for nearly half an hour and Mum still couldn't decide on the coat. She turned around again, in front of the mirror, her hands in the pockets. On the ground next to her was her old Aer Lingus case, the one she'd used on overnights that I'd loved to play with. Some time last month, she'd taken it down to breakfast and since then it had come everywhere with her. Last night I'd emptied it of twigs, leaves and an empty Capri Sun packet. By now it was probably full again.

'I don't know,' she said. Her face frowned back at us from the mirror.

'It's lovely on you,' Lily-Anne said, 'I know you have your other black one, but this one would be nice for going out. It's dressier.'

Where would Mum be going that she needed a dressy coat? I didn't say anything, fixed my smile. In the background Slade were wishing everyone a merry Christmas and it seemed, suddenly, as if the song was playing on a loop, over and over. Another woman came into the dressing room and Lily-Anne picked up Mum's Aer Lingus case to give her room, holding it totally unselfconsciously, as if it were a Prada handbag.

'I'm going to leave you to it,' I said. 'I've to get something for Rhonda. I'll walk home after.'

'Don't be silly,' Lily-Anne said. 'Meet us at the car when you're finished. There's no rush.'

'You'll probably be longer than me though,' I said, 'I don't mind walking.'

Mum came back to us, holding her arms out straight. 'What do you think of this coat, love?'

'It's lovely, Mum. You should get it.'

It was the fifth time she'd asked and the fifth time I'd replied, saying the same thing. In New York she'd always been quick at shopping, decisive. I couldn't stop my eyes rolling.

'Look,' Lily-Anne said, 'I've to go up to the library to bring a book back. Why don't you do that for me and we can meet you there in, say, twenty minutes?'

She was rooting in her crocheted bag before I'd had time to agree.

'The library? Is it still there?'

'Oh, yes,' she nodded, 'all mod cons, these days, the Internet and everything.' She took out a book with a navy cover and handed it to me.

I read the spine, Pema Chodron, *When Things Fall Apart*. Audrey had mentioned it in yoga, I was sure she had. 'Uplifting title,' I said.

'It's wonderful,' Lily-Anne said. 'I read it every year, at least once. Not that I'd dare to suggest you should look at it.' She smiled. Ever since my accusation that she was trying to be my shrink she had been extra careful not to recommend anything.

'OK, I'll see you there,' I said. 'Just, please, for the sales assistant's sake, make sure she buys that coat.'

*

Coming to the library had always been our Saturday thing to do, Dad, Suzanne and me. As I walked up the semi-circular steps the building looked exactly the same, as if nothing had changed in twenty years. Inside, it smelt the same too, and I couldn't see any of the mod cons Lily-Anne had mentioned. I found myself drawn in, past the desk, to the narrow aisles of shelves. I pulled out a hardback book, covered with plastic, the little stamped sheet inside, just like always. A sudden memory – I had insisted on joining the adult library at the same time as Suzanne and pretended I didn't mind there was no Enid Blyton. It was Dad who suggested that I take books out from the children's library as well as the adults', he said that I was at a special age where I could have the best of both.

Handing Lily-Anne's book back, I found myself asking about joining, and before I knew it, the girl was filling in information on her computer, making me a card. In the corner I spotted carousels of CDs and I wandered over to Meat Loaf, Christy Moore, Pavarotti. No sign of Homespun Heroes: they hadn't quite made it in library circles. I pulled out a CD case with a cracked cover, Antony and the Johnsons. I'd never heard of them and it was appealing then, the idea of listening to music I didn't know, that Eddie probably didn't either. By the time Mum and Lily-Anne arrived I'd picked up three more to join it.

'Mission accomplished!' Lily-Anne said, holding out two big Shaw's bags. 'We're ready when you are.'

In the quiet her voice was loud and I glanced around. 'Give me two minutes, until I get these out.'

'Oh, you joined?' Something about her tone made me wonder if that had been her ploy all along. 'Carla joined the library. Isn't that great, Coll?'

Mum's head was tilted back, she was scanning the shelves of books from the ground to the ceiling. 'I used to envy them every Saturday. I used to watch out the window as they piled into the car.'

Lily-Anne frowned, confused. I was about to say I didn't know what she was talking about until I realised that, of course, I did. I'd never wondered why she wasn't in the library memory. It had never crossed my mind that she might have wanted to come. I felt a tinge of guilt. 'Why was it you never came with us, Mum?' I asked.

Her eyes travelled down the bookcase to Lily-Anne, to me. She pulled her Aer Lingus bag up close to her chest. She was going to answer me. I hoped she would.

'It was silly, really, spending all the days at home getting ready for going away again,' she said. 'I might've been better off just being where I was.'

It was the most I'd heard her say in a long time – the most that made sense. Lily-Anne held out her hand but Mum ignored it, walking past her towards the CD racks.

I followed. 'I never knew you thought that,' I said. 'You never said.'

When she turned to face me her eyes were different, sliding across my face and back to the CDs lined up in front of her. I knew, from her eyes, that she'd gone somewhere else.

'I need to get a coat, love,' she said. 'When are we going shopping?'

Two

The fire was low, almost out, but neither of us moved to put on another briquette. After the whole day of burning, the heat was trapped in the sitting room. I thought about getting up to open a window, but my body felt like it was moulded to the chair.

'I thought I'd seen this one before,' Suzanne said, gesturing towards the TV, 'but I don't remember it.'

On screen Harry Potter was in a cave, jumping from stone to stone.

'I'm not sure how I managed to escape the whole phenomenon but I'm glad I did,' I said. 'Is this really the best thing on?'

Suzanne picked up the paper with the TV listings and tossed it over to me. 'Here,' she said.

I put down my glass and scanned the programmes. There were other movies but they were older than this – and not old enough to be any good.

'I always remember films on Christmas Day being amazing,' I said. 'They don't have *The Great Escape* on or *Willy Wonka* or anything.'

'The new *Willy Wonka* was on earlier,' Suzanne said, 'but it's not the same.'

'No.'

I reached across for another chocolate from the tin. I didn't want one, after all the mince pies and pudding, but I took it anyway, unwrapping it slowly before popping it into my mouth.

'Want one?' I held the tin out to Suzanne.

'No, thanks.'

'Go on.'

'No,' she said, 'thanks.'

'I can't believe how good you've been. I thought the diet would've gone out the window, today of all days.'

She turned around and smiled. She was growing her hair and it was long enough to tuck behind her ears now. I'd changed earlier, after dinner, into a tracksuit, but she was still wearing the black dress that showed off the weight she'd lost. It suited her. It made her look even more like Mum.

'Ah, I did break it,' she said, 'or at least I bent it a lot, but I didn't want to throw it out the window entirely, not after all my effort.'

'Mm.'

I nodded, my mouth full of chocolate. On the arm of my chair the screen of my mobile phone lit up. I waited until the light went off, then picked it up. The message took a second to open. It was going to be Eddie, I knew it was. Please let it be Eddie. It opened, a Happy Christmas message from Rhonda, with some picture of Santa done in xs and os. I put it back on the arm too quickly so it slid on to the floor.

'Who was that?'

'Rhonda,' I said, reaching down to pick it up, so she wouldn't see my face.

'Did you speak to Eddie earlier?' She didn't look at me as she asked, her voice high, deliberately casual.

'Yeah,' I said.

'What's he doing today? Going to his mother's?'

'Yeah,' I said, 'the usual.' I picked up my glass and drained what was left. The wine left my mouth dry. I'd lied, I hadn't talked to Eddie and wondered if she could hear it in my voice. I checked the clock again, eleven – six in New York. There was still time for him to get in touch, plenty of time.

'Will I open another bottle?' Suzanne said, after a bit. 'Would you have another glass?'

I had been thinking of going up to bed at the next ad break, but she looked hopeful, like she wanted me to share one with her. Or maybe just someone to share one with her. 'If you're having one,' I said. 'But just one.'

'Ah, yeah, let's,' she said, standing up. 'It's Christmas.'

Left alone in the living room, I checked the phone again and reread Rhonda's message, then Ange's before it. I'd even got a text from Sean, my driving instructor. I'd done that thing last night that I hadn't done for ages, checked Eddie's Myspace. The band were back in New York, playing three nights over New Year so I was probably right with my guess that he'd be in Bonnie's. Janie should be there – it was her year with Bonnie – so it would be just the three of them. Unless Bonnie was seeing someone new. I took another chocolate and bit into it, the strawberry filling oozing over my tongue. Or Eddie was.

From the kitchen I heard Suzanne laughing. I nudged the TV volume down, and there it was again, definite laughter, and then her voice, talking low. I wondered if maybe Mum had got up and come down, until I realised I could only hear one voice. She must be on the phone.

On the TV, Harry was running through dark hallways, his red-haired friend slack-jawed at whatever they had seen behind them. I turned the volume back up but I couldn't concentrate. An image of Dawn had come into my mind and stuck there. The more I tried not to think about Eddie seeing her, the more I thought about it, could imagine her next to him at the table in Bonnie's tiny apartment, getting all her photography and music references in a way I never had. Eddie and Dawn had gotten together on the tour, that was why he hadn't been in touch, nothing to do with my e-mail. After eleven Christmases – eleven years of shopping for presents, eleven carefully chosen cards, eleven trees put up and taken down together – why else would he not have even sent so much as a text message?

But I hadn't texted him either.

The door opened and Suzanne came in, her glass already half

full and the bottle in her other hand. She was pretending not to smile. 'Here you go,' she said, pouring wine for me.

'Thanks.'

'Sorry. I took a while, I was just on the phone.'

I drank some wine. She wanted me to ask her who was on the phone, she wanted to tell me, I knew she did, and I wanted to ask her, but something stopped me.

'Do you think Mum enjoyed the day?' I said instead. 'She didn't mind not seeing all the relations?'

'I'm glad we didn't take her round there,' she said. 'It would've been too much for her, too many people. I think she was happy with us and Lily-Anne and Joe.'

'And Chips,' I said. 'Don't forget Chips.'

Suzanne laughed. 'As if I could. Did you ever think we'd see the day that we'd have a dog in this house for Christmas?'

'No. Do you think she even really knew what day it was?'

'I think so, but you wouldn't be sure.' Suzanne shrugged, 'Sure after all my worry about what to do about the cake she never even brought it up this year. I almost wish she had.'

She was turned towards the TV again but something in her body had shifted since she came in, a heaviness in the way she sat back in the chair, her wine glass cradled in her lap. I wished I hadn't brought Mum up, that I'd let her talk about her call.

'So, who were you on the phone to?' I asked casually, the same way she'd asked me about Eddie.

At first she pretended not to hear, delayed her reaction, but then she glanced at me. 'What was that?'

'I asked who you were on the phone to. In the kitchen.'

She flicked her hair behind her ear and smiled. 'Oh,' she said. 'Just a friend.'

'A friend?'

She nodded, then sipped her wine.

'Are you going to tell me about this "friend"?'

In the light from the tree I saw she was excited, happy.

'He's just a guy from work. Simon.'

'And?' I said.

'And,' she said, twisting her glass between her hands, 'we kind of got together at the Christmas party.' She kept her eyes on her glass.

'Which one?'

She smiled her wide smile. 'Well, we had a conversation at the department one, and I thought maybe he liked me, but nothing happened so I wasn't sure. At the company one, we bailed straight after the meal, just left and went to a bar.'

When she looked up, her cheeks were flushed. I shifted in the chair and my phone slid down between the arm and the cushion. I didn't bother to take it out. 'That's great, Suzanne. What's he like? I want to know all the details.'

'Oh, he's lovely. He's over from the UK office and he has a gorgeous accent. He's so smart – that's what I noticed first. In meetings with him I really had to know my stuff.'

'Meetings? Who cares about meetings? Is he cute?'

'Ah, yeah. He's a lovely smile and dark hair although it's going grey now. He's a bit smaller than me, but not much.'

'How old is he?'

She looked away into the fire and back to me. 'Forty.'

'Forty!'

'I know what you're thinking, but I'm nearly thirty-five. It's not that much of a gap.'

Forty. Only five years younger than Dad had been when he died.

'No,' I said, 'it's not. I just don't know when we all got to be so ancient.'

'Speak for yourself, little sister,' she said, raising her glass to me. 'Because for the first time in ages I don't feel ancient.' She laughed again.

She was wearing it like her new dress, her happiness, on show for everyone to see and I couldn't blame her. I'd seen the change in her over the past few weeks, although part of me hadn't wanted to. 'That's great,' I said. 'I'm really happy for you.'

'Oh, thanks, Carla,' she said. 'But with everything that's happening with Mammy I feel guilty, you know, to be happy. Like I don't care enough about her or something, do you know what I mean?' Her smile faltered and she fiddled with her glass.

'Yeah,' I said. 'I think so.'

'But it's OK to be happy, isn't it? Just because we're happy in our own lives doesn't mean we love Mammy any less.'

She was looking to me for a patch of reassurance to put over the nasty leak in her balloon of elation. I'd said I was happy for her and I was, but even as I listened to what she was saying, some other part of me was already in the future, a future when she and Simon were married, had children and moved to England and that part was terrified, absolutely terrified of where that would leave me.

'I lied earlier. I never spoke to Eddie, I never heard from him all day.'

I'd said the words before I'd realised I was going to, the timing all wrong as they clashed with the end of her laugh.

'Oh, no,' she said. 'You never called him?'

'No. But I thought he'd get in touch, at least text. It's Christmas Day.' I shook my head. 'I have this horrible feeling, Suzanne. What if he's seeing someone else?' I laughed, a sound that might have been a cry.

'You don't know that.' She put her wine on the mantelpiece and moved to perch on the arm of my chair. I wasn't expecting her closeness, we didn't do that. Her hand on my shoulder was hesitant but she left it there, and after a minute her grip tightened. She pulled me towards her and I leaned into her, just a bit. The tears were there now, not falling but on the edge.

'It's ridiculous for me to get so upset – it's just that it seems to have finally hit home today. This isn't a break, or time apart, or whatever we dressed it up as. It's been months now and neither of us has made a move to get back together. This is it, Suzanne, we're splitting up. He probably wants a divorce.'

'Hang on,' she said, 'you're jumping the gun. You don't know it's definitely over.'

Over. I leaned forward in the chair, away from her touch.

'I mean it's bound to be difficult, you here, him on tour. When you sit down face to face, talk things through this—'

'No,' I said, 'it's not just that. Things weren't perfect before – far from it.'

'But you always seemed to be getting on OK. You never fought.'

Why did everyone think not fighting was a gauge of fucking happiness?

'And things were going well enough for you to get married.'

It was a statement, not a question.

'So things were going well enough. "Well enough" isn't "brilliant", though, is it? It's not "madly in love". "Well enough" isn't a reason to get married.'

Anger came then, and it was better than the other feeling. Suzanne's hand hovered in mid-air, as if she wanted to touch me again but was afraid to. She picked up her wine and went back to her own chair. Dad's chair. I waited for her to say more, to tell me Eddie and I shouldn't have got married, to ask me why we had.

'Carla, I know it's none of my business but you might need to talk to Eddie about this. I know you don't want to be the one to get in touch but you might need to so you can figure out what to do next.'

'I don't want to talk about it.'

'You're married, you can't leave it like this. I know it's not the same as with me and Ian but I really needed closure before I could move on.'

Ian had broken up with Suzanne, I'd never really known why. Eddie and I hadn't even got that clarity it seemed; sometimes I wasn't even sure which of us had ended it. I snapped the lid off the chocolates, reached in for another. 'Suzanne, what part of not talking about this do you not get? It's Christmas Day. Can you just leave it for now?'

'Fine,' she said. 'OK.'

We sat in silence then, and I became conscious of the music

from the TV, the fact that the credits were rolling. I glanced at the fire. There were no flames left now, only red embers around the edge that ash was slowly eating away. It was time to go to bed, to finish the night, only I didn't want it to finish, not like this.

'Do you think there's any life left in this?' Suzanne shoved the poker into the grate so orange sparks flew up into the blackness of the chimney. Without waiting for me to answer, she put on another briquette and prodded it until a new flame licked up at the back.

'Pass me that paper,' she said. 'Let's see what's starting next.'

I hadn't asked her to stay up with me, hadn't expected her to. I was about to say that when I noticed the other feeling, relief that she wasn't heading up to bed yet, that I wouldn't be left on my own.

'Probably just another twenty-five Harry Potter films,' I said.

'Nah. Too late for that. I bet there's something good on. Half the time the best films don't start till after midnight.'

I reached down and picked up the paper. As I held it out to her I smiled and she smiled back, so for a second the two of us were smiling, our hands both on the paper before I let it go.

THREE

When I turned off the hairdryer I could hear voices, the sound of a baby. I grabbed my scarf from the bed, checked my coat pocket for gloves. Coming down the stairs I could see them all packed into the hall. Mum standing, arms folded, Suzanne on her hunkers in front of the buggy, Ange behind it, leaning over and shaking her curls at Emily, who tried to grab them with a pudgy hand.

'Hi,' I said. 'Sorry, I didn't hear you arrive.'

Ange grinned. 'Did we get you out of bed?'

'No – I was at yoga.'

Ange raised an eyebrow in Suzanne's direction. 'All this yoga. I'll show up one day and you'll be wearing robes.'

'Between Mammy and Carla I'm lucky they haven't turned the house into a Zen temple!' Suzanne turned to include Mum in the joke.

'Look at Ange's baby, Mammy. Her name's Emily. Isn't she gorgeous?'

'She's a dote,' Mum said. She flicked her hair behind her ear. A few seconds passed. She pulled it free again.

'Thanks, Mrs Matthews,' Ange said. 'It's nice to have a girl, not that I don't love the boys to death, but it's different.'

'Oh, I know.' Mum nodded, flicking her hair behind her ear. 'You're right there.'

You're right there. It was one of the things she said all the time now, something I could never remember her saying before. Words that filled space and meant nothing. She clung to them, like a few phrases in a foreign language.

'Come on, let's go,' I said to Ange. I opened the door and sunlight streamed through the glass porch.

Ange kissed Suzanne.

'Don't be a stranger,' Suzanne said. 'Drop in any time.'

'I will,' she said. 'Saturday mornings are perfect. Pete takes the boys swimming and I drop over to see Dad. Carla, Em and I have earmarked it now for our walks.'

I wheeled the buggy into the porch, eased it down the step. Ange was saying goodbye to Mum, hugging her.

'Nice to see you, love,' Mum said. 'Come back again soon.'

Love. Everyone was 'love' now, not just Suzanne and me. I hadn't noticed when it started but it seemed to be her default tag, as if it was better to welcome a stranger in rather than risk offending a friend.

'I will, Mrs Matthews,' Ange said, still holding Mum's arm. 'It's nice to see you.'

Mum smiled, a practised smile that didn't reach her eyes. A smile for passengers she'd never see again. A smile that probably meant she had no idea who Ange was at all.

*

Up on the hill the car park was packed and I was glad I wasn't driving. Ange circled it again, barely noticing how close she was to the other cars, the wall. A people-carrier with steamed-up windows pulled out and she jerked to a stop, waving it on. Seconds later she'd reversed in, without pausing in the story she was telling me about Pete's promotion.

'I don't know how you do that,' I said.

'What?'

'That manoeuvre. You make it look so easy. I could be there for ever and I wouldn't get the car into that space. I couldn't get a toy car in there.'

'I take it the driving lessons are going well?'

'It's so hard, Ange! The other cars, pedestrians. Bloody cyclists! How do so many people learn to do it?'

'It's practice, that's all. How's your instructor? Still texting you day and night?' She took a woolly hat from her pocket and put it on, checking it in the mirror.

I felt heat creep into my face. 'No!'

When she turned to look at me her curls were already starting to escape. 'I don't believe you. He sounds mad keen. You should go for it. Why not?'

'Maybe because he's twenty-four.'

'Could be just what the doctor ordered.'

Ange got out without giving me a chance to respond. As I put on my gloves, I giggled. It was ridiculous even to think it. Sean probably had no interest in me at all. And yet there was something about the conversation that made me feel better, lighter. Through the window I could see Ange bundling Emily into a fleecy hat that fastened under her chin. Maybe it wasn't to do with Sean at all. Maybe it was just that it was a conversation we'd had so many times about so many different guys. Their names and faces changed, but our friendship remained the same.

As I stepped out of the car the January air hit me like icy water and I wished I'd remembered a hat. I headed for the path we always took, around the front of the hill where you could see the sea, and the estates laid out next to each other, tiny Monopoly houses.

'You coming or what?' I called to her, where she stood by the car.

'Can we go the other way?' She jerked a thumb over her shoulder.

'Why? We always go this way.'

'Not any more,' she said, pointing at the buggy. 'There's steps that way.'

Of course there were, I'd forgotten. 'Sure,' I said, 'we can go whichever way you like.'

★

The path was narrow and Ange pulled the buggy in for another to pass. Behind the bare trees the sun was low in the sky. I checked my watch. Just after twelve – it was as high as it was going to get today.

'Your mum seems pretty good,' Ange said.

I scuffed my foot in the leaves at the side of the path. 'Yeah,' I said.

'I hope this doesn't sound terrible, but I'd been a bit afraid meeting her. You know, just in case she didn't know who I was.' Ange laughed, then stopped. 'But she seemed fine. If I didn't know, I'd never have noticed anything.'

I dug my hands deeper into my pockets, squeezed them tighter. Even in my gloves they were freezing. 'It can seem like that, when you see her for a short while. It's only when you're with her for longer that you start to notice it.'

I heard the echo of Suzanne's words on the day I'd first come home. Behind us I heard a jogger and stood back to let him bounce past us and disappear around the corner. Ange's breathing was heavy as the hill got steeper and I slowed down a little. I didn't have the heart to tell her that Mum's friendliness, her hug, probably hadn't meant anything.

'I know it can't be easy,' she said, 'working and looking after her. Do you get time for much else these days?'

'Actually, I've signed up for a writing class. I'd tried a few in New York but I'd end up missing half of them because of Eddie's gigs or work. This one's on Tuesdays, when the restaurant's closed so I'll have no excuse.'

'That sounds like fun, a good way to meet new people.'

I made a face. 'Sometimes I feel like I know too many people here already. I don't know if I want to meet any new ones.'

'Yeah, well, I think it's great, what you're doing, you and Suzanne, balancing everything, taking care of your mum. Not everyone would be so good.'

The buggy tyres swished over leaves. When I didn't answer her I felt her turn to look at me. 'What?' she said.

'I'm no saint, Ange. I feel guilty saying this but she drives me mad half the time. It seems like not a day passes without her developing some new annoying habit.'

'Like what?'

'Oh, I don't know,' I said. 'Everything, nothing. She's got this obsession with paper – envelopes, paper bags, pages from the calendar. She folds them up into these tiny squares and then she hides them in her bloody Aer Lingus bag or down the back of the couch.'

'She could be doing worse things.'

'Ah that's only one. She's so fidgety all the time. She's always fiddling with something, her hair, a pen, tapping something. For someone who used to be so still, she can't be quiet for a second now. It puts me on edge.'

Ange made a sound as though she understood, but I knew she didn't because I wasn't explaining it properly.

'And every time we go for a walk by the sea, she thinks she's back in Rosses Point in Sligo. She actually stops to look for that statue out in the sea – the Metal Man.'

Somewhere through the trees I heard a dog barking, a raw sound in the cold air. Even though it felt bad to talk about Mum, it felt good too, and once I'd started, it seemed I wasn't going to stop.

'Did you notice her thing with her hair? She does this thing where she flicks it behind her ear, leaves it for maybe ten seconds, then loosens it out again. Flicks it behind, takes it out. It drives me crazy, that and the sniffing. I'm always at her to blow her nose but every time I give her a tissue she just folds it up or shreds it. There's bits of tissue all over the house.'

'You should come to mine. That'd be the least of your worries. In any given place you can find Play-Doh, orange peel, crayons. Pete had a conniption the other morning because he sat on jam in his good suit.'

I remembered her kitchen, my hands sticking to the table. 'They're kids. It's a phase, they'll grow out of it. With Mum – well – it's different.' As soon as I'd said that I wished I could pull the words back in. It was a phase with Mum too, just that she was going the opposite way. I didn't want to think about what came next.

I heard Ange sigh, and when I turned she was hunched over the buggy – it was taking all her strength to get it up the hill. 'What?' She shook her head. It was hard to read her expression through the bouncing curls.

'Nothing,' she said. 'Look, I'm not saying it's not tough, Carla, but at least you still have her. Hair flicking or no hair flicking. At least she's still there.'

★

We were at my favourite part of the hill now, the grey-white tower of the Obelisk behind us, the whole bay laid out in front. All the way down the waves were crashing on to the shore but we were too high up to hear them.

'Thanks for the coffee,' I said. 'I didn't think to bring money – didn't know there was a coffee shop up here.'

'It's new,' Ange said. 'Thanks for watching Emily – she seemed quite taken with you.'

I glanced at Emily in her buggy behind us, chewing a dried apricot that Ange had produced from a ziplock bag. 'She's cute,' I said. 'While you were getting the coffee, some woman admired her, assumed she was mine.'

I leaned out further over the railing, so it dug into me just above my ribs. A little way out and down, birds were flying in a circle, six, seven, eight, whirling together, the sea far below. The coffee cup in my hands had warmed my fingers and I drank a sip. It tasted good. Everything about this moment tasted good.

'What's the latest with Eddie? Any word from him?'

Eddie. Hearing his name made me realise I hadn't been thinking about him. I waited for the pain to come and it did, but it was different, as if maybe I hadn't been waiting for it, it might have forgotten to show up. 'Nope, not a dicky bird.'

'Wow,' Ange said, leaning against the railing beside me. 'It must've been weird not to be in touch over Christmas.'

I was about to answer on auto-pilot that it hadn't been that bad, that I'd been fine, but at the last minute I said, 'It was really shit.'

294

Honesty brought relief, and I laughed into the wind. After a second, Ange joined in. 'I'm sorry,' she said. 'I shouldn't laugh.'

'It's OK,' I said, wiping a wind tear off my cheek. 'It's not OK, clearly. I mean, we're married, we can't just leave things. We need to sort them out.'

I didn't say the word but it was there, under all the others.

'What about your visa?' Ange said. 'What would happen to that?'

Divorce. She didn't say it either, didn't have to. I looked down at my feet, boots poking under the railing. Under the boot, under my socks, the tattoo was still there, infinity, a reminder of my own stupidity in hoping, thinking, things were ever certain.

'When I went to the embassy six months after I'd got here they gave me another six, so I guess I'll have to go back, prove Mum's still sick.'

'Well, she is.'

'Yeah, but I have to show them I'm still married. What if they contact Eddie and he says our marriage is over, that he's planning on marrying someone else?'

'He won't,' Ange said, 'not just like that. But you need to talk.'

'That's what Suzanne said.'

'She's right,' Ange said. 'Not knowing what he's thinking might make it even worse.'

I pushed down harder into my feet. There were too many things to talk to Eddie about, that was the problem, too many questions to ask. Earlier, in yoga, I'd imagined tree roots growing from my feet through the building and into the earth below. Now I was standing on a concrete step. Beneath it there were rocks, earth. Remembering that made it easier somehow, to believe that some time we'd make a start on those questions, even if we never found any answers. 'I hate to say it but I guess you're right. Both of you.'

My hair blew across my face and I let it stay there, watching the bay through strands of brown. Only seconds before Eddie'd been so far away he mightn't have existed at all. Now he was like the birds, flying in circles, close enough almost to touch.

'Anyway, enough of all that,' I said. 'How are things with you?'

'Ah, you know. Grand. Same old, same old.'

She looked down at her hands where they were gripping the railing, swung a little back and forth. Her movements were so familiar, tiny details that I must've carried in my head for years, meaningless until a moment like this when they weren't meaningless at all. I waited for her to tell me what was wrong.

'I'm seeing a counsellor,' she said, glancing at Emily and back to the sea. 'Ah, it's nothing really. I've just been down since everything with Mum. Pete thought it was a good idea, that it might help me.'

What I said next was important, the balance between being interested and prying. Too many questions and she'd clam up, never mention it again. Too few, and I'd seem not to care.

'And does it?' I didn't look at her when I asked, faced the water, the curve of the shoreline.

'No!' She laughed suddenly. 'I was grand before I went, and now it seems I can't stop crying.'

I thought of Mum's office, the box of tissues next to the clock. 'Maybe that's a good thing,' I said. 'Maybe it's a sign you needed to go.'

Ange sighed. 'That's what she says, Niamh. That's her name. She thinks I haven't grieved for Mum. Apparently there's all these stages and if you don't go through them you never get rid of it, the grief. It just gets frozen or something. That's her theory anyway.'

'It makes sense,' I said.

She turned to me, and I knew what she was going to say.

'I don't remember you crying after your dad died. Did you? You must have.'

The conversation was dangerously close to one we'd had over pints of Heineken in the Buttery, when Ange had told me she thought I was doing too well, that I should have been more upset.

'I suppose I did, but I don't remember crying much,' I said. 'Suzanne did, she went to counselling. It's got to help, having someone to talk to.'

'It does.' She reached into her pocket and pulled out a tissue.

It was hard to say what I said next, but I knew I needed to, that I should have before.

'And I know it's not the same, but you know you can always talk to me, if you want. I always felt bad, that I wasn't there for you, when it happened.'

'Thanks,' she said. 'I know I could. I just feel so bloody miserable all the time and you've enough going on, you don't need me moaning on too.'

I was about to tell her that that didn't matter but as she blew her nose, a gust of wind came, whipping her hat into the air, past Emily, whirling it down behind her.

Ange ran around the buggy and pounced, but it was too fast for her, a rolling blur of blue and purple that she had to chase across the grass. I couldn't help but laugh at the shapes she made swiping the air. Over the wind I heard her curse. As suddenly as the wind had come it fell away again, dropping the hat on to a bush. She snatched at it, not realising it was snagged on a briar.

'Look at that! The wool's all pulled,' she said, walking back, breathless. 'And I love how me being so unfit is giving you such a good laugh.'

'Emily, did you see the state of Mummy running after her hat?' I said. 'She looked funny, didn't she?'

Emily looked from me to Ange and stretched out her little gloved fist.

'There you go, love, you mind that for Mummy,' Ange said, handing her the hat. 'It's good to see you laugh like that,' she said to me. 'Remember how much we used to laugh all the time?' She took her hat back from Emily and rammed it into her pocket.

We turned to walk back the way we had come. An old couple were walking towards us, arm in arm, the woman pointing at something through the trees. The man had glasses, a hat with fur pulled over his ears and a peak. If Dad was alive he'd be getting old, wouldn't be far off that man's age. I couldn't imagine him ever wearing a hat like that.

'Do you remember that picnic we went on up here, years ago?' Ange said. 'With Pete and Damien?'

'No,' I said.

'Ah, you do.' Ange elbowed my arm. 'Remember Nosy Rosie's hamper?' She looked at me expectantly, a twitch of laughter back in her face, and an image surfaced: a wicker hamper, weighed down with real plates, cups and saucers, and silver cutlery.

'Yes! I do! It must've weighed two hundred pounds!'

Ange's giggles fizzed up. 'Pete tried to act all macho, took it from Damien, but he could barely lift it either. It took the two of them to get it up here and we ended up eating just beyond the car park!'

It was before Dad had died, I knew by the colour of the memory, the summer before. I remembered it all then – the botched plan to liven the picnic up with a naggin of vodka Pete's brother had bought for him, that we couldn't drink it because we were too much in view of everyone who came and went.

'I don't think I've ever laughed so much as when Pete's mum's bridge partner came along with her dog and he spilled what was left of the vodka all over himself,' I said. 'I don't know how she didn't smell it.'

I expected to see Ange crack up too, but her laugh seemed to have frozen. Her eyes were serious, Emily's eyes in a different face. 'What?' I said.

'I was just wondering,' she said, 'what life might have been like if you and Damien had stayed together. Do you ever think about that?' As soon as the words were out, she covered her mouth with her gloved hand. 'Jesus, sorry, what a stupid thing to say! What a ridiculous thing to bring up.'

'It's OK,' I said.

'It's not. Me and my big mouth. Christ. Forget I said anything.'

Underneath our feet the path was more of a slope now and her hands gripped the buggy tightly. I wanted to say something to change the subject but as our footsteps clipped down the path I couldn't think of a single thing.

From around the grey stone of the hill, the car park came into view, more cars, more children, different families. If I'd stayed I could have been there now, with Damien, in a car just like one of those. I loosened the scarf around my neck.

We reached the edge of the tarmac and waited for a gap in the traffic.

'I've really enjoyed the walk,' Ange said. 'Can we do it again next Saturday? I hope I didn't ruin it, bringing up that stupid thing about Damien.'

'No.' I smiled. 'Don't be silly. Damien was a hundred thousand years ago. I don't mind you bringing him up. Honestly.'

As I said it, I realised that it was true, that in fact I was glad she'd asked, because if she hadn't, I mightn't have asked myself the question and I was glad now that I had. Glad that I had realised, no matter what I decided to do now, there had been no way, back then, that I could have stayed.

No way at all.

FOUR

I tucked the sheet over the bottom corner of the mattress and pulled it towards the top. It stopped halfway because I had it the wrong way round. Changing the bedclothes had always been the job I hated most of all. I yanked it off and started again.

The housework had been an endless source of arguments between me and Suzanne and eventually she had resorted to drawing up a schedule that she stuck on the fridge, next to the list of phone numbers. At first I'd thought it was ridiculous, another example of her over-planning, but I was getting used to it. And now I only had to change Mum's bedclothes every other week.

This time the sheet fitted and I smoothed one side, then pulled the bed out so I could do the other. In the background, my housework music was playing, a CD I'd taken out of the library by a band called Ash. I'd never heard of them before so they slotted in well to my Eddie-free music strategy. It was the beginning of 'Candy', my favourite song on the album, and I danced between the bed and the wall.

The sheet's elastic was nearly gone so I pulled it tight under the corner so it wouldn't come out. Suzanne ironed them when it was her turn, but who had time to iron sheets? 'Candy' was getting to the best part now, the line about it being all right to be alone. I sang loudly, drowning the lead singer's voice.

I went around to the other side and pushed the bed back in so it would line up flush with the wall. As I did, a book fell from the bedside locker. One week I'd put them all away, those books, but

Mum had taken them back. Even though she didn't read any more, she seemed to take comfort from having them around her, just like she always had.

I bent down to pick it up. *When Things Fall Apart.* It was the same book I'd brought back to the library for Lily-Anne, the one Audrey had mentioned. It seemed to be following me around. Maybe it was a sign. I sat down on the bed and it fell open at a page near the middle, marked by some folded paper. I took the paper out and started to read a chapter called 'Growing Up', then closed it. It was more of the same, I could see that in the first line, these books were all the same. I put it on top of the others on the locker and went to slide the folded paper back inside, when something made me open it.

It was handwritten, Mum's writing, the shape of a letter. There were two sheets, not one, and when I put the back one to the front I saw the first line: *Dear Carla.* I folded the paper again and shoved it into the back pocket of my jeans. I picked up a pillowcase, flapping it out to straighten it, before pushing the pillow inside as if nothing had happened. Ash had moved on to another song, one I wasn't as keen on, and it was too much now, the music, taking up all the space in my head. I turned the stereo off, the silence sudden. Standing there, I bit my lip, as if I'd forgotten what to do next.

I reached back into my pocket, pulled the paper out, sat down on the bed. I could hear the heating pulsing in the house. I had been warm a second ago but now there were goosebumps on my skin. I looked at the two sheets of white paper, folded in my lap. I could throw the letter away, never know what it said, what she'd once wanted me to hear.

I wanted to read it but my fingers didn't take the order from my brain, wouldn't move to open the letter. Fear, that was what it was, in my body, just like in yoga when I tried to do a handstand. There was always something to be afraid of. I took a breath, slowly opened the pages.

The writing was moving about and I realised my hand was

shaking. It was dated, I hadn't noticed that before, 21st March, nearly four years ago. I rested the paper on my thigh.

Dear Carla,

I'm writing this letter to you from the conservatory. You've never seen the conservatory but I think you'd like it. At the moment the door is open so I can feel the breeze that is making the heads of the daffodils outside nod. From next door I can hear the sounds of the children playing and laughing and the occasional scream! It reminds me of the parties you and Suzanne used to have. There's nothing quite like the sound of children playing, is there?

Something about the line, the order of words, took my breath from me and I had to stop. Outside, the wind was blowing the top of the McCarthys' oak tree. The house was so quiet I could hear its leaves rustling. 'Rustling unselfconsciously'. The phrase came into my head from something I'd read, or written for my writing class. Some part of me was already turning this into a story, making up the end, but the rest of me knew it wasn't a story. I went on with the letter.

I've just spoken to you on the phone and you sound in good form. You told me about the new demo Eddie's band are making and you sounded excited. I think it was the excitement in your voice that stopped me telling you what I'd called you for. I think that's the reason I started to write this letter.

Even as I wrote that last line I was aware that it sounded melodramatic and might not even be true. What's more likely is that I was looking for an excuse not to tell you. I'm still not sure — even as I write this — whether I am writing a 'DNS' or a real letter. Do you remember I told you about DNS? 'Do Not Sends' — that's what it stands for and I sometimes encourage my clients to write them to express their feelings — things they can't or for some reason won't say. Often these are things the recipient couldn't hear or doesn't need to hear. But sometimes the act of writing is enough. Anyway, those are DNS letters but this can't be a DNS because I need to tell you something, something real, that you need to know, regardless of how either of us feels about it. So here goes: I have been diagnosed with early-onset Alzheimer's disease.

There, it's said. It doesn't get any easier, you know, writing it or saying it. Something about it reminds me of after your dad died and I had to tell people I was a widow. A widow. It came as a surprise every single time I said it, as if I was finding out for the first time myself all over again. It was a hurdle, looming in a sentence, that I had to jump again and again and again. And so far this disease — Alzheimer's — feels, in some ways, the same.

Before I go on I'd like to apologise, Carla, for telling you this in a letter, for not being able to say it on the phone earlier. For not being precise and concise about it, for rambling around the point. Let's get to the facts.

They call it early onset because I am not sixty yet and also because I am in the early stages. For a disease that impacts on so many millions of people they seem to know remarkably little about it. There are many stages that take place over years, decades for some people. I am lucky to be in the early stages. The symptoms are mild – hard to spot. I forget people's names, place names, words, but who doesn't at times? Mostly I cover it up, find another word, get reminded of a name. So far the impact on my day-to-day living has not been too much, other than giving up my practice, of course. The doctor said I could've kept on working with my clients, that I didn't need to stop yet. But once I knew, I couldn't continue. They rely on me, I need to be so fully there for them. Better to help them reach an ending with me now than slowly let go later.

So, what else? Suzanne doesn't know yet. Once I send this, I will tell her. I wanted to tell you both together, but this is as 'together' as our little family seems to get any more. Facts, Collette, stick to the facts.

I'm on medication. I have been since I was first diagnosed. The medication I'm on has proven effective at managing the symptoms in the early stages. Some patients have even reported a reversal of symptoms. It's not a cure – you'll see as soon as you look up Alzheimer's on the Internet that there is no cure yet – but it's the best they have right now. And all the doctors say a cure is close, imminent. And even without one, people last for years with this disease, ten years, longer. So try not to worry, there's no need to worry.

So those are the facts. What about feelings? How do I feel? You'd think being a therapist I'd have some notion of how to answer that but the reality is my feelings are like one of those old-fashioned spinning tops, a whole mix of things spinning so fast they blend into one most of the time. I'm frightened, but I'm coping. I found a support group on the Internet and talking to them online helps. I'm working with Lily-Anne to develop a mindfulness practice around this, to approach this disease with the curiosity and openness that I've worked to approach everything else in my life. There are days when this approach works, when I can see this disease as the ultimate opportunity to be present, to live each and every moment. On those days I am reminded of my grandfather and the walks we took together around Sligo when I was a little girl. We had to walk slowly because of his hip and I can still see him, drawn in by every detail – a bird in a hedge, a raindrop on a line of web – stopping to notice everything. I used to be impatient until I saw things through his eyes, listened as he explained how important it was to pay attention, to look, as well as see.

So, on the good days, I feel like I look as well as see and I am walking with my grandfather again. But not every day is like that. There are days when I feel the worst thing about this disease – the very worst thing – is knowing that I have it and I wish, more than anything, that I could go back to a place of not knowing, that I hadn't pushed the doctor for a diagnosis. On those days I feel gutted, sick, despairing, angry, robbed – not only of my own future but of yours and Suzanne's too. And most of the time I feel a little bit terrified of losing you, both of you, and of losing myself.

Oh dear. I fear that this has turned into a DNS letter after all. I just read back the last paragraph and it's not what

I wanted to say, not why I was writing to you at all. Maybe I'll rewrite it and take that last bit out or maybe I'll send it to you anyway, by express post, just as it is. Or maybe I'll call you back, right now, and tell you all this. But you'll be on your way to work now so maybe I'll call tomorrow, or at the weekend, or maybe I'll book a flight over so I can tell you myself. Maybe Suzanne will come over too.

If you're reading this, it means I didn't have the courage to do any of that, that I took the easy way out and let these words on this page do what I couldn't do. And if you're angry, please forgive me. And if you're upset and worried about the future, stay in today as much as you can.

We've been through tough times – we both know that – and we've always coped, haven't we? We're not given things in life that we can't handle, I believe that, and I remind myself of it every day. And remember, Carla, that everything – absolutely everything – passes.

Always know I love you.

Mum

x

She'd never sent the letter by express post or any other kind. She hadn't taken the easy way out. Instead she'd taken an easier one – she hadn't told me at all, at least not until she had no other choice. An urge came over me to crumple up the paper and fling it across the room, but I let it pass. Instead I laid it on the bed next to me.

A conversation in March four years ago, Eddie making a demo. Four years ago we were living in Greenpoint, in a basement apartment I'd never liked. Dawn was in the band then. I'd no recollection of a demo, but they'd made so many demos. I tried to remember Mum's phone call. The brightest room in that apartment was the little kitchenette and I'd liked to sit on the window ledge. That was where I would have been sitting, on the phone to Mum, and I could imagine the call, but there was no way I could tell where imagination stopped and memory began.

What would have happened if she'd told me that day? If she'd sent the letter? Would I have quit my job? Moved home? Would Eddie and I have got married? Would everything have turned out the same anyway?

I read the letter again, slower this time. Each paragraph sounded different from the one before it, one confiding, the next detached. My eyes stopped on the line about there being no cure. She sounded formal, objective, as if she was writing an article on Alzheimer's, not talking about something she actually had.

I put the letter down, rubbed my eyes hard, picked it up again. All this stuff about approaching it with curiosity and openness. Did she really try that? Had it worked? There was no way to tell now.

I stood up and folded the paper, put it back into my pocket. I picked up the second pillow, found the pillowcase behind me on the bed. Outside it was almost dark, nearly time to get ready for work. I had to iron a shirt first. There was one downstairs, fresh from the line.

Thoughts came and I was aware of each one, standing alone in my head, another forming. I was aware of my movements, slow and steady, making the bed. I was aware of the letter, the words, in Mum's writing, burning through the denim into my skin.

Facts and feelings, that was how she'd structured the letter. Now I knew some more facts and I was aware, as I straightened the duvet, that the feelings hadn't come yet.

But I wasn't fooled. They wouldn't be far behind.

FIVE

My eyes were starting to close and I jerked them open. On my lap, the book was about to fall, and when I moved, it slid on to the floor. Yesterday I'd gotten through a whole chapter but today I'd been reading the same paragraph, the same line, over and over and it still wouldn't penetrate. I'd thought the book might help, that there might be something in it, some clue as to why Mum had never sent the letter, but if there was I couldn't find it.

I didn't have the energy to bend down and pick it up, just let it sit there in the lines of light the blinds made on the floor. The cover was like so many other of these books, trees reflected in still water, *When Things Fall Apart* in big blue letters. When had Mum bought it? When she was diagnosed? How long before? Underneath the title there was another line, made to look like handwriting: 'Heart advice for difficult times'. So far the only advice I'd found was to sit with it, breathe, let go. Just like with all the other books. Was that really all there was?

Sinking back into the chair, I thought of Mum's letter, how having Alzheimer's had reminded her of being with her grandfather, looking and seeing. What a crock of shit. This was a disease, a terminal fucking disease, that robbed you of your memory, your dignity and your personality. No amount of mindfulness was going to change that. She'd been wasting her time, wasting all that fucking time that she could've spent with Suzanne, with me.

'Fuck it, anyway!'

The anger brought a surge of energy and I lashed out with my foot, kicking the book, pages flapping.

'Fuck it, fuck it, fuck it!'

I was on my feet then, kicking it again so it rolled over awkwardly from one corner to another like some banjaxed football. Twice I missed it, so my shoe scuffed the rug, which stoked my rage even brighter.

'Fuck you!'

I picked up the book and flung it across the room so it landed by the fireplace. I didn't know who 'you' was, or if the noise I was making might wake Mum from her nap, but there wasn't room to care about any of that. On the couch the cushions were smooth, plumped up, and I took a run at them, pummelling them with my fists. I didn't stop to pull the curtains or wonder who might be looking in as I bent low to get a better impact, so I could really feel its resistance, the strength of my punch.

My fists took up a rhythm, I was almost enjoying it, my breath and words pushed out along with the motion.

'Fuck you, fuck you, fuck you!'

In my room I'd stuck bullshit affirmations on the wall, positive sayings to start the day. Today's had been 'I focus on my many blessings'. I punched harder. I kneed one of the cushions from the couch and it bounced on to its side. I kicked it again and again and again.

When it was over I sat on the floor. I didn't cry, just sat there wrapped in a quiet calm. It was nothing like the calm at the end of yoga or even after a run. It was an empty feeling, as if there was nothing at all left. I lifted my T-shirt from my chest and felt the dampness on my skin, ran my fingers over my forehead to touch the sheen of sweat. I thought about Mum upstairs and when it would be time to wake her and what time I needed to put the dinner on. I heard next door's TV and hoped they hadn't heard me through the wall and what they would think if they had.

I didn't cry.

After a while I put the couch back together so it looked as if nothing had happened. I remembered our old couch, being curled up on it at the end Mum had said was too close to the TV. I used to take the cushions off it for games of war, using them as sandbags or as rafts to carry me down the river rapids. It was still there when I went to America and I wondered what had happened to it, when it had been replaced. The thought brought a sudden sadness, for the old couch and for the new one – I'd spent so much aggression on it even though it wasn't its fault.

'I'm sorry,' I said, hugging one of the cushions tight. 'I'm sorry.'

I picked up the book from its spot on the floor. The binding was loose at one end and some of the middle pages were crumpled. I flattened them with my hand, pushing them back so they'd stay where they were supposed to. I found my bookmark by the chair on the floor, from the Strand Bookshop, one of my favourite nooks in New York. I slipped it into the book, hiding it. I didn't want to think about New York.

I held the book to me and walked to the window. The brightness was nearly gone from the day but even in this light I could see the overgrown borders straggling on to the gravel driveway. In the shadow from the wall I couldn't see the flowers, dead from the winter, but I knew they were there.

We'd do that tomorrow, I decided. If the weather was nice we'd spend the morning in the garden, getting it ready for spring. The book was still in my hand but I didn't feel like going upstairs. If I left it in here, Mum might see it, remember the letter and wonder what had happened to it. Maybe she'd ask me about it. As the thought formed, I knew she wouldn't, that I was only pretending. Hoping. Even so, it would be better to bring it up to my room where she wouldn't see it.

Just in case.

Six

The driving lesson had gone better than before, the best yet and watching Sean turn the car and drive away I felt a little elated, as if someday I might be able to do that on my own too. When I opened the front door I heard Lily-Anne's voice and I remembered what day it was. I walked down the hall and into the kitchen and felt the elation pop and fizz away.

The room was a mess. The long cupboard door was open and it seemed like everything had been emptied out. Every surface was piled high with baking tins, mixing bowls, trays. Lily-Anne's smile split the streak of flour that went down the side of her face. 'There you are! You're just in time to taste the mixture. We decided to make an apple tart too, while we were at it, didn't we, Coll?'

Mum picked up the rolling pin from the counter and moved it to the table. A strip of dough dangled from it, then fell on to the floor.

'Great,' I said. 'That's nice.'

Under the extractor fan I could hear the burble of the radio. I walked over and turned it off. Lily-Anne held out a wooden spoon with some brown goo. 'Try some – it's chocolate. Suzanne's favourite!' I saw more of the mixture in her hair.

'No, thanks.'

Mum picked up a cake tray that they weren't using and took it over to the sink. Once she'd put it in, she turned to me, her face serious. 'It's Suzanne's birthday,' she said. 'Don't forget now, sure you won't?'

If it hadn't been for me she wouldn't have remembered. No

one would. I leaned into the fridge to find the Diet Coke, but it wasn't there. Beside the bin I saw the empty bottle, waiting to be recycled. I closed the door harder than I needed to. 'I won't forget,' I said. 'I've taken the night off, remember?'

'And I'm sure she appreciates it,' Lily-Anne said. 'How was your driving lesson? You must be nearly ready for the test by now.'

'Grand,' I said, as I filled a glass with water. 'I've only one left after this.'

Lily-Anne started to say something else, but Mum cut across her.

'I always tried to be here for their birthday parties,' she said. 'One time I nearly missed Suzanne's but I switched with Jeannie. I was supposed to go to Madrid and she was supposed to go to Paris. She preferred Paris, we all preferred Paris. But she didn't mind.' She flicked her hair behind her ear and loosened it again.

'I'm sure Suzanne was glad to have you here, Coll. Carla's taken tonight off work as well, so she can be here.'

Lily-Anne sounded interested but I knew from the way she pummelled the cake mixture that she'd heard the story already. 'Are you busy, Carla?' she said.

Her words caught me when I was at the door, my hand already on the handle.

'I was about to go online, sort out about my driving test. Sean says it's the quickest way to book.'

She was going to ask me to do something, to stay, I knew she was, and even though I was just in I needed to get out again.

'You wouldn't be able to do me a favour, would you?' Lily-Anne smiled. 'We bought some balloons earlier, for the party, and we were hoping you'd blow them up for us before Suzanne gets home.'

'Balloons? Seriously? She's going to be thirty-five, not five!'

Lily-Anne laughed her loud laugh. 'You're never too old for balloons. Are you, Coll?'

'No.' Mum shook her head, flicked her hair. 'You're right there.'

It would have been churlish to point out that four people didn't make a party, that Suzanne would rather have been spending the evening with Simon than with us. I made room on the table for my glass of water and put it down. 'All right, then. Just a few. Mum, pass them over to me, would you?'

Mum handed me a tube of fairy-cake cases. They weren't making fairy cakes.

'No, Mum! The balloons. Pass me the balloons!'

She put the fairy-cake cases down, and looked at everything else on the table: a bar of cooking chocolate, butter, hundreds and thousands. Her hand hovered in mid-air and she glanced at me, then back at the table.

'Never mind, I'll get them.' I stood up and reached past her, my hand finding the balloons just before hers did. From the corner of my eye I could see Lily-Anne watching me. Mum walked over to her, standing close to the counter. When she turned I saw that flour had made a line on her jumper, the hand-wash one I'd just washed. 'Lily-Anne, you might want to put an apron on her,' I said, 'although it's probably a bit late now.'

I opened the packet of balloons, sat back down and picked out a green one. I stretched it long, short, long, and started to blow.

'I always tried to be here for the birthday parties,' Mum said. 'One time I would've missed Suzanne's only Jeannie switched with me. I was supposed to be on the Madrid flight, she had Paris. She didn't mind, though.'

Patience. I timed the word with each blow. Patience, patience, patience. I tied a knot in the balloon. Mum was smiling, half looking out into the garden. Her hands picked up the greaseproof paper and unrolled it on the counter.

'Was it difficult for Jeannie to switch?' Lily-Anne said.

She spooned the cake mixture into a baking tin, looking at Mum as she asked the question, as if she really cared about the answer. I wanted to be able to do that, to be like her, but I wasn't like her. I was only me.

'Lily-Anne, watch her, will you? She's going to unravel that whole thing.'

Lily-Anne gently lifted the greaseproof paper from Mum's hands, rolling it up, then giving it back to her. I picked up another balloon, stretched it. I let go too soon and the rubber stung my knuckles, right where my skin was raw and red from the cold weather. 'Shit!'

Mum swung around, her face concerned. 'Are you all right, love, did you hurt yourself?'

'I'm fine,' I said. I picked up the balloon again and started to blow. It squeaked in my hand, expanding in one breath. It wasn't fully inflated but I tied a knot in it anyway, put it on the chair and reached for another.

Lily-Anne was smoothing the top of the cake mixture. For my birthday last year Suzanne had got a cake in Tesco at the last minute. Everyone would have forgotten if I hadn't dropped some hints. I knew I had to stop thinking like this, comparing, raking over the embers of anger long gone cold. I knew I had to stop but somehow, I couldn't.

There was something wrong with the balloon and it wouldn't blow up, the air getting stuck in the tube. Lily-Anne opened the oven door and a blast of hot air rushed out. Mum was standing by the counter, licking the mixture off the wooden spoon.

'You never let me do that,' I said.

Mum stopped licking. 'What, love?'

I threw the balloon to one side and picked up another. 'You never let me lick the wooden spoon. You always said it was unhygienic.'

Lily-Anne stood between us, wiping her hands on a tea-towel. 'It probably is,' she said, 'but sure as long as we give it a proper wash, it'll be fine.'

Mum put the spoon down on the counter and I felt a flicker of guilt.

'Those balloons are looking good, Carla,' Lily-Anne said, leaning down to put her hand on my shoulder. 'Maybe when your

314

mum and I have cleaned up the kitchen you can put them up. A couple around the picture maybe. And the door. We got some "Happy Birthday" bunting too.' She picked up a brown bag and took out the bunting, unfolding it to reveal a red glittering 'H' a silver 'A' a purple 'P.' 'Before you say it, I know it's tacky. My choice, not your mother's, but we both thought Suzanne would get a kick out of it!'

I kept blowing. Balloons and cake and bunting. Who was this party for? Mum smiled her wide smile at me and Lily-Anne, flicking her hair behind her ear. 'One time I nearly missed Suzanne's party. I always liked to be here for their birthdays. Jeannie was supposed to have the Paris flight—'

'Jesus Christ!' I yanked the balloon away from my mouth so the air farted out of it. 'We know! You were meant to be going to Madrid, only you swapped and you came home and you made the party and Suzanne was delighted and you all lived happily ever after! We know!'

Mum looked from Lily-Anne to me. She was upset, confused, but I didn't care. *I* was upset, *I* was confused. Why was it always about *her*?

'Carla,' Lily-Anne said, her hand reaching out for me again. I jerked my arm away before she could touch me.

'What? Don't act like I'm the only one who's driven crazy by her repeating all this crap over and over. You've had it all day – you must be fit to swing for someone by now!'

I'd gone too far. Even as I was saying the words I knew I was going too far but they were spilling out everywhere, all around me, and like the air from the balloon Mum stood there, completely silent, no hair flicking, nothing, just calm. And then she ran past me, throwing open the door into the hall. I heard it bang off the wall, the thump-thump of her feet on the stairs.

Lily-Anne didn't say anything. She took the apron off slowly, holding her ponytail in one hand so it didn't get caught on the strap. She hung it over the back of a chair and went into the hall, closing the door behind her. I was left on my own. Just like I wanted.

★

The water was too hot, scalding my hands, but I didn't care. The mixture at the edge of the bowl had already hardened and I scrubbed at it with the back of the brush. Behind me, I heard the door open, then close again. It was Lily-Anne.

'I know what you're going to say,' I said.

In the sink the suds were nearly all gone and I added more washing-up liquid, more water. I churned it around so some splashed on to my jumper. Lily-Anne found a tea-towel, picked up a cup and started to dry it. 'Those mind-reading skills must be coming along well.'

I took the bowl out of the water, saw it was still dirty and put it back in again. 'It's not her fault. She's sick. She doesn't do it on purpose. I should be more patient with her. I know that. I know.'

The bowl would have to do. I left it to drain on the rack and reached for a stack of plates. Next to me, Lily-Anne was silent, only the squeak of tea-towel on bowl.

'I hate when I lose my temper with her, I literally hate myself. She's my mother. She's sick. There's nothing you can say that will make me feel worse than I already do.'

'I wasn't going to try and make you feel bad,' Lily-Anne said. 'I was going to ask you what was wrong.'

In the dark of the window I saw her reflection, next to mine. Dad used to wash and Suzanne and I took turns to dry and put away. I'd always liked putting away.

I fake-laughed. 'Where will I start? My mother has a terminal illness. My marriage is over. I'm back waiting tables, only for less money. What could possibly be wrong?'

Saying all that out loud sounded good, as if even a saint would have lost it under those circumstances.

'That's all very challenging,' Lily-Anne said, carefully wiping the inside of the bowl. 'But I was wondering if something else had happened. You haven't been yourself these last few weeks.'

I was glad that my face was red from the heat, that she wasn't able to see into my eyes. I decided to spit it out, to ask her.

'When Mum first found out she was sick, did she ever do those support groups online?' I made myself sound casual, kept my hands busy in the water. I was flying through the plates now, standing them up, one by one, like soldiers.

Lily-Anne had stopped drying. She put down the tea-towel and leaned her hip against the counter to face me. 'Why?'

I wanted to tell her but I didn't want to as well.

I sighed. 'I found a letter a few weeks ago that she'd meant to send to me, telling me about her diagnosis. In it she said that she was part of some support group online. It's no big deal.'

Nearly all the suds were gone and in the water my hands looked pale.

'It doesn't sound like no big deal.'

'OK, so it's a big deal. Ever since I found the damn letter I haven't been able to stop thinking about it, what would've happened if she'd sent it. Every time I go online, I find myself searching through archived posts on all these Alzheimer's sites as if I'll find her there or something. Even earlier, when I said about the driving test? That was what I really wanted to do on the computer – look up Alzheimer's sites. It's bullshit, a waste of time. But I can't seem to stop.'

A line popped into my head that I'd seen on one of those sites, the one I'd been trying to forget. Something about the 'unrelenting grind of emptiness', the 'absence of something still there'. The person who had posted it called herself Missus Happy. The line didn't make sense, didn't mean anything, yet every time I thought of those words, they brought me to tears. I wiped my eye with my wrist.

Lily-Anne held out the tea-towel. 'Here, dry your hands. We've time for a cup of tea before we finish the rest of these.'

★

Sitting at the table, I watched Lily-Anne boil the kettle, take out two cups, open a new box of teabags. Simple steps that Mum couldn't do any more. 'Here you go,' she said, sliding mine in front of me, a red tag dangling from the cup.

'Thanks. I didn't think we'd any of these yoga teabags left.'

She picked up her own tag and read it. '"Happiness is taking things as they are." That's a timely reminder. What does yours say?'

Usually they cheered me up, the little sayings with each teabag, like wise fortune cookies, but I wasn't in the mood. I read it quickly. '"To learn, read; to know, write; to master, teach."'

'Teach?' she said, raising an eyebrow. 'Interesting you got that one. Coll told me you used to want to be a lecturer.'

I yanked the teabag from the cup and dumped it in the saucer. 'I'm sick of all these bullshit sayings that mean everything and say nothing. I feel like all I ever do is read all this crap, in books, on teabags. It's not working, Lily-Anne. Nothing I'm doing is working.'

She squeezed her own teabag with a spoon and laid it gently on her saucer. 'And what would it be like if things were working?' she said.

'No! I'm not your client, we're not going to get into one of these conversations.'

She smiled, blew on her tea. 'Sorry, force of habit. Do you want to tell me about the letter? This stuff you read online?'

I sipped my tea. It was too hot.

'I'm not trying to be your therapist, Carla. I'm really not, but I just thought it might help you to talk about it.'

I spread my hand on the tabletop, pushed down into the pads of my fingers, like Audrey always made sure we did in yoga.

'Ever since I read the letter, it's like I'm raging all the time. I'm angry with her all over again for not telling us, but I'm angry about other things too. Irrational stuff that happened decades ago. It even feels like I'm angry with her for getting sick.'

Lily-Anne's blue eyes were on mine, watery. 'Maybe you are.'

I hit my hand off the table. 'But so what if I am? It doesn't change anything. It's still there. And don't say I should sit with it,

318

accept it. Feel it. I feel like I'm doing nothing but fucking feeling it.'

Over on the dresser there was a card, an invite to a christening from Mum's friend Pauline, her first grandchild. When I'd shown it to Mum she'd held it briefly, then started to fold it into squares.

'Carla, listen, I know all this stuff hurts, but it's the only way through it. Believe me, I know.'

'I wish I could be like you, Lily-Anne, have your patience. I'm trying. But she's your friend, not your mother. It's not the same. The feelings aren't the same.' I fiddled with my cup, turning it in its saucer. Part of me felt bad for saying it but it needed to be said. Lily-Anne acted like family, but she wasn't. That was what made it different. It had to.

She was silent for a minute. Then she said, 'I never told you, did I, that I had my own daughter?'

She knew she hadn't. I tried to catch her eye, but she was examining her hands, crossed in front of her, on the table.

'Pamela,' she said. 'Joe and I had tried for years and it seemed like it was never going to happen for us. All our friends were having babies, little boys and girls, and you'd go to the christenings, congratulate them and smile. You had to smile.'

'That must've been hard,' I said.

She nodded, drank some tea.

'I remember one summer when everyone seemed to be pregnant. It was a scorcher as well. One Saturday, I was on O'Connell Street and I saw this pregnant woman with a baby in a buggy and two other little tots in tow. I'll never forget it. She went into Easons and left the buggy right there, at the bottom of the steps, with the baby in it. All alone, in that heat! I went right up and looked in at him. I swear to you, Carla, I nearly took him.'

She was biting her bottom lip, but smiling too.

'Can you imagine, the size of me making a run down O'Connell Street with someone else's baby? She probably had some bruiser of a husband in tow as well.'

She giggled and I did too. The laughter felt good, brought the air back in.

'By the time Pammy came along it was years later. The funny thing was, I think we'd both made peace with it by then, accepted that it wasn't going to happen for us.'

She'd smiled when she said her name but there was pain in the smile. Pammy. Her hands kneaded each other on the table.

'You don't have to tell me this,' I said.

'She was late starting school, nearly five, because she was born in June, like you. And a few weeks later she got sick. I thought it was something she'd picked up from the playground – you know how kids come down with everything when they start school.'

I was squeezing my cup so hard it might shatter.

She looked across at me and took a breath, as if she had to take a run at what she was going to say next. 'It was leukaemia, the acute kind. They didn't have the same treatments back then. She died four days before her birthday. She would've been seven.'

I imagined the presents already bought, the wrapping paper, the card. A silent tear slipped down Lily-Anne's cheek, through the smear of flour. I searched for something to say, something that would make it better, but nothing could make it better.

'I'm sorry.'

She wiped the tear away, blew her nose. Some of her white hair had fallen into her eyes.

'Talk about anger? I was so angry. Livid with everyone, everything, God. When that started to wear off the guilt set in and that was worse.'

'Guilt?'

She sighed. 'I blamed myself. I told myself I should've noticed sooner, taken her for a second opinion at the start. What kind of mother was I that I let her get so sick? Maybe I wasn't meant to have children.'

'Lily-Anne, that's ridiculous.'

'I know that. Sure, part of me even knew it at the time. But I couldn't seem to shift it, couldn't even talk to Joe about it. And

320

he's always been the first person I talk to about everything.'

Through the kitchen window darkness was hiding the garden.

'So what did you do?'

'I pushed it down, kept busy. The usual. I got a job as a receptionist in a hotel. Every day was so packed, all these Americans and businessmen over from Europe, I'd no time to think. I liked it, I was good at it.'

I couldn't picture Lily-Anne behind a reception desk – the leggings, the long hair.

'And I thought, because I was able to do all that, I was fine. That I was coping. Until one night I couldn't push it down any more. And lying in bed, next to Joe sleeping, I felt like I was turning into some block of a thing, some hard thing, as if the anger and the blame were freezing my heart and my body. I was breathing, but I was as dead as Pammy was. Rigor mortis for the living.'

She folded and unfolded her hands.

'What did you do?' I asked.

'I let myself feel it.'

Outside I could hear wind, rain on the window. Inside, the heating pulsed. 'I always felt guilty after Dad died.'

The words were out before I knew they were coming. I'd never said them before, to Eddie, to Ange, maybe even in my own head. I blew a ripple across my tea.

'Why?' Lily-Anne said.

'It sounds ridiculous. It *is* ridiculous.'

I waited for her to interrupt, to tell me it wasn't, but she didn't say anything. I rehearsed the words in my head but I couldn't say them, not even to her, so I said something else instead.

'We used to be so close, you know, when I was younger. But the last few years – I hadn't spent much time with him. I'd kind of ignored him.'

I flattened my hand on the table, into a star shape.

'You were a teenager, Carla.' Lily-Anne leaned across and held my arm.

'I never thought for one second that he – wouldn't be around. If I'd known—' I couldn't say the rest.

Lily-Anne's fingers tightened. 'I know.'

The tears had come properly by then and I didn't wipe them away. On the table I made suction cups with my hands. Lily-Anne didn't let go.

'I just feel like I wasted all the time I had left, only I didn't know it.'

'Did you ever talk to anyone about it?'

'Like who?'

'Your mum? Suzanne?'

I shrugged, like a kid, like a teenager.

'Suzanne fell apart and Mum spent her time looking after her. I wasn't going to be more of a burden on her and, anyway, I was OK. I was fine.'

'Fucked-up, insecure, neurotic and emotional.'

'What?' My head jerked up.

'That's what I say to my clients when they tell me they're fine.'

Lily-Anne smiled a little. I reached for my tea again and she let go of my arm.

'Your dad knew you loved him. He died because he had a heart condition. It wasn't your fault.'

I glanced up at her. I'd never said it was my fault. 'Of course. I know that.'

'I know you know it up here, but do you know it here?' She gestured to her forehead and then her chest, her heart. I thought of what she said, the rigor mortis. The heating ticked. The kitchen smelt of cake. It must be ready by now. My eyes slid to the clock on the cooker, and back to hers again.

'Someone once told me that the longest journey you'll ever make is from your head to your heart.'

'What does that mean?'

'It means it's not enough just to know it, you have to feel it.'

I swallowed. When I spoke I could barely hear my own words: 'What if I don't know how to do that?'

My eyes were on the table in front of me. My two hands like a triangle, around the cup and saucer. She took my arm again and I let her squeeze it. 'None of us do,' she said. 'But we get there in the end.'

SEVEN

I reached for Mum's arm as we went down the steps but she jerked away from me. I walked behind her, watching her feet, hesitant on each step. At the start of the journey, she'd been clear: she knew where we were going, even told me a story about Dad, how shocked he had been the first time he suggested they meet at Front Gate and she wasn't sure which one it was. I'd laughed at that story and so had she. We were in Salthill station then so I knew it was somewhere between there and Booterstown that I'd lost her. I'd asked her a question and she hadn't responded, her eyes fixed somewhere out the window on the wash of the waves.

At the doorway to the street I tried to link her again and this time she let me. The green man was flashing but we stopped at the edge of the kerb, waited for him to come around again. A man in a suit pushed past us and darted across the road, just as the traffic began to move.

'He's lucky he wasn't hit by that car.' As I spoke, I heard my voice, it had sounded just like hers. I didn't know what had made me say that, about the man. I didn't even mean it, didn't even care. We headed towards the corner, the new entrance through the sports centre. Behind a sheet of glass a wall stretched high, the people climbing it held by coloured ropes as they stretched towards the next foothold, almost in slow motion. I thought I'd have to let go of Mum but the entrance was wide enough for both of us. Inside, nothing was familiar, and if it hadn't been for the students swarming out past us it would've been easy to pretend we weren't in Trinity at all.

Mum slowed down, and suddenly we were surrounded by a group of girls, in the middle of their voices, their conversation. Then they were gone, speeding ahead of us. Now that I looked properly there were some old buildings too, which I recognised, shoulder to shoulder with their new glass and granite neighbours. The students ahead of us veered to the right and we followed them past a row of bikes and then we were there, really there, the green of the sports pitches, the Trinity I recognised, all stretched out in front of us.

Under my feet there were cobblestones now, slippery from the rain, and I slowed down, almost stopped. As I forced myself to walk on, I was glad that we'd arranged to meet Lily-Anne for lunch here, that there was no way I could cancel, steer Mum around and head towards Grafton Street instead.

'Here we are, Mum, Trinity,' I said. 'You remember being here?'

She released herself from my grip so she could bend down to pick up something from one of the flowerbeds, a dented cap from a beer bottle. I watched as she held it in her palm before placing it carefully in her Aer Lingus bag. This morning when I'd emptied it I had come across something different alongside her usual junk. Inside the pocket, I'd found some paper, so old and soft that when I opened it it tore where the creases were. I'd recognised my writing, a version of my writing, the heading underlined twice in green pen, 'A Thing of Beauty is a Joy For Ever'. An essay, a story I'd written about cowboys and treasure in the Nevada desert. How had I ever had the confidence to write about cowboys in Nevada? I read it over my coffee and it wasn't bad, I didn't think it was bad.

Mum veered off the path towards the cricket pitches.

'Come on, Mum,' I said. 'We're going to be late for Lily-Anne.'

She answered without turning. 'We have time.'

She was right, but I didn't want to stop, to hang around. It was better to keep moving, keep walking through it all. Mum reached up to one of the branches of the trees, cherry blossom, her fingers on a bud that was just a bump of green. I always loved the blossom even though Dad said the students didn't because by the time it was on the trees it was close to their exams, too late to start studying if they hadn't already.

Mum sat down on a bench next to a couple, who shuffled up to make room. She stretched her legs across the verge, towards the line of white at the edge of the pitch. 'She's always late anyway,' she said.

I took a seat next to her on the arm, which felt damp through my jeans. She might've been talking about Lily-Anne, but it could just as easily have been Olivia, her mother, some friend from Aer Lingus days. 'Yes,' I said, 'that's right.'

The grass needed a cut but it was too wet to do it today. On the other side, behind the railings, rows of buses lined up, double-deckers just like the one I'd come in on. Sitting there, scanning it all, it was strange to realise that it all really existed, just like it always had. The Microbiology Building, the Pav. Ange had always liked the Pav, could never understand why I preferred to hide in the Buttery, with its low ceilings and smoky air.

Mum was saying something about a wall, maps, taking them down. The couple next to her got up and left. 'He couldn't leave,' she said. 'He loved every stone in this place. I took the maps down, when he was at work.'

I turned to look at her side profile, her nose, her chin, cut out of the green behind her. She was talking about Dad. She hardly ever talked about Dad.

'What maps, Mum?'

'He couldn't leave. He loved every stone in this place.'

'What maps?'

When she looked at me her eyes were bright, different from how they'd been on the train. 'The ones on the wall, silly.' She laughed. 'The maps for our trip. Remember?'

I couldn't have remembered because I wasn't there – only then I did remember, a Christmas in Bonnie's, her annoying boyfriend. Mum telling him about travel plans, plans that had never happened.

'It was his home, here. He couldn't leave.'

I took her arm and pulled her up, started to walk towards the Dining Hall. She kept saying it, that line over and over how he loved every stone in the place. I tried to ignore her, to tune in instead to the students who swarmed past us; a snatch of conversation about Manchester United, a sponsored cycle. A girl showed her friend a text, asking what she thought it meant, but I never heard the answer.

Past the Arts Block, taller than I remembered, past the new white Lego cube of a building – Dad would've hated that. All around me the landscape of my memory was coming to life, the same and different. The only thing to do was to keep walking through it.

'He loved every stone,' Mum said, 'every brick.'

'This way, Mum.'

We were at the Front Square, busy today, not like on Sundays when it was only ever Dad and me and our footsteps on the cobblestones. I remembered the shock of being here that week of mid-term, all the students, boys in long black jumpers and groups of girls who stopped him to ask questions about books or poems or what might come up in the exams. I'd been so excited to be with Dad at work for a whole week, glad that Suzanne had hockey camp, almost glad that Olivia was in hospital, but I hadn't realised I'd have to share him with all of them as well. I remembered hopping on one foot while I waited for him to answer their questions, wishing he'd hurry up, but he always took ages, wanting to make sure that what he said was exactly right. I pretended I didn't mind, answered the girls politely when they asked me what class I was in at school, as if it was the first time anyone had asked me, smiled up at Dad every time he told them that I was going to teach English in Trinity when I grew up, just like him.

Outside the Dining Hall, Lily-Anne was on tiptoe, waving frantically, even though we were only a few feet away. 'There you are,' she said. 'I wondered if I was in the right spot, I always get confused in here.' She hugged Mum first, then me, her perfume strong as ever. She'd run into some psychology professor apparently, someone she knew from way back, whom Mum knew too. She talked a mile a minute, telling us everything he'd said. Mum and I followed her through the atrium and into the hall, joining a queue of students. Mum was in front of me and I watched her the way she watched Lily-Anne take a tray, water, cutlery, copying everything she was doing. I copied them both too, as if *my* mind wasn't capable of making a decision right then, so the three of us ended up with soup, salad, brown scones and chocolate fudge cake.

In the queue for the cash register, Lily-Anne turned to me. 'Everything OK?'

'Sure,' I said. 'Fine.'

I led the way past the long tables at the front, all full, towards a quieter one at the back. From the wall the oil paintings watched us, heavy dark paintings of men in the olden days. We'd eaten in the Dining Hall a few times that week, Dad and I, because I wasn't allowed upstairs where he usually ate. He'd made up stories about the paintings – he had funny names for every one of them, names I couldn't remember any more.

I pulled a wooden chair out for Mum, one for me.

'Is this where you ate when you were in college?' Lily-Anne said, unloading her tray.

'Not really. I'd usually go up town.' I opened the packet of butter, tried to spread it on the scone but the top came away in crumbs, on the knife. 'The food here wasn't great.'

Lily-Anne tasted the soup. 'Seems decent enough to me, don't you think so, Coll?'

'You're right there.'

I took a bite of scone, chewed, swallowed. It was fine. The food had always been fine. That week he'd bought me dessert every time we'd come and one for him too so we could sample both. Flan was the worst, we decided, followed by trifle. Our favourite, by miles, was the Black Forest gâteau.

I pushed the chair back hard, so it made a squeal on the floor. I stood up too fast, bumping into the edge of the table so the knife scuttled off the plate. 'I'm not feeling too well.' I said, 'I've been a bit off all morning. I'm going to get some air.'

Mum looked up at me, concerned. 'Are you OK, love?'

'I'll be fine.' I started to stack the food back on my tray. The spoon jangled in my bowl of soup.

'Don't worry about that,' Lily-Anne said. 'We'll do it. You go.'

'Thanks,' I said. 'I'll be fine.'

She nodded. 'I know you will. Take your time. Call us when you're ready. We're in no hurry.'

I grabbed my jacket and retraced my steps across the hall. When I glanced back, Lily-Anne was looking after me but Mum was buttering her scone, saying something. Watching her, I wondered if she remembered that I was ever there with them, and I envied her then, the easy comfort of forgetting.

★

Outside, it was raining. My umbrella was on the floor in the Dining Hall, under my chair. I tipped my head back, felt the rain on my skin. This wasn't working, I shouldn't have come. It wasn't going to work.

My feet were taking me towards Front Gate, the quickest escape route. I'd head up to Grafton Street, wait for them there. Mum needed new makeup, I could buy that while I was waiting. What had made me think anything would be different from before? I shouldn't have come.

Under Front Arch a group of tourists in yellow plastic sheets stood sheltering from the rain. Mum's words were on a loop in my head, just like they seemed to be in hers. *He loved every stone in this place.* Well, I did too, he'd made me love it until I couldn't love it any more.

I skirted around the tourists, their voices echoing off the vaulted ceiling, the walls plastered with overlapping posters for societies, sports clubs, socials, stuff for sale. I'd tried. I'd done my best. Every day I'd come here for a full year. I'd never bunked off. I'd joined the Literary Society and the basketball club, just like I'd always planned to. Somehow I'd even managed to pass my exams.

I'd really tried. And it hadn't worked.

Outside, the rain was coming down hard, bubbling on the cobblestones. Two girls ran from the gate, screeching as it soaked them, despite the bags they held over their heads. Beyond it the umbrellas were jostling on Dame Street. A woman waited at the taxi rank, waving her hand into the gridlocked traffic.

Leaning against the wall, I took a breath, gave it a minute to ease off. Next to me a poster was half torn off the wall, blue with white writing: The Yoga Society. Underneath was a picture of a girl, her arms stretched high above her head, her front leg bent at the knee. Warrior pose, I liked warrior. There hadn't been a yoga society at Trinity when I was there.

Outside the railing a bus stopped and the tourists moved off in a group, following someone in a navy raincoat. If they could head out in this, so could I. Rain bounced off their plastic sheets. It probably looked worse than it was.

I stepped outside, held my bag over my head like the two girls had. The rain found my hands, my hair, ran down my sleeves, spots of it on my jeans. Water seeped through the canvas of my runner, my sock. Halfway to the gate, I turned, ran back to the shelter of Front Arch. I stood there, locked in indecision. In the Dining Hall, Mum and Lily-Anne were eating lunch, warm and dry. I could join them. I touched my fingers to my back pocket, my old student card, so long out of date, the wrong year, the wrong colour. Now that I was here, I didn't know what I'd been thinking, going to the Admissions Office. I'd thought that maybe it would be different now, all these years later, with all these changes on the campus, but nothing had changed, nothing had changed at all.

I don't know how long I stood there for, watching the lines of rain, breathing in its smell. It was my bladder, in the end, that forced me to move, to make a choice. Grafton Street was too far,

I didn't want lunch on my own, but going back to the Dining Hall, surrounded by my memories, Mum's memories, was worse, so much worse.

I'd never been to the Admissions Office, didn't think I had. I was only going to see, that was all, just to ask. It wasn't like there was any obligation. And they'd probably have a toilet. I was still talking myself into it, still deciding, when some part of me decided the decision was already made.

I hitched my jacket over my head, stepped back into Front Square and made a run for it.

EIGHT

The waiting room was beige, everything in it, beige carpet, beige chairs, beige-wood reception desk, even the walls were beige. I flicked through the pages – white hotels next to indigo seas, aquamarine seas, royal blue seas, hotels perched on clifftops, beaches, islands. Normally I loved magazines like this, choosing where I would go, but today I couldn't concentrate. I should've brought his letter.

Next to me, Mum rooted through her bag, picked out a toilet roll insert, a stone and a pine cone, lining them up on the seat next to her. There was no point in trying to stop her, not here. Across from us a lady in a lime-green suit was made up like she was going to a wedding, not a doctor's appointment. Over my magazine I watched her watching Mum before she went back to her book. I hadn't seen her turn a page.

Behind us a door opened and the quiet room was suddenly full of voices, laughter. Two men in tweed were shaking hands with a woman in a white coat, the younger one smiling. It was the first time I'd seen her, the famous Dr Glavin, and I liked the way she shook the older man's hand too, holding it between both of hers.

I put the magazine down. 'Clear up your stuff, Mum. We're next.'

She picked up each thing, placing it carefully in her bag. I was grateful for her calm. Earlier, she had refused, point blank, to come, wouldn't put her coat on or her shoes. The taxi driver had been at the door and she was still in tears in the kitchen, and I hadn't noticed the envelope at first on the mat in the hall. It was only when Suzanne and I were on either side of her, getting her out the door, that I'd seen it, the American stamp, the slanty black handwriting that had once been as familiar as my own.

Dr Glavin walked over to Mum and me, a folder in her hand. Behind her green-framed glasses her eyes were kind, just like her smile.

'Hi there, Collette. And you must be Collette's other daughter?' She shook Mum's hand first, then mine.

'That's right. I'm Carla. Suzanne couldn't make it today. She'd a big thing at work.'

'Sure not to worry,' Dr Glavin said. 'Lovely to meet you, Carla. And Collette, how are you? You're looking great, anyway.'

'Thank you, Doctor,' Mum said. 'So are you.'

Under her white coat Dr Glavin was wearing a navy dress with a long silver necklace. Mum would've liked that dress and I wondered if she'd meant it, or if it was just something she remembered you were supposed to say.

'That's kind of you to say so, Collette. Will we go and get started?'

I grabbed my bag and stood up too, realising as soon as I did that I'd read the situation wrong. Dr Glavin's voice was gentle: 'You can relax here for now, Carla, while Collette gets on with a few tests. I'll call you in when she's ready.'

'Oh, OK, of course.'

I sat down again, feeling stupid. Suzanne could've told me that, not that we'd much time for any chat this morning. If I'd known I was going to be waiting for Mum to do tests I'd definitely have brought the letter.

The two men in tweed got ready to leave, the younger one holding his father's elbow. He looked like him, the same shaped face. He smiled at me as they went past and I wondered if he worried too that he'd get more from him than his slack chin, how long it might be till he was the one being accompanied to a place like this.

Outside the window the wind was blowing harder, so the trees were nearly horizontal. The woman in lime took out her phone, started texting, the phone bleeping every time she misspelled a word. I picked up the travel magazine, flicked past a waterfall, a sunny hammock, markets as colourful as patchwork quilts. Why hadn't I brought the stupid letter? What had made me leave it on the shelf in the hall?

At the back of the magazine they had a feature on yoga holidays, columns of words around a photo of a woman doing a sun salutation on a rock by the sea. I started to read but the words wouldn't stick. He wanted a divorce. That was what the letter would say. Why else would he write to me? What else, after all this time, could he want?

I put the magazine back on the pile, picked up a gossip one instead. They were all this month's. No wonder Dr Glavin was so expensive. Above the reception desk the clock's minute hand was between twelve and one. Mum hadn't even been in for five minutes yet.

My phone rang, and I knew before I checked that it would be Suzanne again. I took it from my bag and hit the silent button. There was no news and, anyway, I wasn't meant to have it switched on in here. It wasn't my fault that she felt guilty she hadn't been able to make it. As I unzipped the side pocket of my bag to put it away, my hand brushed against something I'd forgotten about. My notepad had been there since last week's writing class.

I flicked through the pages, the bits and pieces I'd written. The teacher was a little scatty but she seemed good. Every week we got homework, a specific exercise. This week's was to put ourselves in a train carriage and see where it would take us. The class was tomorrow and I was working tonight. I wouldn't have a chance to do it.

Across from me the woman in lime got an incoming text. Looking up I saw there was a box of toys next to her that I hadn't noticed before. I hoped they were for children. I checked the clock. Five past. My mind bounced to Mum, behind the door of Dr Glavin's office – what if she couldn't do the tests? From there to a white envelope with black writing on the hall shelf. Eddie wanted a divorce, I knew he did.

I pushed my feet into the beige carpet. I couldn't do anything about any of that right now, none of it. What I could do, though, was my homework. I rooted in my bag, found a pen and opened my notepad.

★

Work was a washout, too many of us on, more waiting staff than customers. After a ten-euro tip from my table of eleven, I called it a night, heading home early. A train pulled in just as I got to the platform, the best thing that had happened in a really lousy day.

My plan had been to make a cup of tea before I read the letter in the quiet of Mum's therapy room but as I came up the hill I saw Lily-Anne's car outside. From the hall I heard her voice in the sitting room along with Suzanne's, serious low tones that matched their faces when I came in. I didn't want to join them in one of their endless discussions about Mum, her test results and what they meant but I knew I had to. It seemed pointless to me, all this talk. Mum was deteriorating – we knew that already, we didn't need some doctor to tell us. As they talked on and on I found it hard to listen, to find anything at all to say. If it hadn't been for the weight of Chips' head on my thigh, the rhythm of his panting as I twisted my fingers through his fur, I might have forgotten I was in the room at all.

When I sat on my bed, the clock said eleven-thirty. My fingers held the corners of the envelope. It was light in my hands, one page, maybe two. It wasn't the right day to open it, not after everything else, but I had to. My fingers started to rip at the paper before I was ready. My heart speeded up. He was with someone else. That was why he wanted a divorce. He was with Dawn. They were getting married. He'd loved her all along.

My fingers felt inside, only one page, folded over. I focused my

335

mind, told myself to think positive, as if somehow my thoughts could morph the words Eddie had already written into something else. I flattened the paper on my knee. Whatever was on it, I would cope.

Hey Carla,

How are you? All is good here on this side of the pond. I think this must be the first letter I've written in a hundred years, probably since you were in Montauk. I've never been good at letters, yours were always better, but then you're the writer, right?

So the tour was cool! We had such amazing crowds. Portland and San Diego were especially awesome! Austin wasn't as good as we hoped though and as for San Antonio, let's just say I couldn't care less if I never see that place again!!!

We're back in New York for six weeks off now before we head to Europe. We'll be releasing a single over there. We're supposed to be recording a new album but we're all beat and we need a break. I'm staying with Mom, which was pretty OK until this new guy of hers shows up, Lee, from some place in England. She's trying to help him find a job over here or something. I don't understand a word he says so I can't see him getting one anytime soon!

So guess where our last gig is on the tour? Yep, you got it, Dublin! Crazy! We're starting in Germany, then Denmark, Holland, France, Spain, England and Scotland. Maybe you saw it on our Myspace? We're in Dublin on May 9th. I hope you can come. Bring Ange or whoever,

I'll get you backstage passes. It'd be cool to hang out. I miss you, Carls, I don't know if I'm supposed to say that but I do. It blows my mind that it's been a year, time is so crazy – the tour sped by but now it's on a go slow since we came home.

I hope you're doing well too. And your mom. I ran into Rhonda and she told me you're learning to drive. That's cool, maybe you can drive me around Dublin when I'm there?!

I'm gonna go now. I have no idea where the post office is, I'm going to have to look it up online!! I'm only here for a few more weeks so just email me or post something on our Myspace about how many passes you need!

Take care out there!

E

x

I read the letter a second time, then again and once more. *I miss you, Carls* – every time I got to that line I held my breath, just a little, had to work a little harder to hold the tears back. I missed him too, that was the truth of it. I hadn't realised how much until I saw his writing, his stupid exclamation marks. He didn't want a divorce – he hadn't even mentioned it. He wanted to meet up, for me to drive him around Dublin. He remembered the letters he'd written to me in Montauk and so did I, picking them up from the General Delivery Office. He missed me, I missed him. We missed each other; maybe we still loved each other. Maybe we could work this whole thing out.

I smiled. The relief, after the stress of the day, was physical. I went back to the first paragraph, read it again, slower this time. As I did, the letter seemed to change, different things jumping out, things he didn't say. He was missing me now the tour was over, when he was bored and pissed off staying with Bonnie and this Lee guy.

I finished the letter and turned to the start again. He'd assumed I'd show up at his gig, he could get as many passes as I wanted. Who did he think we were? Old college roommates? Each time I read it, my emotions seemed to change, a swirling barometer going from elation to sadness to anger to rage. It seemed like everything, our whole relationship, was in the letter, everything that had ever been right with it and all the things that had gone wrong. It was all about him, his music, his tour, his mother, his feelings. I could post something on his Myspace, like some little fan. Fuck him! *Hope you're doing well too. And your mom* – he couldn't even bring himself to ask directly how she was.

I crumpled the letter into a ball and threw it on the carpet. It rolled and stopped by the wardrobe. Lying back on my too small, too soft bed, I stared at the ceiling, the pink paper lampshade covered with dust that I'd had for as long as I could remember. Funny how I'd been back more than a year and it hadn't occurred to me to change a single thing about this room.

I rolled on to my side, my arm under my head, the way we did in yoga. I could see the letter still there, a ball of paper and words. The truth was, there were no words that would've been any better than the ones I'd read. Even as I fantasised about us getting back together I knew that we wouldn't. I thought I knew that. I was starting to know that.

May was two months away, not today, not tomorrow. I didn't know how I'd be feeling in May but I knew enough to know it wasn't going to be the same set of feelings I had tonight. Last night in yoga, Audrey had said there were only two questions we ever needed to answer: where we were and what time it was. She'd laughed at us when we all turned to look at the clock, said we didn't need it to find the answers. As I picked up the letter from the floor, I repeated them in my head. *I am here and it is now.*

I folded the paper, put it back into the envelope. All day long I'd been somewhere in the future, worrying about Mum getting

338

worse, about Eddie wanting a divorce, even about how one day I might be coming to see Dr Glavin, or someone like her, about myself, not Mum.

The future was coming and there were decisions to be made, about Eddie, about Mum, and I'd make them. But for right now I just needed to remember the answers to Audrey's questions, always the same.

I am here and it is now.

NINE

In the car's headlights the fog looked white. It was all around us, as if we were driving through the middle of a cloud.

'Put the fog lights on,' Sean said.

'I have them on.'

'No, you don't, you've the main lights on. Remember I showed you how to do the fogs?'

I fumbled at the lights control. Ahead the fog got brighter.

'Not that one! They're the fulls!'

'Which one, then? There's so many bloody switches on this thing, no wonder I can't find anything!'

'It's a Nissan Micra, Carla, not the Starship Enterprise!'

'Oh, fuck off, Sean!'

The words just came out and I started to giggle. I was afraid to look at him to see if he was annoyed. I twisted something else, making two lines of light that pierced the fog.

'I can't believe you just told me to fuck off,' he said. I listened for the smile in his voice and heard it. 'I've never had a client tell me to fuck off before.'

I glanced at him and then back to the road. In the light his curly hair made a silhouette high on his head. Telling him to fuck off had reminded me of Eddie, all those years ago on the beach, but it was a good kind of memory. The lights made a difference and I could see a couple of feet ahead. It wasn't perfect but it was the best visibility since we'd left the house.

'Yeah, well, maybe if you treated me like a client, I'd treat you like my instructor.'

The car in front was braking, turning the fog red, and I braked too, slowing down at the junction.

'Turn left,' he said.

I indicated and turned too quickly so I didn't see the car that came up fast around the bend. The driver blew his horn, stayed inches from my bumper so that his lights poured through the back window.

'I know,' I said, gripping the wheel tight. 'I'll fail if I do that tomorrow.'

I slowed right down and the car overtook me, swerving over the solid white line.

'Idiot,' Sean said.

From the corner of my eye I could see his hand on his leg, his fingers threading the seam of his thick cords. I waited for him to say something else.

'So, how do I treat you, if I don't treat you like a client?'

The question had an edge to it, the slow way he said the words. I'd thought he was flirting with me once or twice before but I could never be sure. This time I wasn't imagining it: he'd wanted me to hear it. Whatever had been between us all these weeks, this contained, hidden thing was unfolding now, filling the car.

'Oh, I don't know,' I said. 'Like a sister?'

'A sister?'

I laughed at the pitch of his voice. 'OK, not a sister then, a friend.'

'A friend?'

'Yeah,' I said. 'A friend.'

'So you're not one of these people who thinks that men and women can't be friends?'

We were stopped at traffic lights and I didn't know where we were. Behind the fog the buildings were only shapes, familiar but utterly unrecognisable.

'Should I keep going straight?'

'That depends,' he said, 'on where you want to go.'

When I looked at him his eyes met mine. His little beard was new, a line of hair that traced his jaw, giving it more definition. It made him look older than twenty-four. But he was still only twenty-four.

The lights changed and I drove straight, focused on the rear lights of the car in front. We came up to a roundabout and he still didn't give any direction so I took the second exit, down past a row of houses, a pub I'd never seen before.

'I hope you know I've no idea where we are,' I said. 'Are you going to give me any directions?'

'I'm waiting for you to answer my question,' he said.

'What question?'

'About whether a guy and a girl can be friends.'

His voice was teasing and in the silence of the car the pounding of my heart seemed way too loud. I took a left, realising too late that we were going uphill again. I changed the gears down so they made a terrible grinding sound. I felt him wince.

'Sorry,' I said. 'I still can't get that.'

'You will,' he said.

At the top of the hill the road levelled out and I recognised the curve of the wall, the school gates. I knew my way from here. Sitting back in the seat, I relaxed, pushed the car into third.

'To answer your question,' I said, 'I've had loads of guy friends over the years. One of my best friends in New York – Murray – was a guy. He was gay, though, so maybe that's different.'

Sean laughed. 'That definitely makes it different.'

'I think some guys and girls can be friends, some can't.' As I said it, an image of Eddie and Dawn flashed into my mind, the two of them in the kitchen one day when I came home from work. He was sitting on the counter playing the guitar, while she sang softly. She was leaning into him, I remembered, so close that her long necklace was grazing his thigh through his shorts.

'So,' Sean said, 'are we the type of guy and girl who can be friends?'

I was driving towards home now and the car felt like it was doing the work, not me. 'Yes,' I said. 'Definitely.'

'Why so sure?'

'Because,' I said, turning into the estate, 'for one thing, you're twenty-four.'

We were at the bottom of the hill, only one more road to go, and I managed to stall the car. It jerked and the lights on the dash went out. 'Shit!'

I put the handbrake on, turned over the engine. Another car came up behind me, one of the neighbours, to witness me making a balls of it. I took my foot off the clutch too fast and the car jerked once, then again, bunny-hopping up the road.

Next to me, Sean was laughing.

'Very supportive,' I said.

'I'm sorry,' he said. 'It's just you haven't done that in weeks and you do it the night before the test. It's kind of funny.'

At the top of the hill I veered left, reversing the car back across the driveway. Upstairs the curtains were open and I could see the light reflected on the wall of my room from the hall below. I pulled up the handbrake, turned off the ignition.

'So what's the second thing?' he said, unfastening his seatbelt. 'You said, "for one thing", what's the second?'

I fiddled with my beads. The second thing was that I was married, only I wasn't really married any more. Maybe I never had been.

'I can't remember,' I said. 'There is no second thing.'

'Oh,' he said. 'OK.'

Something had changed between us, being here outside the house, looking at each other rather than at the road. In the bright streetlight he looked younger, years younger than he had earlier.

'You're still OK for me to use the car tomorrow in the test?' I said.

'Yeah, I told you. I'll pick you up at half two. That should give us loads of time.'

'Great.'

I hated this part, the paying part. Usually we sat in the car for a while, had a chat, but tonight he was down to business, reaching

343

into the glove compartment for his receipt book straight away. As I watched him fill in the white slip, I thought maybe I'd been wrong about the flirting. That he'd only been friendly, that I'd made a fool of myself thinking it might have been anything more.

I dug into my jeans for the money, my fingers finding it tightly folded into a square at the bottom of my pocket. As I looked up I saw he'd put his receipt book away and I barely had time to register that he was leaning towards me before I felt his hand in my hair and he kissed me.

★

I ran out of the test centre, taking the last two steps with a jump. I thought he'd be sitting on the wall where I'd left him, but he wasn't. I swung around and there he was, strolling towards me, smoking a cigarette. Before he reached me he threw it down and ground it under his runner.

'So?' He pulled his mouth into a flat line, like it was going to be bad news and I realised in a flash that he'd thought I'd fail.

'So,' I said, 'I got it! I passed! Can you believe it?'

'You passed?! That's amazing!' He threw his arms open, then wrapped them around me and I hugged him back. It was a good hug, tight and close. It was good to have someone to hug.

'When I saw you had the moustache guy, I thought you were done for,' he said into my hair. 'You must have driven perfectly. You're brilliant, that's what you are, fucking brilliant!'

I hugged him tighter, then let go, embarrassed suddenly to be hugging in the middle of the car park in the afternoon. 'Give me one of those,' I said, pointing to the packet of Camels in his pocket.

'I didn't know you smoked.'

'I don't any more, but this is a special occasion.'

He lit a match for me, cupping his hands around it, and it blew out before I could get the cigarette lit. We tried twice more and eventually I got it, inhaling deep. The smoke hit the back of my throat in a way that I'd forgotten, and for a second I thought I might be sick.

'You OK?'

'Yeah. It's just been a while.' I took another drag.

'We should go celebrate,' he said, 'have a drink somewhere.'

'Where?'

'I don't know – go into town?'

I looked down at my T-shirt, my cardigan. 'I'm not exactly dressed for town.'

'Dressed for town?' He frowned. 'What does that even mean? Am I?'

He held out his arms and did a twirl so I could inspect him, the T-shirt hanging low under his army jacket, the same cords as he was wearing last night. In Brooklyn no one ever got dressed up to go out, we were the same people all day long, wherever we went. I laughed.

'What's funny?'

'Nothing. You're right. It just seems like ages since I've been out, had fun.'

He smiled, took my hand. It felt warm, a little sweaty but nice.

'Well, we'll have to put an end to that,' he said.

*

I didn't think I'd slept, but I must have because when I opened my eyes the room was bright. Rolling on to my back, I saw a triangle of the sky. At first I couldn't figure it out, the shape, until I saw that a corner of the brown sheet that had been tacked over the skylight had come away. Every molecule of sun seemed to be shining through that triangle, right into my eyes.

My mouth, my teeth, were ashy, grimy. Oh, Christ, I'd been smoking. I tried to run my tongue over my dry lips but there was nothing there, no moisture left in my whole body it felt like. I dangled my hand over the edge of the bed and on to the carpet in the hope of finding water but there was nothing. Slowly, I looked to my left, taking in the rest of the room, the open drawers with clothes falling out, the Star Trek poster, the Apple Mac. Next to it a pint glass, half full, so close but miles away.

Beside me I could feel him, his leg against mine, squashed together and sticky. I was wearing something with a collar. I looked down and saw blue material, silky, a football shirt. The realisations all came together: this was a single bed; we were in his room in his dad's house; his dad had been here last night when we came home. My stomach made a terrible sound. For an awful minute I thought I was going to be sick. I lay still, held my eyes open, kept breathing. The moment passed.

Sean wasn't snoring but I could tell by his breathing that he was still asleep. The night came back in snatches, everything after the first pub just a series of images. We'd been to a club – it was downstairs, I remembered the steps, holding on to the railings, only us on the dance floor. Oh, my God, we'd been kissing on the street. Some guys had wolf whistled but we hadn't stopped, Sean's back pushed up against a window.

He rolled over, throwing his arm so it draped across me, putting pressure on my stomach. I lifted it a little higher. His arms were thin, skinny. Eddie was skinny but his arms were heavy. Last night it kept tricking me, in the dark, this body that felt like Eddie's and wasn't; his touch, the way he held me, just the same. But the way he kissed was different and there were patches of hair where there should have been smoothness. We'd bumped our heads at one stage, I remembered that, I thought I did. I moved my fingers to my forehead, just to check, and it was tender.

I swung my legs out from under the covers. The bed creaked. Before I could stand his arm grabbed me, tight, around my waist. 'Where are you going? You can't escape!'

It was a put-on voice, deeper than his usual one. I loosened his fingers and stood up, made it to the water. When I turned he was sitting up in bed, his hands folded behind his head. After a night's sleep his hair was bigger than ever, an Irish Afro. He was smiling.

'I didn't know you were a Chelsea fan,' he said.

I held out the bottom of the shirt so I could see it properly. 'Nor did I.'

'Can I have some?'

He held out his hand and I passed him the glass. He didn't say anything and I picked my jeans up off the floor, my knickers and my T-shirt. I couldn't find my bra.

'You're not going already?'

'I have to. I'm working later.'

'Tonight? We've loads of time. Come back into bed.'

He patted the sheet next to him, smiled his slow smile. I contemplated it briefly, then shook my head. 'No, really, I can't. I have a nasty feeling I promised my sister I'd look after Mum this morning. Do you remember if I called her last night to say I wasn't coming home? I can't find my phone.'

'It's probably in your bag, there on the chair.'

My bag. I hadn't even thought about it but there it was. 'Have you seen my bra?' I said.

He shuffled under the covers, reached down, pulled it out and dangled it on a finger. 'You'll have to come and get it . . .'

I laughed, snatched it from him and turned away to get dressed, glad of the football shirt to hide me. From downstairs I could hear noise, a radio. His dad.

'Will you walk me downstairs?' I said. 'I don't want to meet your dad.'

'Seriously, you're going right now? Wait a few minutes and I'll jump in the shower. I can take Dad's car.'

'No, it's fine, you don't have to—'

'Come on, Carla, I want to.'

He was out of bed and on his feet, skinny in black boxer shorts, his feet and legs long and white. He put his arms around my waist, nestled his mouth into my neck.

'Okay then,' I said. 'Don't take too long, though, will you?'

'I won't, promise.'

He kissed me lightly before pulling a dressing-gown from the wardrobe behind me, navy with light blue stripes, the kind an older man would wear. Maybe his dad had bought it for him. In the bottom of my bag I found my phone, the screen black.

'Fuck!' I said. 'The stupid thing's dead.'

From behind he rested his chin on my shoulder. 'Want to use mine?'

'No, it's fine.'

'I have credit. Your sister might be worried.'

'She knew we were going out. I'm thirty-one years old. I don't need to ask anyone's permission to stay out all night.'

The words came out sounding harder than I'd meant them to.

He stepped away, dug his hands deep into his dressing-gown pockets. Something about the gesture made him seem younger than ever. 'Sure, course. Whatever.'

I knew he thought I'd been making a dig at him, about living at home with his dad, but I couldn't tell him it was nothing to do with him, that it was myself I was trying to convince. 'Listen,' I said, 'I had fun, yesterday – at least, I think I did.'

He scratched at his chin, the line of beard. Late in the night he'd admitted he'd grown it for me. 'You really had a good time?'

'Yeah.' It was true. I might not be able to remember it all but I knew we'd had fun in a way I hadn't since Brooklyn. 'I did.'

'You want some tea while I'm in the shower? Toast?'

He was smiling again, cute, eager to please. It would've been easy to stay, but I had to go home. My stomach made another horrible noise.

'I don't suppose you have any Alka Seltzer?'

TEN

Parked outside the house it was a funny kind of role reversal, Sean behind the wheel, me the passenger. Driving up the road I wondered if anyone had seen us. Thank God Nosy Rosie didn't live here any more.

I cracked the door open, let in some air. It was a relief that the journey was over, that the nausea that swirled in my stomach as we went around every roundabout, every bend, hadn't become vomit sprayed all over his dad's car.

'So,' Sean said, rubbing his hand along his cords, 'got you home in one piece anyway.'

'Yep,' I said. 'I'm glad I wasn't driving today.' I glanced at the house to escape the needlepoint of sun in my eye. The curtains were closed still, downstairs and up, except for my room. I checked my watch. It was after ten – it wasn't like Suzanne to let Mum sleep late, even on a Saturday.

Sean was chatting on, laughing about something from the night before. I'd never noticed his laugh was so high before, so sharp.

'So, I'll give you a call,' he said.

'Yeah, do.'

I had no idea right then if I wanted him to or not, but it didn't matter. What mattered now was getting out of the car without being sick. I pushed the door all the way open and he lunged across the seat to kiss me, and there was nothing to do but kiss him back. When I pulled away I saw Mrs McCarthy struggling to get her black and brown Labradors past the tiny space between the car door and the wall.

'Morning, Carla,' she said.

I pulled the door so they could get by. 'Hello, Mrs McCarthy.'

As soon as she was past I grabbed my bag from the floor. 'Bye,' I said to Sean. 'I'll talk to you soon.'

I hurried up the driveway, feeling his eyes on me as I dug deep in my bag for my keys, fumbled with the bottom lock, the middle one. The top one stuck and I snapped my wrist hard, willing it to open. My headache, a seam of pain that had slowly crept across my head all morning, started to throb just before the lock gave way and the door opened. I turned and waved one last wave before I closed it.

Suzanne hadn't cleaned the kitchen – that was the first thing I noticed, the teapot and the half-full cups on the table, two more in the sink. She must've had people round last night; that was why she wasn't up. Maybe I'd missed my chance to meet the famous Simon. I wanted my bed, darkness, sleep, but I knew the trick to getting my body back on track. I needed food – the greasier and starchier the better.

The grill was coated with yesterday's grease but I lined up the rashers and sausages anyway. To think that she was always going on about the grill, nagging me if there was even so much as a crumb left on the pan. It was almost nice to see it so dirty, to have some ammunition for next time she was having a go at me.

Under the flames the sausages spat and hissed, loud in the silence of the house. Ten-twenty. It must've been a late one, Suzanne never stayed in bed past nine. I filled the kettle, clicked it back on its stand. On the counter next to it the phonebook was out. When I picked it up, the underside was damp. The wet had crept through the cover and into the dense, tight pages so they had warped a little. I dried it off and put it on a chair.

I was buttering my toast when the door opened behind me. I cut a sausage lengthways to line it up on the bread. In the window I saw Suzanne's reflection.

'Good morning,' I said. I almost made a crack about it being nearly afternoon but I knew I'd only leave myself open for her to get in a dig about me being out all night. I laid some rashers on top of the sausage, took a bite and turned. She was still in her dressing-gown, the pink silk one, arms folded, watching me. A strand of her hair was stuck to her cheek, a line of dark on light.

'So you decided to come home, then?'

I turned back to my breakfast. I'd seen it in her stance, the judgement, and I might have ignored it, but I couldn't ignore it in her voice. My mouth was full and I was glad of the chance to let a few seconds pass before I answered. 'Looks like it.'

She walked around the table, so she was facing me, her arms still folded. The V of skin the dressing-gown showed was patchy red. 'Is that all you've got to say?' she said. 'You waltz in here and make yourself a fry, like nothing's happened?'

I took another bite, chewed and swallowed. My stomach gurgled. She sat down opposite me, pushed her hair off her face. This was a Suzanne I hadn't seen in a while, so long I'd nearly forgotten what she could be like. 'What's your problem, Suzanne?'

'What's my problem?'

'I'm an adult. I'm single. I never say a word to you when you stay over at Simon's.'

She stared at me. 'I hardly ever stay over – I feel so guilty leaving you with Mammy – and when I do, I tell you, I give you notice.'

'Well, maybe not everyone else's life is as planned as yours. Sometimes people go out and have a good time and stuff happens. Some people just let life happen.' I crunched into the toast. It was almost nice that she was reacting like this, that she was back being the Suzanne I knew, had known, all along. I knew who to be around this Suzanne. I fell into the role easily. 'I'm thirty-one years of age. I can spend the night with whoever I want.' I cut up more sausage, chewed, swallowed. 'And, by the way, that grill was filthy, full of grease. I'd to clean it up before I could use it.'

I glanced away so she wouldn't see the lie. When she didn't answer, I knew I'd made my point. I looked up at her so she'd see

I didn't care what she thought, what she said. It was only then that I really saw her, the patches that had spread up her neck, red, like the rims of her eyes.

'You didn't get my voicemails,' she said. 'Did you?'

In the split second before I spoke, every detail came together to make a picture – the closed curtains, the phone book, even the grill.

'What voicemails? My phone died.'

She reached into her dressing-gown pocket, pulled out a shred of tissue and blew her nose, hard. In the heat of the kitchen I was suddenly cold. I put my knife and fork down. 'Is Mum OK? Did something happen?'

Suzanne sighed. 'Mammy went missing last night, Carla.'

'Missing? Missing where?'

I gripped the edge of the table. Went missing. It wasn't the same as 'is missing'. Suzanne covered her mouth. In the bright kitchen lights her tears were shiny but she didn't seem to notice she was crying.

'Suzanne, what happened? Where is she?'

I got up from my chair, went over to her, got down on my hunkers next to her. She shook her head as she started to speak. 'The bang must've woken me – the door. I thought it was you. The wind had caught the curtains, blowing them into the hall. It was horrible, Carla, like something from a horror film.'

I could picture the hall, the curtains and I didn't want to. I rocked back on my heels, put my hand on her arm.

'Suzanne, where's Mum now?'

Her crying became sobbing, fast snuffles of breath and snot, no room for words. An undigested piece of sausage hit the back of my throat. I was going to be sick.

'She's upstairs. They found her, the police did. In one of the gardens on the main road.'

'Was she hurt? Is she OK?'

Suzanne grabbed another tissue. 'She's OK.'

'Thank God. Jesus. Thank God.' Pain was biting my knee and

I hauled myself up, holding on to the table. 'You're sure she's not hurt?'

'No, but it was four in the morning, Carla. She was in her nightdress – anything could've happened.'

I bounced my leg to chase away the pain in my knee. Mum was home. I took a breath. She was safe. The knowledge was starting to trickle in. I'd been here before, I knew what to say next.

'But nothing did. She's OK.' I put my hand on her shoulder. 'I was the same way, blaming myself after the National Concert Hall thing, but it wasn't your fault – don't make it worse by blaming yourself, imagining what might have happened.'

Under my fingers I felt her muscles grip bone. 'Don't blame *myself?* Are you for real?' Her head snapped up. 'Why would I blame myself when you were the one who asked me, begged me, to leave the locks off the door? You were the one who said you were on your way straight home.'

With each 'you' she poked her finger at me. I felt as if she was jabbing me hard in the chest, instead of in mid-air. Seeing the confusion in my face, she laughed. 'Jesus, you were so hammered you probably don't even remember the conversation, do you?' She screwed up her face, put on a silly high voice: '"I'm on my way home, Suzanne, please don't do all the locks, I hate those locks." I should never, ever, have listened to you.'

My body was made of lead, it was made of water. My legs weren't enough to hold me and I sat down, hard, on my chair. My fault again. Even when I wasn't here, things were still my fault.

Suzanne was still talking, talking, talking, talking about the door banging in the hall, the curtains, finding Mum's bed empty. I didn't want to hear it, to picture what it was like to wake up alone in the house, to find everyone gone. 'I'm sorry,' I whispered. 'Suzanne, I'm so sorry.'

She went on through her tears, as if she hadn't heard me, taking me through every long, lonely step of the night before. I could feel the gravel, freezing under her bare feet, hear her voice echoing along the empty street calling Mum's name. I held my hands loosely in my lap, looked down at my jeans. When I'd put them on yesterday I'd hoped they'd be the jeans I'd be wearing when I passed my driving test. I didn't know they'd be the jeans that Sean would take off me later, when I decided to sleep with him, that they were the jeans I could've been wearing when I found out that I'd lost my mother, really lost my mother.

Upstairs I heard a noise: the shower coming to a stop. I hadn't realised it was on.

'Mum's up?' I said.

Suzanne stopped, frowned. 'After the doctor left he gave her a sleeping pill. She won't be up for hours yet. That must be Simon.'

It took me a second to register what she'd said. 'Simon? Oh. Simon's here?'

Suzanne smoothed her hair with a hand. 'Yes, he's here. Your phone was going to voicemail and I called him. I didn't want to call Lily-Anne at that time, not when Joe's been sick all week. Who else was I supposed to call?'

It made sense, of course it did, that she'd call her boyfriend but somehow I was surprised. Part of me hadn't realised they were at that stage, that he'd be the one she'd call in a crisis. Who would I have called? Ange? Rhonda? As I went through the names in my head I realised that, without Eddie, there was no one any more, not really. Was that what I wanted from Sean?

The thought was too much and I covered my face with my hands. 'I'm so sorry, Suzanne. I'm really, really, sorry. You shouldn't have had to go through all that on your own.'

I let the tears come, tears for everyone. Suzanne stopped talking and I heard her push her chair back on the lino, felt her hands on my shoulders, just like mine had been on hers. 'It's OK. It's really not your fault. It's mine too. I don't know why I didn't just lock the door anyway. I knew at the time that I should have.'

Suzanne handed me a pack of tissues. As I blew, she went to fill the kettle. She raised her voice over the sound of the water. 'When I thought about it after, I was raging with myself. There was music blaring in the background and you sounded locked. You must be in bits.'

'I'm dying.'

She smiled a little and I did too until she folded her arms, suddenly serious again. 'Look, the truth is, what happened wasn't your fault or mine. We're doing our best, but things are getting out of control. Too much for us to handle.'

I picked up a cold sausage, bit into it. 'Suzanne, I don't want to talk about this, not right now.'

'I know and neither do I, but things aren't working, Carla. She can't be alone now, even for half an hour. This week, with Joe being sick, we've barely coped without Lily-Anne—'

'But he's much better now. He got good results from his tests.'

'That's not the point,' Suzanne said. 'She's done so much already and she's not getting any younger. Mammy's getting harder to handle. I think it might be time to look at proper help.'

A nursing home, that's what she meant, even if she didn't say it. The kettle boiled and switched itself off. Suzanne reached up to the top cupboard for a cup, her hair grazing her jaw. She could've been Mum then, she looked so like her, doing something I'd seen Mum do so many times before, exactly the same reach, the same movement. More than anything I wanted to go back to just one of those times, Mum reaching for a cup, a saucer, a bowl. Something so ordinary, so taken for granted.

'Knock-knock! Can I come in?'

His voice caught me by surprise, not just the timing of it but the sound too, a flat English voice, familiar, like someone from the TV. I turned to see him, his fingers around the door, a shy smile on his face.

'Come on in, Si,' Suzanne said. 'This is Carla. I'm just making you some tea.'

I rubbed away the rest of my tears, remembering too late that it was a hand-shaking occasion. I wiped mine off my jeans before I took his outstretched one. He was smaller than me, smaller than both of us.

'Lovely to finally meet you,' he said. 'I've heard so much about you.'

His accent made him sound very formal and I found myself feeling formal too. 'I've heard all about you too.'

His handshake was good, firm. He let go and put his hands in the back pockets of his jeans. They were from Next or Marks & Spencer probably, matched his navy V-neck jumper. His hair was short, cut tight to cover the fact that he was balding, the patches left were grey. I knew he was older than Suzanne, but this wasn't just older, this was old.

'I've been filling Carla in on last night,' Suzanne said.

He shook his head. 'Bloody nightmare. Thank God they didn't take too long to find her. We were in an awful state.' He glanced over at Suzanne and gave her a little smile. I was glad he'd been there, that Suzanne hadn't been on her own.

'I feel terrible that I wasn't here,' I said.

Simon moved his hands from his back to his front pockets. 'I'd probably feel like that too,' he said, 'if it was my mum. But the timing was a bugger, really. It was just one of those things.'

A bugger. One of Dad's words. Maybe that was who his voice reminded me of, the dips and inflections, the timing of his words.

He walked over to Suzanne, put his hand on her waist and kissed her cheek. *Just one of those things.* People's parents got sick, old, went into nursing homes. Died. That's what happened, I knew that, of course I did, it happened every day.

Simon was right; it was just one of those things. But it didn't feel like that. It didn't feel like it at all, not when it was happening to me.

Eleven

There was only one parking space outside and Suzanne reversed into it easily, despite the minibus parked along the wall. 'I could've driven,' I said. 'I wouldn't have minded.'

'We were running late,' she said, her arm around my headrest as she finished the manoeuvre. 'It was easier for me to take it.'

'You can trust me with your car, you know. I passed my test.'

She opened the door and pulled the seat forward so Mum could get out. 'It's nothing to do with that. Drive home if you want.'

I didn't know why I was making a big deal about the car. I didn't even want to drive. It was just something to talk about, other than what we were all trying not to talk about.

We walked up the wide path, Suzanne and I on either side of Mum. Our reflection in the double doors made us look like bouncers. When we were nearly at the door, Mum stopped. 'This isn't the right place.'

It was the first thing she'd said since we'd left the house. All the way in the car she'd been silent and now she sounded so certain.

'What?' I said.

'It's the right place, Mammy,' Suzanne said. 'Remember we told you where we were going?'

Mum walked up to the window, flattened her hands against the glass and peered through. Inside, I could see an empty reception area, a desk with no one at it. When she took her hands away there were smears of her finger prints left behind.

'This isn't the place,' she said.

Suzanne had found the buzzer on the wall and pressed it. I stood next to Mum, my hand on her arm. She'd been here before, Lily-Anne had told us last week, when we sat down to discuss what to do next. When she was first diagnosed, Mum had been around lots of places, nursing homes and respite centres. This was the one she had said she liked best. What if we had made a mistake? What if this was the wrong one?

From a room at the back, a woman came out, waved at us. She was probably my age but her pink uniform made her seem older. The colour didn't suit her freckly skin. When she smiled I saw a gap between her front teeth. She pressed something on the wall on the other side and the doors opened inwards in slow motion.

'You must be the Matthews,' she said, stepping back. 'Welcome. I'm Siobhan.'

Suzanne took charge, her hand on the small of Mum's back as she ushered her in. 'I'm Suzanne. This is my sister, Carla, and this is our mother, Collette.'

'Lovely to put faces to the names,' Siobhan said, working through each of us, shaking our hands in two of hers.

'Lovely to meet you, Siobhan,' Mum said, shaking her hand. 'I'm Collette.'

She had remembered her name. It amazed me that she could forget mine and Suzanne's yet retain the name of someone she'd only just met.

'And I'm delighted to meet you, Collette.' She sounded as though she meant it.

On the walls of the reception area there were photos, collages of patients and staff, smiling in a garden with flowers. I picked up a leaflet and sat down in one of the chairs.

'Are you going to wait here, Carla,' Siobhan asked, 'or come in with us?' She said it in a nice way, like some people might just wait outside.

Embarrassed, I stood up. 'Sorry. Of course I'm coming in. I just thought maybe we'd have paperwork or something to do first.'

'We can do all that later,' she said. 'There's a sing-song on at the moment. We may as well get stuck straight into that.'

She flicked a switch with her security tag and held open the door she'd come through for us. I could hear voices, a guitar. Inside, the room was bright, hot, the walls all glass. It didn't smell like a hospital. Siobhan took Mum's arm and led her towards the singing. Suzanne and I followed, side by side. I tried to catch her eye but she wouldn't look at me.

This room was a little cooler, despite the crowd of people sitting in a circle singing 'Danny Boy'. I'd always hated 'Danny Boy'. A man with a white beard was leading the chorus, his head tipped back as his voice rose higher. He didn't need the ring binder of lyrics that the nurse next to him was holding on his lap, the words and the notes and the pauses came in all the right places. Some of the others joined in, sharing the sheets of lyrics between them, others just sat and nodded. Across from me a woman held a baby doll high on her shoulder, as if she was winding it.

'Music is so important,' Siobhan whispered to me. 'Does your mother like music?'

'Yes,' I said, 'she does.'

'We find people are great for remembering song lyrics, even when they struggle with other things.'

I'd discovered that. I'd been in the kitchen mopping the floor to Neil Diamond, when Mum came in and started to sing along. We sang our way through 'Sweet Caroline' and 'Red, Red, Wine' and did some crazy uncoordinated waltz to 'Song Sung Blue', the lino getting dirtier and dirtier instead of cleaner, full of our wet footprints. I thought about telling Siobhan but she was busy pointing out the paintings on the walls to Suzanne.

The song had ended and everyone had switched to the Beatles' 'Ob-La-Di, Ob-La-Da', all except the white-bearded man who was still persevering with 'Danny Boy'. Despite his best efforts, he was drowned out as the tempo increased.

Mum was standing a little away from us, her hands resting on one of the women's chairs. Her shoulders were swaying a little with the music, just like they did at home, her fingers drumming the back of the chair, as if she might play the piano on it. She seemed transfixed by the man on guitar, the energy of him, the way he leaned forward and back with the music. Another nurse came over to her and led her to an empty chair in the circle, sitting her down between a man who seemed to be sleeping and a woman leaning forward, clapping and singing with all her might.

Siobhan's hand was soft on my arm, but firm too. 'Do you want to see the rest of the place?'

It felt wrong, leaving Mum there, even for a few minutes, but as I glanced back over my shoulder, she was smiling and singing too, timing her claps with the woman next to her. It scared me how quickly she could slot in with them. These people weren't like her, they were nothing like her and yet she was sitting there in this circle, as if she was one of them.

I turned to follow Siobhan and Suzanne back into the room with the glass walls. It seemed even hotter now. Siobhan pointed out the couches, the television, the fake fireplaces. We walked past shelves full of books, a piano, a room with a mobile hanging from the ceiling, fluorescent stars stuck on the walls. All the time Siobhan was explaining the rationale to make it look and feel like home. Except it wasn't home.

'Down here is the residential unit for long-term patients,' she said. 'I'll show you.'

'Oh, no, thanks,' I said. 'We're only looking for respite, daytime care. She won't be staying here.'

Suzanne glanced at Siobhan and then to me. 'We may as well have a look, Carla, while we're here.'

As she followed Siobhan down the corridor, I trailed behind until I stopped by a long window, facing the garden. An image came into my mind from a video I'd seen online of end-stage patients, one that Mum had caught me watching before I'd turned it off. I didn't need to see that in real life, not yet. Outside it was nice – tulips, patio furniture, a raised flowerbed with a fuzz of green coming through where Siobhan had explained patients could plant their own. Mum would like that. The thought came and I pushed it back to wherever it had come from. That was how it started, thinking things like that, believing Mum would be happy here. Once we started thinking like that, who knew where it would end?

Siobhan and Suzanne were back, chatting quietly as they walked over to me.

'The bedrooms are lovely, Carla,' Suzanne said. 'Some of them are shared but there are private ones as well, with their own bathrooms. They put the patients' photos and names on the doors, so they know which is theirs.'

'That's nice,' I said.

'It's just a little thing,' Siobhan said, 'but we find it helps. People can be a little disoriented at first, so we try to make things as familiar as possible.' She glanced at her watch. She didn't have much more time for us, there were other things for her to do.

Suzanne raised her eyebrows. 'So,' she said to me, 'what do you think?'

I folded my arms. From behind us the music was getting louder. A man came out, shuffling slowly in the direction of the bedrooms. Despite the heat he was wearing a thick wool jumper.

'Where are you off to, Tom?' Siobhan said. He stopped and looked at the three of us. It seemed to take him a minute to understand that she was talking to him. 'Were you not enjoying the sing-song?'

'I'm waiting for someone to come,' he said.

'Who, Tom?' Siobhan said. 'Who's coming?'

He took his glasses off and put them back on again, staring at us as if maybe we were who he'd been waiting for. Eventually he answered her: 'I can't remember.'

'Ah, it'll come to you, Tom, don't worry.' Siobhan walked over to him and touched his arm. 'Tom used to drive buses, didn't you, Tom? There were a lot of people who used to wait for you, didn't they?'

'They did,' he said, nodding, 'but never for that long. As the fella said, we were always very regular.' He laughed at his own joke, and as Siobhan joined in, I saw her turn towards the male nurse standing by the door of the music room and mouth something to him. He came over and led Tom away, in a slow shuffle, down the corridor.

'Carla, I was saying to Suzanne that we have different activities every day. Baking, movement to music, things like that. And we encourage families of our clients to volunteer. Do you have any hidden talents you'd like to use?'

She looked at me expectantly and I shook my head, buried my hands in my jeans pockets. 'I'm afraid not,' I said. 'We're not a very talented family, are we, Suzanne?'

I was waiting for Suzanne to laugh, to make some joke, but instead she smiled as if she'd just had the best idea ever. 'I was just thinking, maybe you could do a yoga class.'

'You're a yoga teacher?' Siobhan said, her face lighting up.

'No,' I said, 'I'm not.'

'Carla does yoga every morning with Mammy,' Suzanne said. 'Mammy used to love yoga and I think it really helps that she can still do it, with Carla's lead.'

'I was only reading something the other day about how yoga can be good for people with Alzheimer's,' Siobhan said. 'Lots of people in the States are doing it. Carla, it would be wonderful if you could run a little class.'

'I'm not a yoga teacher,' I said, glaring at Suzanne. 'I'm not qualified or anything. I'm not even very good.'

'You wouldn't need to be a teacher, it'd just be very gentle,' Siobhan said. 'We've a slot free on Tuesday afternoons. Just think about it.' Her hand squeezed my arm as if we'd made an agreement.

I dug my hands into my pockets. 'No,' I said. 'I'm sorry, but I really couldn't.'

'No problem, just thought I'd ask,' Siobhan said, smiling so I could see he gap in her teeth. 'Sure you can always let me know if you change your mind.'

★

'I thought I was going to drive.'

Suzanne looked at me briefly, then flicked her eyes back to the road. 'You should have reminded me before we left,' she said, glancing into the rear-view mirror as she changed lanes. 'There's no point telling me now, when we're halfway home.'

I sighed. The radio was playing ads so I flicked to another station. More ads. I hit the CD button and Westlife came blaring out. I shut it off. Sighed again.

'What?' Suzanne said. 'You think your ears might shrivel up and fall off if you listen to a few minutes of Westlife?'

'I wish they would.'

I didn't need to look at Suzanne to know she was rolling her eyes. A cyclist in a high visibility vest passed by so close he nearly took off the wing mirror.

'I can't believe you gave that woman the impression that I was going to teach a yoga class. I'm not a yoga teacher. I'm not even any good at yoga.'

'Sorry, it just came out. Anyway, I thought yoga wasn't about how good you are. Isn't that the whole point?'

I closed my eyes, leaned my head against the window.

'If she asks again you can tell her you can't do it. You can just say you don't have time.'

'I know what I can say.'

'Well, then, what's wrong?'

I hit the window harder than I'd meant to, my ring making a rap on the glass. I turned to look at her, really look at her. 'What do you think is wrong?'

She slowed through the gears, glancing in the rear-view mirror. 'You didn't like the place?' she said.

I tried to say no but I couldn't. I couldn't say anything so instead I shook my head hard, kept staring out of the window. It was starting to rain. I wanted to tell her I hated the place, hated everything about it, even the things I liked.

'I was pleasantly surprised,' she said. 'Much nicer than I'd expected. Did you not like Siobhan?'

I jammed my lips together, twisted my ring on my finger. I thought of the people there, the woman I'd just met, who had told me she'd never forget me and kissed my cheek, Tom the bus driver, waiting for someone who was never going to arrive. 'She was OK,' I said.

The lights went green and Suzanne drove off again, turning the wipers on. 'Well, I don't think we're going to get anywhere nicer than that. They have a great reputation. And Mammy liked it.'

When we'd got back to her, Mum had been holding hands with the woman next to her, both of them singing. Since we'd left she hadn't spoken.

'Did she, Suzanne? How do you know? What if she hated it? What if she was scared there? What if we put her there and they abuse her or something and she can't even tell us?'

I heard the panic in my voice. As I opened my mouth to speak again, I felt a hand on my shoulder, a familiar touch, heavy and calming. When I put mine up to feel the fingers they were cold. Mum's fingers had always been cold.

I turned to her and she was smiling her wide smile. It reached her eyes. They held mine.

'Love,' she said. She kept her hand where it was for a moment, then took it away. She sat back in her seat to watch the traffic.

'Mum?'

I kept watching her, wanting more, and her eyes returned to me, but now they were different, not her eyes at all.

'Is Mammy all right?' Suzanne said.

I didn't answer her, there was no answer for her. Instead I kept my eyes on Mum, wondering what had passed through her mind as she'd reached out to comfort me, if she knew why I was upset or if she was remembering a time she comforted me years before.

And as I looked at her, sitting in the back of the car, buckled in and safe, I thought that maybe it didn't matter why she'd comforted me. Maybe it was enough to know that, even for those few seconds, she had been there. Really, really there.

Twelve

My feet were quiet as I came down the stairs. In the hall, I checked the locks. I pulled the curtains halfway before I realised what I was doing, that through the squares of glass I could still see daylight. It was too early for Mum to be in bed but she was in bed anyway. Suzanne's routine, which I'd fought so hard against when I'd first come home, appeared to have broken down completely, and now that it had, I wanted it back.

Around me, the house was silent. I checked the kitchen first, then the living room. No sign of Suzanne, but her car was still outside. She was never in the back room but I checked it anyway. At first I didn't see her, but then I did, through the open door of the conservatory, sitting on the patio.

She turned when she heard me coming.

'Mammy went down OK?'

On the table next to her was a bottle of wine, two glasses already poured, a bowl of crisps beside them.

'Like a light,' I said. 'What's all this?'

'Thought we deserved a drink, after the day we've had.'

I took one of the glasses and sat down. She took the other but we didn't chink them. The metal chair was supposed to have a cushion, but I sank into it anyway. In Brooklyn I'd hardly ever drunk wine but here I was getting the hang of it, starting to like it. I took a sip. It was heavy, warm, the same way the glass felt in my hand.

'I'm not surprised she went down so easily,' Suzanne said. 'It was a big day for her, meeting all those new people. A big day for all of us.'

'I suppose.'

'Lily-Anne called to see how we'd got on. She said she'd always liked that place.'

'Really?'

So that was why she'd set this up, the wine, the crisps, so we could sit and talk about Mum and the home and make ourselves feel better about whatever it was we were doing. I didn't want to feel better about it.

'She said of all the places she and Mammy saw together they both liked that one best.'

Along the wall the daffodils were dead, drooping heads of crispy yellow tinged with beige. Soon the beige would become brown and brown would take them over, until the flowers would fall away and the stalks would die back into the ground.

'I wish you'd say something,' Suzanne said, 'I feel like I'm talking to myself here.'

'Like what?'

'I get the feeling you didn't like the place. If you have reservations, I'd like to know what they are.'

I thought of the woman with the doll, her baby. Mum holding her hand. I took another sip of wine, counted the dead daffodils. 'It just freaked me out, how easily she fitted in there. Everyone seemed sicker than her. I don't know – it didn't seem like the kind of place she's going to get better.'

'She's not going to get any better anywhere, Carla.'

'Jesus, Suzanne, I know that. Of course, I know that.' I took another mouthful of wine and swallowed it fast so it burned my throat. 'I'm not explaining it right. What I mean is, I don't like the idea of sending her off to some place that's going to make it worse.'

Suzanne swirled her glass. When she spoke her voice was soft. 'Let's just take this slowly. We're only talking about help during the day, remember? Not full-time care.'

'Today, that's what we're talking about but that's what's next. Only last year she was saying that everything was fine, that she had ten years, maybe more.' It seemed so long ago. Had it really been just a year? Suzanne leaned across and refilled my glass, then hers. A little drop of wine dripped from the bottle and landed on the stone, red on cream.

'None of this is easy,' she said. 'And I've had more time to get used to it. Ages before you came home I could see something, even though I didn't want to. I kept telling myself she was fine, that I was being paranoid.' Her hair came loose and she fixed it back again. 'And sometimes, it was easy to think I'd got it all wrong. She'd have days when she'd be totally fine, absolutely nothing wrong at all. And I'd think, what made her OK today? And I'd try and do everything the same again the next time – like if we just kept doing things the same way, everything would be fine.' She laughed. 'It probably sounds crazy to you.'

I thought about me and Eddie, heading back to Coney Island even in winter, like a pilgrimage, as if being on the same beach where we'd once been so sure of each other would somehow make us sure again.

'No,' I said. 'It doesn't sound crazy.'

'Well, maybe it wasn't crazy, but it was stupid. Because something would always happen. She'd forget to meet me. Or ring me three times about the same thing. No matter what I did, she got worse anyway.'

I tried to imagine what it had been like, what it would be like for me to go through this alone, without her, without Lily-Anne. I took a breath.

'I never really said it, but I'm sorry you had to deal with so much of this by yourself,' I said. 'I know I wasn't too much help at the start.'

I didn't look at her while I waited for her answer.

'That's OK. It was a shitty situation. You had your own stuff going on.'

'Still though, I probably could've done more.'

The words were out and I was glad I'd said them. She tipped her head back so it rested on the chair. It looked comfortable and

I copied her. Above us, the sky was still blue, but darker. Indigo, teal. Leaning back further, I saw the wall of the house, windows. Mum's bedroom over our heads.

'I hate that she's up there and neither of us even think to lower our voices any more,' I said.

Suzanne sat up and sipped some wine. She pointed her toe towards the flowerbed. 'You know what I hate?'

'What?'

'Those!' She jabbed her foot. 'I hate those fucking flowers!' She let her leg fall, stamping on the patio for emphasis. Next door's dog yapped. A car slowed on the street outside. I followed her gaze along the wall.

'The daffodils?' I said.

'Yeah,' she said. 'I can't fucking stand them.'

I rolled my glass between my fingers. 'Me neither.'

It felt as though my breath had slowed right down, had become barely the faintest trickle of oxygen to keep me alive. She hated daffodils. I hadn't known and I was afraid to ask her why in case it wasn't the same reason. But it had to be the same reason.

She drank more wine, and her glass was nearly empty. When she spoke she directed her words at the garden, not at me. 'You know that first spring day every year when the sun is out and everyone's saying how gorgeous it is? I hate it. I really fucking hate it. Give me rain any time. Give me sleet.' She turned to me, her eyes on mine. 'Do you know what I mean?'

Of course I did. It was the trick of those days, all sunshine and brightness wrapped around a core of death. If he'd had to die, why couldn't it have been raining, grey, even one of those flat, colourless days when the sky is white? I knew what she meant, I knew exactly, but I'd never thought that anyone else could know it too.

I took a breath before I spoke. 'I hate the sound of lawnmowers. I'd forgotten – living in Brooklyn – but since I've come back it seems like everyone is always out there, always fucking mowing. All the fucking time.'

Suzanne opened her mouth and closed it again. When she found the words, she spoke them slowly. 'I wondered if it brought things back, for you, being here.'

I stretched my legs out so they almost reached the edge of the patio, my toes nearly grazing the grass. We were less than two feet from the spot where he had lain. I could still see it – I thought I could – the imprint his body had left on the grass after they had taken him away, the blades flattened, the daffodils broken. I remembered a memory of after – how long after? – standing here, trying to see it, the shape he had made, the impulse to find it, lie down in it, to take the shape myself.

The dog yapped louder. We listened to it whining, a scratch of claws. A door opened and closed. Silence. Suzanne put her empty glass on the table. Neither of us had touched the crisps. We'd never talked about this, the fight we'd had on the night before I was supposed to go back to America didn't count. Looking at her, leaning towards me on the arm of her chair, it seemed important to answer her, to say something real.

'I suppose it has. Some things you can prepare for – you think you can – like the day I went into Trinity with Mum and Lily-Anne. Then others catch you off guard. A lawnmower. A Van Morrison song on the radio.'

Suzanne refilled her glass. 'It's funny,' she said, 'the things you remember. I don't remember hearing a lawnmower. In my memory, everything was completely silent.'

In her memory. She had a reel in her head, like I did, only different. I didn't want to run my reel, yet it was already running. The silence of Mum and Dad's room just before I'd looked out the window, my hand on the banister coming down the stairs, the grass damp under my bare feet.

'You're right,' I said. 'Thinking about it, his lawnmower was switched off, so I couldn't have heard it. Maybe that's what woke me, hearing it stop.'

Was it really the silence that had woken me or had he shouted out? Called my name?

'It wasn't silent once I arrived and started screaming my head off.' She said it like a joke, but I didn't laugh. I couldn't joke about that scream, a sound so painful there might have been blood in it.

She wiped her eye with the heel of her hand. 'You were so calm,' she said. 'You knew what to do.'

'I didn't have a clue.'

'I was older. I was the one who should've been more together. You were right – those things you said before. You did everything. You called 999. Olivia. Even afterwards, in her house, I wouldn't come down to talk to anyone until Mammy got back.'

I'd always loved Olivia's house but not that day, me still in my pyjamas and Mum's tennis shoes until Ange had arrived with some clothes. I'd wanted to stay in the hospital, I remembered that, not wanting to leave, even when we knew for sure there was no reason to stay.

'Where was Mum?' I said. 'Madrid?'

'Rome,' she said. 'It was nearly seven by the time she got there. I left you to deal with everyone, call everyone, while I lay in bed. I felt guilty about that after.'

Guilt: once you scratched the surface it seemed to be everywhere. I pictured what it looked like, collecting in people's heads, people's bodies, sticky strands that wound around their brains, gloopy goo trailing down the gaps between shoulder-blades, pooling in the hollows of collar bones.

'I felt guilty too.' My heart knocked and I gulped some wine, held it for a few seconds on my tongue before I swallowed.

Suzanne shifted in her chair, the legs scraping on stone. 'Why?'

On the grass in front of us a small brown bird landed, swooped away again on to the wall. When I was little I was fascinated by birds, how they could fly away any time they felt like it, halfway around the world if they wanted, to escape our cold weather. I pushed the words out fast, before I could stop them.

'I was supposed to help him that morning, did you know that? I'd promised to give him a hand in the garden. Only I didn't get

up. I'd been out in Stargazers the night before, with Damien and
Ange and Pete.'

Inside my runners I wiggled my toes to remind myself they
were still there. My bladder twinged.

'Stargazers. Jesus, remember that place?'

Inside my chest my heart kept beating, marching forward.

'He came up to call me twice. But I fell back asleep. The
second time, he was pissed off. I remember he leaned against the
door frame and he looked all red and sweaty.' I paused, took a
tissue from my pocket, dabbed my nose. 'It was heavy going, that's
what he said, and would I not get out of bed and give him a hand?
He said it was taking for ever, that he'd no energy, that he didn't
feel well. He said he didn't feel well, Suzanne.'

I was focusing on the patio, my feet. I could feel my heart, my
breath. As soon as I'd said it, I wished I hadn't told her, wished I
could take the words back.

'Carla, you weren't to know.'

I moved my runners close together so the toes were touching.
Along the wall the daffodils were still dead. Seven, eight, ten,
twelve of them.

'Carla, you were a teenager, having a lie-in. I'd have done the
same thing.'

We both knew that wasn't true.

'You couldn't have known, Carla. There was nothing you
could've done.'

'Not lying in bed – but what if I'd got up? What if I'd called
an ambulance sooner? It was half an hour since he'd called me.
What if he was lying there all that time? Calling my name while
I was fucking sleeping?'

'Don't go there, Carla.'

But I already had, picturing his heart filling up with blood,
corpuscles, all those words long lost from my biology book, red
blood cells turning black, congealing, clogging up his heart, his
poor, poor heart. I shredded the tissue in my lap, just like Mum
did.

'Carla, seriously, don't.'

'I didn't know he was really sick, that it was his heart.'

'You couldn't have known. Sure none of us knew.'

'I thought he was just hung-over. I think I might have even said that to him, that he was probably only hung-over.'

I sneaked a glance at her and she had her head tilted to the side, smiling a little. What was there to smile about?

'He probably *was* hung-over,' she said. 'He'd had his night out with the boys. Remember Roisin giving out hell to Noel about the state he'd been in the night before? She went through him for bringing whiskey to Olivia's.'

Noel drinking whiskey while we had tea and toasted batch loaf. I'd known that, yet somehow I'd forgotten. 'Did she?'

'Oh, yeah. I remember Olivia saying you'd think she'd cut him some slack on that day of all days but she never let up.'

We both laughed then, the two of us, and I wasn't really sure what was funny but it didn't matter. There'd been too much crying lately, enough to make you think that was all there was.

'What happened to Daddy was terrible, Carla, and I don't know how I'd feel if I'd been in your shoes, but it wasn't your fault. The doctors said afterwards that it was a massive heart attack, that he would've died instantly.'

I remembered that, had said it in my head, but somehow it was better hearing it in Suzanne's voice. She emptied the rest of the wine into my glass and handed it to me. 'It wasn't your fault.'

We sat there in silence then, watching the night take over the garden, the trees at the end shapes of dark, darker even than the sky behind them. After all this time it was hard to believe that I'd said the words – that I'd said them to Suzanne – and that she was still here, that we were both still here.

After a while, she spoke. 'Talking about all this reminds me that I didn't bring Mammy up to the grave on his anniversary this year. With everything else going on, it just slipped by. Do you think we should bring her at the weekend?'

I heard the 'we'. I was meant to hear it. I hadn't been back, not since that day in March, the day the sun beat down hard, reflecting on the stone all around, so people had to hide their eyes behind sunglasses.

'I don't know,' I said. 'It might not be such a great idea. She hasn't mentioned Dad in ages. Imagine she didn't remember that he was dead?'

Or if she didn't remember him at all. I held the thought back, didn't let it become words.

'I know. But she never missed it. Maybe it's not up to us to make that decision for her.'

We were already making so many decisions for her, would one more make any difference? That was what I wanted to say, but I knew that if I did, it would be about me, not about Mum. The moon was half hidden behind a cloud, the same moon that shone down now on Dad's grave, only a couple of miles away. In my mind it was a pile of earth, sloped on either side. But it wasn't like that any more; maybe it never even had been. Maybe that was a picture I'd made up in my mind. It was only a place to remember him. A memorial. He wasn't there any more than he was in Trinity, than he was lying on the grass in front of me.

Behind Suzanne, the kitchen window was a rectangle of light, making her almost a silhouette.

'So, what do you think?' she said.

In the dark her teeth were shiny white. She was waiting for an answer. 'Maybe,' I said. 'Let's have a think about it.'

THIRTEEN

I turned off the ignition and pulled up the handbrake. Already I was doing things in the wrong order, forgetting everything Sean had worked so hard to teach me. In the back, Suzanne was leaning across Mum, unbuckling her seatbelt. 'We're here, Mammy,' she said.

Mum looked out the window. 'Are we going home?' she said.

'After this, Mammy,' Suzanne said. 'We'll take you home after this.'

I took the plant from the passenger seat and walked on ahead of them. It was four o'clock already. How had it taken so long to go to the garden centre and pick up a plant? At the gate I stopped, watching Mum dither at the car with a surge of impatience. I didn't want to do this. I was doing it for her, for Suzanne. The least she could do was to help to get it over with quickly.

I checked the gates for opening and closing times, but there were none. Inside, it was deserted, no one else around. Through the funny-shaped trees on either side of the pathway I could see the grey stone of the headstones.

I was about to go and see what was taking them so long when I saw their shadows, long on the ground, heard Suzanne talking low before they came, linking arms, through the gate.

'Here we are, Mammy,' Suzanne said. 'Carla has the plant, don't worry. You did a good job picking it out. We'll give it some water when we get there.'

I jangled the car keys from one finger. 'Do you know what time this place closes?'

'Probably not till six or so. It's very quiet, isn't it? Usually there are more people around.'

'Gives me the creeps,' I said. I led the way up the narrow path. Something told me they weren't behind me, and when I looked around, Mum had stopped again to pick a leaf from one of the trees. I watched her take it in her hand, move her thumb over its surface. I held my breath, exhaled, turning my gaze to the line of headstones, an uneven mismatching wall of grey, white, black.

'Suzanne, we don't want to get locked in here,' I said. 'Come on.'

She took Mum's arm, pulled her gently back on to the path. 'What type of trees are they, Mammy?' she said.

Mum opened her hand and closed it again, exposing and hiding the deep green of the leaf, before putting it into her jacket pocket. 'Those are always in these places . . .' She ran out of words, glanced back over her shoulder.

'In graveyards?' Suzanne said.

I stood back, let them walk past me, took up the rear.

Mum took the leaf out of her pocket, rubbed it with her finger. 'They mean something, the branches, when they fall, the branches mean something . . .'

'Maybe they're a symbol,' Suzanne said. 'Let's look it up on the Internet, later, when we get home.'

'When we get home,' Mum echoed.

Ahead of us the path got narrower, a tiny lane between the headstones. A magpie landed on one of the taller ones, eyed me and flew away.

'I hate these places,' I said.

'It's kind of eerie today, with no one around,' Suzanne said.

As I walked, I realised it wasn't only that I hated being surrounded by all that death, it was the colours too, all that concrete, the sunken stones. We spent our whole lives trapped in concrete, in shopping centres and offices, and someone had decided we had to spend our time after in it too.

Up ahead, Suzanne and Mum were in a rhythm, walking

quickly now. Even their walks where the same, the same hip movement, the same pace. Suzanne slowed down, stopped, and I saw a man coming down the hill, so old, so hunched, he was nearly an L shape. He thanked us as he passed. When we started walking again I examined Mum's shoulders under her denim jacket, the slope where, despite all her yoga, they were starting to round.

Suzanne was saying something, but I couldn't hear her properly. Alongside us the headstones were newer, the 1980s, it looked like. Not too many rows between us and the back wall and things were starting to look familiar, or was I imagining that? No, I remembered this, I thought I did, the slant of the path away to the left, the red rooftops behind the back wall, ordinary tiled roofs so close to all this death.

Suzanne took a turn to the left, walking faster now than she had all day, Mum too, staying close to her. After all my haste I wanted them to slow down, to stop, to get lost, so we might never get there.

My shoulder ached and I switched the plant to the other hand. We were in the 1990s now, passing graves from 1992, 1993. His year would be next. I glanced behind me and we were up high, high enough to feel the breeze that rattled the aerial on one of the houses behind the wall. It'd be quicker to get back to the car, all downhill. I wished I'd found a loo before I came.

Suzanne stopped then, so suddenly that Mum walked into her. They were in front of a grave with a shiny black marble headstone, shaped like a scroll. I stopped too, at the grave next to it, one with a built-in statue of Mary. The name on it was McCann, Sheila and Ivor; they had died in the same year. A picture of them was embedded in the stone but water had got in somehow so their faces bulged; hers obscured completely.

Suzanne was on her knees, clearing something from the grave, and when she stood up I gave her the plant. She took the cellophane off and handed it to Mum, putting her hand on her back to bring her in closer. There wasn't enough room for all three of us and I stayed where I was, next to the McCanns.

'Carla?'

Suzanne stood back, gesturing for me to move in but my feet were stuck, my runners on the gravel. From nowhere I had a sudden picture of the shoes I was wearing that other day, black slip-ons I'd never really liked, even when I'd bought them. I hadn't wanted to get close then either, wanted to be invisible in the crowd, but Mum had held me there, trapped at the front, her fingers like claws on my arm. I hadn't forgiven her by then, for not including 'Mr Tambourine Man' in the service, for not even considering it. I remembered wanting to rip her hand away, kick off those stupid shoes and run barefoot down the gravelly path so I wouldn't have to look at the gleam of brass down there in the blackness, to listen for the silence of the rose as it fell.

Mum knelt at the edge and brushed the headstone with her fingers. Above her the sky was whitish-grey, the same colour as the graveyard, a giant graveyard in the sky. That other morning it had been bright, a sweep of cloud, and the only way to escape had been to look for the colours in it, but there was only blue.

I could feel Suzanne's eyes on me. I wrapped my arms around my stomach, took a breath and walked a step closer, close enough to read what was written there.

Nathan 'Nat' James Matthews
7 September 1948 – 26 March 1994

I didn't know they'd put that on, 'Nat'. When I was little, I used to think it was spelled 'gnat', like the insect. He'd laughed when I told him that, made a buzz-buzz sound close to my ear for ages afterwards. I used to push him away when he did it, yell at him to stop, but that only made him do it more because he knew that really I was enjoying it, that I was only pretending.

Mum was tracing out the letters, her finger following the curve of each one. There were more words, something underneath.

Teacher, father, husband, friend
Rest in Peace

I felt a prickle at the top of my nose, bit my lip. They'd started with 'Teacher' and for a second I wondered why but then I knew: of all the things Dad had been, that was what he had been first. Maybe that was what he had been most.

I looked at Mum, balancing on her hunkers, thought of what it might say for her. The list of all the things she'd been was too long for that little space. Wife, mother, friend, teacher, traveller, therapist, musician, yogi. There wasn't enough room for all the things she'd been, all these things she was forgetting she ever was. Did it matter that she didn't remember these versions of herself? The fact that she'd done these things, lived these lives, was that enough?

She turned and looked at me, straight on. 'He died,' she said. 'Did you know that he died?'

I swallowed. 'Yes, Mum. I knew.'

She reached out for the headstone again, traced his name. Nat. Gnat. Buzz-buzz. When she looked up again, her face was confused, sad. 'Do you miss him?'

The question was so obvious, yet no one had ever asked me before. The answer, when it came, was instinctive and absolutely true. 'Yes,' I said. 'I miss him. Every day, I miss him.'

It was so simple it was almost a relief. I missed my dad. He had died, the person I loved most in the whole world had died, and I missed him. I still did. No matter what happened, no matter where I went, I was never going to stop missing him. And maybe I didn't want to: maybe missing him was the best way to show him I'd never forget him.

Mum was on her feet, one step, two, until she was next to me. She spread her arms wide and I let myself step into her embrace, let her pull me close. Her jacket smelt of her perfume and I buried my head in it, let my tears fall into the denim that still held her scent.

And standing there, her hand rubbing my back in circles, there was something about it that I remembered from some other time, I didn't know when, it wasn't even a proper memory, only the feel of her, her smell, crying hard into her softness. And the memory brought more tears and I let them come as well, tears on top of tears, and I didn't pull away even though part of me wanted to.

I let myself stay there, in my mother's arms, at my dad's grave with my sister watching, and I didn't pull away.

FOURTEEN

Under my hands the steering wheel felt thinner than the one in Sean's car or Suzanne's. The windscreen was still fogged up and I crouched lower in my seat, focused on the bits of road I could see through the ovals in the steam. Suzanne thought we should sell Mum's car, get me a new one, but I liked driving her old Volkswagen. There was something comforting about rust around the lock, the dent over the back wheel arch. Enough things were changing. It was nice to have something that stayed the same.

In the back, Mum was sleeping. I slowed down to turn the corner and her head pitched forward, then rolled back, but she didn't wake up. I felt myself relax. That happened about half the time, on these late-night drives, and it was better than when she stayed awake and wide-eyed, her hands clutching the back of the passenger seat, asking if we were nearly there, if she was nearly home.

I turned the radio on low. The Eagles. In front of me the windscreen was finally clearing so I could see the road ahead, empty, orange pools of light. I could've turned around, driven back to the house, but now I was out I felt like keeping going, didn't feel like dealing yet with waking her up, in case she started again, the pacing, the endless questions about when she could go home. It was only a couple of weeks since it had begun but it felt like months. We'd tried everything: reasoning with her, arguing, music, even medication. None of it had worked. It was Ange who had made the suggestion, in the end, to take her out for a drive in the car, like she used to do with Mikey when he was a baby.

The road was getting narrower, but I didn't mind it at night, without the rest of the traffic. I liked the way it swirled and dipped and curved, like a computer game, the closeness of the ivy-covered walls, the whoosh of the tyres on the tarmac. The car was taking me towards Bray, it seemed, and that was OK, after the long day, the busy night at work, I could use some sea air.

Ahead the light was red and I stopped. No grinding. Sean would be pleased. He'd been calling a lot and we'd had good chats, but each time I'd turned down his invites into town to meet his friends. I had plenty of excuses to choose from – my writing class, work, teaching yoga in the respite centre. He laughed when I told him that, said he knew I'd relent. He offered to come down one day for moral support, and he'd sounded like he meant it. All I had to do was ask, he said.

The Eagles had finished and the radio was on ads. I changed the station. Thin Lizzy were 'Dancing in the Moonlight'. In the rear-view mirror I could see Mum's head tipped back against the seat, she was starting to snore. Her words from earlier came into my head: *She'd never have left him*. She was sick, she hadn't meant it. I flicked the radio station again, but it was still ads everywhere. I went back to Thin Lizzy.

Ahead there was a sign for a roundabout and I slowed down, pulling the steering wheel in my hands, ten to two. *She'd never have left him, the way she left me.*

Back on the straight road now, past the new apartment buildings, a taxi with its light on. At first I hadn't known she was talking about me. I'd thought she meant Olivia. That was who she was looking at in the picture. It was only when she'd said the next thing about going to America that I realised, and as she'd turned the page of the photo album I wasn't sure which was worse – knowing that that was what she'd always thought or that right then, for that moment, she'd no idea who I was.

I hit the steering wheel with the heel of my hand. It hurt. I did it again. In the back, she slept on. I could remember the conversation when I'd told her I was staying in America, the words and silences. If that was what she'd thought, why hadn't she said it at the time? Or, better still, never said it at all.

Past the garage, the factory with the chain-link fence that used to fascinate Suzanne and me when we were little. Dad had made up stories about the elf families who lived on its grounds and I remembered how we drank in the details, our breath hot on the car windows as we drove past. If Dad had been alive would I have stayed? Would things have been different? That was a stupid question. If Dad was alive everything would have been different.

At the turn to the seafront the lights were red. As I slowed down, stopped, a motorbike overtook me and went through anyway, sudden and noisy in the dark. Daft bugger. That was what Dad would've called him. On the radio Thin Lizzy had turned to Westlife and I flicked stations again, then again. That was the drawback of this car: it only took tapes. I flicked a third time. A drum beat, a guitar. I didn't know the song but I liked it, I liked the shape of it. The light changed to green. I made a left.

The tune was catchy. I tapped my fingers on the gearstick. At first I didn't recognise their voices, blended together. It was during the chorus that I started to listen to the words, two lines repeated.

> I can feel my soul rising,
> Can you feel my soul rising?

As it changed into the verse there was something familiar about the transition. A guy singing on his own now, a light voice. High, but not girly. I turned it up.

> If we'd left space between you and me,
> Would there have been someone left to be?
> But we took up all the air
> Still it hurts, that you're not there.

My breath snagged in my throat. It was Eddie, not just someone who sounded like him, definitely him, a different-sounding Eddie I hadn't heard since that 'Fallen' song, the first night in O'Dowd's. I turned it up louder, not caring if Mum woke up, but the song was back in the chorus, repeating, fading, already working towards the end. I waited for the DJ's voice to come on, to confirm what I already knew, but it went straight to an ad break.

I turned the radio off. In the silence I could feel the tremor of the engine, my heart. I was on the seafront. It was almost a surprise to find myself there, all the parking I wanted. I drove up towards the bandstand. Now that I was here, I wanted to go home, to find the song online and play it again. I wanted to know what it meant, even though I knew already, I thought I knew.

I indicated, slowed down and turned the car into the space. In the mirror one of the white lines had disappeared and I reversed, straightened, pulled in again. Mum was still snoring, leaning slightly forward against the seatbelt. I thought she might wake up when I opened the door, closed it, but she didn't. I hesitated before locking the car but I locked it anyway – couldn't risk leaving it open.

As I walked towards the water, Eddie's song seemed to expand in my head. It was good, this new song. There was depth to it, the sounds and the spaces adding up to something different from the songs he'd written before. Above the sea the moon was low. Eddie's song was about me, about us. A song that was playing on the radio, to people in cars, in kitchens, at work. Thousands of people, maybe millions, would listen to those lyrics, learn them, sing them, make them about their own lives instead of about us.

My work shirt flapped – I was freezing. I should've brought a jacket. At the end of the beach, Bray Head was a dark mound against the silver sky. I counted the ribbons of waves on the moonlit water, seven, nearly always seven, before a break. I wasn't going to look up the song online, didn't want to. It was his way of trying to figure out what had happened, what had changed, just like my way had always been to come to places like this.

As the thought formed so did a memory, of another night like this one, standing on a boardwalk, looking at another sea. I'd stayed on the Q train that night, let it go by Prospect Park, Avenue M and Ocean Parkway until I was at Coney Island. It had been silly to go there alone so late, dangerous, but it was that September when everything in New York was dangerous. I was volunteering in St Paul's Chapel, had been there all day and even though I was exhausted it had been so hard to leave. Maybe something about volunteering there was why I had let myself see the truth that night, that although we were still so many things to each other, we weren't the important thing. We were a history, a story, a team. We were many things, but we were not in love.

On the beach the stones glistened. The thought was different now; with distance, I could hold onto it, turn it over in a way I couldn't at the time. Back then, the thought was an ambush, overwhelming, a thought I didn't even link to the days I was spending with exhausted men, massaging life back into their feet through thick wool socks, wiping ash from their faces, ringing round for more supplies of lip balm, of gum. Now I could see it, clear as the stones on the beach, how it was spending my days steeped in their truth that made it so much harder to lie.

A cloud drifted in front of the moon, obscuring it briefly. I rubbed my arms through my shirt. What would have happened if I'd left him then? If he'd been out that night, instead of on the couch where I found him, just waking, his hair sticking up, his face concerned and creased from sleep? If I hadn't let him hug me, take my hand and lead me to bed, would I be long over him by now instead of dreading our meeting next week?

Behind me, I heard a noise. When I turned, no one was there. I watched for a minute, just to be sure, my eyes on the car. I made out Mum's shape. She was still asleep.

She'd never have left him, the way she left me.

Her words and Eddie's song were lodged in my brain. I wished I could cut them out and leave that part of me behind on the beach. She hadn't meant it, but she had too. Even if the memory was gone, the feeling was real, just like Eddie's song. It was the first real song, maybe, that I'd ever heard him sing. A reviewer in the *Village Voice* had once called him the great imitator. I'd felt guilty for reading it, guiltier still that from then on I heard echoes of

Dylan and Springsteen and Bowie in all his music. I buried my hands in my armpits. Out of the eleven years of things we'd done together, it had taken breaking up for him to find his voice.

The realisation had clarity and sadness. I waited for tears, but they didn't come. I rolled it around again, just to make sure. Yes, it was sad, but somehow the sadness wasn't everything – there was room for something else. Hope, maybe. Or trust.

I was cold all over now, cold and tired, but I was glad I'd come. I took a last breath of sea air before making my way across the grass and back to the car to drive my mother home.

FIFTEEN

He was sitting in the corner of the lobby, texting. As I walked towards him, I was glad he hadn't seen me yet, that I had a head start on taking him in – the line of his shoulders in his black and green check shirt, the angle his right foot made crossed over his left knee. His hair looked shorter on top and when he looked up I saw it was shaved tight, that the sideburns were almost gone. His eyebrow piercing was the same though, and so was his smile.

'Hey!' He stood up, his arms stretched wide, the phone still in his hand. 'How are you?'

'Good,' I said. 'I'm good!'

The hug was different, we held ourselves a little apart, a protective seal of air between us. I pulled away first.

'You look great,' he said.

'Thanks, you too.'

He rubbed his hand over his hair, from back to front, the way he always did. Now that it was short, it didn't stick up as much. 'I have a mirror in my room, Carls. I know I look like shit!' He laughed and I saw the tiredness in his eyes.

'You look like you could use some sleep,' I said.

'I'm wiped out after this tour,' he said. 'But you look great. I like your hair like that.'

I folded a strand behind my ear. 'It's not much different really, I just went back to my natural colour.'

'It was that colour when we first met,' he said. 'I really like it. I'm not just saying that, even though I probably would have anyway.'

He smiled and I did too. I'd forgotten his disarming honesty. It was a script and I was supposed to produce a sarcastic comeback, only when I reached for one, it wasn't there.

'You want to grab a coffee?' he said. 'The waiter was just right here.'

The bucket chairs on either side of the low table were deep and far apart. Whatever it was we were going to do, I didn't want to do it here.

'Why don't we go for a walk?' I said. 'We're right next to Stephen's Green.'

'What's that? A park?'

'Yeah, just across the road.'

'Oh, I saw it. The entrance looks like the Washington Square monument?'

The idea made me giggle, a sound that annoyed me as soon as I made it. I shoved my hands into my pockets. 'Yep, that's the one.'

'Sure, I haven't seen anything yet except the inside of some club last night – Reynolds?'

'Reynards.'

'Yeah, that's it,' he said. 'To be honest, I can't remember too much about it, but I'm pretty sure the music sucked.'

Last night I'd been working, glad of the distraction after my afternoon with Ange when we had talked through every possible outcome of meeting him. Later, on my way to bed, I'd found myself online, looking at photos of us, trying to prepare myself for how it would feel to see him. But instead of looking at Eddie my eyes were drawn to the girl with the changing hair, the girl who was always smiling. Who was that girl who looked like me? What was she feeling? Or did she feel anything at all?

Eddie was signing a slip of paper on the table. He shoved his phone into the back pocket of his jeans. 'So, let's go.'

'You'll probably need a jacket,' I said. 'It might be May, but it's chilly.'

'Some girl last night was calling it monsoon season. Said it hadn't stopped raining.'

Some girl. Some girl in Reynards.

I shrugged. 'It's Ireland, we get a lot of rain.'

He stood there, waiting for me to say more. When I didn't, he jerked his thumb over his shoulder. 'I'll go grab it,' he said. 'You wait right there.'

I turned away to watch the street through the floor-length window. Outside, people hurried past into their Dublin Saturday morning, to work, to shop. I could walk out there and join them, fall into the slipstream of the crowd and let it carry me down Grafton Street, on to South Anne Street and across the road to where the car was parked. There was nothing stopping me. No one was making me do this.

Behind me, the lift pinged. Was he back already? An American couple stepped out, overweight in shorts and sneakers. The kind of couple we'd used to joke that we'd never be, and we were right: we never would be like them, we'd never be any kind of couple any more. I took a deep breath, tried to clear my head. I took my phone out of my pocket and read the text message I'd written for myself last night. *To thine own self be true.*

I sensed rather than heard Eddie behind me. When I turned, he was there, his hands deep in the pockets of a beaten-up leather jacket I'd never seen before.

'Who are you texting?' he asked, arching his pierced eyebrow.

I was about to tell him I wasn't texting, until I remembered I didn't have to. 'That's none of your business,' I said, with a smile. I put my phone away. 'Come on.'

He followed me into the same segment of the revolving door and, squashed between the glass panes, I could smell his aftershave; since when had he started wearing aftershave? Outside the sun was bright and I was glad of an excuse to put my shades on.

'I see what you mean,' he said, zipping up his jacket. 'Not exactly the Caribbean.'

He said it the way he'd always said it, the way all Americans said it, but somehow it sounded wrong. He turned towards Grafton Street but I pulled him back. 'We're crossing here,' I said.

Waiting for the lights to change, it seemed we'd run out of conversation already, that we only had enough words to get us to the edge of the kerb. The woodpecker wait noise marked our silence, like a metronome.

'So, how did the tour go?'

'Too bad you couldn't make it last night.'

We spoke at the same time. We laughed and the light went green. He answered as we crossed. 'It was pretty cool. We got some decent crowds, especially in Germany and Belgium. England was kind of disappointing – most of the crowd didn't show up until after we'd finished.'

'That's a pain,' I said, leading us towards the gate. 'But, still, it must've been a thrill. Some of those stadiums in England are huge.'

'I guess. But it's hard to get the crowd going when the space is half empty. That's what sucks about playing support. Next time, we'll headline. Now that would be awesome.'

We turned into the Green through the main gate. There had been a time when playing any kind of tour was awesome, support or not. The path split into three and we took the one towards the lake. It was easier walking next to him than being face to face. I took him in in little glances, his runners, his jeans, the soft skin above the collar of his jacket.

'Hey,' he said. 'I almost forgot. I brought you something.'

We stopped while he unzipped his jacket, held out something square, black and green. I recognised the cover from their fan site.

'Do you have it already?' he said. 'It came out here last month.'

Surprise twisted with guilt. Did he really think I'd have bought his album? Should I have? I turned it over to look at the track list and he leaned in close, pointing at something so his finger nearly touched mine. 'That's the first single,' he said. '"Soul Rise". Have you heard it? Last night the crowd seemed to know it.'

I thought about pretending I hadn't. 'Yeah,' I said, 'it's getting good airplay over here.'

'Really?' He smiled. 'You like it?'

By the lake a woman with a shopping trolley was throwing bread into the water. Seagulls joined the crowd of ducks and pigeons scrabbling for crusts. As I watched them I felt his eyes on me. I had the power right then to hurt him. He still cared what I thought. I knew him well enough to know that.

'It's really different,' I said. 'I like it. A lot. I think it's one of your best.'

We started to walk and he said something about the lyrics, but it was hard to hear him over the din of the birds. I knew all about the lyrics. I'd given in to temptation and looked them up online, but he didn't need to know that, just like he didn't need to know that I changed the radio station every time I heard the first guitar chords.

We crossed the bridge. Two little boys pulled themselves up onto the wall so they could lean over the edge and look into the water. The CD wouldn't fit in my pocket and it was awkward holding it in my hand. He was talking about the tour again, some problem they'd had with the bus that had nearly made them miss their London date.

'Too bad you couldn't make last night,' he said again. 'They'd set up this awesome backstage party. It would've been fun, like old times.'

I flipped the CD from hand to hand, made a noise that sounded like a laugh.

'What?' he said.

We'd walked as far as the fountain and stopped next to it. On the other side, a group of Spanish students were jeering at each other, trying to push one guy in.

'When I think of those old times I think of you deep in conversation with some music journo and Nick on the prowl while I minded whatever girl he'd ditched.' My heart beat through the words, steady, loud. I wasn't afraid to say it like it was, for him to know how I'd felt.

'Ouch,' he said, folding his arms. 'I always thought you enjoyed those parties, you came to every single one.'

'I came to support you, because those gigs were important to you.'

'You didn't have to, I never asked you to.'

It stung to hear him say that because there was truth in it. He never *had* asked me to. Sometimes I'd wondered if he wanted me there at all. I shook my hair out of my face, practised in my head what I was going to say next, so it would sound light, breezy.

'So, how are Nick and Dawn?'

He trailed his fingers on the stone rim of the fountain. 'They're good. They both say hi. They would've come to see you today but they had to leave at eight for some daytrip to the west coast.'

'Did you not want to go?'

He looked into the fountain and back to me. Smiled. 'I didn't want to feel like the third wheel.'

It took a second for the words to make sense. I frowned. 'Third wheel? You mean . . .'

'Yep. Crazy, huh?'

Nick and Dawn, not Eddie and Dawn. Nick. 'When did that happen?'

He shrugged. 'Before the tour, so six months ago, I guess. Maybe longer. They're still at that stage where they can't keep their hands off each other. I've had enough of being around that.'

Behind him a young couple were kissing on one of the benches, the boy's hand twisting a strand of the girl's hair, making it a curl. They were young, younger than we were even, when we first met.

'Anyway,' Eddie said, 'I didn't want to go. I wanted to hang out here, with you.'

Hang out? Were we spending the day together? I'd said I'd be back for lunch, that we could get on the road for two. But maybe we could leave a bit later – the roads were so much better now. Suzanne and Lily-Anne would understand.

He was still talking. 'I was kind of gutted that you couldn't come last night, but I was psyched when you said we could hang out today. I've missed you, Carls. It's been hard, you know.'

I folded my arms, looked into the water.

'I thought I was going to go crazy at Mom's with that asshole Lee. You're probably the only one who'd get how annoying her boyfriends can be and it was so hard not to be able to see you, even talk to you.' His voice cracked a little.

I pictured him stuck in Bonnie's apartment, alone and upset. I shouldn't have sent that e-mail about how I didn't want any contact, it had been too much, too harsh. Guilt washed over me, a wave of it, guilt and pity and love that threatened to pull me under, until another part of me stepped in, gave me something to hold on to, a part that reminded me of all the things I had gone through without him.

I scuffed the ground with my runner. 'Jesus, Eddie!'

'What?'

'Listen to yourself. It's all about you – your music, your tour, your mother. What about mine? Do you even want to know how she is? How *I* am? Do you care at all?'

His face showed his shock. He stood up straighter, put his hands into his pockets. 'Of course I care!'

'It sounds like you didn't even notice I was gone till after your tour, till you were feeling a bit left out when Dawn and Nick got together.'

'You're twisting what I said.'

'Well, that's how it sounded! As if we can pick up where we left off and hang out like old times, as if nothing's changed.' My words tumbled over each other. 'Everything's changed, Eddie, don't you get it? Everything.'

In all the blueprints Ange and I had made of how the conversation would go, it was never meant to go like this.

He lowered his head. 'We're still married, aren't we? You're still my wife.'

A man stopped close to us, hand in hand with a little girl. He rooted in his pocket, handed her a penny. She looked at it and gave it back to him. He leaned down, showed her what to do, his hand on hers, they threw it into the water. We watched them in silence, until they walked away.

'Eddie, technically I might be your wife but I'm not in any real way, am I? Not in any way that matters.' We were in the middle of it now, the part of the conversation I'd been dreading most. I took a breath and kept going. 'Sometimes I wonder why we got married at all.'

He looked up, flicked his eyes away and back to me. 'I married you because I loved you.'

A leaf was floating on the water, green with yellow edges. A tree was shedding its leaves already. Love, a word that shouldn't have a past tense.

'I loved you too, Ed. Part of me still does. But it's not the same as being in love, is it?'

'I don't know. How are you supposed to know?'

'I think you're supposed to be happy. I wasn't happy.'

He laughed a hard laugh. 'No shit! You think I didn't know that? How miserable you were that you'd given up school, your family and everything for me?' His eyes were dark. 'You think I didn't know it was my fault? That I didn't feel it, every day – every fucking day, Carla?'

'Eddie,' I said, 'it wasn't your fault.'

'Well, it sure felt like it. Like everything that ever went wrong with your life was somehow down to me.'

'No, no, it was down to me.' I sat on the edge of the fountain, stretched my feet in front of me. 'I don't even know why I was unhappy. I wish it was easier to explain.'

He sat next to me, his fingers drumming on his thighs. 'Try.'

I took a deep breath, pushed my hands into the stone. 'It was just like being afraid all the time, of the future that kept coming so fast. Of my life being over before I'd done all the things I wanted to do. But I didn't even know what those things were, so it was kind of easier to do nothing at all.'

His runners tapped up and down.

'That probably doesn't make any sense.'

He stood up and faced the fountain. 'I think I get it.'

I stood up too. In the water there was a reflection of cloud.

'It's like it was easier to focus on you and the band than my own shit. I guess I got so caught up in all that I ended up resenting it, resenting you a little. Even though it was my fault, not yours.'

He waited a second before he answered. 'We were so young when me met, only kids. I guess we kind of grew up together, in a way.'

I shook my head. 'We didn't, though, did we? We were supposed to grow up but we stayed the same. Or I did.'

He tilted his head back to look at the sky. In the corners of his eyes I saw tears and I was glad for my shades. I wanted to touch him, comfort him, but I didn't know how any more. Once we'd been so close, part of each other, and now he was the hardest person to touch in the whole world.

'Come on,' I said. 'Let's walk.'

We took the path through the circular flowerbeds, the white hyacinths like soldiers, guarding the roses in the middle. He asked me about Mum, and I told him how she seemed to like the respite centre, how she was showing them all how to do yoga. When we got to the railings we doubled back down the shaded path by the edge. He was asking me about my job, my driving test, my friends. 'You seem pretty settled here,' he said. 'You think you'll ever come back to New York?'

Across the Green the main gate looked just like the monument in Washington Square Park, like he had said. I'd been in and out of it a thousand times and I'd never noticed that. For a second I panicked that I might start to forget New York, until I realised I could never forget New York. 'I will, but maybe not for a while,' I said. 'I'm going back to Trinity in September.'

His smile was a real one. I'd always loved his smile.

'That's great,' he said, and bumped his elbow against me. 'I always knew you'd go back to school. You doing an English major?'

'Yep,' I said. 'The longest degree in history.'

'Who gives a shit?' he said. 'That's what you want? Go for it.'

He meant it. I knew he did. I was glad then that he was the first person I'd told.

'What about the visa?' he said. 'Where's all that at?'

I buried my hands in my pockets, watched my feet on the gravel, one foot, then the next. 'I got an extension because of Mum. But I only have till September if I want to try and keep it. I'd need to go back, have another interview. Convince them she's still sick, that we're still married.'

'I'll do that with you,' he said, the words out of his mouth even before I'd finished.

'Really?'

Two teenagers in tracksuits passed us, whispering together and looking at him. He pretended not to notice, but he straightened his shoulders a fraction, and I knew that he had. 'Sure, it'd be fun. We'd convince them, no problem. I'll just tell them about your smelly feet – make you take your shoes off to prove it!'

'Hey!' I hit his arm. 'I'll have no choice but to tell them about your flatulence issues – I'll lace your food with raisins before we go in.'

'Not the raisins,' he said, holding his hands up. 'Remember the time I ate that packet of Raisinets on the way to DC?'

'A family pack, if I remember,' I said. 'Christ, that was the longest journey. And you tried to blame it on Rob.'

We were nearly back at the start, and if it had to end, this was how I wanted it to, with the two of us laughing.

'Seriously, though, whatever you need, I'll do it. It'd be fun to have you in the city. I'll definitely have a new place by September, so you'll have somewhere to stay.'

I was glad of my sunglasses then, that he couldn't see the tears. This was the end but it felt like he didn't get it.

'Thanks,' I said, 'but I'd stay with Rhonda.'

He nodded, buried his hands deeper in his pockets. 'Sure. Whatever. I just mean I'm in no hurry to get divorced or anything.' He raised his eyebrows. 'Unless you're in some crazy rush up the aisle?'

I laughed. 'Are you kidding? I'm off relationships. A casual fling is too much for me right now. What about you?'

As soon as I asked the question I wished I hadn't, wished I could've just left it there. Before he answered, I knew. I knew by the way he looked slightly over my shoulder. I knew by the jut of his chin.

'You know me, Carls. I've never been good at being on my own.'

I bit down hard on my lip.

His voice, when he spoke again, was lower. 'Some people aren't good at being on their own.'

Dawn wasn't the only girl in New York, of course she wasn't. I wasn't surprised. I'd known he'd be with someone, that it was over between us. So why did it still hurt so much?

We walked out on to the street.

'I'm starving,' Eddie said. 'You want to get brunch somewhere?'

I checked my watch, already eleven thirty. It wouldn't make much difference if we got on the road at three, instead of two. I could call Suzanne, explain to her that I needed a bit more time. She'd understand. Only maybe I didn't, maybe I'd had enough time.

'Listen, Eddie, I'm sorry. I didn't realise you wanted to hang out for the day. I've to get back. We're taking Mum away for the night, to visit Sligo where she's from.'

He folded his arms. 'Oh, right, that's all day?'

'Yeah, it's over on the west coast,' I said. 'A couple of hours' drive, maybe longer with me behind the wheel.'

He bounced on the balls of his feet. 'Maybe you'll run into Dawn and Nick.'

'Anything's possible.'

Sunlight glinted on the glass of his hotel and it was inconceivable suddenly, that he was going to go back there alone, that we might never see each other again. The idea of the visa interview together was comforting, of definitely seeing him again. Part of me wanted to arrange that, to set it up right now, but even as I was clinging to that idea, I knew it was better to trust, to let go.

'I guess I won't see you again before I head back — I fly out Monday morning.'

'We get back Monday night,' I said.

'Right,' he said. 'So I guess this is it.'

We'd come to the bit I'd been dreading for so long, maybe even since the first night we'd met. We'd been such a big part of each other's lives, we'd moulded each other, but now we were going to say goodbye because that was what people did.

Looking at him standing in the May sunshine, I wondered who I might have been if I'd never met him. If he hadn't decided to play a second night in Montauk that summer, if we hadn't been at the bar at that exact same moment. Had I always been destined for New York anyway? Had I made up my mind that day in Coney Island or had I made it up years before, lying on the carpet watching TV when I was seven, eight, nine? Or maybe I'd made it up on a Saturday morning when I'd heard my sister scream. Maybe it didn't matter, maybe they were all connected, all the things that had bumped me along, brought me away, brought me back until I was right here. Maybe right here was where I was supposed to be.

'Whatever happens, Carls, I don't want to lose you from my life.'

I couldn't answer him, couldn't tell him that he already had, that we'd both lost something along the way. I reached out to hug him, a proper one this time. I held him and let myself be held. I felt myself waver before I let go.

'Bye, Eddie.'

I waved my hand with the CD and turned away quickly while I was still in control. One step, two. On the third, I heard his voice, calling me: 'Carla?'

When I turned back he was smiling, his hand making a visor for his eyes. 'I forgot to ask. Are you writing?'

I made a snapshot of him in my mind then, the shadow on his face, his jeans hanging from his skinny hips the way they always had. I knew all the tattoos under those jeans, all his clothes. He'd always have an infinity symbol on his ankle, just like the one I'd always have on mine.

'Yes,' I said. 'I am.'

He nodded, raised his hand, and I waved too, then walked away before he could say anything else. At the kerb the lights stopped me and I could feel him there, the pulse of him, still watching. His words floated in my mind: *I've never been good at being on my own.* He'd said it like it was a fact, that there was nothing he could do about it, but if you weren't good at being on your own how would you ever be good at being with someone else?

The traffic stopped and I stepped off the kerb, crossed the road, heel, toe, heel, toe, just like Jan said. I was far enough away that he wouldn't be able to see me any more, but I didn't look back. The crowd on either side of me was a blur behind my sunglasses, behind my tears. I kept walking, one foot, then the other, heel, toe. I'd done it. It was over.

I didn't look back.

Sixteen

Chips barked as he disappeared over the top of the dunes, running down towards the sea. I couldn't see it yet but it was loud today and I'd been able to hear it since I got out of the car, could taste the layer of salt on my skin. In front of me, Lily-Anne wobbled in the sand, tried to use Mum to balance before she pulled her down too, the two of them laughing into the wind.

We were all giddy after the confines of the journey, and my own laughter almost toppled me when I pulled them up.

Getting towards the top I could see the first line of the ocean, grey, like the smoky sky, white tips of waves. Up there the wind was a roar, a sting of air.

'Here we are, Mum,' I shouted. 'Does this remind you of your summer childhood days at the beach?'

She didn't hear me or maybe she just didn't answer. Standing on the ridge of dune, her back to us, her hands on her hips, she looked strong, certain of where she was, why she was there.

I wondered if she knew that she was finally home, if she felt different here. Suzanne was coming up behind me, her footsteps deep in sand. I glanced around in time to see her face change, and when I turned back I saw Mum had disappeared, following Chips.

Lily-Anne whooped, the first to follow, and Suzanne ran after her, passing me. I followed them over the top and down towards the waves, my feet sliding in the sand, knee deep, shin deep, ankle deep until I reached the flat wet sand of the beach.

Chips had doubled back, running in circles around us, barking into the wind that was flattening his fur. Out in the sea there were specs of black, purple and blue on the water, people rising and falling between the waves and the sky. Kite surfers: I'd seen them on TV but never in real life before. The Metal Man was out there somewhere too, balancing on the water no matter how hard it tried to pull him under. After all Mum's sightings of him I was looking forward to seeing him in real life as much as she was, maybe even more.

'Mammy, no, it's too rough! No, Mammy, you can't get in!'

Mum had shed her coat and was hopping on one leg, pulling at her shoe.

Suzanne's hair whirled around her face as she looked from Lily-Anne to me. 'Tell her! Mammy, it's too rough and cold. We said we'd only get in if it was nice.'

Lily-Anne reached out for Mum's arm but she jerked away. 'Suzanne's right, Coll,' she said. 'It's supposed to be nicer tomorrow. We can go in then.'

They were both right. And yet as I watched Mum pull her jumper over her head, the energy in her body that I hadn't seen in such a long time, I couldn't make her stop, couldn't take that from her as well.

'Come on, Suzanne,' I said. 'Don't you remember when we were kids? We'd never have let a bit of wind stop us, a few waves.'

Before I could think too much about it, I started to pull off my jacket, my hoody. The wind found the line of skin between my T-shirt and jeans. Mum was nearly undressed, down to her navy swimsuit. I'd helped her put it on, before we left, but right now she didn't need any help, knowing what she wanted to do next as she ran towards the sea.

I undressed faster, my jeans getting stuck around my ankles. I'd watched her running into the water so many times, the last time in Montauk, the same run, the same swimsuit, now that I thought about it, even the same ocean. The wind caught one of my socks and blew it along the beach. In Montauk the sand was hot, packed tight, like demerara sugar. At Rosses Point it was wet and cold, already sticking to my feet.

'This is crazy, Carla,' Suzanne said, bending over to gather Mum's clothes. 'Madness!'

'I know!' I said, throwing my jeans on to the sand.

'Look after her, Carla, won't you?' Lily-Anne said. 'Don't let her go in too far.'

'I can't get in even if I wanted to,' Suzanne said. 'I left my togs in the car. I didn't think we'd go swimming, not in this.'

'Get in anyway!' I called. 'I dare you!'

I started to run, just like Mum had, my feet making a spanking noise on the hard sand. Closer to the water it had the pattern of waves, the ridges sore under my feet, before it gave way to softer, wetter sand. Ahead of me, Mum's footsteps were disappearing already, shapes full of sea water, and I knew mine would be gone in moments too.

I stopped at the edge. Lapping at my ankles, the sea was freezing, liquid ice. I pushed in further and it crept up my shins, my knees. My legs were goosebumped and white, a plucked chicken. This was the worst bit, the bit where Dad had always run straight in, splashing through the froth in awkward jumps. *Don't think about it too much, run straight in.* That was what he'd always said. *Get down fast, and once you're down, keep swimming.*

The last time I'd been on this beach, he'd been with me, all the times I'd ever been here, leading the way. As the thought formed I realised he was still here, in the call of the gulls, the rush of the wind in my face.

Water over my thighs, my waist, the shock of it. A wave was coming, a big one, a rise of grey water, full of my fear. *Don't think about it too much.* I forced myself into the centre of it, felt my feet leave the seabed. I hated this, being under, my eyes clenched shut, the churning silence. I broke the surface, a rush of noise. All I could see was water, water and sky, darker now than before. Rain had started to fall, fat drops, pocking the waves all around.

Where was Mum? I couldn't see her. I moved through the water in panicky splashes, my timing and my breath all wrong as I snapped my head one way and then the other trying to find her.

On the beach Lily-Anne was calling something and I turned to see Mum bobbing up and down. She'd found me. 'Look, love,' she said, pointing towards the shore.

I looked and saw Suzanne, wearing her pink T-shirt that she pulled down with one hand to cover her knickers as she half ran, half skipped towards the waves. Mum and I were beyond the places where they broke and it was easier then, to rise and fall with the sea. I watched Suzanne get as far as her knees, her arms folded across her middle. Behind her, Chips was racing along the water's edge, his barks lost in the wind.

Suzanne was up to her waist. She hesitated. A wave crashed into her shoulder that nearly knocked her down. She looked back towards the beach and, just as I thought she was going to get out, plunged head first into the next wave. She disappeared, then surfaced.

'C'mon, love!' Mum turned to me before starting towards Suzanne, her body in front of mine white in the water. I followed her, the cold not so bad now that I was moving. Mum was faster than I was and she glanced back every now and then to check that I was still there, smiling. Beyond her, I could see Suzanne smiling too, her T-shirt a bubble of pink behind her.

It was a perfect moment, the kind of moment I'd hoped we'd have here, the three of us together. It was the kind of moment I wanted to freeze-frame, even as it was happening, so that things could stay exactly as they were, but things weren't going to stay exactly as they were.

Behind me a wave came, a big one. I closed my eyes, let it rise over me and gulped air on the other side. When I opened them again I saw that Mum had already reached Suzanne and they turned to look at me, two heads side by side above the water, two smiles. This moment might be perfect but it would change and change and change again. I couldn't stop it changing, no one could.

There was only one thing to do, the thing Dad had taught me, the thing I'd known and somehow forgotten.

I took a deep lungful of air, kicked my legs and kept on swimming.

ACKNOWLEDGEMENTS

I dedicated this novel in part to my grandmother, Sarah Bowe, who passed away in 2001 after a long battle with Alzheimer's. It was a disease that seemed to be shrouded in silence, and I knew that I wanted to write about it, to incorporate it somehow in the story of one of my characters. It's taken me a decade to figure out just how to do that.

It is very important to me that the portrayal of the journey of the Matthews family deeper into this disease is accurate, both factually and emotionally. To do my best to achieve this I conducted a lot of research – reading as much as I could, watching films and documentaries, joining in discussions online and carrying out personal interviews with those, who like me, had felt the impact of Alzheimer's in their own lives.

Along that path, a number of people were very influential in shaping how Collette's story unfolds. Specifically, I'd like to thank Serena Ferguson and Margaret Howard who so openly and generously shared their own personal experiences with me. I hope I have represented you well. Thanks also, to all the staff at The Orchard Respite Centre in Blackrock, Co Dublin, who were so welcoming and flexible in allowing me to volunteer and spend time with their clients. That such a place of warmth and kindness exists gives me great comfort.

This novel has more characters, themes and layers than my first and I called on many people for their input. I'd like to extend my thanks to the following people whose support and help was invaluable:

Steven Byrne, Norma Cairns, Maura and Paul Cassidy, Michael Collins, Yvonne Cullen, Orla Dempsey, Clare Farrell,

Bernie Furlong, Carla McBeath, Emma McEvoy, Kathleen Murray, Karen O'Neill, Aisling O'Sullivan, Orlaith O'Sullivan, Lorraine Reid and Maresa Sheehan.

Special thanks to Eoin and Jill Dempsey for allowing me to 'borrow' their City Hall wedding story down to the detail about the rings, Danielle Mazzeo for her eagle eye read through and relentless fact checking, Martha O'Hagan for her patience in answering my endless questions about Trinity College and to Hazel Orme, my copy editor for her attention to detail .

Among all those who helped me along the way, there were two people to whom I turned for feedback on an early draft. I turned to them because as readers they bring insight, an understanding of what it is I am trying to achieve and an unerring knack of helping me realise this. For their encouragement, keen observations, suggestions and wisdom, I'd like to extend a huge 'thank you' to two very fine writers: Dominic Bennett and Eileen Kavanagh. I look forward to returning the favour for you both, very soon.

As always, a big thank you goes out to my agent Broo Doherty for all her hard work and of course, to my editor, Ciara Doorley, for her patience, her guidance, her trust and most of all her belief in my work. Thank you, Ciara, for once again, helping me make this book the very best it can be.

And finally, thanks to everyone in my life who provides the love, support and encouragement to keep me on this path – I could't do it without you and I wouldn't want to.